ALLEGHENY HOPES

JANICE A. THOMPSON

BARBOUR
PUBLISHING

Red Like Crimson © 2007 by Janice A. Thompson
White as Snow © 2007 by Janice A. Thompson
Out of the Blue © 2008 by Janice A. Thompson

ISBN 978-1-60260-584-8

Scripture quotations are taken from the New King James Version®. Copyright © 1982 by Thomas Nelson, Inc. Used by permission. All rights reserved.

Scripture quotations are taken from the King James Version of the Bible.

This book is a work of fiction. Names, characters, places, and incidents are either products of the author's imagination or used fictitiously. Any similarity to actual people, organizations, and/or events is purely coincidental.

Cover photographer: altrendo nature/Getty Images

Published by Barbour Publishing, Inc., P.O. Box 719, Uhrichsville, Ohio 44683, www.barbourbooks.com

Our mission is to publish and distribute inspirational products offering exceptional value and biblical encouragement to the masses.

Printed in the United States of America.

Dear Readers,

Thank you for choosing to read my "colorful" stories about the state of Pennsylvania. Setting these three "red, white and blue" tales in such a beautiful place just came naturally! My sister lives in the Philadelphia area and we've often visited the Amish Country together. My desire was to write stories that would reflect the theme of freedom, which resonates throughout Pennsylvania. I wasn't thinking of freedom in the traditional sense, however. I wanted each of these stories to be about people who had been set free in a spiritual sense. You will notice that each story has a prologue set in the past and then the first chapter jumps to the present. Perhaps you can relate. I pray that, in reading these stories, you will let the Lord release you from the pain and/or sin of your past. May you, through the freedom He offers through His Son, step boldly into the future. And may you, like these characters, know what it means to have a mountaintop experience with Him—one as magnificent as the Alleghenies themselves!

Sincerely,
Janice A. Thompson

RED LIKE CRIMSON

Dedication

To all those who hope to leave the
past in the past...when it belongs.

Prologue

Virginia Beach

The small linen envelope contained a simple "Dear John" letter. Nothing more. So why did Adrianne's hands tremble as she slipped it underneath the door? Why did she struggle to press down the accompanying lump in her throat?

Surely in her three years at the university, she'd faced tougher writing assignments than th is brief, handwritten note. Last week's philosophy paper, for example. And the term paper for her humanities class last spring. Yes, she had certainly completed lengthier projects. But never one more personal.

Adrianne stood and brushed her palms against her jeans, as if by doing so she could wash this whole, ugly thing from her memory before turning and walking away.

And yet it hadn't all been ugly, had it? She allowed her mind to visit the hidden places as she eased away from the door. No, most parts of it had been wonderful. Completely wonderful. Even pure. But somewhere along the way, things had taken an ugly turn, and reality had come around full circle.

Now she must face facts, though facing them surely meant releasing every dream she'd ever held tucked away in the recesses of her heart. She couldn't stay. Not one day more, in fact, even if it meant leaving college in the middle of the semester.

As Adrianne inched her way along the corridor, she tried to avoid the eyes of fellow students passing by. Many laughed and talked together. Their voices layered on top of each other, creating a cacophony of sounds, much like a symphony coming into tune. Such chaos among the students she had grown to expect, even appreciate. But one voice she could not squelch.

"Come now, and let us reason together. . . ."

The all too familiar words from the Bible she had loved since childhood rose to the surface again, and the lump in her throat became unbearable.

"I've spent all morning reasoning," she whispered to the skies. "I've tried to be logical. But, Lord, surely You can see this is the only way."

"Though your sins are like scarlet. . ."

A cool breeze whipped through the courtyard outside the dormitory, not unusual for early autumn in Virginia Beach. The leaves, in varying shades of red and gold, rippled through tree branches overhead, as if begging to be released. She understood their pain.

At that moment, a light breeze caused many to tumble down in colorful array. A sign, perhaps, that moving on—letting go—was the better choice?

"Oh, Lord. I'm so sorry. So very, very sorry." She closed her eyes and whispered a good-bye to Virginia Beach. In just a few short hours she would return home— to Philadelphia. For good. There, much like those fallen leaves, she would face the cold, hard reality of winter, and would surely come to terms with the consequences of her sins.

"Though they are red like crimson. . ."

Adrianne stopped walking and stood a moment in silence—wanting to look back, and yet knowing she could only move forward.

If only her heart would move forward with her.

Chapter 1

Philadelphia, eight years later

Adrianne rushed around the apartment in a tizzy. "Have you seen my shoe?" she called out. "I'm missing my right shoe!"

Her daughter appeared at the bedroom door with a comical look on her face. The vivacious seven-year-old dangled a dainty black pump from her fingertip. "You lose *everything*, Mom." She rolled her eyes, but Adrianne noticed a twinkle there.

"I know, I know." Adrianne pushed aside the wispy strands of her daughter's light brown hair as she reached to plant a kiss on her forehead. "You're the mother and I'm the daughter. Right?"

"No way!" Lorelei's face erupted in a smile and her green eyes danced with mischief. "I want to be the kid. I don't want to have to go to work." She passed off the shoe, then sprang onto the bed.

Adrianne gazed into her daughter's face with the most serious expression she could muster. "School is better then?"

Lorelei nodded, eyes widening. "Indubitably."

"Indubitably?" Adrianne repeated the word, to make sure she'd heard it correctly. "Since when do you use words like *indubitably*?"

"Grandma says it all the time."

And you're using it in context. Not bad for a seven-year-old.

Adrianne hopped up and down in an attempt to get the wayward shoe into place. Once she had it secured on her foot, she glanced up at the mirror above the oak dresser. "Oh, my hair. It looks awful." She attempted to press the dark curls into place with her fingertips, but, as always, her unruly hair had a mind of its own and would not cooperate.

Before another word could be spoken, Lorelei bounded from the bed and handed her the hairbrush. "Your hair is *so* pretty, Mom." The little darling let out an exaggerated sigh, one Adrianne had grown to anticipate during such mother-daughter conversations. "I wish my hair was pretty like yours."

Lorelei joined her at the mirror, mother and daughter now standing side-by-side, staring at the glass. "Better be careful what you wish for." Adrianne spoke to her daughter's reflection as she pulled the brush through her wayward curls. "I used to wish for a little girl. And look what I got. . . ."

"The best kid in the world!" Lorelei hollered out.

"Puh-leeze!" Tossing the brush aside, Adrianne reached over to tickle her precocious daughter, and they both broke into raucous laughter. Seconds later, the neighbor from the apartment next door banged on the wall.

"Enough, already!" Mr. Sanderson hollered out, his voice somewhat muffled through the thin layer of sheetrock. "I'm trying to sleep over here. Don't you people ever stop?"

With a finger to her lips, Adrianne led her daughter from the room, tiptoeing all the way. They gathered up their belongings and headed out of the apartment to face the day.

Moments later, they stood at the bus stop together, waiting for the school bus to arrive. In the field to her right, the first fall leaves had tumbled to the ground. Adrianne closed her eyes a moment, remembering another autumn, years ago. *"Though your sins are like scarlet. . ."*

"Mom, I'm c–cold." Lorelei spoke through chattering teeth.

Adrianne snapped to attention and buttoned her daughter's jacket, then wrapped her in a warm embrace. "Is that better?"

"Mm-hmm."

At this point, Adrianne released her hold, opting for a game of distraction, one they often played together on mornings like this. "Name five great things about living in Philadelphia," she coached.

"That's easy." Lorelei giggled. "Philly cheese steak."

"Philly cheese steak tops your list?"

"Mm-hmm. And the Liberty Bell."

"Good girl. What else?"

The youngster's nose wrinkled. "Grandma and Grandpa."

"Naturally. Although, your grandmother will be devastated to learn she's so far down on the list. What else? Or should I say *who* else. . . ?"

"You."

"I was beginning to wonder if you'd forgotten about me." Adrianne glanced at her watch. *7:34? If that bus doesn't come soon, I'm going to be late for work.* "Name one more thing."

A pensive look crossed the youngster's face, followed by a shrug. "I don't know, Mom. I can't think of anything else."

"Excuse me?" Adrianne crossed her arms and presented her most serious face. "You can't think of anything else about living in Philadelphia, Pennsylvania—the very birthplace of freedom?"

Lorelei shrugged.

"Let me see if I can refresh your memory then." Adrianne slipped into teacher mode. "One of our country's founding fathers once lived in this very spot." She pressed a hand to her heart, feeling the swell of patriotism.

"Mom, puh-leeze!"

Undeterred, Adrianne carried on. "He was a printer, a postmaster, and an inventor. Some claim that he discovered electricity by flying a kite in a storm. He signed both the Declaration of Independence and the Constitution of the United States." Here, Adrianne's shoulders rose in pride. Her voice intensified as she finished. "And your mother currently works as a curator at the museum named in his honor."

"I know, I know." Lorelei's eyes narrowed as she gave the matter some thought. "The Ben Franklin Museum."

"The Franklin Institute, to be precise," Adrianne admonished.

Lorelei groaned, clearly tired of this part of the game. "You tell me all the time."

"And I'll go on telling you, too. Until you remember every detail."

At that very moment, the bus arrived. Adrianne reached to give her daughter a peck on the cheek, then the youngster climbed aboard en route to school.

Not one minute too soon. With no time to spare, Adrianne settled into her car and headed downtown. As she drew close to the familiar museum, excitement grew. She had adored this place since childhood. She loved the artifacts, the paintings, and the clothing displays. She loved the hustle and bustle of tourists as they made the rounds from one venue to the next, oohing and aahing over all of the wonderful things the facility had to offer.

More than anything, she hoped to instill this same love for America's rich history into her daughter. Whether the little monster wanted it or not.

"Girl, you're late!" Dani Jennings looked up from her paperwork with a scolding smile as Adrianne entered the museum lobby.

"I know, I know. Lorelei's bus was late. Again."

Her petite coworker shrugged. "At least you don't have to worry about Mr. Martinson chewing you out. He thinks you hung the moon."

"Hardly."

"One of these days he will retire and you'll be senior curator. Wait and see." Dani winked.

Adrianne tried to suppress a smile. Perhaps one day soon she would work her way up the ladder. For now, she was plenty happy to carry on as an associate. Thrilled, in fact.

"What does the morning look like?" Adrianne stepped behind the counter and noticed a stack of papers.

"Quite a few tour groups, but Joey is here. So's Brenna. A school bus just pulled up with fifty third graders."

"Saw that." Adrianne shuffled through the papers on the top of the stack, noting several RSVPs for the upcoming fundraising banquet.

Dani continued on, oblivious. "We've got a private group coming in at ten thirty. A wedding party. They'll be lunching at the bistro afterward. They've already placed their order."

"Ah. Okay." What was it, though, about the words *wedding party* that brought a sigh to Adrianne's lips?

"For the life of me," Dani went on, "I don't understand all of these wedding groups coming through. As much as I love this place, I can't imagine bringing my bridesmaids to a museum as a form of pre-wedding entertainment. I can think of a thousand other places I'd take them, but. . .a museum?"

Adrianne offered up a shrug. "Oh, I don't know. It's something fun to do together." And why not? Usually the bride or groom hailed from the Philadelphia area and simply wanted to show off the historic aspects of the city he or she loved. Nothing wrong with that.

"I'm just saying that if I had a life outside of the things of the past"—Dani gestured to the inner sanctum of the museum—"I'd stick to the present. Especially on the week of my wedding."

"If I had a life outside of the past. . ."

Dani turned her attention to the school group. Adrianne shrugged off her friend's words and headed to her office, where she dove into her paperwork with a vengeance. She would sooner do anything than focus on the past, today of all days.

To Adrianne's amazement, the morning flew by. She spent a little time looking over plans to update the Wright Brothers display, and then telephoned the professional party planner she'd hired to take care of the upcoming fundraising banquet.

In the midst of that conversation, Dani appeared at her office door, breathless. "Adrianne, I hate to interrupt, but this is important."

Adrianne looked up from the phone and, with a raised index finger, whispered, "Just a minute." She finished the call, then turned to face Dani head-on. "What's up?"

Her friend's pretty blue eyes sparkled and the pitch of her voice rose as she shared her news. "Mr. Kenner is here to talk to you about the consultation grant."

"Ooh!" Adrianne gasped. "You're kidding. I didn't expect him till next week."

"I know. But he says you're going to want to talk to him now." Dani's face broadened in a smile. "Sounds like good news."

Adrianne felt her heart rate quicken. Perhaps her most recent prayers for the museum had truly been answered. "I sure hope you're right." She fumbled with her purse, reaching for the tube of lipstick. "I'll be there in just a minute."

She pulled open a compact and dabbed on the rosy-colored lipstick, then sprinted in the direction of the meeting room at the back of the museum. As she rounded the corner just beyond the electricity display, she ran headlong into Joey, who happened to be leading the bridal party tour.

"I'm so sorry." She offered up a shrug. "Going too fast for my own good."

"Not a problem." Joey flashed a broad smile and gestured to the group, his spiked blond hair standing at attention. "But let me introduce you to these fine people."

Adrianne drew in a breath, a little frustrated at the interruption. What should she do about Mr. Kenner, who waited in the meeting room? For weeks, she'd awaited news from him, and now he waited on her. She didn't want to keep him long, not with so much at stake.

"Ladies and gentlemen," Joey spoke with flair, "I'd like to introduce one of our most admired curators, Adrianne Russo. She's been with the museum for four years, and has made improvements to several of our displays, including the one you're viewing right now."

She took note of the words *most admired* with a sigh, and then looked across the group of people with a rehearsed smile. Which one was the bride? *Ah. The one with the glow on her face.* And the groom must be the one to her right with his arm around her waist. A cluster of lovely bridesmaids stood nearby and. . .

She glanced to her left to take in the group of groomsmen. Her gaze ran from one young man to the next, finally landing on the taller one at the end of the line.

As their eyes met, Adrianne's heart flew into her throat. For a moment, she could scarcely catch her breath. *No! Not here. Not like this.*

From just a few short yards away, the man she had once loved more than life itself stared back in stunned silence. And in that moment, eight years of unspoken words traveled between them.

Chapter 2

Christopher stared at Adrianne in disbelief. Except for the length of her dark brown curls and the uncharacteristic professional attire, she looked every bit as she had the day he'd seen her last.

Virginia Beach. Eight years ago. Eight years of questioning, wondering, worrying. Eight years of trying to figure out if his actions had driven her to leave town, with no notice other than a note under his door.

"I—I. . ." Adrianne's face paled and she turned away from the group and sprinted down the hallway. Christopher pulled away from the rest of his group and followed after her, unable to still the hammering of his heart.

Still running? Why, Adrianne? Why?

On she raced, a woman on a mission.

"Adrianne, wait." When she didn't slow, he called out, "Please!"

She came to a halt, then slowly turned to face him, her eyes filled with tears. "I'm sorry, Chris. I—I can't talk right now."

Can't or won't?

"I have a meeting." She shot a glance at her wristwatch and looked back up with a pained expression. "I'm sorry, but I don't have any choice."

"Well, then, I'm going to wait for you," he managed, pushing aside the lump in his throat. When she started to argue, he added, "I don't care how long it takes. I've waited eight years. I can wait a little longer."

She drew in a deep breath and nodded. Then, without a word, she disappeared into a door on the right.

Chris leaned against the wall to collect his thoughts. *Why now, Lord? After all this time? After all of my unanswered letters?*

At that moment, his best friend, Stephen, appeared at his side, a look of intrigue on his face. "Something you want to tell me, man?"

"Um, I. . ."

Stephen shrugged. "She's a knockout, but she doesn't look familiar to any of us."

She wouldn't.

"Doesn't resemble you, so she's definitely not your sister. A long-lost cousin, maybe?"

"No. Not my sister or my cousin." *Almost my wife.* Chris slid down the wall and sat on the floor.

14

Stephen looked down at him, clearly intrigued. "Interesting game we're playing," he observed. "Wish I knew how it was going to come out in the end."

"You and me both." Chris closed his eyes and tried to make sense of all this. How could he begin to explain? When Adrianne had bolted from his life years ago, the hole in his heart had been huge. For months, he had grieved the loss of both her love and her friendship.

And her respect.

His breaths grew faster as he thought about it now. How many letters had he sent to her parents' home in Philly those first two years? Fifteen? Twenty? And how many times had she responded?

None.

"When you're ready to talk, I'm here." Stephen crossed his arms and cast a pensive gaze his way.

"When you're ready to talk. . ." Chris's mind flashed back to a phone message he'd left for Adrianne nearly eight years prior. He had spoken those same words. *"When you're ready to talk, Adrianne, I'm here."* Apparently she hadn't been ready then. And judging from the look on her face, she wasn't ready now, either. In his heart, he suspected the reason for her leaving. He had blamed himself all these years—and rightfully so.

"I tried to tell her I was sorry." He spoke the words aloud now and brushed the mist from his eyes.

Stephen stared down at him, a concerned look registering on his face. "Sorry for what?"

"We dated for nearly two years," Chris whispered. "And I promised her—promised God—that we wouldn't. . ."

"Wouldn't what?" Stephen sat on the floor next to him.

Chris sighed. "We were going to wait until we got married. We promised each other. I'm not sure when things started to slip, but they did. I take full responsibility. I should have stopped it, should have. . ."

"Chris, it happens to the best of us," Stephen said with a look of understanding in his eyes. "We all make mistakes."

"But we were in Bible college. I was going into the ministry. Missions, no less. If anyone needed to stay pure. . ."

"Chris, God calls all of us to live in purity," Stephen said. "Being in the ministry doesn't make you more accountable. But it does make you more vulnerable, at least to some extent."

"I disagree." Chris shook his head. "Being in the ministry *does* make me more accountable. And I take full responsibility. I'm completely to blame here. No doubt about that. Somewhere along the way I. . .we. . .crossed a line. And I lost her because of it. She left."

"Left?"

"The school. The relationship. Everything. Just. . .left." Chris closed his eyes and thought back to the note she'd left under his door. "Adrianne said we couldn't turn back the clock, couldn't go back to the way things were before. She said she had to"—he swallowed hard—"had to get her life back on track. When I read her letter, I just broke. My mistakes cost me the one person I loved above all others."

"Look"—Stephen reached over to give him a squeeze on the shoulder—"I don't claim to have the answers. But I know you, and I know you're a good man. A godly man. I'm sure you've made mistakes along the way. We all have."

Chris looked up, hope setting in, and whispered, "Thanks."

"You've already made things right with the Lord. And it's not too late to ask for Adrianne's forgiveness." Stephen stood and offered him a hand up. "Maybe that's why God has led you here."

"Maybe." Chris contemplated the possibility. *Lord, are You behind all of this?*

"I don't believe in coincidence."

"Me, neither." Chris stood alongside his friend and sighed. "And I thought I was in Philly to be your best man."

"Always a groomsman, never a groom." Stephen chuckled.

Chris groaned. "I know. Don't remind me." How many times had he played this role through the years? Four? Five?

"Your day is coming." Stephen patted him on the back. "But in the meantime, it looks like the Lord has given you an opportunity to get some things off your chest."

Chris nodded, unable to speak.

"I'll be praying for you, my friend." Stephen glanced down the hallway. "But right now I'd better get back to my bride-to-be. I'm surprised she hasn't come looking for me yet. And you. . ." He gestured Chris's way. "When you're done meeting with Adrianne, join us in the restaurant, okay?"

"Okay."

Stephen headed off down the hallway, turning as he reached the end. "By the way," he called back, "that 'always a groomsman' remark was just a joke!"

Chris forced a smile. "Yeah, I know. Don't worry about it."

For now, he would happily play that role. Perhaps, one day, the Lord would shift him into another.

Chapter 3

Adrianne tried to focus on Mr. Kenner, tried to stay tuned in to the excitement in his voice as he told her about the incoming grant money. On any other day, she would have jumped for joy. But today, with Chris on the other side of the door, her thoughts volleyed between joy, intrigue, and sheer terror.

"Are you okay, Miss Russo?" Mr. Kenner reached to pat her arm, a look of concern on his face.

Adrianne nodded in silence.

He chuckled, then broke into a broad smile. "I can tell you're in shock. I understand. It's a huge amount of money. I'm sure it's going to take awhile to sink in."

Another nod.

"I'll be in touch within a day or so to fill you in on the details," he added. "In the meantime, feel free to share the news with your employees. Looks like we'll have a lot to celebrate at the fundraising extravaganza."

Adrianne snapped to attention and extended her hand. "Mr. Kenner, I can never thank you enough." Tears erupted, but she didn't even try to force them down. "That grant money means the world to us." She managed a smile as he gripped her hand.

"I've told you"—he made direct eye contact and gave her hand a gentle squeeze—"to call me James."

"James." She stared into the man's eyes about three or four seconds, just long enough to grasp his all-too-personal meaning. At that point, she withdrew her hand from his and returned to a more businesslike stance. "I'll look forward to your call."

"And I, as well." He offered another pat on the arm as he turned to leave the room. Her gaze followed the handsome thirty-something as he left, but her mind never shifted from another man—the one standing outside the door.

Christopher Bradley. The love of her life. The one who still took her breath away, still drained every ounce of normalcy from her at the very sight of him.

And he hadn't lost a bit of his charm or his shocking good looks.

Adrianne closed her eyes a moment and tried to collect her wits before walking out into that hallway to face him head-on. For some reason, her thoughts gravitated to his beautiful green eyes. How they had once swayed her with their love.

17

But no more. No, she was a grown woman now, a woman capable of looking forward, not behind. What was it Dani had said? Ah yes. *"If I had a life outside of the things of the past, I'd stick to the present."*

"Thank You, Lord, that I'm not ruled by my past," Adrianne now whispered. Certainly there were many issues to dredge up, if she cared to do so. But all of the mistakes of yesterday had been washed clean away, dealt with once and for all.

Hadn't they?

A little shiver ran down her spine and she offered up one last prayer before leaving the room. "Father, not my will but Yours be done." And then, with a resolute spirit, she tiptoed out into the hallway to see if Chris had, indeed, waited for her, as he'd promised.

Yes. She couldn't help but smile as their eyes locked. He'd waited. And the look on his face told her he would have stayed till midnight, if necessary.

"Adrianne..." His eyes misted over and he reached to take her hand. It wrapped hers perfectly, like a glove. Nothing had changed there.

"Chris." She gestured for him to join her in the meeting room, and he followed like a puppy on her heels as she ushered him inside. Adrianne closed the door behind them, then offered him a chair.

Once seated, Adrianne drew her hands into her lap and clasped them together. A protective habit, really. Even after all of this time, she still inwardly longed for the feel of his hand in hers. Nothing could ever replace that.

"I'm sure you have a thousand questions," she began.

"Probably more than that." He offered up a weak smile. "But I only want you to say what you're comfortable saying."

Only what you're comfortable saying... How could she say anything at all, since the very things to tumble forth would surely reveal years of untold truths?

Adrianne took a deep breath and pushed back the tears that threatened to erupt. *Lord, I sense Your timing here. I don't want to blow this.* She gazed into Chris's beautiful eyes and began.

"Leaving you was the hardest thing I've ever done in my life. I need you to know that."

His eyes misted over right away and he nodded a bit before speaking. "*Losing* you was the hardest thing I've ever been through."

She instinctively glanced down at his left hand, in search of a ring. Surely, after all these years, Chris had married, started a family. Surely he wouldn't still be single.

Nope. No ring.

For whatever reason, a wave of joy washed over her. She fought to suppress it.

"Before you go on," Chris said, interrupting her thoughts, "there's something I have to say to you. I've waited a long time to say it, but I can't let it go any longer.

I know the Lord has brought me all the way from Nicaragua to Pennsylvania to speak these words. I'm. . .amazed. Grateful. But I'm terrified."

"Terrified?" She was the one who owed him an explanation, not the other way around.

Chris placed his hand on her arm as he spoke. "Adrianne, you were the love of my life. And I wanted to treat you with the respect and dignity every woman deserves. I wanted to marry you, to make you my wife."

A lump grew in Adrianne's throat and her gaze shifted to her hands as he continued.

"I'm so ashamed," he said. "I let my physical desires get in the way of what God wanted. I took advantage of the situation, and I took advantage of you." He reached to lift her chin so that they were now eye to eye. "And in doing so destroyed any hope of a relationship with the one person I loved above everyone else on the planet."

Her heart felt as if it had been pressed upward from her chest into her throat.

"I don't blame you for leaving," he continued. "You were right to leave."

"Oh, Chris. . ." *If only you knew. . .*

"I read your letter a hundred times. And the things you said were right. We couldn't have turned back the clock, couldn't have gone back to the way things were before. My mindset was so wrong back then. I tried to justify everything. Told myself we were going to get married. Told myself you were already mine. . ."

I told myself those same things.

"I need to ask your forgiveness," he whispered. "I've wanted—needed to do this for eight years."

"You weren't the only one who messed up," she said. Whether she wanted to voice it or not, Chris hadn't taken advantage of her. She could have drawn a line in their relationship. But she had willingly participated. Willingly. And doing so had changed not just her relationship with him, but everything.

"Losing you nearly killed me," he went on. "And I want you to know—I *need* you to know—that I really tried to reach you. Multiple times, in fact. I sent letters. A couple dozen."

"I know." Tears began right away. "I read them."

"You did?" His face lit with joy. "You read them?" She nodded and he reached to squeeze her hands. "Adrianne, why didn't you let me know that you were okay? I knew the relationship was beyond repair, but I was so worried about you."

She shook her head and brushed aside the tears. "I—I. . . It's complicated. I was so scared."

"Scared of what?" He gazed into her eyes, begging for answers.

And he deserved them, didn't he? Hadn't he gone for eight long years without knowing the truth? How could she go on keeping it from him now? "Chris. . . ," she began. "There's something I need to tell you. But I don't think this is the right time, and I know for a fact it isn't the right place." She quickly jotted down her cell phone number on a scrap of paper and handed it to him. "Let's plan to meet while you're in town."

"C–can we get together this weekend?" He fingered the tiny piece of paper, clearly nervous. "I'm only going to be here for the next few days for my friend's wedding."

"Still playing the role of best man?" she asked with a smile.

He shrugged. "Yeah. But please don't say it. I hear it all the time from everyone else."

She wouldn't say it. She wouldn't dare.

No, if she spoke anything at all, it would be the story that began eight long years ago—the story that would change his life forever.

❧

Chris walked toward the bistro, deep in thought. As he and Adrianne had arranged to meet the following day, he couldn't shake the feeling that she had something specific on her mind, something she might have shared today, if circumstances had been better. She had stopped short of telling him something of major importance. He sensed it to the core of his being.

Lord, I feel like I'm shooting in the dark here. But I know You see everything. Help me see it all in Your time.

Chris continued on down the hallway alone, reflecting on everything that had just transpired. What a miracle to stumble across Adrianne after all these years. Seeing her had sent his heavy heart into flight. Her lyrical voice. The way the end of her nose tipped up. The light in her rich doe-colored eyes when she spoke. Nothing had changed.

And yet, with the very next breath he had to conclude the obvious. . . .

Everything had changed.

Chapter 4

W here's that girl of mine?" Adrianne entered the familiar spacious living room at her parents' house, but couldn't find a soul. "Hello?" She wound her way into the kitchen, which was still decorated in shades of the 1980s. Country blue wallpaper lined each wall, and her mother's now infamous collection of ducks abounded. Adrianne couldn't help but chuckle as she remembered her mother's enthusiasm over "all things country." The fad had ended in most homes by the '90s, but not in her mother's kitchen, oh no.

"Hello?" Adrianne called again.

Nothing. No one.

"Hello?" She tried one more time.

Through the sliding glass door at the back of the house, she saw wisps of smoke rising into the early evening sky. *Ah. Dad's barbecuing again.* She opened the door and peeked outside, a delicious smell greeting her.

"Hey there!" she called out.

"Mom!" Lorelei squealed and ran her way. The youngster wrapped herself around Adrianne's waist, as always, bouncing up and down all the while. "You're home!"

Funny, how her daughter still referred to her grandma and grandpa's house as home, even after years of living in their own apartment.

"Were you good for your grandpa?" Adrianne asked.

"Gooder'n gold." Adrianne's dad turned from the barbecue grill long enough to respond. "But then again, she always is. That girl's the apple of her grandpa's eye."

"I know, I know." Adrianne sighed. "She can do no wrong." *Little monster. She can get away with anything where her grandparents are concerned.*

"Grandma, Mom's here!" Lorelei's lyrical voice rang out, and Adrianne turned to see her mother coming out of the back door with a tray of corn on the cob in her hands.

"I heard you come through," her mother said with a smile. "But I was on the phone in the bedroom. One of the ladies at church is in the middle of a crisis, and you know I'm the one who heads up the prayer chain."

"Yes. Of course."

"Anyway, I'm glad you're here," her mother added. "You're just in time for dinner."

"Mom, you don't have to feed us. I'm perfectly capable of. . ." She wanted to say she was perfectly capable of caring for the needs of her daughter on her own, but that would be wrong. Adrianne's parents thrived on helping out with Lorelei. And Adrianne thrived on letting them.

"Help me out with this, would you, honey?" Her mother passed off the tray. "I need to get back inside to work on that cheesecake we're having for dessert."

"Mmm. Yummy!" Lorelei clapped her hands. "I love cheesecake." The youngster bounded off into the house with her grandmother, and Adrianne approached her father at the grill.

"More food here for you to cook." She nodded as she set down the tray.

He opened the top of the grill and pushed aside large, juicy pieces of chicken to make room for the corn on the cob. "If you think this looks like a feast, you should see the baked beans your mother's made. And the salad. You'd think she was feeding an army."

"What's the special occasion?"

"Ah. You've forgotten then?"

Adrianne racked her brain, trying to remember. *Not their anniversary. No one's birthday.* "What?"

"Today marks the eight-year anniversary of the day you came back to Philly to be with us." He gave her an endearing look.

"Ah. Yes, you're right." Funny, since this morning she'd completely forgotten.

"Seems like just yesterday."

"Not to me." An exaggerated sigh escaped her lips. "Seems like a lifetime ago." She pulled her jacket a bit tighter, fighting off the evening chill.

"I remember the look on your face the night you sat me down to tell me you were expecting Lorelei." Tears filled her father's eyes as he spoke.

"Oh, Dad. I'm so sorry. I'm *still* sorry for hurting you and Mom."

He shook his head. "I'll admit it was a hard pill to swallow. Your relationship with the Lord had always been so strong, and I knew your convictions were, too. And I could see how disappointed you were in yourself. I guess that's why I responded like I did."

He'd responded with all the love of a father aching for his baby girl to be made whole again.

"You showed me love when I didn't deserve it," Adrianne whispered.

He dabbed at his eyes with the back of his hand. "How many times has God done that for me? He would ask me to do no less for you."

"Dad"—Adrianne pushed back the lump in her throat, grateful for his response—"I need to talk to you about something. I need your advice." A little shiver worked its way up her spine as she mustered up the courage to forge ahead.

"You do?" His lips curled up in a pleasurable grin. "It makes the old man feel good to know his little girl still needs him. What kind of advice are we talking here? Something to do with the museum?"

"No. Nothing that easy." She waited a moment, then finally the words came. "Chris is in town."

Her father immediately lifted his spatula from the grill and turned with a pensive stare. "Are you sure?"

Adrianne nodded. "He showed up at the museum today."

"Looking for you?" The spatula trembled in his hand and he set it down on the side of the grill.

"No. He's in town for a wedding."

"Still playing the best man, or. . ." Her father paused. "Is this *his* wedding?"

Adrianne tried to gauge her father's expression. "Best man. But he didn't come looking for me. We just stumbled across one another at the museum—a coincidence."

"Hmm. Doesn't sound like one to me." He shook his head, albeit slowly. "More like a God-incidence, maybe?"

"Maybe." She offered up a shrug.

They both stood in silence for a while. Adrianne knew what her father must be thinking. He finally cut through the stillness with the question she knew he would ask.

"Does he know?"

"No." She whispered the word as if afraid the evening wind might pick it up and carry it off across the city to wherever Chris was. "He has no idea."

Her father's brow wrinkled. "Don't you think it's time, honey? I mean, don't you think God has arranged all of this? I'm sure you're nervous, but. . ."

"I've always wanted him to know he has a daughter." Adrianne pulled up a seat and leaned forward with her elbows on her knees. "I mean, I struggled with telling him when I was pregnant. And I let the months go by when I probably should have said something right away, especially in light of all the letters he sent that first year. But I was so worried about him pulling away from the ministry. . . ."

"I remember."

"When Lorelei was an infant, I called the school to see if anyone knew where he'd gone. I was told he was on the mission field in Nicaragua." Her heart twisted as she remembered the regret she'd felt that day. And yet, in the same breath, a certain amount of excitement had registered, too. How many times had he shared his dream of reaching out to the people of Central America with the gospel message? And how many times had she hung on his every word, like a starry-eyed schoolgirl?

Her father's face registered his shock at this news. "Why didn't you tell us?

We always thought you didn't want him to know."

Adrianne pondered his words. She had been terrified. At the time. But keeping the truth from him just felt wrong.

"I tracked down the name of the mission organization," she explained. "And when I found it, they told me he was out in the field, training the locals to dig water wells—hours outside of Managua." She still remembered the swell of pride she'd felt upon receiving that news. "He was doing what he'd always dreamed of doing," her voice drifted off. "And I didn't want to take that from him. Besides, they said he couldn't be reached unless it was an emergency."

"And you didn't think it was?" Her father closed the grill and gazed into her eyes with compassion.

"I—I don't know. At least, I didn't at the time." Her next words were rushed. "I wanted to tell him, I really did. That's why I tried so hard to find him. But relaying a message through someone else. . . I don't know. It just felt wrong."

"Well, it looks like he has found you."

"Yes."

At that moment, the back door opened and Lorelei bounded out, her voice rising in glee. "Grandma bought me a present!" she squealed. She held up a DVD case with one of her favorite new movies inside.

Adrianne shook her head. "Good grief. It's not your birthday."

Her mother appeared at the door. "I know that." She shrugged. "But in a way, today is like a birthday for us. This is the day we got our daughter back. And it's the day we found out about little birdie-bye here." She ran her fingers through Lorelei's soft curls.

Silence permeated the backyard for a moment as that thought sank in. Eight years ago tonight, Adrianne had stood on this very porch and spilled her story to heartbroken parents. Amazing, how far they'd all come.

"So, what were you and Daddy talking about out here?" her mother asked, as she placed pieces of chicken from the grill onto a large serving plate.

"Oh. . ." Adrianne glanced at her daughter, knowing better than to delve into this with Lorelei looking on. "We were talking about—"

"The past," her father interrupted. "And the future."

"Oh?" Her mother's eyebrows arched. "Something specific going on I need to know about, or is this father-daughter stuff?"

It's father-daughter stuff, all right. Adrianne looked down into Lorelei's sparkling eyes—eyes that mimicked her daddy's in full—and struggled to contain her emotion. How much more specific could you get than the life of a child?

"I have some things to tell you, Mom," she whispered on the sly. "But not right now. Right now"—she raised her voice—"right now, I feel like eating."

And with that, they turned their attention to the celebration dinner.

Chapter 5

The following day, Chris managed to slip away from his friends for a couple of hours to visit with Adrianne. He had tossed and turned in the uncomfortable hotel room bed for the better part of the night, trying to decide exactly what he would say when he had the opportunity. Nothing could stop him now.

He tracked down Adrianne at the museum, in the Wright Brothers display. She didn't see him coming, so he spent a moment or two analyzing her as she worked alongside a couple of others. Funny, she still pursued the task at hand with that same determined spirit he'd grown to love back in Bible college. How many times had he watched her dive into a project with such zeal? Nothing much had changed there, had it?

And yet, he had to admit as his gaze followed her, this was a much more mature woman standing before him. She handled herself with such professionalism. And even now, as he examined her handiwork, Chris couldn't help but think of how she might have fared on the mission field. Would she have worked alongside him with the people he'd grown to love in the outlying areas of Nicaragua? Would she have been willing to give all of this up to see his dream come true?

Snap out of it, Chris. He drew in a deep breath and called her name.

Adrianne turned abruptly, her face awash with surprise when she saw him. "Chris."

"Hey."

She nodded but said nothing, though her eyes registered an interesting mix of excitement and nervousness. Was she happy to see him?

"I waited till lunch time to come," he said with a shrug. "I was hoping maybe. . ."

"Ah." She bit her lip, a habit he'd grown to love years ago.

"I was thinking maybe we could sneak off to the restaurant," he suggested. "Is that a possibility?"

She looked around, a look of anticipation on her face. "I guess that would work. But I can't be gone very long. We're trying to get this display finished before next week's fundraising dinner."

"Any amount of time you can give me will be great." His heart raced as the words were spoken. *Even two minutes with you would make my day.*

She stepped out of the display and ran her fingers through her somewhat messy hair. "I'm sure I look awful."

"No." He shook his head, unable to speak another word for fear the words would reveal too much of his heart. Instead, he reached up with a fingertip to help her brush a curl from her eyes.

Big mistake, Chris.

The minute his hand touched her hair, those old, familiar feelings returned. He let his palm rest against her brow for a second, his breaths coming a bit more slowly. Until this very moment, he hadn't realized just how much he missed her.

Adrianne's cheeks grew pink and she pulled away. Almost too abruptly, she turned and began to walk down the hallway in the direction of the bistro.

"So," she began. "You're in town for your friend's wedding."

"Yes. Stephen Madison."

"Ah. Friend from work?" She gave him an inquisitive look.

"Not really. I met him through the mission organization when I was raising funds to travel to Central America. He's done some amazing work with the Nicaraguan people, and that's partly because he grew up there. We've been close ever since the day we met, like brothers, really."

"Nicaragua." She whispered the word, and her face appeared to pale. He couldn't help but wonder why.

"Yes."

They arrived at the bistro and walked to the counter, where Chris turned to Adrianne. "What would you like to eat?"

She shook her head. "I'm not really hungry."

"Are you sure? Please eat with me." He put on his best puppy-dog face and she laughed, then ordered a turkey sandwich with Swiss on wheat.

"Mayo, not mustard." They spoke the words aloud, in unison, and she turned, her face reflecting genuine surprise.

"You remembered."

"There are a lot of things I remember." *Like how beautiful you look in blue. How those brown eyes sparkle when you get mad. How you love working like a maniac to get the job done. How you get silly if you stay up too late.* Chris wanted to say more, but when Adrianne's cheeks flashed pink, he turned, instead, to place his order.

When the food arrived, they made their way through the ever-growing lunch crowd to find a table. He spotted one off in the distance and gestured. Adrianne nodded and they eased through a group of kids to reach it.

"I've never seen so many elementary students in my life." He looked around the room in awe, the voices of children ringing out on every side.

"You should try coming on a Monday." Adrianne glanced down at the children and smiled. "It's pure chaos in here. Heavenly chaos."

As they sat next to each other at the small table, Chris turned to look at her one more time. Her eyes certainly lit with joy as she watched the children playing together. Not much had changed there, either. She'd always loved teaching the little ones at church, back in Virginia Beach. *She would be great on the mission field.* In his mind's eye, he could see her working with local children in the villages. They would take to her like flies to a piece of watermelon.

Just as quickly, he stopped himself, lest his hopes soar through the roof.

"I've thought about your work in Nicaragua a thousand times," she acknowledged, as if reading his mind.

His heart skipped a beat. "You have?"

Adrianne nodded. "In your last letter, you told me you were headed down there to work. I. . ." Her hands trembled as she opened her napkin. "I called the missions organization, hoping to find you, but you had already left."

"No way." He stared at her in disbelief. "You tried to track me down after I left? They never told me."

She shrugged. "I never gave them my name. And by the time I called, you were already there, out in the field, no less. I hated to bother you."

"Hated to bother me? Are you kidding? I would have flipped the world upside-down to get to a phone if I'd known you were trying to reach me. Didn't you know that?"

She stared down at the table. "Maybe. Maybe that was the part that scared me the most. I was so confused back then. Dealing with so much. . ."

As her voice trailed off, Chris couldn't help but notice a tear on the edge of her lashes. He reached to lift her chin and gazed into those haunting brown eyes. "You'll never know how much it means to me just to hear that you tried to reach me. Thank you for telling me." His fingertips traced the edge of her chin, and she leaned her cheek into his palm. Chris's heart quickened at her tender response.

"I. . ." He offered up a shrug. "I can't believe you never married."

He shook his head. "No. I couldn't."

"Couldn't?" She gave him an inquisitive look.

Chris pinched the napkin with his fingertips. "I. . ." He dared himself to speak the words. "I've never loved anyone but you. Not ever. I probably never will." Where the courage came from, he had no idea.

In response, her eyes seemed filled with love, and Chris knew, in that moment, she'd connected with his words.

"I'm so sorry," she whispered.

He reached to grasp her hands. "Sorry for what? We were two mixed-up kids who lost our focus. That's all."

"That's not all." A pained look filled her eyes, and she pulled away.

"What are you saying?"

"I–I'm. . ."

27

"Does this have something to do with what you were saying yesterday?" he asked. "You said you had something to tell me. Are you. . ." *Is she involved with someone else? Is she afraid to tell me?*

The hurt in her eyes let him know he'd crossed a line. At that point, a man he recognized as yesterday's tour guide appeared at the table. For whatever reason, Chris released Adrianne's hands immediately.

"Adrianne!"

Chris looked on in curiosity as Adrianne glanced up at her coworker.

"Hi, Joey." Her face lit into a smile.

A nervous energy laced Joey's words. "Is this private, or could I join you?"

If he sits down, I might have to punch his lights out.

"I, um. . ." Adrianne shrugged. "I think it might be better if you didn't right now. Chris and I are talking."

Thank You, Lord.

"Ah." Joey's eyes reflected his disappointment, but he moved on to another table.

"Sorry about that," Adrianne whispered. "W–where were we again?"

Chris shook his head, trying to figure out how to jump back into such a delicate conversation. He opted for a diversion, choosing instead to talk about the children he'd met on his various jaunts into the backwoods of Nicaragua. He told story after story, doing his best not to carry the full weight of the conversation.

Every now and again, Adrianne would chime in, giving her opinion or offering up an *ooh* or *ah*.

Finally, the moment arrived. Chris could delay no longer. His breath caught in his throat as the words raced out. "Stephen's wedding is Saturday afternoon, but there's a rehearsal dinner tomorrow night. It's late, after the rehearsal."

"Uh-huh." Her eyes reflected her curiosity.

"I was wondering. . ." *I want you to go with me. I want to spend every available minute with you, don't you see that?* "Would you go with me?"

Her lips pulled into a smile. "I'd love to."

Relief flooded his soul. "Thank you." He reached to give her hand a squeeze, though he couldn't help but notice the strained look from Joey, who sat a couple of tables away.

"I'll pick you up after the rehearsal," he started.

"No." Her abrupt answer threw him. "I, uh, it's not necessary for you to come to get me, not on such an important night. I can meet you."

"Are you sure?"

She gave a slight nod. "Yes. It's not a problem. I know this city like the back of my hand. It's the least I can do."

"Okay. Well, we've got reservations at the Penn's View Hotel. Do you know where that is?"

She nodded. "Of course. This is my city, remember?"

He nodded and smiled.

"I love that place," she said with a dreamy look on her face. "It's beautiful. Historic."

"Right. Well, just ask for the Conner party. That's the bride's last name. We'll be in the restaurant—the Ristorante Panorama." He loved saying the words; their Latin flavor reminded him at once of the language that flowed like water from his lips as he labored alongside his Nicaraguan coworkers.

Though he'd only been back in the States a couple of weeks, he already missed the excitement of the language. And he missed the people, though he hadn't acknowledged that to anyone aloud. If only Adrianne would marry him—go back there with him—they would work together to reach the people and—

"Mmm. They have great veal." Adrianne's eyes sparkled mischievously.

Chris shook himself out of his dream state. He could hardly think about food. Not right now. Not when she'd just agreed to spend the evening with him. He tried to calm his heart as he continued on. "Come around eight o'clock, okay?"

"I'll be there." Adrianne glanced at her watch and pushed back her chair with an anxious look. "I have to get back to work."

"I understand." *But not yet. Please. One more thing.* Chris reached to grab Adrianne's hand one last time and the words just flowed. "Adrianne, I need to know that you've forgiven me. Please. I have to know."

"I told you yesterday."

"I know, but. . ." He drew in a deep breath. "I need to hear the words. I have to hear them before I can move on."

For a moment, neither of them said anything. Eventually moisture rimmed the edges of Adrianne's lashes and she dabbed at her eyes with her napkin. "God has forgiven me of so much." Her hoarse whisper seemed to grate across her throat. "How could I not forgive you?"

Chris worked to push back the lump in his throat as he thanked her.

She looked at him dead-on. "It's not that easy, Chris. I need your forgiveness, too."

He shook his head. "No. No, you don't."

"I do," she whispered. "You'll never know how much."

He gave her hand a loving squeeze. "Adrianne, you've got it. I forgive you. Though, for the life of me, I don't know what I'm forgiving you for."

❧

"I don't know what I'm forgiving you for."

Adrianne pondered Chris's words for hours after they parted ways. For some reason, she couldn't shake the image of his eyes—eyes that reminded her in every way of Lorelei's—from her mind.

Soon, he would know the truth. She would tell him. Tomorrow night.

Chapter 6

"M om, you look so pretty!" Lorelei joined Adrianne at the mirror and stared in exaggerated admiration.

"Do you like my dress?" Adrianne twirled in a circle for effect.

"Mm-hmm." The youngster gave a brisk nod. "Is it new?"

"Sort of. I bought it for the fundraiser dinner next week, but decided it was too pretty to wear only once."

"So, where are you going?" Lorelei asked, her innocent eyes staring up in awe. "Someplace special?"

To see your daddy.

For the first time, the word *daddy* sent a shockwave through Adrianne. Soon—tonight, in fact—Chris would know he was a daddy. And soon enough, Lorelei would meet her father. *Lord, help me. I've already made such a mess of things. I only want to make things better now. . . .*

"I–I'm going to a restaurant in a fancy hotel to meet an old friend," Adrianne said with a forced smile.

"A *man* friend?" Lorelei asked, her eyes dancing with excitement.

Adrianne sighed. "Yes. A man friend."

"Mom!" Lorelei's face lit up even more, if that were possible. "Is it a date? A real, honest-to-goodness date?"

"Good grief, you're full of questions." *If I tell her it's a date, she'll have me married off by night's end.* "It's just dinner with an old friend. Don't fill your head with all sorts of ideas, promise?"

"I promise." The youngster's smile shifted to a frown. "But Grandma says you need to start dating. She says—"

"Never mind all that now." Adrianne tried to put a stop to the conversation. "You'd better get busy with your homework. We'll be leaving soon."

"Am I going with you?" Lorelei's eyes broadened to saucer-width.

"Um, no." *Not hardly.* "You're staying with your grandparents. But homework comes first. So get busy now, while I finish dressing."

Her daughter reluctantly left the room, and Adrianne completed the task of putting on her jewelry and makeup. She shot one last glance in the mirror before leaving. *I've aged so much since our college days, Chris. How in the world you might still find me attractive remains a mystery.*

30

Immediately, Lorelei appeared at her side. "Mom, you're the prettiest lady I know."

Her words startled Adrianne. *Were you listening in on my thoughts again, you little imp?* She reached down to give her daughter a hug. "I'm not sure I'd agree, but I appreciate you for saying that. Kind of makes an old woman feel young again to be told she's pretty."

"You're not old." Lorelei giggled.

Adrianne sighed as she glanced in the mirror, wondering if Chris thought she looked older. *Stop worrying about that,* she chided herself. *Stay focused.*

At that very moment her cell phone rang. Adrianne's heart flip-flopped as she contemplated the possibilities. *Is it Chris?*

She answered it on the third ring, but her heart sank as she heard James Kenner's voice instead.

"Hi, Adrianne, I hope I'm not interrupting anything."

"Oh, I. . .well, I'm just getting ready to go out."

"Ah." His downcast voice caught her off guard. "I guess it's too late to ask you to dinner then."

Ask me to dinner? "Well, I have plans to meet an old friend," she explained.

"No problem. I was just thinking it would be fun to get together and talk about the plans for the fundraiser dinner. I know Bob Martinson wanted my input."

"Oh?" Why in the world would her boss want James Kenner's input regarding the dinner?

"Well, I can see you're busy," James said. "I won't keep you. Maybe one of these days we can get together. Soon, I hope."

"M—maybe." She thanked him for the invitation and quickly ended the call.

"Was that him, Mom?" Lorelei asked.

"No."

"Who was it?"

"Someone else. Someone from work."

"Oh." Lorelei's downcast face spoke volumes.

Adrianne finished the task of getting ready. Soon thereafter, she and Lorelei headed out for the evening. "Did you get that homework done?" she asked as they climbed into the car.

"Almost."

"I hope you brought it with you then. Make sure you finish it."

"Grandpa will help me. He likes spelling."

"Yes, he does."

Adrianne tried to stay focused on her daughter's words but found her mind drifting to the inevitable. She looked over at Lorelei and drew in a deep breath. *Lord, help me through this night.*

Forty-five minutes later, Adrianne stood outside the beautiful, historic Penn's View Hotel. A bellman met her at the door.

"Good evening, miss."

" 'Evening." She offered a polite nod. "I'm meeting friends at the Panorama. A wedding party."

"Just down the hall to your left." He gestured, and then shifted his attention to another customer.

Adrianne took in the beauty of the place as she made her way down the elegant hallway. She loved Philadelphia so much, particularly the exquisite historic buildings like this one. It wasn't just the architecture, though that certainly took her breath away. It was the fact that so many amazing things had happened here throughout the years. History was made in places like this.

Perhaps tonight's meeting would make the history books, too. At least the ones featuring her life story.

Within a minute or two, she stood at the entrance of the lovely restaurant. A hostess, dressed in black, met her with a smile. "Can I help you?"

"Yes. I'm here to meet the Conner party."

"Ah. The wedding party."

Wedding party. Why did the words shake her? "Yes."

"They called from the church to say they'd run into a bit of a problem. Something about the minister not showing up for the rehearsal on time. They'll be here shortly. Would you like me to seat you?"

"Um, no thank you." She looked around, feeling a little lost. "I think I'll just look around the hotel a few minutes."

Disappointed, Adrianne turned back toward the hall with a sigh on her lips.

❧

"Can't you drive any faster?"

"What's your hurry, Chris?" Stephen asked. "You'd think this was your rehearsal dinner, not mine."

"Sorry." Chris glanced down at his watch: 8:23. Would Adrianne still be at the restaurant, or would she have given up already and headed home? He prayed it was not the latter.

"It's that girl, isn't it?" Stephen looked over with a crooked grin. "Adrianne?"

"Yeah."

"Don't worry. She'll still be there. How could she leave my good buddy hanging in the lurch?"

It wouldn't be the first time. Chris thought back to the day she'd left Virginia Beach. "I just don't want to take any chances. I really feel like God has given me an opportunity here, and I don't want to blow it."

"Then listen up." Stephen's voice grew serious. "If it's really God, you won't have to worry about what you do or don't do. This is in His hands. His. Meaning, you couldn't blow it if you wanted to."

"I'm not so sure about that."

"I'd like to go on record as saying"—Stephen looked over at him with a mischievous grin—"the next wedding will be your own."

I pray you're right.

"Then we'll be sitting in traffic with your bride-to-be three cars back with a group of chattering, overdressed bridesmaids, and you and I will be driving together with the guys. Again."

"Yeah. I hope so, anyway."

Stephen dove into a complicated speech about marriage, and Chris tried to relax. His friend was right, at least about the part where Adrianne would still be at the restaurant, waiting. If the Lord was in this thing. And if He wasn't...

If He wasn't, Chris thought perhaps his heart would break in two.

Chapter 7

Adrianne's nerves reached the breaking point as Chris and the others rounded the corner. *Lord, help me through this night. Please.* The look in Chris's eyes made things all the more intriguing, which certainly didn't serve to calm her down in the slightest.

He took her by the hand and shook his head, almost as if he couldn't believe his eyes. "You're. . .breathtaking."

She felt her cheeks warm, and she tried to shush him, but he would not be silenced.

"No, you're absolutely beautiful." His eyes brimmed over, and she was glad for the distraction of the maitre d' seating them.

Chris made introductions as they took their seats. Stephen and his bride-to-be, Julie, welcomed Adrianne, and she offered profuse thanks for the invitation.

"We're happy to have you." Julie gave her a knowing smile. "I really believe it's a God-thing, don't you? I mean, how romantic that the two of you would meet again after all these years."

Adrianne felt her cheeks flush as she offered up a mumbled response. Did everyone here see her as a potential love interest for Chris?

Did *she*?

Within minutes, everyone in the wedding party chattered merrily, but Adrianne and Chris only had eyes for each other. They reminisced, talking about college professors, courses they'd taken, and their common dislike for math.

At one point, Stephen chided his best man with a "Hey, glad you could join us, Chris," but even that did little to pull the two apart. Adrianne didn't mind the noise going on around them. In fact, other than the beat of her pulse in her ears and the lulling sound of Chris's voice as he shared his stories, she heard nothing. Absolutely nothing.

And still, as the evening wore on, one problem remained. The obvious. The inevitable.

Just as the dessert arrived, Adrianne took Chris by the hand. He gave it a squeeze and stared into her eyes.

Her gaze shifted at once to the table. "I have something to tell you." The words vibrated in sync with her hands.

"Tell me." He gave her fingertips a loving squeeze. "Whatever it is, you can tell me."

She shook her head. "I need to know if you'll come to my parents' house with me for a little while. We can talk there."

He gave her a curious look. "O—okay."

"I'll bring you back to the hotel after." Adrianne tried to keep her breaths steady, but her heart continued to race. "I promise. But I need you to come with me. And I know my mom and dad have been looking forward to seeing you."

"You told them I was here?"

"Yeah."

"It will be good to see your parents again," he acknowledged. "I've missed them a lot."

"They've missed you, too." Adrianne started to push back her chair, but Chris leaped to his feet to assist her.

"You're ready to go? Right now?"

"Mm-hmm." As she stood to her feet, the cloth napkin floated to the ground. Her heart seemed to hit the floor alongside it.

He reached down to pick it up, a gesture of kindness. "I, um. . ." He glanced over at the others. "I just need to tell Stephen. I know he's expecting me to stay here at the hotel with the rest of the guys."

"I'm sorry. Do you mind?"

"No. It's not a problem." Chris leaned over to whisper something into Stephen's ear.

Adrianne watched as the two men exchanged a quiet conversation, then Chris gave Stephen a quick shrug as he looked her way. *Sorry.* She mouthed the word. She hated to interrupt the fellow's rehearsal dinner, but she simply couldn't put this off one moment longer. Her heart wouldn't allow it. She'd waited eight years too long. Not one second more would do.

Julie looked her way. "Leaving so soon?"

"If you don't mind." Adrianne reached to give her a hug. "Thanks so much for having me."

"Thank you for coming. Will we see you tomorrow?"

"Oh, I, uh. . ."

"Please say you'll be there, and come to the reception, too. You can bring a friend if you like, if it would make you more comfortable."

Adrianne shrugged. "I don't know."

Someone called out the bride's name and her attention shifted. Adrianne and Chris took advantage of the opportunity to slip out of the room. Moments later, they pulled away from the hotel in her car. She shivered against the chill.

"Cold?" Chris reached to turn on the heater.

She shook her head. *Not cold. Just a sudden, horrifying case of nerves.*

Her foot vibrated against the accelerator as she pulled out onto the turnpike.

"So, we're going to your parents' house," Chris started. "Do you live with them?"

"No. I have my own place."

"Ah."

"There's something I need to take care of there." She whispered the words. "Something big."

Chris sat in silence, but she felt his gaze as it bore a hole into her heart. *He's got to be wondering what in the world is wrong with me.*

A painful silence filled the car for a couple of minutes. Chris broke it with a question. "I've always wondered if you went back to school."

She startled to attention. "W–what?"

"I mean, you left just after starting your senior year. I've always wondered if you finished up, got your degree."

"Oh. Yes, actually, I did." She didn't give him any details. Perhaps later she would tell him about going back to school in Philly the year after Lorelei was born. One thing at a time.

Adrianne tried to shift the conversation back to Stephen's wedding, but she didn't do a very good job. Her words surely sounded strained. Contrived. Chris must've picked up on her subdued mood, because his light-hearted responses all but disappeared.

Within minutes, she pulled up in front of her mom and dad's house, parking just underneath the street light. Chris unlatched his seatbelt and started to open his door, but she reached across to take his hand in an attempt to stop him. "Wait. Please wait."

He turned to face her. "You're scaring me, Adrianne."

She tried to force back the lump in her throat but it would not be squelched. It, along with the tears that now rose to her lashes, gave her away. "Chris, I need to tell you something. It's something I should have told you years ago. Something I *tried* to tell you years ago."

He offered up a silent stare, along with a shrug. The blank look in his eyes spoke of his desire to understand. She would make him understand.

Adrianne closed her eyes and whispered a prayer. *Oh Lord, please help me through this. I want Your will. I'm so sorry for taking things into my own hands.*

"When I left that note under your door," she started, "it was because I knew I had to leave Virginia Beach."

Chris nodded. "I know. You told me."

"No." She shook her head. "You don't know. You know only half the story. I had to leave because. . ."

The tears came full force now, and Chris leaned over to slip his arm around her shoulder. She wondered if she should shrug it away, or give in to the comfort it brought.

"Were you in love with someone else?" he whispered, his voice strained.

"No." She gazed up into his eyes. They were filled with pain. *Oh Father. They're about to be filled with even more pain, aren't they?* "I never loved anyone but you. I never have."

Relief flooded his face and he drew her close. "Then tell me, Adrianne. Whatever it is, I can deal with it. Were you sick? Had something happened back home?"

She shook her head and drew in a deep breath. "No." The words flowed now. She couldn't have stopped them if she'd tried. "I—I left Virginia Beach because I was pregnant."

He stared in stunned silence. "W—what?" His arm loosened around her shoulder and he pulled back, a look of horror in his eyes.

"I was pregnant," she whispered. "With your baby." This time, she didn't give him time to ask questions. She raced through the story, feeling it afresh as the words tumbled forth like those autumn leaves of that awful day so long ago. "I left Virginia Beach the day I found out. I couldn't think straight. I came home to be with my parents. I knew they would help me, tell me what to do."

"But, Adrianne. . ." She read the rejection in his eyes as he pulled away. "You. . . you. . ." He shook his head, unable to continue as tears filled his eyes.

"I'm so sorry." The words sounded lame, even to her.

"You had no right to do that—just leave without telling me? You. . ." His voice trailed off. "You should have come to me. I would have done the right thing."

"I know that." She hung her head in shame. "But I was so young, and so scared. You have no idea how scared. I knew you were headed to the mission field. And the mission board wouldn't have let you go. Not if they'd known the truth. It would have ruined everything for you."

"That's. . ." He shook his head, and anger laced his words. "That's ridiculous. W—we could have *made* it work."

She shook her head. "No. You would have given up on your dream."

"*You* were my dream." He spoke the words so emphatically, they scared her. "You. Yes, I wanted to work on the mission field, but my ultimate goal was for the two of us to minister together, to work hand in hand. When I left for Nicaragua, I felt emptier than I'd ever felt. Part of it was the fact that I'd drifted from God, at least in part. I thought being there would fill the emptiness, but it didn't."

"I–I'm sorry." She whispered the words.

"And your explanation makes it sound like you did all of this *for* me. That's. . . ludicrous." His pensive stare sent daggers through her heart. She wanted to respond, but no words would come.

For a moment, neither of them said a word. Finally, he asked the dreaded question. "Th–the baby?"

Adrianne's heart lifted a bit as she shifted her conversation to Lorelei. "She was born that next spring."

"She?"

"Yes. Lorelei. She was born in April."

"Lorelei." He whispered the word. "Like the Lorelei that we learned about in lit class? The one who sang along the rocks of the Rhine River?"

Adrianne nodded. "I knew you loved that story."

Chris's voice seemed to tighten even further, if that were possible. "So my daughter was born in April. I was still in school in April. You could have called me. You *should* have called me. I would have come to Philadelphia. I would have flown halfway around the world to be with her." He choked back tears. "With you."

"I know, I know." Adrianne leaned her face into her palms and wept openly. How many times had she picked up the phone to call? Ten? Twenty?

"You said you got my letters," he whispered. "And you still didn't tell me? Why? You knew I loved you. You knew it. And you. . .you *stole* this from me?"

"I'm so sorry." She took a breath. "I was so, so scared. I knew I would eventually tell you. And I tried to. I really did."

"You tried to? When? How? I'm just not seeing it, Adrianne."

"That June, when Lorelei was still tiny, I tried to call your apartment. It was something my dad said that gave me the courage. He told me that from the day I was born, his heart would swell with pride whenever he looked at me. He said he would always think to himself, 'There's my little daddy's girl.' So I called. I did. June 24. Lorelei was two months old that day."

"June 24." He whispered the words. "I'd already left for Nicaragua."

"Yes." *Oh Lord, please help him understand.* "I talked to your roommate. He told me you'd left. I never told him why I was calling, but he was great. He gave me the number for the mission organization in Managua. I called them that same day. Remember, I told you. . . ."

"Yes, you told me you called them, but you left out a very important detail. You never told me *why* you called." His breaths were coming quicker now. She could hear them and could sense the strain in his voice.

"I–I'm sorry, Chris. I am. But. . ."

He shook his head and anger laced his words. "They could have reached me. Might have taken some doing, but they could have reached me."

"Yes," she said, "but I couldn't relay a message like that through other people. This was something I had to do myself."

Chris leaned back against the seat and closed his eyes. Adrianne reached over to grasp his hand.

"Chris. . ." She gave him an imploring look. "Don't you see? You were already there, doing what you were called to do. I was here, and things were going okay.

My parents were helping me. It would have been wrong to stop you midstream. I should have told you sooner, not later."

"So, you decided not to tell me at all?" His words carried an icy chill. "You were going to let me go the rest of my life not knowing I had a daughter? You felt that was the answer?"

Adrianne shook her head, trying to explain. "No. When your letters kept coming, I tried again. I called your parents' home."

"You did?" His voice had an air of disbelief, but Adrianne couldn't blame him. "When?"

"Your father had just passed away. Your mother was very broken. Hurting. She said that you would only be back in the States long enough to attend the funeral. The timing was. . . awful."

Chris nodded.

"I tried again when Lorelei was three." Adrianne smiled, remembering. "My parents had been praying all the while that you and I would. . .well. . ."

He gave her a curious stare.

"They really loved you."

"In spite of my flaws?"

"They always loved you. Still do."

"Even though I got their daughter pregnant?"

Adrianne sighed. "They're grace-filled people. More so than I deserve." She sat a moment, remembering the love her parents had poured out on her those first few years. "I tried to track you down in Nicaragua, the year Lorelei turned three," she continued. "By then we were told you'd moved on to a different organization. No one in Managua had your contact information. It was like a trail of evidence leading. . .nowhere. But I wanted to find you. I always wanted to find you."

The sound of Adrianne's heart pounding in her ears proved deafening. "If I *had* found you," she said finally, "I'm not sure what I would have said. How I would have said it. It would have been so. . .so hard."

"What are we going to do?" He gave her a blank stare. Underneath the lamplight, his eyes seemed vacant, hollow.

Adrianne gave a little shiver. "I think we need to take this one step at a time. First things first. You need to meet your daughter."

He shook his head without responding.

Please don't say you won't see her.

"Does she know about me?" he asked quietly. "Does she even know I exist?"

"Yes, she knows she has a daddy." Adrianne chose her words carefully. She'd been very limited in what she'd told Lorelei, naturally.

"But does she know I'm here? In Philadelphia?"

Adrianne shook her head. "I couldn't think of a way to tell her. I needed to tell you first. But my parents know. They've been praying for this day for years."

More silence.

Then, with a deep sigh, Chris turned his gaze toward the house. "They're probably wondering what we're doing out here."

"No. I'm sure they've figured it out. They'll want to spend a few minutes with us before we wake Lorelei."

"Lorelei." He whispered the word again, then leaned back against the seat and closed his eyes. "Lorelei."

The sound of their daughter's name running across his lips was pure music to Adrianne's ears.

Chapter 8

The trembling in Chris's hands hadn't stopped for a good ten minutes, ever since receiving the news.

I am a father.

I have a daughter.

The words hadn't fully permeated his heart, at least at this point. He wondered if they ever would. In fact, as he eased his way out of the front seat of Adrianne's car, he contemplated pinching himself. Would he wake up from this dream-like state to discover life was exactly as it had been ten minutes before?

No.

One pinch was all it took.

As they made their way up the front walk to the door of Adrianne's parents' home, Chris fought to understand. Why would she have kept this from him? *How* could she have kept this from him? How she could have kept his *child* from him?

Just as quickly, guilt swept in. His sin, the very thing he'd agonized over for the past eight years, had caught up with him. There was no simple apology. No asking for forgiveness and watching it go away.

No, in this case there were certainly consequences.

If you could call a child a consequence.

All of these things, and more, filled his head as they approached the front door. The silence nearly deafened him. He wanted to yell. At the top of his lungs. Wanted to cry out to God. . .to Adrianne. . .to anyone who would listen.

Instead, his lips remained sealed.

But his heart did not. In fact, it felt as if it had been ripped from top to bottom. Chris wasn't sure if he'd ever felt such raw pain before. Or betrayal.

Yes, Adrianne. Betrayal. You lied to me. You stole seven years of my daughter's life from me.

Just as quickly, his anger shifted to joy. When he contemplated the truth— that he had a daughter just beyond that door—his heart nearly burst with anticipation.

"A–are you ready?" Adrianne whispered, as if in response to his thoughts. She lifted her key to place it in the door.

"Wait." Chris reached to touch her arm, needing just a minute more. "I have to know this. Is she. . .is she like me? In any way at all?"

Under the porch light, he could see Adrianne's face come alive. "Oh, Chris. . ." A glistening of tears tipped over the edges of her lashes as she spoke. "Your daughter is the spitting image of you. She has your features, your hair. . ." Adrianne's lips turned up in a loving smile. "Your goofy personality. Especially that. She's funny, Chris. A real clown sometimes. But smart. Really smart. And she has the most giving heart you've ever seen. Just like you."

He pressed down the lump in his throat as he nodded his head. "Does she know the Lord? Have you. . . ?"

Strangely, in light of his past sin, the question seemed oddly out of place. And yet he had to know.

"She knows." Adrianne grinned. "She's very passionate about her faith, especially for being so young. I told you, she's so much like you it hurts."

Hurts. A word I understand.

"Are you ready?"

He offered up a lame nod, and Adrianne opened the door to the living room. Almost immediately, her mother and father swept him into their arms. He heard his name from both their lips, but their excitement made it nearly impossible to distinguish one voice from the other.

Finally, Mrs. Russo paused long enough to plant a kiss on his cheek. "We thought this day would never come." She put her hand over her mouth and shook her head in silence.

"Son. . ." Mr. Russo extended a hand. "We're glad to see you."

Why? How in the world could you not hate me?

As if in response, Adrianne's father wrestled him into a tight bear hug. He could feel the man's chest begin to heave, and sobs came. For both of them. Soon enough, they were all four in tears. Mrs. Russo ushered them to the sofa, where they sat in a puddle until someone finally broke through the ruckus.

"What happened? Grandma? Mama?"

Chris looked up through tear-stained eyes at the beautiful little girl who'd just entered the room. Her light brown hair glistened under the lamplight, and as she rubbed at her eyes with the backs of her hands, he couldn't help but notice the color of those eyes. Green. Same as his. Immediately, his hand went to his mouth, and he fought to keep from crying aloud.

"Lorelei." Adrianne rose from the couch and stepped in the child's direction. "We didn't mean to wake you, baby."

"I heard crying." The youngster looked around the room, a sleepy expression on her face. "What happened?"

"Oh. . ." Mrs. Russo stood and ran her fingers through Lorelei's hair and forced a smile. "We're just happy. You know, adults cry sometimes when they're happy."

Lorelei didn't look convinced. "What are you all so happy about?" Her gaze shifted from person to person until it came to land on Chris. His heart flew into his throat the minute their eyes locked. For a moment, no one said anything. Finally, Adrianne spoke up.

"Lorelei, this is the friend I told you about. Chris."

"Ooh." Lorelei's eyes widened in merriment. "The one you went on the date with?"

Chris couldn't hide his smile.

"Um, well, yes." Adrianne nodded. "We went to dinner together."

"He looks like that man in the picture, Mom." Lorelei took a step in his direction, but Chris's gaze shifted at once to Adrianne.

"What picture?" Adrianne's eyes grew large.

"You know." Lorelei crossed her arms, a pensive look on her face. "That picture you hide in your underwear drawer."

Chris's heart almost sang aloud at her words. So, she had been thinking about him. Even after all these years, she'd kept his picture close by.

Adrianne leaned her head into her hands, then looked up with a sheepish smile. "Yeah, he does kind of look like that guy, doesn't he?"

"Mm-hmm." She—his daughter, his Lorelei—gave him another once-over and he attempted a smile.

Mrs. Russo opted to shift gears, though her red-rimmed eyes still gave her away. "I've got a German chocolate cake in the kitchen. Anyone hungry?"

Chris didn't know that he could ever eat another bite of food as long as he lived, but he followed along on her heels as she led them into the kitchen. All the while, he stared at the remarkable youngster to his right. *My daughter. My little girl.* His heart swelled until he thought it would burst. Suddenly, much of the anger he'd felt—even the sting of betrayal—seemed to lessen. When he looked at this little angel, he was suddenly filled with possibilities, nothing else.

As they settled down at the table, Lorelei chattered merrily about a dream she'd been having before they'd awakened her. Something about singing on a big stage somewhere. He couldn't seem to focus on her story. No, he was blown away by her very presence. She looked remarkably like Adrianne. And yet she shared so many of his characteristics, right down to the eye color and the hair. The nose was Adrianne's, to be sure. And the lyrical sound of her laughter. Just like her mother.

At one point, she looked his way, cheeks flaming pink as she announced, "My mom wore her brand-new dress just for you."

"She did?" Chris peered over at Adrianne, whose expression still seemed guarded.

Adrianne nodded. "Yeah. I did."

"*I* want to get dressed up and go out on a date," Lorelei said with a pout.

"Oh no. You're never dating." Chris and Mr. Russo spoke in unison. Chris clamped a hand to his mouth the moment the words were spoken. Where had they come from?

Lorelei gave him a quizzical look. "How come?"

"Well, I, um. . ." He looked to Adrianne for support.

"When you're old enough," she explained, "then you can date."

"But I want to look pretty like my mom." Lorelei leaped from her seat and pressed herself into her mother's lap, where at once she began to play with Adrianne's hair.

Adrianne's mom chuckled. "You don't have to date to look pretty. You look pretty right now."

You're beautiful, in fact.

"I want my mom's hair."

Chris watched it all in silence, his throat suddenly constricted. *My daughter and my. . .* The word *wife* entered his mind but then disappeared just as quickly. *Lord, you know my heart. You know my greatest desire right now is for—*

"No one has prettier hair than you." Adrianne buried her face into Lorelei's hair after speaking the words. Her tears started again. She wept in silence, but Lorelei wasn't fooled.

"Are you happy again, Mom?"

Adrianne glanced across the table at Chris and nodded. "I am."

"She must really like you a lot." Lorelei bounced from her mom's lap and approached him. Chris wanted to scoop her up into his arms, wanted to plant kisses on her forehead. Wanted to tell her that he loved her—more than life itself.

Instead, he nodded lamely. "I like her a lot, too."

"You do?" Lorelei's eyes grew large as she turned to face her mother. "He likes you a lot."

Adrianne brushed away the tears and nodded without responding.

Say something, Adrianne. Say that you love me. . .that we're supposed to be together. Say that. . .

"It's way past your bedtime." As Adrianne stood, the bottom of the chair legs scraped against the tile floor with a squeal. "We should be getting home."

"Do we have to go?" Lorelei whimpered.

Chris's heart echoed her sentiments. He didn't want to go. He didn't ever want to leave this room for fear he would lose everything he had suddenly gained.

And yet another world awaited. The wedding. Tomorrow afternoon. Downtown. He had to be there for Stephen, had to fulfill his obligation.

Fulfill your obligation.

For the first time, he thought about the fact that Adrianne and her family had taken on both the emotional and financial obligation of raising Lorelei up to this point. He would change that. Immediately. He would make sure she was taken care of, that she had everything she needed and more.

Whoa. Slow down, man. You can't change everything in one night.

Lorelei flashed her mother a woeful smile, in an attempt to sway her, no doubt. "Can't we just stay here tonight? Puh-leeze?"

"I have to get Chris back to the hotel."

"Oh! We're driving you?" Lorelei turned to look his way.

"Looks like it," he said, not even trying to hide the smile.

"You sit up front with my mom," the youngster instructed. "I'll sit in the back."

You little matchmaker, you.

"That's up to your mama."

Chris looked at Adrianne, and for the first time saw her through new eyes. She was more than a creative soul, a hard worker, a museum curator. She was. . .a mother. The mother of his child. And she had done a remarkable job of raising this little girl, even without his help.

He swallowed back the pain at the thought of those last few words. He would make up for the lack of help now, if it was the last thing he did.

"Son, it was good to see you." Another bear hug from Adrianne's father felt awfully good, especially in light of the fact that Chris had lost his own father just a few years ago. He pondered that fact for a moment.

I've been without a father.

My daughter has been without a father.

A shiver ran through him as he embraced Adrianne's dad one more time. "I'm so glad to be here." He wanted to say more, but feared he would give away too much in front of Lorelei.

After a hug from Adrianne's mother, they were on their way. True to her word, Lorelei climbed into the back seat, allowing him the front, though he suddenly felt awkward next to Adrianne. Everything had changed over the past hour. Everything.

As Adrianne drove, Lorelei chattered merrily from behind. Chris didn't mind. In fact, the more she talked, the less he needed to, which served his purposes just fine, at least for now. When they arrived at the hotel, he turned to face Adrianne, wanting to say so many things, but unable to speak a word beyond the obvious "Good night."

She gave him an imploring look and reached for his hand. He took it, though mixed feelings still threatened to consume him.

As he climbed out of the car, Lorelei waved from the backseat.

"G'night, Chris! See you soon!" she said with a giggle.

"Yes. See you soon."

The car pulled away, and Chris's heart immediately plummeted. Somehow, in one night, he had gained—and lost—almost everything.

Chapter 9

Adrianne pulled away from the hotel, but a piece of her heart remained behind—with Chris. She couldn't bear the thought of leaving him like this, with no clear resolution. No plan. And yet, what choice did she have? They couldn't exactly talk things through in front of Lorelei.

Lorelei. She looked over at her daughter, praying she would fall asleep. Nope. No such luck. Instead, the youngster seemed to have come alive in Chris's presence.

She's drawn to him. But then she would be. Wouldn't she?

"I like Chris a lot, Mom." Her daughter gave a little giggle, then leaned back against the seat with a deep sigh. "Don't you?"

"Yes, honey, I do. He's a really nice man." Adrianne kept her eyes focused on the road, but her mind wandered all over the place.

"And he's handsome, too!" At this, Lorelei's spurts of laughter grew more animated. "Like the prince in Cinderella."

"Oh, and I suppose he has a glass slipper just my size." Adrianne chuckled at the thought of it.

"Maybe." Lorelei grew silent for a moment, then spoke quite seriously. "You're always losing your shoes, anyway. You *need* a prince."

Adrianne groaned. "Puh-leeze. You've been watching too many movies. It doesn't really happen like that. Not in the real world."

"Grandma says it does."

"Good grief." *How can I argue with that?*

Another sigh escaped Lorelei's lips. "And he likes you, Mom. I can tell."

"Oh?" Adrianne caught her breath, lest she say too much. "Now, how can you tell a thing like that?"

"He said so. Besides, he looks at you a lot," Lorelei explained. "And his eyes are smiling."

"Oh, his *eyes* are smiling, are they?"

"Mm-hmm. When will we see him again? Can he come over for dinner tomorrow night?"

"He's in a wedding tomorrow," Adrianne explained.

"He's getting married?" The disappointment in the youngster's voice was keen. "No way."

46

"His *friend* is getting married."

"Ooh. Okay." Lorelei's voice took on a dreamy quality. "Maybe he can come over the next night?"

Adrianne pulled the car into the entrance of their apartment complex and fumbled for her remote control to open the gate. "Maybe. We'll see."

"Promise you'll ask."

"I promise."

Adrianne couldn't help but smile at her daughter's persistence. Just as quickly, the somber reality resurfaced, taking the place of the joy. She and Chris needed to talk—and soon. Yes, his reaction had been better than expected. He hadn't blown up at the news, though she'd worried over it for eight years. His reaction had been. . .reasonable. That was the word. At least he hadn't turned and run in the opposite direction. Yet.

As they walked toward their apartment door, Lorelei let out an exaggerated yawn.

Adrianne reached over to pat her on the head. "Sleepy?"

"No."

Yes you are, you little goof. Just too stubborn to admit it.

"What are we going to do tomorrow?"

"Well. . ." Adrianne thought for a moment. "The leaves are changing. Why don't we go to the park and take some pictures? I'll use my new digital camera."

"Okay." Another yawn slipped out.

They entered the apartment, and Lorelei dressed for bed.

"Is there any particular reason you chose the Cinderella nightgown?"

Lorelei just giggled.

Adrianne couldn't help but laugh. "Fine. I get your message. But enough with playing around, okay?"

"Okay."

"Brush your teeth, and then we'll say our prayers."

The youngster headed off into the bathroom. Less than a minute later, however, she emerged with toothbrush in hand, her eyes twinkling. "What's Chris's last name, Mom?" she asked, a look of innocence in her eyes.

"Bradley."

"Adrianne Bradley." The youngster giggled. "I like it." Almost immediately, however, her expression changed. "But I'll still be Russo?"

Yikes. How in the world do I respond to that? Adrianne put on her most serious face. "You've got me married off already?" she asked, hoping to shift gears. "Don't you think it's a little early for that?"

Lorelei shrugged. "I dunno." She went back into the bathroom for a couple of minutes, then emerged again, this time with toothpaste smeared all over her lips.

"Still, if you got married, he could adopt me. Right?"

"Could we talk about this tomorrow?" Adrianne didn't even try to stop the groan that escaped from the back of her throat. "I've got a terrible headache." In all honesty, her head did hurt. And if anyone deserved a few moments of peace and quiet, she did. Especially in light of all she'd been through this evening.

Lorelei gazed up with an imploring look. "Can I sleep with you tonight, Mom?"

Oh, not tonight. Tonight I need to be alone, to think, to pray. . .

"I promise not to steal the covers." Lorelei's sheepish giggle did little to sway her.

"I really do have a headache," Adrianne explained. "So I think it's best if you. . ."

The look of sadness that swept over her daughter's face did the trick.

"Oh, okay. But just tonight. I don't want you to get in the habit."

"Thank you, thank you!" Lorelei jumped up and down, and Adrianne immediately put her finger over her lips to shush the youngster, lest Mr. Sanderson take to pounding on the wall again.

"Promise you'll go to sleep right away?"

"I promise." She gave a little twirl and the Cinderella nightie caught Adrianne's eye one last time. Perhaps there would be a "happily ever after" in both their lives. If only. . .

Hmm. There were too many if-only possibilities to ponder right now. Instead, she tucked her daughter in for the night and they prayed together. Then, after just a few minutes, Lorelei's words grew slower, quieter. Finally, her breaths came in long, steady succession, and Adrianne knew she'd fallen asleep.

At this point, Adrianne quietly dressed for bed and slid under the covers alongside her daughter. As she leaned back against the pillows, the tears threatened to come again. She tried to push them back, but finally relinquished. It might do her good to cry, all things considered.

Still, she must do it silently. And with as little movement as possible. Not an easy task.

After a few moments, she dried her eyes and tried to rest. Her mind would not be silenced. So many questions to be answered. . .

Will Chris forgive me?

Will he want to get to know his daughter?

She took her hand and gently ran it across Lorelei's back. The youngster stirred, then settled back down again.

How will I tell her? How will we tell her?

This was not the first time she'd worried about Lorelei's reaction to the news. Adrianne had played out multiple scenarios in her mind over the years. Still, she couldn't come to grips with how—or when—to tell her. Up until now, Lorelei had asked very little about her father, only once or twice questioning his existence. Adrianne had managed to get by with a limited explanation of his work in another country.

But now. . .

She's going to put it together. She's a smart little girl. And she's seen his photograph. It's only a matter of time before she. . .

Her prayer came in rushed whispers, more mouthed than spoken aloud: "Lord, I've made such a mess of everything. I've asked Chris to forgive me. I know one day Lorelei will have to learn to forgive me, too. But tonight, Father, I ask for Your forgiveness. Forgive me for not doing the right thing in the first place. Forgive me for keeping Lorelei from her father. I should have told him right away. Then she would have known him. I've taken that from her."

A familiar wave of guilt washed over her as she pondered her sins of the past. *"Though they are red like crimson. . ."*

She reached over to turn on the tiny bedside light, then reached for her Bible. She opened to the book of 1 John, chapter 2. When she glanced down at the words, amazed at their appropriateness, she knew she must have been guided to this scripture by the Holy Spirit's prompting.

" 'My little children,' " she whispered, " 'these things I write to you, so that you may not sin. And if anyone sins, we have an Advocate with the Father, Jesus Christ the righteous. And He Himself is the propitiation for our sins, and not for ours only but also for the whole world.' "

She read the words over again, letting them sink into her spirit. " '*My little children. . .*' "

The Lord was calling her His child. And tonight, with her past so clearly staring her in the face, she felt a bit like a child, caught in her own actions.

And yet. . .

The Lord had already done a work in her life, had already dealt with so much. Hadn't He?

She checked her heart to see if there was something left undone, some small area she hadn't given over completely to Him.

"Oh Lord," she prayed in a near-silent whisper, "I've been afraid to give You my lingering guilt over not reaching Chris with the news. I could have done more, Lord. I should have tried harder."

She looked at the words once again, allowing them to minister to her. "Thank You, Father, for sending Your Son, Jesus, as an atonement for my sins. Thank You for washing me white as snow. And thank You for this precious child of mine." She reached out once more to run her hand across Lorelei's back, and felt a wave of emotion run through her. "Thank You for the blessing she has been to me, and thank You that her future is blessed. Keep her in the palm of Your hand, Father."

Immediately, she felt the Lord's presence as He wrapped His arms around her. She sensed His forgiveness and His peace. Right away, a new burst of energy sent her prayer sailing forward.

"Lord, I know Your Word says You make all things new. That's what I'm asking for tonight. Make things new. Give us a fresh start. Give Chris a desire for his daughter. Give me a. . ."

She wasn't sure what to pray next. A second chance with the man she loved? Did she deserve such a thing? Did she even *want* such a thing?

A muffled ring drew her attention from the other room. Her cell phone? Who would be calling this late?

She tiptoed down the hallway into the living room, where she fetched her phone from her purse. An unfamiliar number lit the screen. She answered hesitantly. "Hello?"

"Hey." Chris's voice greeted her. At once, her heart flew to her throat. "I had to talk to you," he said.

"I'm so glad you called," she confessed. "I couldn't sleep."

"Me neither."

For a moment, neither of them said anything. Adrianne finally broke the silence. "I was just praying."

"Me, too."

More silence.

"I, um. . ." She fought to get the words out. "Chris, I'm so sorry about everything. I don't know if I can ever tell you how sorry I am. You don't know how much I wish I could just go back eight years and do all of this over. I'd change so many things. I promise I would."

"Me, too. This is really all my fault. I'm the one who, who. . ." His voice trailed off.

Adrianne came up with a plan and voiced it right away. "Let's make a deal. No looking back."

He paused a moment before offering up a hesitant "Okay."

"It won't do any good, anyway. And besides, we have to think about where we are. Right now."

There was an undeniable weariness to his voice as he responded. "I've been thinking about it. All night. Needless to say, I don't think I'll be sleeping."

"You have to. You're in a wedding tomorrow."

"Oh, the wedding." He changed gears. "You're coming, right? I really want you to."

"But they hardly know me."

"They know me," he explained. "And that's enough. Besides, Julie sounded pretty insistent."

"I don't know, Chris. I just don't think I could handle it right now. And besides, I've got Lorelei."

"Bring her. Julie said you could bring a guest, right?"

"Chris."

"Seriously." His voice intensified: "Bring her. I know that Stephen and Julie would love it. The wedding is going to be at Christ Church at two o'clock. Do you know where that is?"

"Do I know where that is?" She couldn't help but laugh. "I'm addicted to historic Philly, Chris, you know that. And it just so happens that Ben Franklin attended Christ Church. So did Betsy Ross. And a host of other famous Americans."

"Well then. . ." She could hear the weight lift from his voice as he carried on. "I'm sure they would want you to spend your Saturday afternoon at the place where they were inspired with some of the ideas that made this country what it is today. And besides"—his voice faded a bit—"*this* famous American wants you there. Please?"

A sigh rose up from the back of her throat. How could she resist an invitation like that? "Christ Church at two. I'll think about it."

He whispered a soft "Okay," followed by, "Good night," and then ended the call.

Adrianne clicked the phone shut and made her way back down the darkened hallway into the bedroom. As she slipped beneath the covers, Lorelei rolled over, eyes wide open. Her words very nearly knocked Adrianne clean out of the bed.

"See, Mom," the youngster said with a giggle, "I *told* you he liked you."

&.

"Are you okay, Chris?" Stephen's voice shattered the darkness as Chris entered the hotel room, cell phone in hand.

"Oh, I didn't mean to wake you. I got back to the hotel a long time ago, but was restless, so I went for a walk."

"In the middle of the night?" Stephen flipped on the lamp and sat up in bed.

"Yeah. Then I sat in the lobby long enough to work up the courage to call Adrianne."

Stephen shook his head. "I've been worried about you. When you didn't come back, I didn't know what to think."

"Ah. Well, I didn't mean to worry you, especially not tonight. You've got a big day tomorrow."

Stephen gave him a pensive look. "Big day or not, I've got plenty of time to talk if you need to. And I'm pretty sure you need to. It's written all over your face."

"Oh?" Chris sat on the edge of his bed and looked across the room at his friend. "You think you know me pretty well, don't you?"

"I do."

"Hmm." He wondered what Stephen would say if he told him everything he'd learned tonight. Might be pretty eye-opening.

"So. . ."

Chris just shook his head and didn't respond. "If I get started now, it's going to be a long night." He glanced at the clock. 2:16. Yikes. "It's already been a long night."

"I don't care how long it takes." Stephen crossed his arms and turned to face him. "So you might as well dive in."

"Right." Just a moment or two of silence was all it took. Then, like a flood, the story poured out. Chris felt a huge sense of relief as he told Stephen the details—right down to the most important one. To his credit, Stephen didn't respond, not vocally anyway. His wide-eyed expression at the news of Lorelei spoke volumes, though.

As he wrapped up the story, Chris opened himself up to his best friend's counsel. He listened as Stephen shared his thoughts, his opinions. And he listened even more intently as his friend—now more serious than he'd ever known him to be—took the time to pray. Aloud. At length. Chris reveled in the fact that the Lord had sent him someone to share this burden.

Somewhere around three thirty, Stephen turned off the light and rolled over. Chris changed out of his clothes and slipped into his bed, unable to fight the weariness any longer. He prayed at length, then, somewhere in the shadows of the night, gave himself over to the exhaustion.

Chapter 10

Chris woke up early, in spite of his rough night. He glanced over at Stephen, who snored soundly in the bed next to his. Unable to fall back to sleep, Chris finally rose and slipped on his clothes. Moments later, he found himself walking the beautiful historic streets of downtown Philadelphia, enjoying the solitude of a Saturday morning in blissful silence.

He had to give himself time to think, time to work out a plan of some sort. His mind wouldn't be silenced. As he made his way toward Independence National Park, he breathed in the crisp autumn air and contemplated the overwhelming beauty of the early-morning sun against the red and gold leaves.

He stopped to pick one up, staring at it momentarily. Its changes seemed to signify the transformation in his life. His past seemed as stained as this deep red leaf, but his present, and indeed, his future, could be filled with God's redemptive power, couldn't it? One season had ended, but another one—a fresh one—had begun.

On he walked, finding the city eerily quiet this weekend morning. Soon, he imagined, the tourists would flood the place, in search of the Liberty Bell. Soon the museum would open.

The museum.

Every time he thought about Adrianne's job at the museum, his heart twisted. He couldn't imagine taking her away from the work she loved so much. Besides, she probably wouldn't be interested in the kind of life he lived out on the mission field. How could she be, when she had already settled into a life that brought her such joy?

Stop thinking like that. Just because you have a daughter in common doesn't mean she's ready to be your wife.

Still his mind would not rest. Even if Adrianne married him, agreed to go with him, how would she feel about bringing Lorelei along? Could he justify taking her out of school, away from her friends, her grandparents?

Instantly, Chris's heart began to break. It seemed there was no solution to this problem. *Lord, You know my heart. I'm a missionary. I want to—need to—reach out to people. But right now, I'm so confused. I feel so lost. I thought I had already dealt with all of the forgiveness issues in my life, but here we are again, facing new ones.*

Guilt washed over him afresh, and the deep red leaf in his hand began to tremble, as if in response. He stared at it, transfixed, thinking all the while about his sins, his flaws. How they had come round to meet him once again.

"Though they are red like crimson. . ."

The familiar scripture played out in his mind, though he couldn't imagine where it had come from.

"Though they are red like crimson, they shall be as wool."

He tossed the leaf toward the ground, but the morning breeze picked it up and danced it across the park. Chris watched it, wondering if it would find a home. At last, it came to land on a concrete bench. Still, it seemed unsettled, as if the next brisk wind would pick it up and take it on to another place.

In some ways, his life was like that. He had known the freedom of bouncing from place to place, going wherever he liked. Doing whatever he liked. He'd never really settled down. Not really.

Settling down.

He pondered the words as he started walking again. What would it be like to stay in one place, to own a home? To kiss his wife each morning and tuck his daughter into bed each night? To attend PTA meetings and slip coins under pillows when loose teeth wiggled free? To dance around the living room with his little girl in his arms? To tell her stories about her grandfather, a man she'd never met?

A little shiver ran down Chris's spine as the early morning breeze brought on a chill. Could he—would he—learn to love such a life? Or would he resent it?

His mind traveled again to the tropical jungles of Nicaragua. In his mind's eye, he could see his coworker, David, hammering nails into a church beam. He could see his good friend, Pastor Alejandro, working with machete in hand to clear the weeds so that they could begin their work on a new water well. Dozens of people gathered around, eager to help. The children, their wide brown eyes, smiling, grabbing hold of his hand, calling out, "Mister, Mister!"

Immediately an ache filled Chris's heart. *Lord, help me through this. I don't have a clue which way to turn. I'm going to need Your direction, maybe more than ever before. I'm so. . .clueless.*

In that moment, a picture of Lorelei's cherub-like face flashed before him like a clip from a movie. Her dimples. Her green eyes, a mirror image of his own. Her soft brown hair, familiar in color and form. Her adorable upturned nose, much like her mama's.

Her mama's.

Chris's heart swelled at the thought of Adrianne as a mother. She seemed to take to the task quite easily. He tried to imagine what her life must be like, balancing a child and a job. He tried to picture what it must be like in the mornings as the two girls—*his* two girls—prepared for the day.

What was it like, he wondered, on those mornings when Adrianne simply didn't feel like getting out of bed and going to work? Who did she talk to on those days when she felt lonely or confused? Who did she turn to for comfort when Lorelei was sick, or acting up, even?

Did Adrianne have someone in her life to love? Someone with whom she could share her hopes and dreams?

Right away, Chris's heart ached. *I would have been there for her, if I had known. I would have.*

I still could be.

But how?

He sat on the bench, deep in thought for some time. Finally, the park began to fill with tourists, just as he'd predicted. He looked across the park at a little boy and his mother, walking hand in hand. The youngster tugged at his mom's fingers with one hand and pointed at the Liberty Bell with the other.

"Look, Mama! Look!"

"I see, I see." She took her place in the now growing line in front of the familiar landmark.

Chris glanced down at his watch: 10:45. Stephen would be looking for him soon. They had a big day ahead.

As he stood to begin the trip back to the hotel, Chris couldn't seem to take his eyes off of the little boy's mother. *She was born for this.*

Just like Adrianne. *She* was born for the role she now played, he had to acknowledge. Born to be a parent.

Born to be a parent.

With a seven-year-old daughter, *he* was surely born to be a parent, too. And it was about time he started acting like one.

❧

Adrianne awoke with a splitting headache. She rolled over in the bed to find Lorelei had already awakened. From the living room, she could hear the strains of a familiar cartoon theme song.

"Ah. She's watching TV."

Adrianne yawned and stretched, wishing she could sleep just a bit longer. She glanced over at the clock and groaned. "No way. Ten fifty?" How in the world could she have slept so late?

On the other hand, she hadn't actually fallen asleep until sometime after four. No wonder she'd slept in.

About that time, Adrianne heard noises coming from the kitchen. "Oh no. Not that."

She bounded from her bed and sprinted down the hallway. As she turned into the kitchen, she caught Lorelei with a fork in hand, trying to pry an overcooked pastry from the toaster.

"No, Lorelei. Don't do that." She grabbed the fork from her daughter's hand, all the while trying not to overreact.

"It's stuck." Lorelei's pouty face would have been cute under other circumstances.

"I know." Adrianne unplugged the toaster, turned it upside down, and weaseled the pastry out. "But you can't put something metal down inside the toaster. You could have been electrocuted. It's very dangerous."

"I didn't know." Lorelei reached to grab the burnt pastry and popped a piece in her mouth.

"Don't eat that," Adrianne scolded.

Lorelei spoke around the mouthful of food. "But I want it."

"I'm going to make a really special breakfast."

"Mmm. What?"

"How about. . ." She thought for a minute. "Chocolate chip pancakes?"

"Yummy!" Lorelei squealed. She opened the pantry door and tossed the pastry in the trash. "I love your pancakes." Immediately, the youngster reached up to the shelf that housed the pancake mix. After that, she opened the refrigerator door and pulled out the carton of eggs. She then snatched the jug of milk in hand and placed it on the kitchen counter.

"Goodness," Adrianne said with a smile. "You've already done half the work. Why don't you just make the pancakes, too?"

"I'll help." Lorelei reached into a drawer in the refrigerator for the bag of chocolate chips. "I like to cook. Grandma says I'm good at it."

"I'm glad one of us is." Adrianne couldn't help but sigh.

"It's okay, Mom." Lorelei turned to give her a more-than-serious face. "Chris will still like you, even if your cooking is bad."

Adrianne turned to face her daughter. Standing there with that hopeful look in her eyes, Lorelei looked, for all the world, like her father.

"Excuse me? Who said anything about Chris?" Adrianne tried to hide the smile from her face, but it would not be squelched. Instead, the more she thought about him, the broader it grew.

"He likes you, he likes you." Lorelei whispered the words over and over as she cracked two eggs into a large mixing bowl. Then she turned to face her mother head-on, startling her with her next words. "And you like him, too!"

Chapter 11

"How do I look?" Stephen fidgeted with his tie and Chris reached over to help him straighten it. No matter how hard he tried, he couldn't get the crazy thing to cooperate.

"You look like a happy man." Chris glanced down at his watch. "A man who's getting married in less than ten minutes."

Stephen glanced in the mirror one last time, checking his hair. "I can't believe it." He turned back to face Chris. "Everyone tells you the whole wedding-day thing is kind of surreal, and they're right. It's weird, almost like it's happening to someone else, not me." His face broadened in a smile. "Are you sure *you're* not getting married today instead of me?"

"Um, no." Chris shook his head. "I'm pretty sure I'd remember that." His heart wrenched as the words were spoken. Whether he wanted to admit it or not, he wished he could trade places with Stephen. His thoughts shifted at once to Adrianne. And Lorelei. *His* Lorelei.

Stephen must have taken note of his change of mood. "You doing okay?" He slipped an arm around Chris's shoulders in a show of support.

Chris looked up, embarrassed. "Oh. Yeah. Just thinking."

"You won't have to think long on this one, I'd guess. I've known you for years, and one thing is for sure—you're a man who finishes well, Chris Bradley." Stephen patted him on the back, then once again turned his attention to his tie.

You're a man who finishes well.

Why did the words shake him to the core? Ah. Because he wanted it so badly, probably. He wanted to finish well, wanted to make up for the mistakes of the past.

Something across the room caught his eye. He walked over to a large glass case and glanced down at the open Bible inside. "Hey, did you notice this?" he asked.

Stephen joined him, looking down at the leather-bound Bible. "Nope. Man, that thing is old. I wonder if it. . . You don't suppose it dates all the way back to the founding of the church, do you?"

Chris shrugged. "I don't know. But it's amazing. Look at the lettering."

"Wow."

They stared in silence for a moment and Chris pondered the possibility that many great men of faith—possibly even America's founding fathers—might have read from this same book throughout the generations.

As Stephen turned back to finish getting ready for the ceremony, Chris noticed for the first time that the King James Bible was opened to the twelfth chapter of Hebrews.

" 'Wherefore seeing we also are compassed about with so great a cloud of witnesses,'" he read aloud, " 'let us lay aside every weight, and the sin which doth so easily beset us, and let us run with patience the race that is set before us, looking unto Jesus the author and finisher of our faith; who for the joy that was set before him endured the cross, despising the shame, and is set down at the right hand of the throne of God.'"

"Amen," Stephen said when he finished. "Great scripture to share with a man on his wedding day—when he feels like the whole world is out there, in front of him—a race waiting to be run." He gave a knowing smile.

Chris sighed. "Great scripture to read on a day when I'm feeling like my past is catching up with me."

"Is that how you feel?" Stephen slipped an arm around his shoulder. "Like a kid who's been caught doing something he shouldn't have been?"

"A little," Chris acknowledged. "But it's such a strange mixture of feelings. I'm so excited about Lorelei. I don't even know if I can explain how excited. And Adrianne. . ." The edges of his lips turned up as he thought about her.

"You still care for her, don't you?"

Chris nodded and forced back the lump in his throat. "That's the strange part. I do. I mean, I thought I'd given the whole thing over to the Lord years ago. But I still care about her. Very much."

"I'd say it's because you gave it over to the Lord that you still have the capacity to care," Stephen added. "But then again, you probably already knew that." He gave him a friendly slap on the back, and then turned his attention back to his tie. "Could you help me with this?"

"Oh, of course." Chris jumped back into best-man gear, finally getting the wayward tie in place. Moments later, the other groomsmen entered the room with guilty looks on their faces.

"Where have you guys been?" Stephen gave his tie a final pat and turned to face his friends.

"Oh, we, uh. . ." George Ferguson gave a shrug. "We had to talk to a man about a horse."

"Sure you did." Stephen's eyes flashed a warning. "What were you up to?"

"Nothing." Phil Sanders, the younger of the two, glanced in the mirror, then reached for a comb. "Nothing you need to worry about, anyway."

"If you were messing with my car. . . ," Stephen started.

George's face gave away their prank before he spoke. "Who said anything about your car?"

"I told you guys not to do it. Wedding or no wedding."

Chris looked back and forth between George and Phil. Neither said a word, but they had clearly "done the deed," as it were.

At that moment, Stephen's father entered the room, carrying boutonnieres. "The wedding planner is in over her head with the bridesmaids," he explained. "So she asked me if I could make sure these made it into the right hands."

All of the guys scrambled, trying to figure out how to fasten the fall-colored flowers onto their tuxedo jackets. A knock on the door interrupted their frenzy.

"Nearly ready?" the minister, a pleasant-looking fellow, asked as he entered the room. "The organist has just started the Brandenburg Concerto and that's our cue. All of the guests are seated." He glanced to his right, noted Stephen struggling with the boutonniere, and came to the rescue. "Let me get this for you. I've become something of an expert over the years."

"Thanks, Rev. Stone." The color seemed to drain from Stephen's face even as he spoke the words.

"Are you okay, man?" Chris asked.

"Yeah. Just feeling a little nauseous."

Rev. Stone finished with the boutonniere, and then went on to offer a bit of advice. "Don't lock your knees."

"I beg your pardon?" Stephen's brow wrinkled.

"When you get out there in front of the crowd, don't lock your knees. Keep them slightly bent." The older man's face softened slightly as he demonstrated the proper stance. "It's been my experience that we lose a lot of grooms when they lock their knees."

"Ah."

"And deep breaths, young man." He faced Stephen. "Remember, it's not about the ceremony. It's about the marriage."

Chris couldn't help but laugh as Stephen took several slow, deep breaths. *He really is nervous.*

"Here we go." Rev. Stone led the way to the door that opened into the large, formal sanctuary. Stephen trailed him, with Chris following along like a puppy on his heels. George and Phil fell into place behind Chris, and within minutes they were standing at the front of the crowd.

As he looked around the magnificent room with its rich historical elements, Chris thought about what Adrianne had said on the phone. *"Ben Franklin attended Christ Church. So did Betsy Ross."* He gaze shifted upward, to the large white balconies and arched windows. They were amazing, really, though noticeably different from the churches he'd helped build in Nicaragua. There they were lucky to have openings for windows. No glass at all.

Yes, this place was great. And how remarkable, to consider the countless historic things that had surely happened here. Great men and women of faith had stood in this very spot, perhaps preached in this very place.

This is a room where amazing things have happened, I feel sure of it. In this room, the Lord has spoken to many of our forefathers.

"Lord," the word came out as the faintest of whispers, "speak to me. Here, in this place. Speak to me. Show me Your will."

Chris's eyes were immediately drawn to the crowd. Had Adrianne and Lorelei come? Were they here?

No, he saw no sign of them. Keen disappointment set in, but it was short-lived. *Stay focused. You're here for Stephen and Julie.*

A change in music signaled the entrance of the bridesmaids. One by one, they entered the room to the familiar strain of Pachelbel's Canon in D. They joined the men at the front, and then the moment arrived. The "Bridal March" began, and the crowd rose to its feet.

As soon as the doors opened and Julie—radiant in white satin walked in on her father's arm, Chris's attention shifted to Stephen. *What does it feel like, to watch the woman you love walking up the aisle? Is your heart so full you can hardly stand it? Are you a nervous wreck?*

The bride literally glowed with joy as she approached and took Stephen's hand. Together, they entered the altar area. Chris felt the sting of tears as he turned with the others to face the minister. Just as he did, however, something at the back of the room caught his eye. Someone—rather, a couple of someones—slipped in the back door unnoticed. Unnoticed by anyone other than himself, anyway.

Right away, his heart soared. *They're here. My daughter and my. . .*

"We've come here this day to unite this man and this woman in holy matrimony." The minister's words rang out across the sanctuary, creating a near hollow sound against the marble floor and the wooden pews. "Marriage is an honorable estate, and not to be entered into lightly. . . ." He continued on with his opening remarks, but Chris found it difficult to focus, at least on Stephen and Julie. No, he saw himself standing in their spot. With Adrianne at his side.

❧

"Mom, look!"

Adrianne glanced over at Lorelei and shushed her.

"But, Mom"—Lorelei pointed at the flower girl, a pretty little thing with blonde ringlets and a beautiful white dress—"I've never been a flower girl."

Right away, Adrianne's finger went to her lips. "We have to be quiet," she whispered. "We can talk about it afterward." She tried to focus on the ceremony, but found her gaze shifting to Chris. He looked remarkable in his black tuxedo. Breathtaking, actually.

Don't do that. Pay attention.

The wedding couple exchanged vows, hand in hand, love pouring from their eyes.

What would it feel like, to stand up there? What would I be thinking. . .doing?

Her gaze shifted to the large columns to her right and left, then lifted to the carved balconies on the second floor. The chandelier overhead cast a warm glow on the room, reminding her of days gone by. Though not as ornate as some of the other churches in the historic district, this one still captivated her more than any of the others. Probably because Ben Franklin had attended church here. Perhaps sitting in this very pew. Just the idea of it put goose bumps on her arms. *How is it that I can be so intrigued with someone from history?*

"*Because he changed lives. He left a legacy.*"

The words nearly rocked her off the pew. Yes, he and the other founding fathers had certainly left a legacy.

And that's exactly what she wanted to do, too.

Familiar words from the minister directed her attention back up to the front of the sanctuary. "You may now kiss the bride."

Lorelei's eyes grew large as Stephen and Julie kissed. "You're going to get married someday, too, Mom. And you'll get kissed, don't worry." Her forced whisper was a little too loud, catching the attention of the elderly lady who sat in front of them. The somewhat matronly looking woman turned with a scolding look on her face.

Adrianne mouthed *I'm sorry*, then turned her attention back to the minister's closing remarks, hoping Lorelei would keep her thoughts to herself.

No such luck.

"Look, Mom!" Her daughter pointed at Chris as he made his way down the aisle, along with others in the wedding party. "I see Chris."

"Yes." Adrianne couldn't hide her smile.

"He looks handsome, just like Prince Charming. See, I *told* you!"

"Lorelei," Adrianne whispered the words, but let her eyes do the begging, "please don't. Please."

Thankfully, the joyous strains of Vivaldi's *Four Seasons* theme drowned out the youngster's voice.

Almost.

Lorelei's jovial attitude quickly faded as she noticed the pretty bridesmaid on Chris's arm. She turned to face her mother, pain registering in her eyes. "Is that his *girlfriend?*"

"Please—lower—your—voice." Adrianne mouthed the words slowly, succinctly.

Lorelei seemed to pay her no mind at all. Instead, she took advantage of his nearness to give him a little wave.

Adrianne buried her head in her hands and wondered if she would ever get over the embarrassment of this afternoon as long as she lived.

She lifted her gaze just as Prince Charming walked by, tuxedo shimmering under the chandelier overhead.

Chris nodded their way and even gave Lorelei a wink. Then he turned his gaze to Adrianne. The love that showed in his eyes nearly caused her to stop breathing altogether, and for a moment—just a moment—she contemplated tossing a glass slipper his way.

Chapter 12

Wphat are you doing, Mom?"

Adrianne dug around in her purse for pennies, finally capturing a few. "Come with me," she said, taking Lorelei by the hand. "I have something to show you."

Together, they scooted around the wedding party at the front of Christ Church and walked around to the old burial ground nearby.

"A cemetery?" Lorelei's eyes widened. "I don't want to go in there."

"Don't worry, we're not." Adrianne handed her the pennies, then pointed out one of the large, flat gravesites several yards away. "That's where Ben Franklin is buried, that gravestone right there."

"Ooh." A sound of admiration rose from her daughter's lips. "Why are there pennies all over it?"

"Well," Adrianne explained, "Ben always had a saying, 'A penny saved is a penny earned.' He's remembered for witty things like that. So tourists come by here and toss pennies. It's a tradition. People have been doing it for hundreds of years. And I thought you might like to try. But you have to do it from outside the fence."

"Cool." Lorelei took aim, then tossed the first penny. It missed by about three feet. She turned back to her mother with a pout.

"Try the other one."

The youngster tried again. This time, the penny came within inches. "Do you have more, Mom?"

Adrianne reached inside her purse once again. "I don't think so. But you were close, anyway."

"I have a penny."

They turned quickly as Chris's voice seemed to sweep over them from behind. He stood closer than her own breath, his brilliant green eyes dancing in the afternoon sunlight.

"I. . .I thought you were busy having photos done," she explained. "And I wanted to show Lorelei something from our history." *Something from our history. Hmm. Probably should have worded that differently.*

He held up a copper penny between his thumb and forefinger and smiled. "Want to include me?"

His words caused her hands to tremble. Yes, she wanted to include him. In her life. In her daughter's life. In her decisions, her hopes, her dreams, her future. Everything.

Lorelei reached up to snatch the penny from his hand. "Can I try again?" she asked.

"You may."

This time she tossed the coin and it landed in the center of the gravestone. "I did it!" She jumped up and down, excitement oozing from every pore.

"You did it." Adrianne and Chris spoke in unison, then turned in laughter, suddenly finding themselves face-to-face.

Adrianne felt his breath warm on her cheek, and for a moment thought of pulling away. But something inside her wouldn't allow it. Instead, she remained still as he leaned in close. Her eyes closed instinctively. She remembered the taste of his lips against hers. Eight years might have passed, but some things would never be forgotten.

"Chris, are you ready to go?" Stephen's voice rang out from around the corner, and Adrianne's heart leaped into her throat as Chris pulled away quite suddenly.

"Mom?" Lorelei grabbed her hand and stared up, eyes blazing with laughter. "See, I *told* you."

"Told you what?" Chris asked, his cheeks flushed pink.

"I *told* you he would kiss you."

Adrianne looked up in embarrassment, only to find Chris's beautiful green eyes riveted on hers. She did her best to shift gears, feeling a little foolish for giving away her feelings in front of her daughter. "Wh–who said anything about kissing?"

Chris gave her a look that voiced his opinion on the matter. She could read the *"I did"* in his expression.

As if in response, Lorelei grabbed their hands and pressed them together. Then, with a smile on her face, she led the way to the front of the church to meet the others.

ॐ

Chris's heart sang all the way to the wedding reception. He had seen the look in Adrianne's eyes. She still loved him, in spite of everything. And he loved her, too. With every fiber of his being.

And Lorelei. . .

He couldn't help but wonder at the youngster's tenacity—or her matchmaking skills. Clearly, she wanted to see the two of them together.

For obvious reason, he chided himself. *Of course she wants to see us together. She's been without a father all of her life.*

He pushed aside the feelings of guilt that suddenly rose to the surface and focused on the activities ahead. Any moment now, he would arrive with the rest of the bridal party at the reception hall, where they would make a grand entrance. Hopefully, Adrianne and Lorelei would stay for a while, until his duties as best man had ended. He had so much to say to her, so much to share.

Within moments, Chris and the others entered the lavish Ballroom at the Ben—and found the room filled with cheering wedding guests. The music started right away and the bride and groom headed off to the dance floor for their first dance as a married couple.

Chris stood off to the side, scoping out the room. *Ah. There they are.* Adrianne and Lorelei—his girls—sat at a table nearby. They smiled his way, and Lorelei waved in excitement. He made his way through the crowd toward them.

"This place is great, don't you think?" Adrianne gestured around the room.

For some reason, he couldn't focus on the room, only her rich brown eyes as they danced in excitement.

"Beautiful," he said with a hint of a smile rising to his lips.

"Those chandeliers are absolutely exquisite."

"Exquisite," he echoed, still paying no attention whatsoever to the room.

"And the gold trim on those archways is unbelievable."

"Unbelievable."

Adrianne looked Chris's way and caught his meaning. Her face reddened. A feeling of warmth rushed over him, and he wanted to sweep her into his arms again. Instead, Lorelei caught his attention, pointing at the couple on the dance floor.

"She looks like Cinderella, Mom."

"Yes, she does." Adrianne nodded. "And look who she's dancing with—Prince Charming."

"No she's not." Lorelei looked up at Chris with a shy face, and he tried to decipher her meaning.

Just then, the music ended and the DJ announced the opening of the buffet line. Lorelei tipped her face upward and grinned. "Food, Mom!"

Adrianne seemed to snap out of her somewhat dreamy state, looking over at Chris with a more practical look on her face. "I—I don't want to keep you from your friends. We'll just sit over here. . ."

Chris let out a sigh. "I guess I do need to sit at the head table with the wedding party. I'm still officially on the clock."

"Always a groomsman. . ." Adrianne started, then slapped her hand over her mouth. "Oh, I'm so sorry. That was totally inappropriate."

"Nah." He grinned. "I'm used to it."

Always a groomsman. But maybe not for long.

The rest of the evening played out just as he'd hoped it would. Though dedicated to his best friend, he managed to snatch some well-deserved moments with Adrianne and Lorelei. And at one point, well after offering the toast, he even managed to ask her to dance. Lorelei, not Adrianne.

The youngster's face lit with excitement as she took him by the hand and they walked to the dance floor together.

As Chris circled around with his daughter's hand clutched in his, tears came. He couldn't control them. *This is my first father-daughter dance. But it won't be my last.*

Through the tears, he glanced over at Adrianne, who sat alone at the table, eyes glistening.

When I'm done, Adrianne Russo, he vowed, *you're next. And this time, I'm not going to let you get away.*

Chapter 13

Adrianne looked up as Lorelei's happy-go-lucky voice rang out above the crowd of people in the fellowship hall.

"I'm going to kids' church, Mom!"

Adrianne turned her attention away from Mrs. Norris, one of the members of her church, to focus on her daughter. She turned back to the older woman with a smile. "Excuse me. Looks like I'm needed."

She finally caught up with her daughter. Taking her by the arm, she asked, "Hey, what's your hurry?"

"I don't want them to start without me."

Adrianne glanced at her watch: 9:15. "Yikes. I didn't know it was this late." Seemed like the whole morning had been a bit "off," what with getting so little sleep last night. Then again, who could sleep, with the crystal-clear memory of Chris wrapping her in his arms for a turn around the dance floor?

"Mom, are you coming?" Lorelei's voice jarred Adrianne back to the present. Together, they made their way through the throng of people to the children's church room. All along the way, familiar faces greeted her. When they arrived, Adrianne stopped for a short chat with Jacquie Levron, director of the children's ministry.

"Are you ready for tonight?" she asked.

Jacquie nodded, but her expression carried a bit of concern. "Pretty much. Some of the kids haven't memorized their lines yet, and Phillip Johnson has strep throat, but you know what they say. . ."

"The show must go on." The two women spoke in unison.

Adrianne couldn't help but laugh. "So, tell me." She lowered her voice a bit. "How do you think Lorelei is doing? She's been practicing every day."

"Oh, Adrianne." Jacquie's voice lit up. "That girl of yours is amazing. Of course, she has a voice like an angel. I've told you that before. But there's something more to it than that. When Lorelei sings. . ." Jacquie shook her head, apparently trying to find the right words. "When Lorelei sings, there's an anointing on her. You can feel the presence of God."

Goose bumps rippled down Adrianne's arms as she nodded in response. "I'm her mom," she acknowledged, "so I thought it was just me—thought I was just reading too much into it."

Jacquie's smiled broadened. "No, you're not reading too much into it. That girl was born to sing. And I'm so glad to have her in our church. Not just because she's talented, Adrianne." Her voice took on a more serious tone. "But because she's a good girl. Genuine. Her walk with the Lord is evident. And it's so pure."

"It's so pure."

Adrianne brushed back the tears as she turned to leave the room. *Lord, how is it possible? This child, born out of my sin, is as pure as the driven snow. She's such a blessing to me, such a joy. What would I have done without her?*

She shifted her thoughts as she headed into the sanctuary. Her parents would be waiting. Probably in the fourth row on the left, as usual. Yep. There they were.

"G'morning, baby. How are you?" Her mother reached over to wrap her in a warm embrace.

Adrianne knew that, no matter how long she lived, she would always be referred to as her mother's baby. She also knew that she loved the reference, for it implied innocence. Purity.

There's that word again.

Snapping back to her senses, Adrianne answered her mother's question. "I'm great. Lorelei and I went to the wedding yesterday."

"Tell me all about it." Her mom ushered her to a seat and Adrianne quickly relayed the whole story—everything from the beautiful ceremony, to the dance she and Chris had shared at the end of the night.

Her father listened in without saying a word, but she observed the look in his eye when she reached the part of the story where Chris had swept Lorelei into his arms for a father-daughter dance.

"He's a good man, Adrianne." Her dad gave a nod. "But I think you already knew that."

"Yes."

Chris Bradley had always been a good man—a man after God's own heart. Yes, he had made mistakes. They both had. But God had restored them, and that meant the past was truly in the past.

The worship team began to play a familiar praise and worship song, and the congregation stood. As Adrianne sang, her heart soared. *Lord, You're so good to me.* A few moments later, the familiar strains of a slower worship song began, a song Adrianne had always loved. She sensed God's overwhelming presence, and closed her eyes, ready to let Him minister to her in any way He pleased.

"See, child. Do you see how much I love you?"

The tears came at once. She didn't even bother to wipe them away.

" 'Though your sins are like scarlet...,'" she whispered.

"I've erased those sins, My daughter. I've forgiven and forgotten, as far as the east is from the west."

" 'Though they are red like crimson. . .'"

"The only crimson I see is the precious blood of My Son, who takes away the sins of the world."

Adrianne drew in a deep breath and brushed the tears away.

"Adrianne?" Her father leaned over with a soft whisper, concern registering in his eyes. "Everything okay?"

She took him by the hand and mouthed the words *Yes. Very okay.*

He gave her fingers a little squeeze, then leaned over to plant a kiss on her forehead. In that moment, a thousand feelings washed over her at once. Poor Lorelei had never known the love of a father's kiss pressed upon her brow. She'd never experienced the comfort of a gentle squeeze of a daddy's hand, or the wink of his eye.

Thank You, God, for my father. Thank You for giving me such an idyllic family life. I don't know what I've ever done to deserve it. . .to deserve him.

As if he'd read her thoughts, her father turned and gave a wink. She nodded his way, then shifted her attention to the front of the room and focused on the pastor. He opened the message with a scripture from the Psalms, one of Adrianne's favorites.

" 'As far as the east is from the west,'" he read, " 'so far has He removed our transgressions from us.'" The pastor forged ahead, his words laced with excitement. "I had another message planned for today," he explained, "but at the prompting of the Holy Spirit, I've gone a different direction. I've titled this morning's message 'From the East to the West.'"

He went on to share one of the most amazing sermons Adrianne had ever heard on forgiveness, honing in on God's ability to forget, as well as forgive.

Oh, if only I could forget! If only I could wipe away all traces of my past.

"Turn with me in your Bibles to the book of Psalms, chapter 32," Pastor Monahan said.

Adrianne turned to the passage and the pastor began to read aloud, starting in the first verse.

" 'Blessed is he whose transgression is forgiven, whose sin is covered. Blessed is the man to whom the Lord does not impute iniquity, and in whose spirit there is no deceit.'

"When our sins are forgiven," Pastor Monahan said, "God can't count them against us. And it's clear why, when we turn to the book of Isaiah, chapter 43."

Adrianne flipped through the pages of her Bible until she landed on the chapter in question.

" 'I, even I, am He who blots out your transgressions,'" the pastor read, " 'for My own sake; and I will not remember your sins.'" He looked up at the congregation as he repeated the words, " 'I will not remember your sins.'"

After a slight chuckle, he continued. "We can't seem to forget offenses that others commit against us, whether they happened yesterday or last year. It's so difficult for us to forget, isn't it? And how much harder is it for us to forgive ourselves when we've broken God's heart? Sometimes forgiving ourselves is the hardest thing of all."

Adrianne squirmed a bit, and her father reached over to give her hand a squeeze.

Pastor Monahan's eyes lit with excitement as he spoke. "How ironic is it," he said, "that the Lord loves sinners, but hates sin? How fascinating, that the price to pay for forgiveness is so very high, but that He was willing to pay it? And how amazing, that God doesn't even keep a record—or a transcript—of our sins. He doesn't forgive in part. He forgives completely."

Adrianne listened intently, thankful for the Lord's reminder that she could not only put the past behind her, but that He would remember it no more.

"How do we receive this forgiveness?" Pastor Monahan asked. "When you come to the Lord, truly repentant, and put your trust in the work done on the cross, your sins are washed away. Erased. Doesn't matter how big. Doesn't matter how bad. The blood of Jesus was—and is—sufficient to wash away any trace or stain of sin."

"Any trace of sin." Adrianne whispered the words. *'Though they are red like crimson. . .'*

As the pastor's words flowed forth, Adrianne couldn't help but think the Lord Himself had planned this message just for her. She would learn to walk in forgiveness—for her sake, and for her daughter's.

❧

Chris's cell phone rang just as he and the other groomsmen finished up their lunch at the hotel. The sound of Adrianne's voice on the other end brought a smile to his lips right away. He excused himself from the table and took the call outside.

"I'm so glad it's you," he said.

He noticed a bit of hesitation in her voice as she responded, "Yeah. I needed to call. We have a lot to work out."

"Right." He pondered that for a moment. Had she called with a particular plan in mind, or was she as clueless as he was?

"How long are you in town?"

"I leave tomorrow afternoon for Virginia Beach. Then it's back to Managua three days later."

"Oh."

Was that disappointment in her voice? He hoped so, prayed so. "Are you free today at all?"

"Well, I was actually calling with an invitation." Her voice seemed to lift a bit with her next words. "Lorelei is in a play at church tonight. She's singing a couple of solos, actually."

"Ah." He grinned. "She is her mother's daughter, isn't she?"

Adrianne chuckled. "Yeah. But, to be honest, I haven't sung in years."

He couldn't hide the disappointment from his voice as he said, "That's a shame."

"Well," Adrianne continued on, "in all honesty, she's far better than I ever was."

"I doubt that." Chris couldn't remember anything clearer—or purer—than the sound of Adrianne's voice as she sang out to the Lord. He had held on to that memory for eight years now. And her performances back in college had mesmerized plenty of people besides him.

"Well, I guess you're just going to have to come and hear her for yourself. Then you'll know I'm telling the truth."

Chris smiled as he heard the pride in her voice. "Just name the time and place and I'm there."

"I was thinking I could come by and pick you up after I drop off Lorelei for rehearsal. That way, we could spend a little time talking beforehand."

His heart quickened. "S–sounds good. What time will you be here?"

"Five?"

"Five. Okay. Dressy or casual?"

"Casual."

"Casual it is." Chris leaned back against the side of the building and paused a moment before saying the one thing he'd been dying to say since he took her in his arms last night. Finally, the courage gripped him. "Adrianne?"

"Yes?"

"I—I still love you. I do." *More than I can stand to say.*

Her silence seemed to go on an eternity. When she finally did speak, he could hear the emotion in her voice and knew she was crying. "I—I know."

Please say you love me, too. Say it, and I'll know what to do.

"I. . ." Her voice took on a more practical sound. "I'll pick you up at five."

Though he suddenly felt the wind had been knocked out of his sails, Chris managed to eke out a quick good-bye. Then, with his back still pressed firmly to the wall, he closed his eyes and allowed the tears to come.

Chapter 14

Chris entered the sanctuary of the inner-city church and looked around in amazement. The architecture of the the Freedom Fellowship Church could hardly be compared to the grandeur of Christ Church, but something about this place just felt—right. Good.

"Wow. This is really cool. I've been to a lot of churches, but never seen one converted from a warehouse like this before."

"It's more of a storefront ministry," Adrianne explained. "We do a lot of inner-city outreaches. And we deal with a lot of homeless people, too. I always like to tell people that we're a little different right off the bat so they won't be surprised. Our church has an inner-city 'face,' if that makes sense. Lots of people with lots of issues. New converts, I guess you'd say."

"I understand. They sound a lot like the people I worked with in Nicaragua. People new to the faith, with a lot of things to unravel in their lives. Lots of alcohol problems, especially."

"Same here." She looked at him, eyes wide. "Sounds like we've kind of been working along the same lines all along. Weird, huh?"

"Yeah."

She led the way to the third row of chairs and gestured for him to take a seat. As he did, an older woman leaned over to shake his hand.

"Welcome."

Chris nodded. "Thanks."

"This is Mrs. Norris," Adrianne explained with a nod. "She heads up our ministry to shut-ins."

"Great to meet you." He flashed a broad smile. Something about the woman reminded him a bit of Alejandro's wife. Her colorful attire, perhaps? Her silver hair swept up in a bun?

"Do you have a child in the play tonight?" Mrs. Norris asked.

Chris's heart almost stopped. Especially when he saw the look that crossed Adrianne's face. If he said no, he'd be lying. If he said yes, the woman would likely ask which child.

"Actually, I've got a—"

Thankfully, the musicians on stage began to play, signaling the beginning of the service. The woman shrugged and took her seat. Chris wiped a bead of sweat from his brow.

"That was a close one," Adrianne whispered.

"Yeah."

At that moment, her parents slipped into their seats next to them. "Sorry we're late," her mother said. "I had a long-distance call from your brother in Kuwait. I finally told him that I had to go, that our little angel was playing the starring role in her first play."

Adrianne smiled in her direction. "It's fine. You didn't miss anything."

Chris made a mental note to ask Adrianne about her brother. *Kuwait. He must be in the military.*

His thought shifted back to the service as the worship leader, a young man in his late twenties perhaps, came to the center of the stage and asked everyone to stand. He led them in three or four worship songs, then turned the service over to the elementary director, whose face shone with excitement.

She introduced the production, and the lights went down. Moments later, a spotlight came up—on his daughter. Center stage. She wore a biblical costume, along with the brightest smile he'd ever seen.

For just a second, Chris was overcome with nerves for her.

No need. She dove into the opening song with great gusto, her beautiful voice ringing out loud and clear. She sang with the joy of a youngster, but the clarity and vocal strength of a grown woman. In fact, she sounded for all the world like her mother, the last time he heard her sing in church. Eight years ago.

Whether he meant to do it or not, Chris could not be sure, but he reached to take Adrianne's hand and gave it a squeeze. She squeezed back, a good sign. He glanced at her out of the corner of his eye. Were those tears?

Yes. She dabbed at her eyes with her other hand, never taking her focus off of the stage. Was she crying because of Lorelei's performance, or had the events of the past few days finally taken their toll? He offered up another gentle squeeze and she responded by gripping his hand.

The play went on, creating both laughter and tears from those watching. Chris couldn't remember ever having so much fun in church. And the fact that his daughter ripped his heart out with her obvious love for the Lord only made the evening more enjoyable.

When the production came to an end, the audience members rose to their feet and applauded. Chris stood, with tears in his eyes, clapping madly. Afterward, once the lights came back on in the auditorium, he caught Lorelei's attention from a distance. She ran all the way from the stage, directly into his outstretched arms.

"Chris! You came!"

He did his best not to let the moisture in his eyes give him away. "I came. And I'm so proud of you."

She wrapped her hands around his neck and gave him a squeeze. "Thank you. It was so fun!" After he put her back down, she pulled at her mother's blouse. "Can we go out for ice cream with everybody else?"

Adrianne looked at Chris with a little shrug. "Several of us like to go out after church on Sunday nights. It's kind of a tradition."

"Will you come, Chris?" Lorelei looked up with a pretend pout, trying to woo him.

"I'd love to. I'm all for tradition." Chris had the oddest feelings run through him as he spoke the words. He was suddenly aware of the time crunch, aware of the fact that he would be leaving tomorrow to return to Virginia Beach, and then on to Nicaragua shortly thereafter. Aware of the fact that he needed to take advantage of every possible moment with Lorelei.

And Adrianne.

He looked over at the beauty on his left. With her dark curls framing the splattering of freckles on her cheeks, she looked like something from a magazine. But there was more to her than physical beauty, for sure. Her inner strength, her passion for life—these were the things that made her the woman she was.

"Do you think it's okay if I go with you two?"

Adrianne's lips curled up a bit as she responded, "Of course."

Right then and there, Chris's heart took flight. Yes, he would go with them. To the moon, if they asked him to.

&

Adrianne had spent the better part of the performance trying to catch her breath. She couldn't tell which had her more unnerved, Lorelei's amazing performance or the delicious comfort of Chris's hand in her own.

Face it. You're a wreck because you're still in love with him. Something about sitting here in church, with Chris at her side, felt so good, so right.

And yet...

The whole thing seemed like a childish dream. In reality, he would leave tomorrow, returning to his work in Central America. Their conversation in the car had revealed that much, though the sadness in his eyes had been evident.

Yes, tomorrow Chris would walk out of her life, just as she had walked out of his all those many years ago. And she and Lorelei would be left alone to fend for themselves. Again.

Chapter 15

After ordering two banana splits and a small hot fudge sundae, Chris and Adrianne joined a couple of others at a small booth in the back of the ice cream parlor. All along the way, he watched her as she interacted with others, fascinating thoughts taking hold. *She's just as social as she ever was. And her face still lights up like a maraschino cherry when she orders a banana split.* Some things really didn't change with time.

"Chris, this is our pastor, Jake Monahan." Adrianne made the introductions with a smile on her face.

Clearly, she admired her pastor. Chris reached out to shake the man's hand. "Nice to meet you."

Jake introduced his wife, Katelyn, whose smile broadened as her gaze traveled back and forth between Chris and Adrianne.

"Any friend of Adrianne's is a friend of ours," she said with a somewhat mischievous grin. "Are you from Philly?"

"No. Just here for a wedding." Chris pondered those words as soon as he said them. This trip to Philadelphia might have started out as a simple wedding trip, but it had rapidly morphed into something else altogether.

Lorelei appeared at the table, licking her lips as she gazed at the hot fudge sundae. "Is that mine?" she asked.

"It is." Adrianne passed it her way. "But you owe Mr. Bradley a thank-you. He was kind enough to treat us tonight."

"Thank you, thank you!" She took the sundae and, after asking her mother's permission, sat at the next table with several of her friends.

Chris turned his attention back to Adrianne as she continued on with the introductions. "Chris and I have been good friends since college. He's in missions work," she explained to the pastor and his wife. "Foreign missions, I mean."

Pastor Monahan's face lit up immediately. "Really? Where?"

Chris swallowed a huge bite of banana and ice cream, then answered, "Central America."

"You're kidding!" Katelyn and Jake looked at each other incredulously.

Chris shrugged, then spooned another bite of the gooey dessert into his mouth. "Nope. Why?"

Jake's voice intensified as he explained. "We've been talking about sending out a team to Central America for ages now, but the timing just hasn't been right. And we didn't really have a connection. Maybe you could give me some information while you're in town."

The two men dove into a lengthy conversation about Chris's work in Nicaragua. At several points along the way, Chris glanced at Adrianne to make sure she didn't feel left out. No, she seemed enthralled, as did Katelyn. Meanwhile, Lorelei, who at some point along the way had shifted out to the playground area with her friends, popped her head in the door every now and again to ask if they could stay longer.

When the adults wrapped up their discussion about water wells and remote villages, Jake looked over at Adrianne and smiled. "I like this friend of yours, Adrianne."

"He's a keeper," Katelyn said with a wink.

Chris noticed Adrianne's cheeks flush, and shot a glance over at the playground, hoping to distract everyone. "Looks like Lorelei's having fun."

"Oh, yes," Katelyn agreed. "She's very social, have you noticed?"

"I have." *Just like her mother.*

Katelyn added her thoughts on the matter. "Now that's one great kid. She has the sweetest spirit. She's the spitting image of her mother."

She is at that.

Jake chimed in with a gleam in his eye. "And I guess it goes without saying she's very talented."

"She is." Chris couldn't help but dive in. "And she sings just like her mother. You should have heard Adrianne back in college. She. . ." He caught himself just before giving too much away. Perhaps Adrianne didn't want her good friends knowing so much about her past.

"You never told us you sang, Adrianne." Katelyn turned to stare at her in surprise. "We would have signed you up for the worship team."

"Oh no." Adrianne threw her hands up in the air. "My singing days are behind me. Trust me."

"I wouldn't be so sure." Jake's smile seemed to light the room as he spoke. "It's a funny thing. Just about the time we say 'never again, Lord,' He opens a door."

"Or just the opposite," Katelyn suggested. "Sometimes when we're convinced that we know exactly what we're supposed to be doing, God sends us off on a detour in a completely different direction."

Whoa. A message for me, perhaps?

Chris leaned back in his chair and listened quietly as the pastor and his wife dove into an animated story of how they'd met on just such a detour. Every now and again, Adrianne would look Chris's way. When she did, her eyes seem to speak something. . . What was it? Hope? Longing?

Just about the time he thought he'd calmed his heart, Lorelei approached their table, stifling a yawn. Right away, Adrianne snapped to attention, glancing at her watch.

"Oh! It's nine thirty. We've got to get you home to bed."

"I'm not sleepy," Lorelei argued.

Adrianne stood, as if in response. "Sure you're not."

Chris stood alongside her, painfully aware of the fact that their time together was drawing to a close. In minutes, she would drop him off at the hotel and they would part ways.

For how long, he had no way of knowing.

&

Adrianne gripped the steering wheel as they pulled away from the Dairy Queen. "Did you have a good time?" She glanced over at Chris, who nodded. She wondered at his silence over the past few minutes.

"I wish I didn't have to leave tomorrow." He turned to look at her, and even in the darkness, she noted the tremor in his voice. "I don't want to go."

"Do you have to leave?" Lorelei piped up from the back seat. "I want you to stay. Forever."

"Forever is a mighty long time." Adrianne tried to make light of the situation, but inside her heart was breaking. If Chris really boarded the plane the next morning, she didn't know what she would do.

Their conversation shifted a bit as they took turns talking about the day. Finally, when Adrianne was convinced her daughter had drifted off to sleep, she whispered a somber, "We need to talk," Chris's way.

"I know." His response, equally as soft, was accompanied by the touch of his hand brushing against her cheek.

She leaned against his hand and tried to still her heart. What in the world would she do without him, now that they'd found one another again?

And yet he had to go. He must return to his work on the mission field. Adrianne knew, beyond a shadow of a doubt, that she could never ask him to give it up, not after seeing the gleam in his eye as he talked to Pastor Jake about it. No, he must return to Nicaragua, and she must return to her life—as a single mother.

For a few minutes, she didn't speak. The lump in her throat wouldn't allow it. Finally, Chris broke the silence. "W–what are we going to do, Adrianne?"

She glanced back over her shoulder to make sure Lorelei was genuinely asleep before answering. "We'll. . .we'll work out a plan. You'll have to come back as often as you can. . . ."

"As often as I can?" The pain in his voice drove a stake through her heart, but she forged ahead.

"Yes. Whenever you're in the States, you'll have to come see us."

"And. . .that's it?"

She kept her focus on the road and willed herself not to cry. "I don't want you to miss out on anything. And you're welcome to be with us. . . ." Here her voice lowered. "With Lorelei. . .as often as you're able."

"And then?"

"I think she needs time to get to know you, and to get used to the idea that you're really her. . ." She mouthed the word *father*. Adrianne pushed back the lump in her throat. "And we both need time to pray and ask the Lord to show us what to do, right?"

"I'm going to do the right thing by both of you." He spoke firmly. "Financially, I mean. And in whatever other ways the Lord shows me. I need you to know that."

"You're a good man, Chris." She paused. "I—I know you're passionate about your work." Another pause gave her long enough to dab at her eyes and force down the lump in her throat. "We've just got to figure out how to balance the jungles of Nicaragua with historic Philadelphia, that's all."

"I don't know." He leaned his head back against the seat and sighed. "I know you love your work at the museum. It's obvious. You're amazing at what you do," he said, reaching out to touch her arm.

"So are you." She whispered the words, realizing all too well what she was saying. Whether they wanted to admit it or not, they were living in two very different worlds, going in two very different directions.

A painful silence filled the car as he released his gentle hold on her arm. The gesture seemed to speak volumes. As much as she hated to admit it, a separation of sorts had taken place. A wall had been erected, and it didn't appear to be coming down anytime soon.

With a sigh, she turned her attention back to the road.

Chapter 16

"Mom, where is Chris again?" Lorelei asked.

Adrianne looked up from underneath the bed where she'd been searching for her shoe. "I told you the last three times. . . ." A groan escaped her lips. "He had to go back to Virginia Beach. He's probably headed to the airport right now."

"Virginia Beach? How far is Virginia Beach?"

"Not close." Adrianne pushed back the lump in her throat and avoided her daughter's penetrating gaze. "Besides, I think he leaves for Nicaragua sometime later in the week. He was only here on a short furlough." She turned her attention back to looking for the missing pump.

"Furlough? What's that?"

"It's when a missionary comes home from the mission field for a short season. But he has to go back to Nicaragua." She spoke as much to convince herself as anything. "That's what missionaries do. They have to go wherever they feel the Lord is leading them."

Lorelei stepped closer, her voice trembling as she spoke. "But, Mom, I miss him. Can't the Lord lead him here?"

Well said, well said. "I suppose that could happen, but I wouldn't count on it."

"Isn't he coming back at all?"

Adrianne stuck her head under the bed once more in an attempt to reach the wayward shoe. Finally snagging it, she rose to her knees and stared at her persistent daughter. "I'm sure he'll be back sometime, but I couldn't say when."

"But, Mom,"—Lorelei sat on the edge of the bed, tears coming to her eyes— "I wanted you to marry Chris. How can you marry him if he's in Nicaragua?"

Once again, Adrianne looked away as she spoke, focusing on the shoe, not the child. "What's your hurry to get me married off?" she asked finally.

Lorelei lifted her chin, defiant. "I want to have a dad. Someone to drive me to school every day. And come to my ballet recitals."

"I walk you to the bus stop every day. And you don't even take ballet."

"I would. If I had a dad."

Adrianne felt the sting of tears in her eyes but quickly forced them away. *She only wants what every little girl wants.* She contemplated her next words as she slipped on her shoe. "Sometime soon we're going to have a long talk about all that."

"We are?" Lorelei's brow wrinkled, as she looked her way.

"Yes." *I think it's about time you knew the truth. But this isn't the time or the place.* Adrianne glanced at her watch. "Oh no, not again. You're going to miss the bus if we don't hurry up."

They donned their jackets and reached for Lorelei's schoolbooks, then raced out of the apartment. No sooner did they arrive at the corner than the school bus pulled up.

"Have a great day, baby." Adrianne kissed Lorelei on the cheek.

"I love you, Mom." Lorelei climbed aboard the bus, then looked back with a wave as it pulled away.

Adrianne caved the moment her daughter disappeared from sight. For once, she didn't even try to hold back the tears. Her heart felt completely broken. She longed to see Chris again, to tell him how much she loved him. Needed him. But how? With his heart in Nicaragua, and hers in Philadelphia, they seemed destined to remain apart forever.

The tears continued to flow as she made her way to the car and then on to the museum. All along the way, she thought about her situation. She examined it from every conceivable angle. Still, no matter how hard she tried, she couldn't find a workable solution.

⧉

Chris boarded the small commuter plane with a heavy heart. He glanced down at his e-ticket as he shuffled through the crowd of people.

Twenty-two E. Oh, great. A middle seat again.

Moments later he found himself seated between a rather large gentleman in the aisle seat and a young girl, probably six or seven, in the window seat.

Not that he had time or energy to focus on others at the moment. His thoughts kept gravitating to Adrianne and Lorelei. *What am I doing on this plane?* The thought rolled around and around in his brain. *Why in the world don't I just get off of here and tell her how I really feel?* "How do I really feel?"

"Excuse me?" The stewardess gave him a quizzical look as she passed by. "Aren't you feeling well, sir?"

"Oh, I . . ." He looked up and shrugged. "I'm fine."

She went on by, and the pilot's voice came on with their flight information. Chris scarcely heard a word. He spent the next several minutes, thinking through everything that had happened over the past few days. In less than a week, his entire life had changed. But how did he feel about all he had learned, really?

Hmm. With the plane now taxiing down the runway, he paused to think, really think, about his heart, his feelings. His love for Adrianne was undeniable. And yet, she hadn't been completely honest with him from the beginning, had she? On the other hand, she had tried to reach him on several occasions over the years.

80

Surely she needed his forgiveness as much as they both needed the Lord's.

And what about Lorelei? Clearly, the youngster adored him. But then again, she didn't know the truth about their relationship either, did she? Would she still love him, once she realized he was her "absent" father—the one she'd done without all these years?

Chris leaned his head back against the seat and closed his eyes. A silent prayer went up—a please-show-me-what-to-do-Lord prayer. He prayed for Adrianne, for her provision, her peace of mind, for direction. He then shifted his attention to Lorelei, praying at length for her well-being, emotionally, spiritually, and physically.

Finally Chris began to pray about the decision he now faced. *Lord, I know You have all of this figured out, but I feel like I'm being torn in two. Half of me wants to be in Nicaragua. Half of me wants to be in Philadelphia.*

Even as he prayed, the image of Lorelei's face flashed before him. He remembered, all too clearly, the look in her eyes as he spun her around the dance floor of the ballroom at the Ben. Was it just two nights ago? Seemed like an eternity. But the image, now fresh in his mind, suddenly reignited his desire to play the role of father.

Just as quickly, Chris saw the faces of all the children he had ministered to in the villages of Nicaragua. After years of mentoring countless boys and girls, he had become a spiritual father to many. How could he leave them now? And who would take his place, if he opted to leave?

With his mind twisted up in knots, Chris turned his thoughts back to prayer. He clamped his eyes shut and dove back into a silent debate with the Almighty.

A few seconds later, a gentle voice from his right roused him from his catatonic state.

"Are you scared?"

Chris looked over at the little girl in the window seat. Her wide blue eyes riveted on his.

"Excuse me?" he asked.

"Are you scared of flying?"

"Oh. No." He offered up a weak smile. "No, I'm not scared."

"You looked scared." She flashed a broad smile, then pointed out the window. "But see? We're already up in the air. There's nothing to be scared of."

"We are, aren't we?" He glanced out of the window and then turned his attention back to the little girl once again. Was she all by herself? Traveling alone at such a young age?

As if reading his mind, she chattered away, answering all of his questions before they were even voiced. Her name was Hannah. She was traveling to Norfolk to see her father for a few days. She and her mother lived in Perkasie, about an hour and a half north of Philly. She had never flown alone before, but needed to get used to it, now that her parents were divorced.

Whoa.

As she rambled on and on, Chris let his thoughts drift. *Lord, I don't want this to happen to Lorelei. I don't want her boarding planes alone, flying halfway across the world just to see a father she barely knows. I want her to know me. I want to know her.*

Just after the pilot's voice came on, informing the passengers of a rocky flight ahead, Chris closed his eyes once more in an attempt to sleep. As the plane began to shake, Hannah grabbed his arm, rousing him from his near-slumber.

"Do you think there's a God?" she asked.

"What?"

"Do you think there's a God?" Hannah's voice grew more serious as she gazed out the window at the clouds.

"I do." The plane continued to vibrate and her grip on his arm intensified.

"Do you think He lives out there?" She let loose long enough to point out to the darkened clouds.

"Actually. . ." Chris smiled, as he pondered his response. "I think He lives in here." He pointed to his heart and Hannah looked over at him in curiosity.

"Huh?"

As the plane rocked and tipped, Chris took the opportunity to explain, in childlike terms, the full plan of salvation. Hannah's eyes widened as he told her about Jesus and His sacrifice on the cross. She smiled broadly when he explained that she could ask Him to live in her heart. And she even whispered a soft prayer to do just that—right there in the window seat.

As the bumpy ride settled down, the youngster turned back to look at the clouds once again. Before long, she drifted off to sleep. Chris closed his eyes and leaned back against the seat once more, finally ready to relax.

"Do you really believe all that stuff?"

This time the voice came from his left. Chris opened his eyes and gazed into the somber face of the man in the aisle seat.

"Excuse me?"

The portly fellow closed his magazine and stuffed it in the back of the seat in front of him. "All that stuff you were spouting. You believe that?"

Chris swallowed hard before answering, not wanting a confrontation, particularly in front of the sleeping child. Still, he needed to address the question at hand. "I do," he said finally.

"Then you're a fool." The man tilted his seat back and closed both his eyes and his mouth, as if that settled the whole thing.

An invitation to spar, perhaps?

"What do you mean?"

The fellow gave him a sideways glance, sort of an I'm-not-sure-you'd-really-get-it look. "I used to believe all that stuff about God," he explained. "About forgiveness. Before. . ." He shook his head, the already-deep wrinkles in his forehead deepening further still.

"Before what?"

The fellow looked over to make sure Hannah was asleep before responding. "Before my wife died of cancer."

Ah. Handle delicately, Chris.

He spent the next few minutes ministering to the man, speaking softly, and asking the Holy Spirit to guide every word. He deliberately chose not to slip into a preaching mode—even when the man, who introduced himself as Pete, got defensive. Chris simply did what he often found himself doing on the mission field; he met the man right where he was.

By the time the plane landed, Pete had opened up, sharing a few of his hurts, his pains. He confessed his anger with God, and his frustration with the doctors involved in his wife's care. He talked about his strained relationship with his grown children, how the whole family had grown apart since their mother's death.

Something interesting happened as the conversation drew to a close. Chris found himself sharing words of love, not as a missionary, but just as a friend. And the Spirit of the Lord rocked him to the core with an interesting new thought as he exited the plane behind his new friend.

"Don't you see, son? The mission field is everywhere—everywhere you happen to be. I can use you wherever you go, whether it's in the fields of Nicaragua or on an airplane. It's a ready heart I'm looking for. That's all."

Funny. Just knowing that suddenly put a lot of things in perspective.

Chapter 17

Adrianne stayed as busy as she could in the days following Chris's departure. The upcoming fundraiser dinner proved to be the perfect distraction. She and Dani worked together day in and day out, settling last-minute issues with the caterer and working alongside the party planner they'd hired to transform the lobby of the museum into a lovely banquet room.

Joey stayed close by, offering both humor and a helping hand. He proved to be a nice distraction, too, always giving her something to laugh about.

Still, in the quiet moments, when no one else was around, her heart ached for Chris. Many times during the day she would find herself wondering where he was, what he was doing. And why he hadn't called.

Frustrated, she forced her attention to the task at hand. Mr. Martinson was counting on her. The museumgoers were counting on her. She wouldn't let them down.

The following Friday night, Adrianne donned the same beautiful dress she'd worn to the rehearsal dinner and prepared to leave for the banquet. She found her nerves in quite a state—in part because so much rode on tonight's event, and in part because she hadn't heard from Chris in more than a week.

Maybe I'll never hear from him. Maybe he'll turn out to be a deadbeat dad, like so many others.

As she prepared to leave the house, her cell phone rang. She answered it with some degree of impatience.

"Ms. Russo?" The familiar voice greeted her. "James Kenner here."

Ah. "Mr. Kenner. Has something happened?"

"Oh no. Nothing like that. I was just wondering. . . ." His voice changed from businesslike to familiar in a flash. "I was just wondering if you might like a ride to the museum."

"Oh." She stumbled a bit through the rest. "I—I don't think that's necessary. See, I have to drop off my daughter at my mom's house, and I couldn't expect you to do that. It's not even on the way."

"I'd love to."

Now what do I do?

"There are some things I'd like to talk over before we get to the dinner—things having to do with the implementation of the grant money. Sorry to have to bore you with business, especially on a night like tonight, but this is important."

Sure it is.

"If you'll give me your address, I'll pick you and your daughter up in, what do you think, twenty minutes?"

"Hmm." Adrianne's mind raced. She grappled with many confusing thoughts, not the least of which was the idea that this guy could turn out to be anything but what he presented himself to be. "Tell you what," she said finally, "I'll meet you at the coffee shop on the corner near my apartment complex. That way you won't have to mess with the code for the security gate. Sound okay?"

"Sounds perfect."

She relayed the directions and he ended the call with a joyous, "See you soon, then."

As she snapped the cell phone shut, Adrianne slapped herself in the head. "Why in the world did I just do that?"

"Do what, Mom?" Lorelei entered the room with a portable video game in her hand.

Adrianne shook her head and sat on the sofa with her shoes in her hand. "That was a man I work with. He's picking us up."

"Why?"

Why, indeed? "It's a work thing," Adrianne explained. "He wants to talk to me about the museum. He's going to drive you over to Grandma's and then we'll go on from there."

"In his car?"

"Yes."

Lorelei shrugged. "Okay, Mom." She turned her attention back to the video game.

Twenty minutes later, mother and daughter entered the coffee shop. The whole place was alive with activity. People stood at the counter, ordering up every conceivable type of coffee. The place, which smelled delicious, calmed Adrianne's nerves at once.

She looked through the crowd until her gaze fell on James Kenner. "Ah. There he is," she said.

"He's handsome, Mom," Lorelei whispered.

Handsome didn't seem to be an adequate word. In his black tuxedo with his dark wavy hair carefully groomed, James Kenner looked like something from a magazine.

"Adrianne." He extended a hand as she approached, his amber eyes alight with joy. "You look amazing." He looked down at Lorelei and smiled. "And you must be..."

"Lorelei." The youngster stuck out her hand, and he took it for a firm handshake.

"Lorelei, it's great to meet you. I'm Mr. Kenner." He offered up a playful smile as he asked, "Are you a coffee drinker?" He gestured toward the crowd of people with countless cups of coffee. "Could I order something for you?"

She giggled. "No. I can't drink coffee. I'm just a kid." She looked up at her mom with a smile, then whispered, "But sometimes my mom lets me have just a little."

Adrianne felt compelled to explain. "Actually, I just give her a glass of warm milk with a teensy-tiny bit of coffee in it."

"It's yummy!" Lorelei added.

James laughed. "You two are funny. I like you." He flashed a dazzling smile in Lorelei's direction. "I'll call you Latte for short. Is that okay?"

She shrugged. "Okay."

James now looked at Adrianne. She felt his gaze sweep her from head to foot, and a flush warmed her cheeks as he asked, "Are we ready to go?"

"Sure." Adrianne draped her wrap over her shoulders. "Let's get this show on the road."

Lorelei chattered all the way to her grandparents' house, telling Mr. Kenner about her role in the church play, her video games, even her passion for cooking. Adrianne wondered if she might be wearing on the poor fellow's nerves, but he seemed to take the youngster's enthusiasm in stride.

"See you later, Latte!" he said as they dropped her off at the house.

"Later, gator!" she responded.

Adrianne glanced at her watch as they left her parents' house. "Yikes. We've got to get going. I'm going to be late."

"I won't let that happen." James chuckled. "No damsels in distress in this car."

They settled into an easy conversation, and Adrianne relaxed, in spite of everything. She took in the man to her left. He appeared to be genuinely nice. Clearly, he hadn't been as interested in talking business as she'd hoped, though he did manage to bring up the grant money and the banquet a couple of times.

As they drew near the museum, James glanced her way, and a shy look crossed his face. After a moment of silence, he finally stammered, "You. . .you look amazing, Adrianne." He offered an admiring gaze. "I really mean that."

"Thank you." She felt her cheeks warm.

"And I haven't had a chance to tell you this yet, but I'm so impressed with the way you've pulled together this evening's event. I hear you've been working round the clock."

"Yes." *Thank goodness. It's kept me sane for the past week since Chris*— No. She wouldn't think about him. Not tonight.

"It's going to be wonderful," James continued. "And a lot of my colleagues will be there. I've encouraged them to be *exceptionally* generous this year."

"Wow." Adrianne tried not to get too excited about his comments lest she be disappointed later. "We really just want people to give because they love the museum or admire our work there."

"There are a great many things to admire." James looked over at her with a penetrating gaze and she understood his meaning at once.

"I—I. . ."

"Promise me one thing, Adrianne." He took hold of her hand and gave it a squeeze. "When this is all over with, promise me you'll let me take you out for a celebration dinner. Say, one night next week?"

"Oh, I don't know—"

"Or the week after. Seriously, I won't take no for an answer. You've worked so hard. You deserve a night out to celebrate. And besides"—he feigned a back-to-business face—"we still have a lot to talk about."

Yes, but we're not talking business now, are we?

Adrianne leaned back against the seat and prayed her stomach would settle down before the evening's events got underway. They arrived at the museum in record time. The entire lobby had been transformed. Adrianne gasped as she saw it, then rushed to Dani's side. "It looks amazing in here."

"I used a lot of your ideas, so of course it looks amazing."

Adrianne looked up at the large swags of fabric and twinkling lights, and then shifted her gaze to the many dining tables, each fully decked out with fine china and crystal. The whole place was absolutely magical—like something out of a. . .a fairy tale.

"Just pray this works," she whispered. "We need funds to come in."

"I've already prayed," Dani assured her. "Stay calm, Adrianne. Tonight is a night for relaxing. Celebrating." She chuckled. "Okay, and maybe a little arm wrestling with a few deep-pocketed patrons, too."

She nodded, then glanced to her right as her boss made his appearance.

"We rarely get to see you in a tux, Bob," she acknowledged.

"Yeah. I can't stand 'em, but my wife made me." He pulled at his bow tie with a grunt. "Said it'd be good for business."

"She was right."

He chuckled, then looked around the room. "Adrianne, the place looks great. Great. I've heard nothing but complimentary things from our guests."

"Really? I'm so glad."

Just then, James slipped in behind her, sliding an arm over her shoulders. "She's quite a girl, isn't she?" The words were meant for Mr. Martinson, but his eyes twinkled in Adrianne's direction.

"She is." Bob gave her a wink, then turned his attention to James. "Mr. Kenner"—he extended his hand—"we can never thank you enough for all the work you did on that grant. You've been a tremendous asset to the museum, and we're all very grateful."

"My pleasure. I've always loved this museum." James released his hold on Adrianne's shoulder to shake Bob's hand. "But never more than lately. There are a great many things here to draw my attention." He shifted his gaze, just for a moment, back to Adrianne.

Bob looked up with a fatherly glance, and Adrianne felt her cheeks flush.

"Well, I should head on over to chitchat with some of the others," he said. "I've got a little hobnobbing to do."

As he moved on to greet the other guests, Adrianne turned to face James. Just as she opened her mouth to tell him that he had embarrassed her, Joey joined them.

"Hey." He gave a little whistle as he saw Adrianne's dress. "You look amazing."

"Thank you." She gave a little twirl but immediately wished she hadn't. The eyes of both men now locked firmly on her.

For a moment, anyway. After just a few embarrassing seconds, Dani cleared her throat. "Well, I. . .um. . .I'd better go check on the caterers."

Adrianne did her best to alleviate the awkwardness. She reached to give Joey's hand a little squeeze. "I know you had a lot to do with this. Thank you so much for helping set up the room."

"No problem. I'd do anything for y— the museum," he stammered. "You know that."

"Well, it turned out great, and I just want to give thanks where thanks are due."

Joey reached over to give her a warm hug, and for the first time since meeting him, Adrianne saw James Kenner's expression shift from genteel to perturbed.

What in the world?

Joey pulled back but never lost his focus. She looked at him with an uncomfortable smile, wishing she could just this once pull a Cinderella and run from the room.

Nope. Too awkward. She must stay put, no matter how difficult. As Adrianne stood there, with one man to her right and another to her left, she suddenly wished, for all the world, she could have the one in the middle, the one on the other side of the world.

Prince Charming.

❧

"Chris, my friend, I can't tell you how happy we are to have you back. We were at a loss without you."

Chris looked across the dinner table at fellow missionary David Liddell and shrugged. "Looks like you did pretty well when I was away. I see a lot of progress."

David shook his head. "Things are never the same when you're on furlough. But I know you deserved the break." He flashed a warm smile. "And I do hope you had a good trip back to the States."

"I did." Chris's thoughts shifted at once to Adrianne. His trip had presented some interesting challenges but some unexpected blessings, as well.

"How was the wedding?"

"Oh, great. Stephen and Julie were wonderful hosts, and the ceremony was beautiful. I wish you could have seen the church. I'm not sure you would have believed it, especially after some of the buildings we've worked on here. It was amazing."

David let out a lingering sigh. "I know Stephen will be happy, married and living in the States, but I just keep thinking about him when he first came to Managua five years ago. I don't remember ever seeing such excitement in a young missionary's eyes."

"Right. I remember."

"We had some great years together."

"We did," Chris agreed, "but God has called him to a different season now."

"Right." David grew silent. Finally, he looked up with a smile. "Did you get some rest when you were in Philly?"

"Um. . .not really. No."

"Hmm. I was hoping you'd come back rested and refreshed. We've got a lot on our plates over the next few weeks. The church in Masaya is really struggling. I'm going to make a trip down there in a couple of days and hoped I could talk you into coming with me."

"Sure." Chris answered more out of rote than passion. For whatever reason, he couldn't quite seem to get back into the swing of things since his arrival in Managua a few days ago.

"I hear Pastor Alejandro is in need of some building supplies," David continued, "so we'll load up the truck before we go. Oh, and one more thing"—he glanced at his watch—"I've got to get over to the airport to pick up Brent in a few minutes. He's on the 8:15 flight."

"Brent?" *Who's Brent?*

"Brent Ferguson. He's from California, originally, but I understand he's done a lot of missions work in Guatemala and has a lot of experience with some of the more remote Spanish dialects. He's married to a nurse."

"Wow."

"He wants to join us for a couple of weeks to see what we're all about."

"I see." *Well, at least we won't have to train him. That's a relief.* "Where is he staying?"

David gave him a knowing smile.

"Oh no." Chris slapped himself in the head. "He's staying with me?"

David offered up a shrug. "It's either that or a hotel. There's too much construction going on over at my place. And I didn't have the heart to ask him to pay for a hotel room for two weeks."

"Two weeks?" Chris groaned.

"Yep. But don't worry, Chris. He's a nice guy, and he loves the Lord. And he has a heart for this kind of work. I know you'll enjoy getting to know him."

"I'm sure you're right."

Chris wished he could garner up even half of David's excitement, but found his attention drawn to other things. He couldn't stop thinking about Adrianne and Lorelei. What were they doing right now, at this very moment? Were they eating dinner? Was Adrianne helping Lorelei with her homework?

Where are they?

And why am I here, so far away from them?

Chapter 18

Adrianne paced across her parents' living room, wearing a path in the carpet. For several minutes, she had struggled with whether or not to tell Lorelei about Chris. Her thoughts on the matter shifted back and forth, much like her emotions over the past week, since his departure.

She muttered her thoughts aloud, grateful the room was empty. "If I tell her that he's her father and he doesn't play that role in her life, she'll be even more hurt, more disappointed than ever."

Back and forth Adrianne walked, her thoughts rambling.

"On the other hand, if I don't tell her the truth about who he is, then I'm not being completely honest with her. And she's old enough now for me to be open and honest, even about something this difficult."

Adrianne paused to look out of the window, thinking she'd heard a car pull up in the driveway. *Just Dad starting the car. He's ready to go and I'm holding him up. And for what? I'm not making any progress, anyway.*

She continued on with her ponderings as she marched from one side of the room to the other. "I'm going to tell her. It's just a matter of time. I need to make sure I do this at exactly the right time and the way the Lord wants me to. I don't want to hurt her. That's the last thing I'd want to do."

"Mom, are you coming?" Lorelei entered the room, dressed in blue jeans and a matching jacket. Her eyes glistened with excitement, and her ponytail bobbed up and down as she clapped her hands in glee. "It's time to go."

"Mm-hmm."

"Grandma says you're lollygagging. What does that mean?"

"She's trying to say I'm taking too much time. But I'm coming now." *If my mom knew what was going through my mind, she would give me the time.*

"Grandpa says all the fish in the river will be gone if we don't leave soon."

"Okay, okay."

As Adrianne started toward the door her cell phone rang. Her heart flip-flopped as she reached to grab it from her purse. *Finally.* She had waited for Chris to call for days, and now. . .

She glanced at the number and groaned. James Kenner. Should she take it or let voicemail pick it up? If she didn't take it, he would probably be offended. She responded on the fourth and final ring with an all-too-cheery hello.

"Adrianne." His voice dripped with sweetness. "I'm so happy you're there. I was hoping I would catch you."

"Actually, we were just heading out," she explained. "My parents are taking us fishing this morning."

"Oh." The usual lilt in his voice all but disappeared. "Well, I understand. I had such an amazing time with you last night, and I was. . .well. . .just hoping we could spend the day together."

"I'm sorry." Adrianne glanced at her watch: 8:15. Her mother and father had already been waiting in the car a good five minutes.

"Wait, I have an idea!" James practically sprinted through the next few words. "I have a great little boat. The *Pocket Yacht*. I keep it at the Delaware River Yacht Club. What if I met you and your family there in, say, half an hour?"

"Oh, James, I don't know."

"Please let me do this, Adrianne." His tone softened a bit. "I want to meet your parents. And I know Latte would love the boat. They were made for each other. Besides"—he sounded remarkably coy, even a little embarrassed—"I really want to get to know you. Outside of our work environment, I mean."

"James, I—"

At that moment, Adrianne's dad entered the room with a frown on his face. He gestured to his watch and then shrugged, as if to say, "What's taking so long?"

"James, my dad is right here. If you'll hold on a minute, I'll run this by him. I'll be right back."

She quickly relayed the information he had given her, praying her father wouldn't take the bait.

"A yacht?" Her father's eyes grew wide. "Are you kidding? Of course we'll go. I'll tell your mother." He bounded from the room, a smile as broad as the Atlantic on his face.

Good grief. Men and their boats.

Adrianne turned her attention back to the call, wishing with everything inside of her that she hadn't taken it in the first place. "James," she spoke with a sigh, "we'll meet you at the Yacht Club in thirty minutes."

At that very moment, another call came through. She didn't take the time to look at it, since James was still talking. "Do you know where it is?" he asked.

Sadly, yes.

The lilt in his voice continued on. "I could give you directions, if you like."

Another *beep* in her ear let Adrianne know the second caller was still trying to get through.

"No, that's okay. I know where it is."

Another *beep*.

"Wonderful." The happiness in his voice was genuine. "I'll see you then."

"Yes. See you soon." As she clicked off, Adrianne tried to take the other call but found the caller had already hung up. She glanced at the caller ID. *Hmm.* "Restricted call?" What in the world did that mean?

Frustrated, she reached for her sweater and then sprinted toward the car.

❧

Chris's heart thumped out of control as Adrianne's voicemail kicked in. He listened intently to it, loving the lyrical sound of her voice. After the *beep*, he left a message, his nerves driving the words.

"Adrianne, this is Chris. I was hoping to reach you. I want. . . no, I need to talk to you. I miss you so much. I miss Lorelei so much. I wish I hadn't gotten on that—" Just as he tried to say the word *plane* a *beep* rang out and the message ended.

"No way." Should he call her back, try her home number?

What he would say when he found her was still unclear. Perhaps the Lord would give the right words in the right moment. One thing was for sure, he couldn't put off talking to her one moment longer. His heart wouldn't allow it.

Just as he reached in his wallet to search for her home number, Brent entered the room. "Are you ready?"

"Hmm?"

"David said we're supposed to be at the church in Masaya by late afternoon. I figured you'd be raring to go."

"Oh, I don't know." Chris clicked the phone off and placed it back on the stand. "To be honest, I'm completely unfocused. I've got a ton of other things on my mind today. I really don't know what good I'd be out on the field."

"I guess I could go in your place," Brent offered. "Or. . ."

Chris looked up, puzzled.

"Or, I could drive and you could talk. I've got pretty broad shoulders, and it looks like you just need someone to bounce things off of. Maybe God has sent me here for that very reason."

"God sent you all the way to Nicaragua to listen to me ramble on about my love life?" Chris chuckled. "Man, you've got a great sense of humor."

"Ah." Brent gave him a knowing smile. "This is about a woman?"

Chris nodded and Brent crossed his arms with a knowing look on his face. "Then I *know* the Lord has sent me here. My wife and I have only been married three years, but I could tell you just about anything you want to know about balancing marriage and missions work. So, let's get a move on. I'll do the driving, you do the talking."

"Okay. I guess." Chris reluctantly agreed, though he secretly wondered what in the world a total stranger might have to tell him about something so personal.

No sooner than they'd climbed into the truck to set out for Masaya, Brent shot a probing stare his way. "Okay, I'm waiting."

"Man, you get right to it, don't you?"

"Yeah. I figure you've got a captive audience, so why not go for it?" His expression softened a bit. "Seriously, Chris. You just tell me whatever you're comfortable sharing, nothing more."

I don't know how comfortable I am sharing anything with a total stranger.

Chris began, tentatively at first, then increasing in both courage and emotion. He told Brent every sordid detail of his relationship with Adrianne, all the way back to the beginning. He shared the part of losing touch and, more importantly, the part about finding her again.

And Lorelei. He shared, with a smile on his face, no less, the story of discovering the daughter he never knew existed. Brent didn't interrupt, but Chris could see the look of surprise on his face as he voiced his story. *Looks like maybe I've stumped him after all. This isn't your run-of-the-mill missionary story, after all.*

After hearing everything Chris had to say, Brent slowed down and pulled the car off the road. Then he turned to give Chris an inquisitive look.

"What is your heart telling you?"

Chris rubbed at his temples, unable to voice the words on his heart. "I don't know," he whispered. "I just know that I can't imagine living without them. Every time I think about it. . ." A lump the size of the San Cristobal volcano grew in his throat. "Every time I think of going one more day without them, I feel sick inside. Everything feels wrong."

"But?"

"But the obvious. My work. I'm called to this organization. I'm called to work with *these* children, here in Nicaragua."

Brent nodded and drew in a deep breath. Then he looked Chris. "I want to remind you of something," he said finally. "Something I know you already know, but probably just need to hear."

Chris looked up, not even trying to hide the moisture in his eyes.

"We are all called to share the gospel," Brent said. "All believers. The Great Commission isn't just for people with special degrees, or men and women who've applied to particular missions organizations. 'Go into all the world' means just that. And maybe, just maybe, the 'world' you're supposed to go into is different than what you thought."

Chris felt his heart drop. "I—I can't believe God would call me away from Central America. I love it so much. I love these kids so much. I just wish I could. . ." He fought for words, but none would come.

"Have your cake and eat it, too?"

He looked at his new friend with a sigh. "Yeah. That's it. I want Adrianne and Lorelei, but I want this, too."

"So, why not do both?"

"Oh, I can't bring them here. It's out of the question." He dove into a lengthy explanation, which Brent quickly squelched.

"I'm not saying you should bring them here. I'm just asking you to consider the possibility that your work here could change somewhat to accommodate a new plan, a plan that includes a wife and daughter."

"I don't know what you mean." Chris stared Brent down.

With a great deal of excitement, Brent began a detailed explanation of just how he felt this whole thing could actually work. Chris listened intently, especially when his new friend asked him to open the Bible and turn to James, the first chapter, verses 5 and 6.

"Read it out loud," Brent encouraged him.

Chris turned the pages to the passage and glanced down at the familiar words, understanding their significance in a new way. " 'If any of you lacks wisdom,'" he read aloud, " 'let him ask of God, who gives to all liberally and without reproach, and it will be given to him.'" Chris glanced over at Brent with a smile. "Sounds so easy."

"Keep reading."

" 'But let him ask in faith, with no doubting, for he who doubts is like a wave of the sea driven and tossed by the wind.'" With a sigh, Chris looked up. "That's what I've been feeling like, a wave tossed around by the wind."

"That's why I love verse five so much," Brent said with a smile. "God has a specific formula for stilling the waves of doubt. Whenever I'm in a position where I don't know what to do, which way to go, I ask the Lord to give me supernatural wisdom. I know He will, because the verse says that God gives generously to all without finding fault."

"Wow." Chris allowed those words to sink in. *Without finding fault.*

"Do you think it's possible"—Brent gave him a pensive look—"that you've been afraid to ask God for the very thing you want the most because you feel in some way you don't deserve it?"

Man, this guy is good. "Well, I—"

"Because we serve a God who longs to give us the desires of our heart."

"As long as they're not selfish desires," Chris threw in.

Brent shook his head. "I don't believe for a moment your desires are selfish. You long to have a family, and you long to minister. Those are two bona fide desires. And they're godly desires, too." He dove into a lengthy dissertation about God's views on family and ministry, sharing more of his thoughts on Chris's specific situation. When he finished, Chris suddenly felt the issue settled in his spirit.

"I know you're right. God has forgiven me for the things of the past, and He loves me. And I know He has all of this figured out."

"Then let's pray for wisdom." Brent prayed aloud as they drove, asking the Lord to reveal His perfect will. Afterward, the two men once again began to talk about the particulars of combining family and ministry. Before long, a full-fledged plan emerged, one clearly sent from on high.

Within ten minutes, Chris couldn't stop the smile from creeping across this face. Within twenty minutes, he drummed his fingertips on the door of the vehicle and bounced ideas off of his new friend. Within thirty minutes, he was ready to catch the next flight to Philadelphia.

Chapter 19

Pastor Jake, could I talk to you and Katelyn for a minute after service to-day?" Adrianne hoped he didn't notice the trembling in her hands as she spoke.

"Sure, Adrianne." Jake flashed a smile. "Want to meet in my office? You know how crazy it gets in the sanctuary after service. Everyone hangs around for ages."

"Sure. That'd be great."

He turned toward the podium and took a few steps, then turned back again with a concerned look on his face. "Is everything okay?"

She nodded slowly, then shrugged. "I just need someone to talk to," she said. "And I know you two will give me great advice."

"Okay. We'll see you there."

Adrianne somehow made it through Jake's sermon, although his "Love Conquers All" theme only added to her dilemma.

So many thoughts rolled around in her head. She reflected on them all—the look on Chris's face the night she'd told him about Lorelei, the pain in her heart when he'd left days later, and the confusion over James's unwelcome attentions, both at the fundraiser dinner and aboard his yacht yesterday.

"Lord, I need Your wisdom. I'm so confused, and yet. . ."

In her heart, she knew the one thing that made sense in the middle of all of this. Sitting in church last week, with Chris's hand in her own, watching their daughter onstage, singing her heart out. . .

Now, *that* felt right.

The service came to a close, and Adrianne sent Lorelei off with her parents so that she could meet with Jake and Katelyn. She beat them into his office but was too nervous to sit. He finally arrived, his wife at his side. Jake settled down in the chair behind his desk, and Katelyn and Adrianne sat in the wing-backed chairs across from him.

"All I have to do is look at your face to see that something is up," Katelyn said. "So what's on your heart, Adrianne?"

Adrianne drew in a deep breath before starting. She wanted to do the best possible job presenting this story, not deliberately swaying her friends one way or the other.

"It's kind of a long story," she said. "And it starts eight years ago."

She told them, no words minced, about her relationship with Chris back in college. Katelyn eyes grew large, but she didn't say anything, not at first, anyway. Adrianne told them both about the sin she and Chris had entered into, and how she had left the school to return to Philadelphia.

"I've struggled with feelings of guilt for years," she acknowledged, "but I know the Lord has forgiven me. He's done an amazing work in my life."

"And in Lorelei's life, too," Jake added. "She's pretty special."

"Yes. She's an angel, that girl." Katelyn offered a reassuring nod.

"I know. But thank you for saying it. I often wonder what I ever did to deserve her." Adrianne dove back into her story, telling her friends about the many times she had tried to reach Chris. When she got to the part of the story where he had "coincidentally" shown up at the museum, Katelyn's eyes widened again.

"Oh, my. Looks like God set that one up."

"Yes. That's what my dad said, too." Adrianne then shared all that had transpired since Chris's arrival in Philadelphia, how she had told him about Lorelei, and how he had responded. She closed out the story with tears in her eyes as she shared the part where he'd left town, heading back to Nicaragua. "I don't know when I'll see him again," she whispered.

Katelyn looked into her eyes, love pouring forth as she spoke. "Adrianne, I want to tell you something. Last week, when we met Chris for the first time, I just had this, this *sense* that he was more than a friend. I'm not sure how I knew, but I did."

"Really?" Adrianne shook her head, amazed.

"There was something about the way he looked at you." Katelyn's lips curled up in a smile. "And, to be honest, your face was lit with joy every time you looked at him, too."

"W–was it? I didn't mean to. . ."

"No," Katelyn said, "this wasn't something you did consciously. This was a genuine caring look, like a wife would give her husband."

Adrianne felt her cheeks flush, but resisted saying anything.

"The two of you are very natural together," Jake agreed. "I definitely saw the friendship side of things, but wondered if there might be more."

"But what can we do?" Adrianne asked. "I mean, really? Is there a solution? We can't take Lorelei to the mission field."

"You already have." Jake looked intently into her eyes.

"What?"

"Every time we do an outreach, every time we bring inner-city kids into the church to see a play, every Christmas when we take gifts to children in the projects, she's on the mission field."

"But you know what I mean," Adrianne implored. "Nicaragua?"

Jake shook his head. "I don't think you'll be taking Lorelei to Nicaragua, at least not for good. But I do think she will see much of the world, once you and Chris are married. So will you, in fact."

"W–what?"

Jake smiled. "Look. Katelyn and I have been talking about this for days, ever since we met Chris. We really liked what we saw in him. And I think he'd be a great addition to our staff here. We could stand to have a missions pastor, especially one who's acquainted with Central America. And from everything he shared last week, I think he would do well, taking charge of all of our local inner-city missions projects, too."

"Are you serious? You had already planned to contact him?"

Katelyn nodded. "We were going to run this idea by you today, in fact. He could work here much of the time—in Philadelphia—and take teams to Central America three or four times a year."

Adrianne shook her head. "I—I don't know. His heart is in Nicaragua. He loves the children there. He could never leave them."

Now Jake shook his head. "I think you're wrong about that. A man with a true heart after God puts the Lord first, his family second"—he glanced at Katelyn—"and his ministry third. I honestly believe that Chris will come to the same conclusion, especially once he's had some time to think about it."

"But how could I expect that of him? He's not my husband. He's just—"

"The man you love," Katelyn whispered. "And the man who loves you. I have no doubt about that, especially now that you've shared your story. I can see the three of you—you, Chris, and Lorelei—ministering together all over the place."

"But how in the world could we minister with our background?" Adrianne hung her head in shame. "People would never accept us. W–we messed up so many things."

"Haven't we all?" Jake stood and began to pace the room. "I mean, no one is immune from a sinful past. No one. 'For all have sinned and fall short of the glory of God.' That's what the scripture says."

She nodded. "Right."

"I'll bet you didn't know that I was away from God while I was in my teens."

"What?"

"Yes. I was on drugs for three years. In fact, Katelyn wouldn't date me during that time—and rightfully so. She knew we were unequally yoked."

Adrianne looked over, amazed as Katelyn nodded. "I steered clear of him, to be honest. And it was hard. I loved him, even then. Prayed for him every day."

"The Lord got a hold of me when I was nineteen," Jake added. "I got cleaned up. Sobered up. And, man"—a look of joy filled his eyes—"I still remember the day I felt the Spirit of the Lord leading me to go into the ministry." He looked at

Katelyn with a smile. "Do you remember that?"

"I do." She looked at Adrianne. "At first, I doubted he was really genuine about laying down the drugs and following the Lord, but thankfully I was wrong."

"Thank God," Adrianne whispered.

"Don't you see?" Jake reached over and put a hand on her shoulder. "That's why I feel so at home in this part of the city. That's why I want so desperately to reach out to those kids on the streets. I can relate to them, especially the ones who are struggling. And I'd be willing to bet Chris, once he really hears from God on the matter, will be the same. It might take some time for the two of you to see yourselves as useable, but don't wait forever. You said it yourself, Adrianne. God has washed away all of your sins. Right?"

"Right."

"And you love this man, right?" Katelyn asked.

"R–right," she whispered.

"Then prepare yourself," Katelyn said with a wink. "Because I have a feeling the Lord has already set the wheels in motion. Just pray, Adrianne. And we'll pray with you."

Jake and Katelyn took the time, right then and there, to pray. With great passion in his voice, Jake prayed that Chris would hear the voice of the Lord as never before. Katelyn prayed that Adrianne would have the faith, and the courage, to be still and allow God to be God.

And Adrianne prayed, too—that God would give her the right words to say to Lorelei, for the time was drawing near.

❧

"Are you ready, Chris?"

"Hmm?" Chris turned to face Brent, his heart beating wildly.

"You've been holding that phone for nearly fifteen minutes. Are you going to call her, or what?"

"Oh, I. . ." He stared down at the phone.

"Listen." Brent approached him and took the phone from his hand. "Let's talk this through. What are you going to say when you reach her?"

"I. . .uh. . ."

"Not great with words, eh?" Brent grinned. "Never fear. I'm here to help. Let me make a suggestion."

"Okay."

"Tell her that you are miserable."

"I am."

"You are. And tell her that God has been speaking to you through your friends."

"Good grief. Can't I just say that He's been speaking?"

"Whatever. Anyway, tell her that you can't live another day without her."

"Sounds like you've been working on this speech."

"I've used it before"—he flashed a grin—"with my wife. Before she was my wife, I mean."

"Ah."

"It's a good speech."

"And the part about the missions work?" Chris looked up for reassurance.

"Just what we talked about the other day. No more, and no less."

"Okay." He clutched the phone, then began to punch in her number. "I can do this. I can."

When Adrianne picked up after only two rings, it startled him so much that he almost dropped the phone. "H–hello? Adrianne?"

"Chris, is that you?" The joy in her voice spoke volumes. "I can hardly hear you."

"We must have a bad connection. But Adrianne, I have something to tell you. I haven't slept for nights, and I won't sleep tonight, either. Unless I tell you."

"Tell me? Tell me what?"

"I—I. . ." He looked up to find Brent nodding in encouragement. Chris stood and began to pace the room. "I have loved you from the day I met you. The first time I saw you walking across the campus, you were wearing a white blouse and a pair of jeans. Your hair was pulled back, but the wind was still blowing little bits of it in your face. I was with my buddies. I pointed across the parking lot and said, 'That's the girl I'm going to marry.'"

"I—I never knew that." The tremor in her voice gave him the courage to continue.

"It's true. And you will never know how scared I was to ask you out on that first date. Do you remember? We went out for pizza. I could hardly eat a bite."

"I remember."

"I remember so many things." His words began to speed up. "Like how much I loved hearing you sing on the worship team. How beautiful you looked whenever you lost your temper."

"Hey now. . ."

"How comfortable you were in my arms. And how amazed I was that someone like you would look twice at a lowly guy like me—a kid hoping to one day be a missionary."

"I was so proud of you, Chris," she whispered. "I still am."

His heart sailed at the words. "Thank you." After a brief pause, to offer up a silent prayer, he forged ahead. "I want to tell you something else, too—something that's easier to say now that I've had time to think. I am so proud of you for raising Lorelei the way you have. She's your clone, the spitting image of her mother."

"And her father."

"When I look at her"—Chris's eyes filled right away—"I see all of the possibilities for what we can be. Together."

"Oh, Chris—"

"Adrianne, I have to tell you something." His pacing stopped and the sweating began. "I have messed up so many things in my life, but I don't want to blow one more thing. I love you. I've loved you every minute of every day for over a decade. And I'm going to do the right thing. I'm going to—"

Just as he reached the pinnacle of his speech, the phone went dead in his hand. Chris looked at it in disbelief. "You've got to be kidding me," he muttered. He tried—panic leading the way—to dial the number again, only to find all circuits were busy. "No way!" He turned to face Brent, a shockwave running through him. "What in the world do I do?"

"Well, I guess there's really only one thing *to* do." Brent faced him head-on. "I guess you'll just have to tell her in person."

Chapter 20

Adrianne hardly slept a wink on Sunday night. Instead, she tossed and turned, replaying Chris's words in her mind. *"I told my buddies, 'That's the girl I'm going to marry.'"*

"*'The girl I'm going to marry.'"*

Her lips curled up in a smile. How she longed to know more. Did he still feel that way now? If so, would he act on those words? Why, oh why, had the phone call ended so abruptly? Would she never know?

A plan, of sorts, rolled through her brain at about three in the morning. At four, she arose from the bed and signed on to the Internet. As she clicked the Web address for airplane flights, her heart raced. "I must be crazy. I can't go to Nicaragua, can I?"

She stumbled around the site, trying to find a direct flight from Philadelphia to Managua. Nothing. She tried again, this time finding a flight with a brief layover in Atlanta.

"One thousand two hundred ninety-eight dollars? No way."

She continued on in her search, growing more frustrated by the moment.

"Slow down."

Adrianne heard the Lord's voice so clearly, it almost scared her. She leaned her head down onto the keyboard and wept. "Lord, I don't feel like slowing down. I want to see him. I want to. . . ," she stammered over the words. "I want to marry this man, spend the rest of my life with him. We've lost eight years already, eight years we could have been a family. I don't want to lose one minute more."

"Trust Me with all your heart. Don't lean on your own understanding."

"But, Lord. . ."

She took a few slow, deep breaths and attempted to calm down. After drying her eyes, the temptation to return to the Internet resurfaced. She resisted and shut down the machine altogether.

After pacing the living room for nearly half an hour, she finally wore herself out. With her eyelids now heavy, she headed back to the bedroom, where, thankfully, she dozed off. A couple of hours later, the alarm went off. She reached over to slap it, noticing the headache at once. After swallowing down a couple of aspirins, she leaned back against the pillows, hoping to catch a few more z's before waking Lorelei. She awoke to the sound of her daughter's shrill voice.

"Mom, I missed the bus!"

"W–what?" Adrianne sat up, shocked. She looked at the clock: 8:45. "No way. It was just six. Wasn't it?"

Lorelei pounced on the bed. "Do I have to go to school today? I'm already late anyway. Can't I just stay home?" She ping-ponged up and down on the bed, eyes blazing with excitement.

"You have to go to school," Adrianne admonished. "Regardless of the time. I'll write a note. Everything will be okay."

With a pout, her precocious daughter headed off to dress for school. Adrianne raced like a maniac around the room, trying to decide what to wear. Her navy suit was at the cleaners. Maybe the black slacks and brown sweater? "Hmm." She looked through her closet, finally settling on a tailored ivory jacket and slacks, with a sky blue blouse.

"Hurry, Lorelei!" she hollered as she dressed. "We're late!"

"I'm hurrying!" The youngster's voice rang out from down the hallway.

Moments later, Lorelei appeared at the bedroom door, dressed in a mismatched purple T-shirt and fluorescent orange pants. Her tennis shoes were a shocking pink, which really made the whole ensemble look more like a costume than school clothes.

"Oh no." Adrianne shook her head. "You can't wear that."

"Why not?" Lorelei looked in the mirror. "I like these colors."

"You can't, because. . . Oh, never mind." Adrianne looked around the room, frustration mounting. "Can you help me find my shoes? I can never seem to find them when I need them."

"The ones you left in the living room last night?"

Adrianne sighed. "Yeah. Probably. Would you run and fetch them for me?"

As Lorelei sprinted down the hallway, Adrianne turned her attention to her makeup. She looked into the bathroom mirror, horrified at her swollen eyelids. "Oh no. Please, no." She pulled out the stick of concealer and ran a line of it under each eye. As she rubbed it in, she thought about her middle-of-the-night escapades. What would Lorelei say if she knew her mother had spent half the night thinking about flying off to Central America? What would her parents say? Would everyone think she had lost her mind?

"I found your shoes, Mom." Lorelei appeared with the familiar pumps in hand. She looked up, a curious look crossing her face. "You were crying, weren't you?"

"What?" Adrianne continued applying her foundation. "What makes you say that?"

"Your eyes are all puffy." Lorelei pointed at the reflection in the mirror. "I can always tell."

"Good grief." Adrianne smeared on some lipstick, then reached for her blush brush. "I didn't get much sleep last night. I tossed and turned."

"Why did you get on the computer?"

Good grief again. Can't a woman have any privacy at all? "I, um. . ."

Lorelei crossed her arms and watched intently as Adrianne applied eye shadow to her swollen eyes. "You're keeping secrets."

"No, I'm not." *It's not like I actually bought a ticket. It's not like I'm going anywhere.*

"How come you couldn't sleep?" Lorelei leaned her elbows on the bathroom counter with an inquisitive look on her face. "Are you sick?"

Lovesick, maybe. "No, not really sick. I'm just—"

"You miss him, don't you, Mom."

"What? Miss who?"

"You know who. Prince Charming. Chris."

"I don't know why you keep saying that," Adrianne said. "And in order to make your little story work, I'd have to change my name to Cinderella."

"Ooh, Cinderella!" Lorelei agreed with a smile. "She's my favorite."

Mine, too. "Well, if I have to play the role of Cinderella, I'll have to dress in rags and sleep in the ash heap."

"Only until he rescues you," Lorelei said with a giggle. "That's the best part."

"And what makes you think I need to be rescued? I'm doing a pretty good job, don't you think? I put a roof over our heads, and the bills are paid."

"That's not everything."

Good grief. She really does sound like the mother, doesn't she?

Adrianne opted to change gears. "What makes you think it wasn't James Kenner I was thinking about?" She crossed her arms and gave her daughter an inquisitive stare.

"Oh, come on, Mom. Puh-leeze!"

"I thought you liked him."

Lorelei shrugged. "He's okay. He's handsome, but—"

"What?"

Lorelei wrinkled her nose. "He doesn't have your shoe size."

"Excuse me?"

"You know. He's not Prince Charming. He won't have a shoe that fits."

"Lorelei, you've been watching too many movies. And reading far too many fairy tales."

Her daughter shrugged. "You told me if I would read more it would make me smarter. And besides, I want you to get married some day. I want to have a dad."

Adrianne groaned. "Honey, we've had this discussion before. And I really don't have time right now. . . ."

Even as she spoke the words, reality, like a bolt of lightning, hit.

Slow down.

That's what the Lord had said. Slow down and. . .

Oh Father. Are You asking me to talk to her? Now? I don't have time. I don't have. . .

A thousand excuses ran through her mind. But less than a minute later, the truth won out. *Yes, Lord. I'll do it. And I'll do it now.*

She drew in a long, deep breath and turned to face her daughter. "You know what?" she said. "I think maybe, just maybe, it's okay to take our time. There's something I need to talk to you about."

"Cool!" Lorelei raced to the bed and sprang up on it, motioning for Adrianne to do the same.

With slow, deliberate steps, she made her way to where her daughter sat. Then, with her heart in her throat, she began.

"I know you've always wondered about your daddy," she started.

Lorelei nodded. "You said you would tell me someday."

"That's right." She swallowed hard. "And today is that day."

Lorelei's eyes grew large. "You're going to tell me about my dad?" She grabbed Adrianne's hand and squeezed it. "Tell me, Mom. I'm big enough. You can tell me."

"I know you're a big girl, and that's a good thing, because what I have to tell you is only for big-girl ears."

Lorelei pulled her knees up to her chest and sat in silent anticipation. Adrianne pushed back the tears and told her the very thing she had put off for years.

"Your father is a wonderful man," she said with a smile. "A man who looks a lot like you. He has your sense of humor." She reached to tuck a stray hair behind Lorelei's ear. "And he has a good heart like you do."

"Really?" Lorelei sighed. "But will I ever get to meet him?"

Adrianne closed her eyes and whispered a silent prayer before saying the words: "You already have."

Her daughter looked directly into her eyes, clearly confused.

"You met him that night at Grandma and Grandpa's house, and you met him again at the wedding the next day."

"Oh, Mom!" Lorelei reached to grab her hand. "Chris is—"

Adrianne nodded, the lump in her throat now the size of an apple.

"My daddy? He's my daddy?"

"Y–yes. He is. It's a long, long story, and one day I'll tell you more. But Christopher Bradley is your daddy. H–he didn't know about you."

"He didn't?" Another look of confusion registered. "Why not?"

"That's a long story, too. But from the minute he found out he had a daughter—from the minute he laid eyes on you—he loved you. He still loves you."

Lorelei's eyes misted over, and within seconds tears began. She leaned her forehead into her knees and sobbed openly. Adrianne slipped an arm around her shoulders and drew her close.

"But he's in another place now." Lorelei looked up, her damp cheeks now shining pink. "Doesn't he want to be here? With me? With us?"

Answer carefully, Adrianne.

"I know he wants to be with you, with both of us."

"He does?"

Adrianne nodded. "I know, because he called me from Nicaragua to tell me how much he misses us."

Lorelei leaned her head against Adrianne's arm. "Mom?"

"Yes?"

"Do you love him? Do you love Chr— my daddy?"

Adrianne smiled, and a warmth like she had never known flooded over her. "Oh, honey, I do. I love him so much. I've loved him for many, many years."

"Is that why you kept his picture in the drawer?"

A slight chuckle slipped out as she contemplated her answer. "Yes. I suppose so."

After a deep sigh, Lorelei looked up with a childlike grin. "I'm so happy, Mom. I am. Thank you for telling me."

Over the next half hour, Adrianne answered many of her daughter's questions. "No, Nicaragua isn't close." "Yes, your grandma and grandpa know." "No, we can't go see your daddy today." She smiled as she answered the last one. "Yes, I hope one day we will both change our last names to Bradley."

As they wrapped up their quiet conversation, Adrianne looked once again at the clock. "It's nearly ten," she said.

"Do I still have to go to—"

"Yes, you still have to go to school."

Lorelei sprang from the bed, her electric outfit catching a shimmer from the morning sunlight at the window. "But I'm too excited."

Me, too. "I know. But we have to keep doing all of the usual stuff."

"Till when?" Lorelei asked.

"Till the Lord gives me clear directions," Adrianne said with a grin.

With a pout, Lorelei asked, "When will that be?"

"I haven't got a clue," Adrianne responded. "But I'll promise you this—when He tells me what to do, you will be the very first to know."

❧

Chris sat quietly among the mob of people in Atlanta's busy airport. Every few seconds he glanced down at his watch. Forty minutes till his flight. Thirty-five. Thirty.

A voice announced over the loudspeaker that passengers could begin boarding momentarily. As he stood to get in line, he toyed with the notion of calling Adrianne.

Nope. Don't call. Just surprise her.

Somehow, the idea of popping in on her just felt right. And the idea of asking her to be his forever felt even *more* right.

Chapter 21

Chris's plane landed at the Philadelphia International Airport at exactly two fifteen in the afternoon. He raced to get his suitcase from baggage claim, then rented a car. All the while, he rehearsed the speech in his head, what he would say when he saw Adrianne. Within minutes he was on the turnpike, headed for the historic district. At three o'clock, he pulled into the Franklin Institute parking garage.

Before getting out of the car, he offered up a rushed but determined prayer. *Father, I put this into Your hands. Not my will, but Yours be done.*

As he made his way into the museum, Chris did everything in his power to squelch the knot in his stomach. It refused to budge. So did the tightness in his chest. No, he wouldn't be the same again until he held the woman he loved in his arms once more. Then all would be right with the world.

He found the museum more crowded than before. Several school groups milled about, hundreds of youngsters with name tags and frustrated teachers calling out to keep them in line.

"Excuse me." He edged past a little girl with red hair and freckles. She turned to give him an inquisitive stare. "Sorry," he added.

A boy with dark brown eyes glanced his way with wondering eyes. "Are you lost?" he asked.

"No," Chris responded. *In fact, I don't know when I've ever felt more found than right now, in this very moment.*

With excitement mounting, he worked his way through the mob and went to the front desk, where he was met by a young woman with a clipboard in her hand. He glanced down at her nametag: DANI.

"Hi." He tried to steady his voice. "I–I'm looking for Adrianne Russo."

"Ooh." Dani's eyes grew wide. "You don't say."

"I do say."

"Well"—her lips curled up in a smile—"your name wouldn't happen to be Christopher Bradley, would it?"

He nodded, unable to speak. The joy at knowing Adrianne had told a coworker about him proved almost more than his nerves could take.

"I had a feeling," Dani said, her smile widening. "What a great day this is turning out to be."

Chris gave her an imploring look. "Can you take me to her?"

"She's working on a new display in the back of the museum," Dani explained. "It's off limits to visitors, but I'll take you there myself."

"Are you sure it's okay?"

"For you?" she said. "It's more than okay. To be honest, I can't wait to see the look on Adrianne's face."

"Um. . .me neither."

He tagged along on Dani's heels, winding in and out through the crowd of tourists. At one point, he almost lost sight of her, she was moving so quickly. They went through the Wright Brothers display and back into an area marked UNDER CONSTRUCTION, where Dani used her key to open a door.

They pressed through that door, and then turned right, where she opened another narrower one. Chris looked around, amazed to find himself inside a large display window. Adrianne stood with her back to him, working diligently to dress a mannequin in a Revolutionary War costume. He wanted to race toward her but resisted the urge.

Dani put a finger to her lips and backed away. As she eased her way out of the door, she gave him a thumbs-up signal. Chris swallowed hard, and then prayed for courage to do the thing he had come to do.

"Adrianne." As the word leaped across his lips, it sounded like music to his ears.

She turned, with one hand on her heart and the other over her mouth. "C– Chris?"

For a second, neither moved. But then everything seemed to advance at warp speed. They met in the middle of the display case, where he swept her at once into his arms and began to plant soft kisses on her cheek. Her arms reached out to encircle his neck and their lips met in a kiss so familiar, it tilted him backward in time eight years.

How have I lived this long without her?

They lingered a moment in each other's arms before Adrianne looked up at him with a shy smile. "I—I knew you would come. I knew it."

"I had to. I thought I'd die if I didn't."

"I understand. You have no idea."

He smiled. "Oh, I think I do."

She brushed a soft kiss across his lips and then leaned her head against his. He reached with his fingertips to touch her cheekbone, tracing a familiar line of freckles. Finally, he pulled back to gaze into her eyes.

"I need to tell you something." When she nodded, he continued. "I didn't get to finish this on the phone, so I'm going to finish now."

"O–okay."

"I told you then that I'd loved you since the day I met you. But I didn't get to tell you the rest—that I'm not complete without you. I'm only. . ." He fumbled to get the words out. "Half of what I should be. Half of what God created me to be. I thought my work would fill the emptiness inside of me, and to some extent it did. But I know now that I could never be truly whole without you."

"Oh, Chris"—she reached to grab his hands—"I've felt that way for eight years. It's been awful without you. I haven't been myself. I've been—"

"Lost." They spoke the word together.

"For a while, I was lost in confusion," she acknowledged. "And then the grief took over. But the worst season of all was the one where I couldn't forgive myself. I lived for years like that. I—I didn't think I could ever shake it."

"I understand, trust me." He gazed into her eyes, wondering what in the world he had ever done to deserve her. "W–what do you think now? About the forgiveness issue, I mean."

"Ah." A lone tear trickled down her cheek. "These past few weeks God has shown me over and over again that He forgave me all those years ago—when I first asked—not just for the sexual sin, but for not trying harder to reach you. I should have done more."

Chris shook his head and kissed the back of her hand.

"His forgiveness I could accept," she continued. "Finally, anyway. *Mine* was harder, because I felt like I somehow had to earn it by being good. And I could never be good enough to please myself. Does that make sense?"

"You *are* good, Adrianne," Chris emphasized. "But it's not your goodness, or lack thereof, that matters. When God looks down at you—and me—He sees two people who are washed in the blood of His Son, forgiven of the past. If He can see us that way, well. . ."

"I know." She sighed, and then gazed up at him once more, love pouring from her eyes. "We've wasted so much time. So much."

"I'm not wasting a minute more." He reached into his pocket to pull out the tiny box. It held the same ring he had purchased—and intended to slip on her finger—ages ago in Virginia Beach.

As Chris dropped to one knee, his foot caught the edge of the curtain that had, until now, anyway, shielded the unfinished window display from the crowd on the other side. He didn't care. This had to be done, tourists or not.

"W–what are you doing?" Adrianne stared down at him in amazement.

"Exactly what I came to do. Exactly what I should have done when we were in college." With the ring box firmly gripped in his hand, he gazed up into her eyes. Pressing down the lump in his throat, he spoke: "Adrianne, I love you more than I ever knew it was possible to love another human being."

"I love you, too," she whispered in response.

Onlookers gathered on the other side of the window, but Chris tried to stay focused. "I've made a lot of mistakes. I know I don't deserve you. But I would be so honored—so honored—if you would. . ." He looked up, encouraged by the love pouring from her eyes. "Will you marry me, Adrianne?" The tears started at once and he reached to kiss her hand.

She knelt beside him and nodded, her tears spilling over. "Yes." She whispered the word, then added, "Oh yes. I will." Her face lit into a broad smile as he pulled the ring from the box and slipped it onto her finger. She stared down at it, then whispered, "It's beautiful." She stared at it a moment longer before looking up at him, amazed. "I–I've seen this before somewhere."

"It was the summer before our senior year," he reminded her. "We were in the mall in Virginia Beach. Remember?"

Recognition registered in her eyes. "Everson's Jewelry."

He nodded. "You pointed to it and told me it was the prettiest thing you'd ever seen."

"I remember. But, a–are you saying. . ."

"Yes." He nodded and she shook her head, clearly confused. "I went back that same afternoon and put it on layaway. Paid on it for weeks."

"I don't believe it," she whispered.

"I paid it off on a Tuesday," he said. "But I wanted to wait till Friday night to give it to you. It burned a hole in my pocket for days," he explained. "But then—"

"I left."

After he nodded, she gripped his hand and gazed intently into his eyes. "I've made so many mistakes, Chris. But this isn't one of them. This is the best thing that has ever happened to me."

Chris's heart began to sing. Adrianne, his Adrianne, now wore his ring. She would soon be his. And they, together, would raise their daughter. "W–when can we tell Lorelei?"

"Today. Right now, if you like."

There, with more than a dozen people looking on, they sealed the deal with a passionate kiss. Through the glass, Chris could hear the roar of the crowd as the applause began. Now, somewhat flustered, he looked out to discover the group outside had grown immensely.

"Um. . .Adrianne?"

"Yes?" She gazed into his eyes. He pointed through the glass. She looked out and offered up a little shrug. "Oh well. They paid the admission price. Why not?" She leaned forward and gave him one last playful kiss, then, together, they turned and waved to the crowd.

꙳

Adrianne danced a jig on the inside as she and Chris left the Revolutionary War display. *He's here! He came for me. And I'm. . .engaged!*

She glanced down at the simple ring, overwhelmed by the thought that he had purchased it all those years ago. Her heart practically sang aloud as she pondered the truth: *He has loved me all along. And I have loved him, too.* Nothing would ever change that.

Hand in hand, she and Chris eased their way through the crowd of people—many still clapping—and worked their way to the lobby. There Dani met them, hands clasped together at her chest and a look of glee on her face.

"Congratulations!"

A chuckle rose up from the back of Adrianne's throat. "How did you hear?"

"Are you kidding?" Dani reached for Adrianne's hand to look at the ring. "Good news travels fast around here. I've practically got the wedding cake ordered. And I assume I'll be a bridesmaid."

"Correct assumption." Adrianne giggled.

"We're planning a wedding!" Dani spoke aloud, catching the eye and ear of a man passing by. When he gave her a curious look, she added, "For this happy couple." She pointed to them.

"Happy couple." We are a happy couple. And we're about to be a family, a real family.

With Chris's arm wrapped around her waist, Adrianne contemplated the great joy that threatened to overwhelm her. *Oh Lord, I'm so grateful. So very grateful.*

After finishing up her conversation with Dani, Adrianne went off in search of her boss, to ask for permission to leave early. *I came in late, and I'm leaving early. Hope he doesn't kill me.* Thankfully, she found Mr. Martinson in a good humor. He looked up as she entered his office.

"Hey," she started.

"Hey, back," he said. "I see you created quite a stir back in the Revolutionary War area."

"Oh, I'm sorry," she explained. "I. . . Good grief. How in the world did you hear so quickly?"

"Didn't hear. I saw it. With my own eyes."

"W–what?"

He grinned. "Security cameras. Recorded the whole thing."

Adrianne slapped herself in the head. "Oh no! I forgot about that."

"Yep. From the second the curtain dropped. Not a bad piece of film, let me tell you." He let out a laugh. "I've watched it twice already. Great stuff. Has all the elements of a great movie scene. Just let me know if you ever want a copy for your children."

She shook her head and dropped into a chair opposite him. "This is so embarrassing. A–are you upset?"

"Are you kidding? I think it's great. And great for business, too. Maybe the papers will pick up the story." His smile lit the room. "And besides, it's about time someone snagged you. I'm just glad it wasn't that Kenner fellow."

A wave of relief swept over her. "I'm so glad to hear you say that. I hope this doesn't hamper his contributions. He's been such an asset to the museum."

"Nah. He won't stop giving. He's been a staunch supporter for years." Bob looked up with a smile. "I think he had designs on you."

"Sorry about that. He's—"

"A guy with too much money to spend and too much time on his hands. You now. . ." He rose from his chair and came to stand beside her. "You deserve much more than that. I just hope this fellow you're marrying is worthy of you."

"Oh, he is." The warmth rose to her cheeks. "He's the best thing that ever happened to me, Mr. Martinson. He's a good man. Perfect for me in every way."

"A good fit, huh?"

"Yes." She smiled, thinking of Lorelei's words. "A perfect fit."

Mr. Martinson gave her a fatherly pat on the back. "Well, you're a great mom, and I know you're going to be a great wife."

"Thank you so much," she said. "That means a lot coming from you."

"You're welcome. Now, get out of here. I'm sure you have things to do, people to tell."

"I do." She turned and with a wave sprinted back to the lobby, where she practically ran into Chris. Ironically, she found him chatting with Joey. *Ouch. This might be tricky.*

Joey looked her way with a shrug. "Hey."

"Hey."

"I, uh, I hear congratulations are in order." He stuck out his hand for a stilted handshake. "Congrats."

"Thanks."

"You're getting a great girl." Joey's words were meant for Chris, but his eyes never left Adrianne's.

"Thank you." Chris reached to slip his arm around Adrianne's shoulders. "I've been in love with this woman for as long as I can remember."

"I understand." Joey gave a curt nod, then turned back to his work.

"Don't worry about him." Dani leaned over to whisper in Adrianne's ear. "I have it on good authority he has a crush on at least three other female employees. His heart will mend."

"Yes, it will. I know the power of a mended heart, for sure. But thanks for telling me that. It helps."

"Something I need to know about?" Chris looked at her, curiosity in his eyes.

"Nah. I just think he was in love with me, is all."

"Ah. I see." He wrapped her in his arms and kissed her on the forehead. "Well,

I can't blame him for that, but he's going to have to fight me to get you. And he won't win, I'll promise you that. I almost lost you once. I'm not going to let that happen again."

"This guy is a keeper, Adrianne," Dani said with a sigh. "He's a prince of a guy if I ever saw one."

"What did you say?" She looked over at her friend, stunned.

Dani shrugged. "I just said that he was a prince. You know, if the shoe fits—"

"I know, I know." Adrianne giggled. "I guess it's unanimous, then." She slipped her hand into Chris's and together they headed off to tell Lorelei the good news.

Chapter 22

Chris pulled out onto the turnpike in the direction of Adrianne's parents' house. He couldn't have stopped smiling if he'd tried. The joy that flooded over him was almost more than he could stand. Several times along the way, he unclasped his right hand from the steering wheel and reached to grab Adrianne's. How perfect it felt, wrapped in his. How right.

"What will we tell Lorelei?" he asked as he kissed the ends of Adrianne's fingertips.

She gave a little shrug. "Let's just see what happens in the moment, okay? No rehearsed speeches. I have an idea God is going to take it from here."

"I'd say He already has."

For the next several minutes, as they made their way along in the traffic, Chris laid out his plan for moving to Philadelphia. "I can still work with the missions organization," he said. "I'll do short-term jaunts, several a year, staying only a couple of weeks each time. And I'll find something to fill the gap on this end, I feel sure of it."

"Funny," she said with a childish grin. "That's just what Jake said."

"Really?"

She went on to tell him about the conversation she'd had with Jake and Katelyn just a few short days ago—how her beloved pastor planned to offer Chris a position at the church.

Chris responded with "Are you serious?" Then he went on to share more from his side. He told her the story of Brent and his wife, of their desire to settle into his home, and his position, in Nicaragua. When he finished, Adrianne looked over at him and simply shook her head, clearly too overcome to respond.

Chris pulled off of the turnpike in the direction of her parents' house. *No. My future in-laws' house.* There he would lift Lorelei into his arms and hold on to her.

Forever.

☙

Adrianne's heart sang as they approached her parents' house. She could hardly wait to see Lorelei, or, rather, for Lorelei to see that Chris had come for them. As they started to get out of the car, Chris took her by the hand and lifted up a heartfelt prayer, for the Lord to guide every action, every word. Then he planted half a dozen tiny kisses on her cheek. "Ready?"

"Mm-hmm."

When they arrived at the front door, Adrianne motioned for Chris to give her a moment inside alone. He nodded in understanding. She opened the front door, surprised to find her mother in the living room alone, reading a book.

"Mom?"

Her mother looked up, surprised. "Oh, I was so engrossed in my story, I didn't even hear you come in." She glanced up at the wall clock. "You're early."

"I know." Adrianne giggled. "There's a reason for that." She cracked the door open a bit and motioned for Chris to come inside. As soon as he did, her mother sprang from the couch with a squeal.

"I knew it! I just knew it." The book dropped from her hand on to the sofa, and she crossed the room to wrap Chris in a motherly embrace.

"Mom?" Adrianne's heart swelled as she lifted her left hand for her mother to see the ring.

"O–oh, oh!" This time her mother captured them both with outstretched arms. "I'm the happiest woman on the planet."

"That might be debatable," Adrianne said with a wink. "I think maybe I've got you beat."

After a few more words of congratulations, they turned their attention to the most important thing.

"Where is Lorelei?" Chris asked.

"She's in the backyard with her grandpa. He's raking leaves."

"Let's surprise her," Adrianne suggested. She looked over at Chris. Nerves had clearly gotten the better of him. "It's going to be fine," she whispered.

He nodded, and they made their way to the back door. She led the way outside, surprised to find her father, rake in hand, but no daughter in sight.

"Dad?"

He turned to face her, a smile erupting the moment he saw Chris standing beside her. He came at once to join them, a teddy-bear hug nearly squeezing the life out of both of them. "This is a happy day, a happy day."

Another minute or two of explanation and congratulations passed before Adrianne voiced the question on her heart. "Dad, where's Lorelei?" She looked around, growing a bit nervous.

"Ah." He put a finger to his lips and pointed to a tall mound of leaves. *She's in there,* he mouthed. Then he whispered, "I think she's trying to hide from me, so I've been playing along."

"Ah-ha."

Adrianne and Chris eased their way across the yard to the heaping pile of autumn leaves. Just as they drew close, a lyrical sound ribboned through the leaves, catching everyone by surprise. The leaves fluttered a bit, and Lorelei's childlike voice rang out, "Someday my prince will come."

Adrianne clapped a hand over her mouth, hardly believing it. "Oh my."

"What's she singing?" Chris whispered.

"I, uh. . .I'm not sure you'd believe me."

His eyebrows elevated playfully as he whispered, "Try me."

She stifled a giggle, then leaned to speak softly into his ear. "Well, it's sort of a. . .well. . .a fairy-tale kind of thing."

"Fairy tale?" He shrugged. "Girl stuff?"

"Um. . .yeah."

Lorelei's song poured out from beneath the colorful mound of leaves, and suddenly Adrianne's breath caught in her throat as reality hit. She turned to glance at Chris, and the reminiscent look in his eyes told her right away that he understood the magnitude of what was happening right in front of them.

"Lorelei," he whispered.

Adrianne nodded, remembering the story, the reason for their daughter's name. Lorelei—the maiden along the Rhine River whose lyrical voice wooed sailors as their ships passed by.

For a moment, neither of them said anything. They leaned against each other, just listening as the song poured forth.

Adrianne stared at the red heap of leaves in blissful silence as another reality hit. *"Though they are red like crimson. . ."* The mound of brilliantly colored fall leaves now stood as a reminder of all God had done. *Red. Crimson.* Lorelei, their Lorelei, was encased on every side by the color red. Not a reminder of the sins of the past, but a clear and vivid picture of the forgiveness God had poured out on them all.

Just then, the youngster sprang up, her purple shirt and bright orange pants creating a fluorescent haze amid the leaves and shouted, "Gotcha!"

Lorelei's face was aglow with excitement—for a moment, anyway. The moment she laid eyes on Adrianne and Chris standing together, a look of confusion registered in her eyes, but only for a moment. In a split second, she bounded from the leaves, shouting the word Adrianne had ached to hear her say for seven long years. . .

"Daddy!"

Epilogue

C an't you drive any faster?" Chris looked over at Stephen, who drove the
streets of downtown Philly like a man possessed.

"I'm doing the best I can. There must be some kind of traffic jam
ahead or something."

"I don't want to be late to my own wedding."

David, who had arrived in Philadelphia only an hour ago, chuckled from the
back seat, then reached up and patted him on the shoulder. "You're plenty early.
Calm down."

"I'm calm."

"Sure you are." David laughed loud and long.

"Remember what I told you the night before my wedding?" Stephen asked.
When Chris shook his head, Stephen reminded him. "I said your wedding would
be next. And I was right."

"Oh, that's right. You did." He remembered now. They'd been racing down a
street on their way to Stephen and Julie's rehearsal dinner.

"If memory serves me right, you were worried about keeping Adrianne waiting
that night," Stephen said with a grin.

"Kind of like today." Chris glanced down at his watch, his nerves a jumbled
mess.

Stephen's expression changed all of a sudden. He gave Chris a pensive look.
"Hey, I just thought of something."

"What?"

"That 'always a groomsman' thing. We won't be able to say that anymore."

"Yeah." Chris smiled. "I'm glad about that."

"It's going to be a great day," David said. "The best day of your life."

"I hope I can remember my vows. And you've got the ring, right?"

"Of course," Stephen said.

"And the limousine company, did you call them?"

"Called 'em." Stephen chuckled. "Deep breaths, my friend."

Suddenly, the church came into view. A feeling of comfort washed over Chris
the moment he saw the building. "There it is. Right there." Over the past six
months, Freedom Fellowship had become more than a home. It was a place he
now loved—and served. "Not the prettiest church in town, but certainly a place

where the Lord moves."

"Hey, it sure beats any of our buildings in Nicaragua," David said from the back seat. "Looks like a mansion to me."

"Just my kind of place," Stephen agreed.

Chris smiled at his buddies. It felt good, right, to have them here, with him on this special day. As they sprang from the car, he noticed a small box on the floor. "What's this?"

"I don't know, man. This is your car, remember?" Stephen laughed. "I was just the assigned driver for today. Something about the groom being too nervous—"

"Yeah. I know." Chris reached down to nab the box and recognized it right away as Adrianne's. "Oh no. I've got to get this to her right away. I'll guarantee you the wedding won't go on unless I do."

"Must be pretty important," David said.

"Yep," Chris agreed. "More important than you might imagine."

➤

Adrianne looked up at her daughter and her bridesmaids with a smile. "What do you think of my hair?" she asked.

"It's amazing," Dani answered.

"Be-you-tee-ful!" Lorelei exclaimed.

Katelyn offered a reassuring smile. "I think you're going to be the prettiest bride I've ever seen. And I've seen a few."

"Thank you." Adrianne looked in the mirror once again, touching up her lipstick. "But I'm not going to look very pretty waltzing down the aisle in this old bathrobe. I think it's about time to put on my dress." She looked over at the beautiful gown, a duplicate of an eighteenth-century ball gown from the museum. A dress she had dreamed of wearing for years.

"Chris is going to flip when he sees you in this," Dani said.

"He flips *every* time he sees her," Lorelei said with a giggle. "Even when she's in jeans and a T-shirt, he still says she's the prettiest girl in the world."

Adrianne felt her cheeks flush. "You're embarrassing me. Besides, we need to stay focused. We don't need to be talking about all of that." She looked around the room, searching for a small, familiar box. "You're all dressed, and I've hardly started. H—have any of you seen my shoes?"

Dani looked up from the mirror, where she had been touching up her mascara. "Your what?"

"My shoes." A familiar frantic feeling gripped Adrianne as she scoped the room.

"Oh no!" Lorelei slapped herself in the head. "Not again, Mom."

"I know they're here," Adrianne said. "I remember distinctly. They were in the—" She racked her brain, trying to remember. "Oh, good grief. I think they

119

were in the car. Chris's car. I meant to get them out last night after the rehearsal dinner."

"What?" Katelyn looked at her. "Are you sure? Want me to see if he's here yet?"

"Yeah, do you mind?"

At that moment, a knock on the door distracted them all. Adrianne gripped her robe a bit tighter and motioned for the other ladies to get it.

"Who is it?" Dani asked through the door.

"Chris."

Adrianne shook her head and gave the women an imploring look. "We can't see each other today. Not before the wedding."

Chris's voice on the other side of the door distracted her for a moment. "I think I have something my beautiful bride might need."

"Oh, thank goodness." She almost went to the door without thinking, but Katelyn stopped her.

"I'll get them."

The door cracked open and Chris's hand appeared with a pair of delicate silver sandals dangling from his index finger. "Here you go, my lady. Your slippers."

"Mom!" Lorelei's eyes widened as she whispered, "He's got your shoes."

Adrianne put a hand to her heart and breathed a sigh of relief. "Thank goodness."

"No, Mom. Don't you get it? He's got your *shoes*." Her daughter stood with hands on her hips, clearly trying to make a point. "I *told* you he was Prince Charming."

She erupted into laughter and before they knew it, they were all giggling.

"Everything okay in there?" Chris asked, his hand still in view.

"F–fine." Adrianne signaled to shush her daughter.

Katelyn snatched the pumps from Chris's finger and sent him on his way with a quick "Thanks so much." She handed them to Adrianne, who slipped them on her feet right away.

"Time to get dressed." Katelyn now took on the role of wedding coordinator, snapping everyone to attention.

Adrianne's hands trembled as she reached for her dress. "I've dreamed of this moment for years. I can hardly believe it's here."

"Believe it, Mom," Lorelei whispered.

"You deserve it, honey," Katelyn added.

Less than five minutes later, Adrianne stood fully dressed in the elaborate ball gown in front of the full-length mirror. She swished to the right and then the left, captivated by the way she felt wearing it.

"That beadwork is amazing," Katelyn said. "I've never seen anything like it."

"There hasn't been anything like it for over two hundred years," Dani said with a smile. "Trust me. It's patterned after a one-of-a-kind gown from the Revolutionary War era."

"Something old *and* something new, all in one gown," Katelyn said. "Gorgeous *and* practical."

"Yes," Adrianne said with a smile. "And I've borrowed this necklace from my mother." She fingered the beautiful piece that draped her neck. "It was my grandmother's."

"It's so pretty," Lorelei said.

"What about the 'something blue' part?" Katelyn asked.

"Right here!" Dani held up the baby blue garter, trimmed in lace.

"Ooh, I almost forgot that." Adrianne quickly slipped it on.

"Almost done. Just one more thing." Dani reached up to fasten the delicate veil into Adrianne's hair, then placed a beautiful tiara on top. When she was finished, they all stood in silence a moment, just staring.

"Oh, Mom!" Lorelei stared at both of their reflections in the mirror. "You look like Cinderella."

"Do I?"

Katelyn and Dani nodded.

"You look like a queen," Lorelei whispered, her eyes wide.

Adrianne gazed down into her daughter's beautiful eyes. "If I'm a queen," she said, "then that would make you a princess."

"Ooh. That's true." Lorelei turned to look at herself in the mirror once again. "I'm a princess."

An abrupt knock on the door interrupted their ponderings.

"It's almost time, honey," Adrianne's mother's voice rang out. "Is it okay if Daddy and I come in?"

"Yes. Of course."

Her parents entered the room and she turned to greet them. Her father's eyes filled at once. "You look beautiful," he whispered. "Absolutely beautiful." He kissed her on the cheek.

Her mother reached into her purse for a tissue. "I told myself I wouldn't cry today."

"It's okay, Mom." She grabbed her mother's hand and gave it a squeeze. "I'm sure by the time this day is over we'll all be drying our eyes."

Katelyn, still playing the role of organizer, handed each woman a bouquet to carry. From outside the door, the familiar strains of "Trumpet Voluntaire" rang out.

"I think that's our cue." Adrianne's father extended his arm. "Are you ready?"

She took it with a smile. "I'm ready."

With her bridesmaids and daughter leading the way, they made their way down the hallway toward the back of the sanctuary. The doors swept open, and for the first time, she saw her groom-to-be. He looked every bit like a prince in his black tuxedo and tails. His face glowed with excitement, and all the more when he finally caught a glimpse of her.

She watched as, one by one, her bridesmaids took their places at the front, and then, with great joy, as Lorelei made her way up the aisle, dropping rose petals all the way. *My little girl. My princess.* Something from the front distracted her. She looked up just in time to see Chris wipe his eyes as Lorelei went by. He mouthed a silent *I love you* to their daughter and she responded with a nod of her head.

As the wedding march began, Adrianne happened to glance down at her flowers. Most would have chosen pastels for a springtime wedding. *But not me.* No, nothing but red roses would do for a day like today.

"Though they are red like crimson. . ."

A wave of joy washed over her as she looked forward—into her bridegroom's eyes. She pushed back the lump in her throat as the Lord reminded her, once and for all, that the past truly *was* in the past.

With a prayer on her lips and a song in her heart, Adrianne took her first step down the aisle—toward her future.

WHITE AS SNOW

Dedication

To Cecilia, the real Gran-Gran.
And to my son-in-law, Brandon.
Who needs football anyway?

Prologue

Los Angeles, California

Brianna Nichols shoved the earplugs from her CD player into her ears and settled back against the airplane seat. She willed herself not to think about the life she was leaving behind. What would be the point anyway?

She opted to squeeze her eyes shut instead of sneaking a peek out of the tiny window. With a resolute heart Brianna focused on the music, turning up the volume to a near-deafening level. "Onward and upward." She whispered the words. At least she thought she'd whispered them. With the music blaring in her ears, she must've spoken a little louder than she thought.

"Excuse me?" The businessman next to her turned to give her a quizzical look.

"Oh, uh, never mind." She fought the temptation to explain. No point in doing so. What would she say? That she'd chosen a college halfway across the country to get away from her father? That he was so busy coaching his latest star players he couldn't even make sure she made it to the airport okay? That a lousy move on his part had caused her to lose the only boy she'd ever loved? That she was now headed to Pittsburgh, where she would be living with a grandmother she hadn't seen since she was fourteen?

No, she would skip the story.

And, if she could, she'd skip the rest of her life, too.

Chapter 1

Pittsburgh, Pennsylvania
Eight Years Later

Brianna unlocked the front door of the duplex she shared with her grandmother, pushed it open, and stepped inside. She wriggled out of her lightweight jacket and hung it on the hall tree, then paused for a minute to brush a loose hair out of her face.

"Gran-Gran, where are you?" she called out. When she didn't get an immediate response, fear kicked in. Her grandmother's age and physical condition were top priority these days. Only one thing brought hope...the pervasive scent of hot frying grease. Gran-Gran must be cooking again.

Brianna made her way past the collection of silver spoons hanging on the wall in the front foyer, beyond the AGE IS A STATE OF MIND sampler and into the living room, where the furnishings were covered in doilies. No Gran-Gran. She continued on, past the dozens of knickknacks and into the narrow hallway, where her grandmother had created a shrine of sorts out of family photos.

"Gran?" she tried again.

Just then her grandmother's lyrical voice rang out from the back end of the house. "I'm in the kitchen, Bree, working on a feast fit for a king!"

A familiar scent wafted through the hallway, and Brianna smiled as she recognized it—Gran-Gran's fried bread.

"Mmm. I'm coming!"

She entered the kitchen and caught sight of her beautiful grandmother, hair as white as snow pulled up into a tight bun. Her faded yellow-checked apron, the same one Bree had seen her wear hundreds—if not thousands—of times before, made her look a bit more like Aunty Em and a little less like Martha Stewart, but Brianna wouldn't have it any other way. She loved this image of her grandmother and hoped it would remain forever embedded in her heart. She stopped for a moment and closed her eyes to capture it like a photograph, just in case.

Gran-Gran picked up a mound of fleshy-white bread dough from a greased cookie sheet and placed it in a skillet filled with hot oil. Once settled, it sizzled and popped then started to swell. Within seconds the bottom half turned a lovely golden color. Gran-Gran flipped it over with a pair of tongs and scrutinized it.

"Not bad, not bad," she said with a girlish laugh.

"Oh, man!" Brianna noticed the platter filled with already-fried circles of bread and snagged one right away. She shoved as much as she could fit into her mouth and talked around it as she asked, "What's the occasion? What's going on?"

Gran-Gran's eyes lit with pure delight. She lifted the piece of bread, now beautifully browned on both sides, and placed it on the platter. She then raised another ball of dough in the air and waved it triumphantly. "Football! The first game of the season is on tonight!" She set the ball of dough in the hot oil, and it began to sizzle right away.

Brianna groaned. How many times had she told Gran-Gran—and everyone else in the city of Pittsburgh, for that matter—that she'd come to Pennsylvania to get away from the sport? But did they listen? Of course not! These Pittsburgh folks were diehards, and Gran-Gran was the leader of the pack. She'd tried for years to indoctrinate Brianna, but, at least so far, the California native remained undaunted. Football and all the hoopla that went with it were a part of her past, not her future. She'd had her fill back in L.A.

"I've been scheming all day." Gran-Gran walked over to the computer on the small desk in front of the window and typed in the Web address for the Steelers, something she did with remarkable ease, considering her eighty-four years. "It's a good thing I'm computer savvy." An impish giggle escaped before she continued. "Those classes at the senior center have worked wonders! I don't know how I'd keep up with the players otherwise. Seems like every year the lineup shifts around on me, and I can't seem to remember one handsome face from another."

"Gran-Gran!"

"Well, the players jump from team to team. Harper's back, ya know. Thought we lost him because of that blown ACL."

"ACL?"

Gran-Gran nodded but didn't explain. "No one thought he'd be able to play this season, but he's back."

"Oh, yeah. I think I heard something about one of Pittsburgh's players blowing out the ligament of his knee last spring. Football is a dangerous sport. That's just one more reason I—"

"Harper, Bree," Gran-Gran interrupted. "*Harper*. Our star quarterback, remember?" She went off on a tangent about his excellent plays last season before the accident, but lost Brianna a minute or two into her dissertation.

"I think I remember hearing Harper's name from the guys at work or something," Brianna acknowledged with a shrug. "Not really sure."

"Honestly. You're hopeless." Gran-Gran gave her a how-could-you-be-my-blood-kin look. "But since you're standing there, why don't you go ahead and flip that bread over for me?"

Brianna reached to grab the tongs, then gently eased the ever-growing mound of dough over in the hot oil. Noting her grandmother had become engrossed in the computer, she shifted her attentions to the oven, where she discovered something cooking inside. She took advantage of the opportunity to open the oven door.

"Mmm." Gran-Gran's famous meat loaf. After easing the oven door shut, Brianna glanced inside a pot on the stove. Lifting the lid, she discovered homemade mashed potatoes. "Wow. You weren't kidding when you said it was a feast fit for a king, were you?"

"Great football food," her grandmother said with a wink. "Just in case we work up a manly appetite—hollering at the bad plays."

"We?" A gnawing feeling let Brianna know what was coming, even before the words were spoken.

"I've invited a couple of my girlfriends over," Gran-Gran said with a mischievous twinkle in her eye.

Brianna looked up, alarmed. "Who?"

"Rena and Lora. But don't fret now. They've promised to be as good as gold this season." Gran-Gran crossed her heart then kissed the tips of her fingers, as if to offer reassurance. "None of that acting up like last year; they promise."

"Humph." Another piece of bread went into Brianna's mouth, a self-protective measure. If she spoke her mind about Rena and Lora, Gran-Gran might take offense, but the two women—each at least ten years her grandmother's junior—drove Brianna a little crazy with their jerseys, pom-poms, and colorful hand towels. And their play-by-play commentaries didn't help either. She just didn't know how much she could take. Even from up in her bedroom their cheers and jeers proved difficult to ignore.

"Rena's bought a new jersey," Gran-Gran said with a snicker. "Ordered it from the Internet. She thinks she's one-upped me, but hers isn't signed by Harper."

"Are you serious? A signed jersey costs a fortune. Tell me you didn't. . ."

"I did." Gran-Gran winked. "Bought it from the Internet, but I signed his name myself. Do you think she'll figure it out?" She reached across the desk for the jersey. Across the back, in rather wobbly handwriting, she'd scribbled out *Harper*.

"Oh, no." Brianna slapped herself in the head. "Now you've gone to plotting and scheming. You'll have to do penance for this for sure, Gran-Gran."

"Aw, it's all in fun." Her grandmother turned her sights to her computer again.

Brianna dropped into a chair at the breakfast table and let out a grunt. To her way of thinking, football was a game where a handful of healthy, fit men ran around a field for a couple of hours, watched by millions of folks who could probably use the exercise. A game her father had sacrificed almost everything to—time, family, relationships. The almighty game of football. Yippee.

Wasn't it bad enough she'd had to grow up on the sidelines in L.A., her father off coaching this game or that? Why had she chosen Pittsburgh, of all places, to get away from the sport? In this city, football consumed almost everyone.

She sighed as she thought about the guys at work. Seemed as if they had nothing better to do throughout the winter months than place friendly wagers on the games and gossip over the various players—none of whom interested her in the least. She'd never joined in their chatter and never planned to. In fact, she never planned to participate in football in any form or fashion. . .not since. . .Daniel's accident. Their senior year.

She shuddered as the memories surfaced, but she quickly pushed them away. She wouldn't think about her old boyfriend tonight. And she wouldn't think about her more recent flash-in-the-pan boyfriend, Andy, either. His fanatical football ways had driven her to the edge. She'd finally put him behind her. Just like Nick. And Matt. And every other Pittsburgh guy she'd ever looked at twice. Not a one of them could see beyond the pigskin to notice she was alive. Maybe they were all like her dad.

"Oh, speaking of news. . ." Gran-Gran glanced up from the computer with a big smile on her face. "Your mother called today to say they're coming out for a visit at Christmastime."

"Really? All of them?" Brianna popped another piece of bread in her mouth. The idea of seeing her mom and brother excited her. Oh, how she wished she could get over the twinge that hit every time she thought about spending time with her father.

"Yes. They would've come for Thanksgiving," Gran-Gran continued, "but your mom said. . ." Her voice drifted off, and Brianna filled in the blank.

Dad can't take time away from the team at that time of year. What else is new?

Just as quickly she offered up a prayer, asking God to help her get beyond these feelings. Maybe her father hadn't changed much since she'd been away, but she had, right? Brianna paused to reflect on the changes in her life since arriving in Pennsylvania. Her commitment to Christ and the teaching she had received from Gran-Gran, Pastor Meyers, and the youth leaders at church afterward did a thorough job of convincing her the past was in the past. . .where it belonged. She'd worked for years to get over the pain of Daniel's rejection after his accident. And she'd worked even harder at forgiving her father for putting Daniel at risk in the first place. Weren't coaches supposed to look out for the best interest of their players?

"Don't look back, Bree," her grandmother always said. "Press on toward the goal."

Yes, she thanked the Lord she had chosen Pittsburgh. She would never have made it this far without Gran-Gran.

Brianna snapped out of her ponderings as her grandmother added, "Your mom said to tell you she's looking forward to meeting your boyfriend."

"Gran-Gran, you know I'm not dating Andy anymore. He never had time for me. That guy is just like every other man I've met since I moved to Pittsburgh. He eats, sleeps, and breathes. . . ."

Brianna didn't say the word.

She didn't dare.

ॐ

The lights above the field cast a Hollywood-like haze over the players' heads. Watching from the glow of the plasma TV he could no longer afford, Brady Campbell sighed. If only he hadn't told his agent to play hardball with Tampa, maybe he could've settled for a little less pay and no respect. At least then he'd be on the field and not on the sofa. But Tampa had slipped through his fingers this season, and he found himself in the one position any second-string quarterback would hate. Out of the game.

So here he sat, nibbling stale chips, his feet kicked up on the coffee table, watching his former team members on television on a lonely Sunday afternoon. He could only stand a few minutes of outside observation before he had to change the channel. Anything would be better than this.

Ah. The Steelers, playing their first official game of the season. Now *this* would be pure joy. All his life he'd dreamed of playing for Pittsburgh. Maybe someday. . .

Brady kept a watchful eye on Harper, Pittsburgh's star quarterback. The guy had a bad knee, a blown ACL. Despite predictions he'd miss the start of the season, Harper had managed to rehab it and return to the game. Who would've guessed he'd be back this quick? But look at him now, sprinting across the field.

The television camera focused on the scoreboard, and Brady groaned as he reflected on the score: 0-3. "Man." Just two minutes left in the first quarter. Would they rise to the challenge?

Less than sixty seconds later, a yelp rose from the back of his throat as he got his answer. A roar went up from the crowd as Jimmy Harper threw the ball for a touchdown. Tight end Jared Cunningham leaped into the air, catching it in the end zone. For a second it looked as if he might let it slip through his fingers, but tenacity won out, and the scoreboard reflected the shift in power: 6-3. One swift kick later and the electric lights boasted a cheerful 7-3. Not bad for a last-minute attempt. Brady turned up the television to hear the roar of thousands of boisterous fans. How he loved that sound!

A commercial cut into the action, distracting him. Instead of switching back to the Tampa game, Brady swallowed down a mouthful of soda and leaned back against the sofa, contemplating his situation. *Lord, I don't get it. I gave You my life, and I trust You, but it seems like everything is falling apart. How am I going to do all those things You've called me to do if I'm not even in the game?*

He pondered his recent decision to trust Christ as his Savior. That one move had changed everything. And yet nothing seemed to be working out the way he'd hoped.

The commercial ended, and Brady kept a watchful eye on the screen as his old college coach, Ed Carter, cheered on the Steelers from the sidelines. After a few seconds of ego-pumping and strategy planning, the players prepared for the next quarter.

Several minutes in, with the Steelers in possession once again, Harper ran toward the goal, ball in hand. Brady rose to his feet, ready to shout. Just seconds short of reaching the line, however, Harper took a hit, shot backward through the air, and landed on his back. He rolled over to his side, curled up in the fetal position, a look of agony on his face. The referee's whistle blew, and the crowd grew silent.

Brady sat back down, his heart shifting to his toes.

From the way Harper grabbed his knee, Brady knew he was done for.

Chapter 2

Brianna leaned back against the driver's seat and focused on the road leading out of the North Hills section of Pittsburgh toward the hustle and bustle of the city a few miles south. She turned the nose of her silver SUV onto Interstate 79 and settled in for the trip.

The strains of a familiar worship song filled the air, and she immediately reached to turn up the volume on the radio. As the words took root in her spirit, she joined in, singing at the top of her lungs. In fact, she got so caught up in the lyrics and the beautiful melody that she almost missed the turnoff for 279 South. She managed to catch it just in time.

Worshipping with abandon on the road was not an unfamiliar routine on the drive to Allegheny Building and Design near downtown each morning. Brianna enjoyed this part of her day nearly as much as her time with Gran-Gran in the evenings. And last night's football saga had certainly proven to be entertaining, if nothing else. She was thankful her grandmother's team had won in the end. Seemed like the ladies had a good time, dressed in their jerseys and waving their pennants like high school cheerleaders gone awry.

The song came to an end, and Brianna shifted her thoughts to the day ahead. She sighed as she reflected on the guys in the office. Nearly every one happened to be enamored with the one sport she was trying to avoid. And now that the season had begun, she was sure to hear of little else. Office pools were all the rage, as were arguments over plays and coaching decisions, not to mention the bantering back and forth about incoming and outgoing players.

Brianna interrupted her morning reverie to glance up at the gray skies over the Allegheny River as she crossed one of Pittsburgh's forty bridges into the area known as the Golden Triangle. "Pittsburgh has more bridges than Venice, Italy." She recited the words she'd recently heard a newscaster speak. Still, no amount of bridges could take the place of the breathtaking Pacific Ocean or the beautiful hills of Los Angeles. She still yearned for them in her heart, even though years had passed, and she'd long since reconciled herself to living in Pennsylvania.

"It ain't exactly L.A.," she muttered, as she did almost every morning. "But it's home."

No, Pittsburgh certainly didn't have that Southern California feel. A long way from it, in fact. No movie sets. No glitz and glam. No red carpets. No starlets sipping cappuccinos at local coffee shops. No paparazzi perched for the latest shot.

Nope. Pittsburgh was just. . .Pittsburgh. A little on the gray side at times, but awfully pretty when the winter snows turned everything to a glistening white. During that magical season, the trees hung heavy with blankets of snow, their branches dipping lower, lower, as if they might one day touch the ground.

Of course, those same snows often resulted in treacherous driving, but she'd even grown accustomed to that. Almost, anyway.

The people of Pittsburgh were amazing—that she had learned very quickly. Brianna had fallen in love with their tenacity, their spirit. And she had certainly never met more dedicated business owners than John and Roger Stevenson, her bosses at AB&D.

She smiled, even now, as she thought about them. The brothers, both in their sixties, did a fine job of managing the company and had built it into Pittsburgh's leading high-end home remodeling company. How she enjoyed working alongside them.

Brianna's heart swelled as she thought about that. Her business degree, coupled with her love of people, had served the company well. Seemed like no matter where she went—the grocery store, the auto repair shop, the mall—it didn't matter. She always managed to run into potential customers—folks looking for a reputable home remodeling company. She carried business cards with her at all times, just in case. And her in-office skills had proven to benefit the company as well. It hadn't taken long for John and Roger to promote her to a nicer office space in the building.

She inched her way along in traffic. Off in the distance she caught a glimpse of the area where Three Rivers Stadium used to stand. As much as she avoided all things related to football, it was a bit sad to know that the once-architectural wonder had lived out its glory years only to be imploded when the need for a new stadium had arisen. For a moment she allowed herself to think about Daniel and all he had lost in one night so many years ago. A little shiver ran down her spine as she contemplated how truly temporary the things of this world could be.

She shook off the memory and focused on more positive things. With a determined spirit, Brianna turned up the radio and sang at the top of her lungs.

❧

Brady received the call from his agent, Sal Galloway, a little before ten in the morning.

"Bad news for Harper means good news for you," Sal said. "Pack a bag. You've got to be in Pittsburgh tomorrow at eleven."

"W–what? I'm playing for Pittsburgh?"

"Well, not officially. But they want to talk to you, so start packing."

Brady's heart went into overdrive. For a moment. As excited as he felt about the upcoming news, he knew it came as a result of an injury to another player.

"I don't understand...," he started. "How? Is Carter behind this?" Surely his old coach hadn't put his neck on the line for a virtual unknown like Brady Campbell.

"Carter got you the interview, but I'm gonna get you the job."

After a few brief instructions Sal hung up. Brady held the phone in his hand, completely stunned. He thought about his bond with Coach Carter back in his college days and marveled at the fact that God appeared to be bringing things full circle. He also laughed as he thought about Sal's words: *"Carter got you the interview, but I'm gonna get you the job."*

"You're wrong, Sal," Brady said to the empty room. *"You're* not gonna get me this job. *God's* gonna get me this job—if that's His plan."

With joy filling his heart, he started packing his bag. He hoped by tomorrow afternoon he'd be packing far more than that.

Chapter 3

Brianna arrived home from work on Wednesday afternoon to find Gran-Gran at work, trimming bushes along the front of their duplex.

"Gran-Gran! You don't need to do that. I told you I'd be happy to hire someone to do the yard work."

"Pooh. You know I love to work in the yard. Makes me feel young." Her grandmother turned and gave her a wink. "And keeps me in shape."

"Still. . ."

"I'm trying to get the house ready," Gran-Gran explained. "We're getting a new neighbor."

"We are?" Brianna turned to look at the twin unit. It had been empty for weeks, though a host of Realtors had brought a few people by. "How do you know?"

"The sign is gone," her grandmother said.

Brianna glanced at the spot where the FOR RENT sign used to be. "Ah, you're right."

"And I saw the most handsome man today," Gran-Gran said with a giggle. "I do hope he's the new renter, not a Realtor or something."

Brianna laughed. "Are you looking for Mr. Right, Gran-Gran?"

"Not for me!" Her grandmother giggled. "This one was your age."

"Oh, no, you don't. Not again." Brianna shook her head, trying to push any such ideas out of her grandmother's head.

"But this one's different."

"That's what you said about Andy. And Nick. And Matt. Remember?"

"Well, I can't get it right every time, Bree."

"At least I knew those guys," Brianna said. "We don't know a thing about this one. What if he turns out to be the last person on planet Earth God would have in mind for me? Then what? I'm stuck living next door to him for who knows how long."

"Oh, he's only signed a six-month lease," Gran-Gran said. "I asked Mrs. Brandt across the street."

"How did she know?"

"Her daughter works as a receptionist at the Realtor's office."

"Have you stooped to spying?" Brianna asked.

"If it means finding you a husband, maybe!" Gran-Gran went back to trimming bushes, and Brianna chuckled as she turned to give the twin unit a glance.

So they had a new neighbor—a man, at that. Though she hated to admit it, Brianna did feel better knowing someone would be so close by, just in case.

She hoped, whoever he was, he'd have a fondness for white-haired women and homemade bread.

꣠

Early Friday morning Brady pointed the movers in the direction of the upstairs bedroom. "Watch your step!" he called out, as the two rotund, whiskery fellows rounded the corner with a chest of drawers in tow. Even with his imagination in play, Brady couldn't picture how both of their bellies could possibly fit into the stairwell with the dresser wedged between them. Surely disaster lay ahead.

"Oh, please be careful," he pleaded. "That's been in the family for—" He never got to say "years." The deafening scrape of wood against sheetrock made him cringe. He looked up to find a gash in the wall, then turned and closed his eyes.

The older man let an expletive fly, and the younger one lost his grip on the tail end of the dresser, nearly causing the family heirloom to tumble to the floor. Nearly.

Brady drew in three deep breaths and walked in the opposite direction, something his mother had taught him to do as a child. How many deliberate breaths had he taken this morning? Thirty? Sixty?

The doorbell rang, mercifully distracting Brady from the scene of the crime. He chugged across the living room, nearly tripping over the large metal dolly the movers had deposited in the middle of the floor—a potential death trap. He caught his balance and continued on beyond a half dozen boxes, past the stack of wall art to open the front door, ready to argue with the man from the electric company on the opposite side. He was supposed to have been there yesterday.

To his surprise an elderly woman—certainly no more than five feet tall—stood on the other side of the door, her white hair coiled up like a mound of pasta atop her head, her whimsical blue eyes twinkling with mischief.

"Hello, neighbor!" she called out in a singsongy voice. "I'm Abbey Nichols. Live next door. Hope you're hungry."

He was. But he wasn't quite sure what that had to do with anything. Until he noticed the plate in her hand. A familiar, tempting smell wafted up to greet him. As Brady glanced down beyond the clear plastic wrap, he noticed pot roast, potatoes, and carrots. And yeast rolls! Just the sight of them made his mouth water.

"Um, I'm Brady," he stammered. "Brady Campbell."

"The name suits you." The older woman took a step in his direction, and he swung the door wide to allow her to enter. Whether he wanted it or not, company had arrived. "I'll just take this to the kitchen." She took a step in that direction, then very nearly tripped over a box. "Can't see the forest for all the trees in here."

"Sorry." He moved a box of his favorite CDs and DVDs to clear a pathway for her.

Just then Mutt and Jeff plodded down the stairs and headed for the door. They stopped short when they saw the plate in her hand.

"Looks mighty good," the first one said with longing in his eyes.

"A man could work up quite an appetite unloading furniture," the second one added as he rubbed his bristly chin.

"Well, you fellas take a load off!" Abbey's voice dripped like honey. "I've got plenty more where that came from. Just sit right down, and I'll be back in a few minutes with two more plates."

She headed for the door, and Brady groaned. How could he tell her he was paying these guys by the hour without hurting her feelings?

The men tipped their caps in her direction then entered the kitchen and plopped down at the table. Abbey disappeared out the front door, assuring them she would return not just with dinner but dessert as well. "Apple pie!" she sang out.

Brady shook his head and whispered a prayer for patience before joining the movers in the kitchen. *Help me to be nice about this, Lord. I'm not sure I can do it on my own.*

He offered the men—whose names turned out to be Jake and Lenny—cans of soda, which they took willingly. Abbey returned moments later, not even bothering to ring the bell. She pressed her way into the room with a smile that seemed to light up the place like the football field at halftime. After passing out the plates, she insisted they join hands and pray.

"You do the honors, young man," she said with a nod. "It'll do you good to chat with the Almighty."

Brady didn't bother to mention that he'd chatted with Him every day for the past eight months. Didn't figure it was the right time. Instead he bowed his head and offered up a quick prayer.

Then the feast began.

Jake and Lenny dove in, barely pausing between bites to say a thing. That left the floor wide open—for Abbey.

"Tell me about yourself, Brady," she encouraged him.

"What would you like to know?" He broke off a piece of the warm yeast roll and stuck it in his mouth.

"Well, it's obvious you're not from the North—that's sure and certain." Abbey laughed. "Where do you hail from, young man?" She gave him an inquisitive look.

"I'm from Tampa," he managed through the mouthful of bread. He pointed at the plate. "This is good. Makes me miss my mom's cooking."

"I do love to cook," she said with a grin. "I'm especially fond of breads. I doubt Bree and I will ever go hungry."

"Bree?"

"Ah." Abbey's smile seemed to widen, if that were even possible. "My grand-daughter. She's lived with me since she was eighteen. She's a transplant, too. From L.A. But she's fallen in love with Pittsburgh." Here her excitement seemed to wane a bit. "Least *most* things about Pittsburgh. But she'll come around on the rest."

Brady was just about to ask for details when Jake and Lenny nodded in the direction of the apple pie. "Do you mind?" Jake asked.

"Be my guest." Abbey pushed the pie in his direction. "I'm planning to bake a chocolate cake for tonight." She nodded in Brady's direction. "These are just leftovers from last night. Would've gone to waste if I hadn't noticed the moving truck out front."

Brady nodded then glanced at his watch. So much for hoping these guys would finish up quickly. Looked as if he'd be writing a heftier check than planned.

As he took another bite of pot roast and leaned back in his chair, contentment washed over him.

Really, what did it matter? Even if he had to pay them for an extra hour, it would be worth it for this meal.

With a smile on his face and genuine peace in his heart, Brady settled in for a long chat with his new neighbor.

Chapter 4

Later that evening Brady caught a glimpse of Abbey's granddaughter for the first time. As he pulled his car out of the driveway, he noticed a tall, slender blond making her way toward the front door of the adjoining house. She wore a pair of jeans and a soft blue sweater that accentuated her narrow waist.

She turned to pull keys from her bag, and he managed to get a good look at her face. Large eyes. Tipped-up nose. In many ways she reminded him of Abbey. Except for the height, of course.

What was her name again? Ah, yes. Bree.

He gave her another look. She didn't seem terribly made-up, like so many of the women who hung around the players. No, this one had more of a girl-next-door appearance about her. Ironic. He loved the fact that a few wholesome girls were still out there. In his line of work...

No, he wouldn't go there.

The setting sun cast an angelic glow above Bree's head. The beauty tossed her blond hair back as she balanced mail in one hand and used the key to open the front door with the other.

Brady couldn't help but stare at her. In fact, his heart seemed to kick into overdrive, a fact that caught him completely off guard.

"Calm yourself, man."

He found himself so preoccupied that he almost backed into the mailbox. The tires let out a telltale squeal as he hit the brake. Thankfully, he missed the metal box by inches. He didn't, however, miss the attentions of his new neighbor.

The young woman turned and glanced his way with a concerned look on her face. She almost dropped the stack of mail in her hands but managed to hang on to it. Her wrinkled brow relaxed when she realized he was okay, and she flashed a wide smile his way.

Brady remembered seeing that same smile on Abbey's face as she'd talked about her granddaughter earlier today. Now he understood it. This was a girl worth smiling over.

"So you're Bree," he whispered. "You must be something else—to keep such a beautiful expression on your grandmother's face."

She nodded her head in his direction as if she'd heard every word and wanted to chime in with her agreement.

He offered up a slight wave in response, then tried to remember why he'd climbed into the car in the first place. Ah, yes. The grocery store. He needed to purchase groceries to fill his empty pantry. Funny, right now he didn't feel much like shopping. In fact, if he had his way he'd pull his car back into the driveway and head next door to return Abbey's pie pan. Would that look suspicious?

Maybe.

Then again. . .

Brady was so struck by Bree's wholesome beauty and her inviting smile that he couldn't seem to remember how to get the car into gear. In many ways the beautiful blond reminded him of the girls back home in Florida. She looked. . . casual. Laid back.

Why weren't all women like that? Why were so many of the ones he'd found himself interested in so high-strung and difficult to please?

Bree gave him a curious look, and he quickly managed to shift the car into gear. Best to head on out for the evening, not give the impression of a gawking schoolboy. There would be plenty of time to get to know her later. After the news reporters picked up the story of his arrival.

On the other hand. . .

He gave her one last look as she slipped inside the twin unit. Why it felt as if a piece of his heart remained behind, he could not be sure.

≥◆

"Gran-Gran?"

As Brianna entered the house, she turned her attention from the new neighbor, handsome as he was, and focused on her grandmother.

"Well, hello, stranger!" Gran-Gran inched her way down the narrow stairs, clutching the rail. Her tightened brow reflected her efforts.

As always, Brianna's heart lurched as she saw her grandmother struggling to make it to the bottom step. "Do you need help?" she asked, rushing to her side.

With a wave of her hand Gran-Gran gave her answer. "Shoo now. Let me do for myself as long as I can, why don't you?"

Brianna feigned offense but then smiled at her grandmother's tenacity. Not every eighty-four-year-old could manage stairs without assistance. Brianna only hoped to be half as spry when she reached that age.

"Have it your way." She offered up an exaggerated shrug as she headed back down again. "But one of these days I'll be calling on you to help me up and down these stairs, and I hope you'll come rushing to my side."

"Oh, pooh." Gran-Gran stepped gingerly down to the bottom step, then reached over for a warm hug, which Brianna returned with great joy.

She glanced up at the sampler on the wall, the adage of which she had

memorized less than a week after arriving as a teen. THE OLDEST TREES OF-
TEN BEAR THE SWEETEST FRUIT. Hadn't made much sense back then, but she
certainly understood it now. Some of the sweetest things she'd ever learned had
come from this beautiful grandmother of hers.

"Are you hungry?" A little wink followed Gran-Gran's words, which explained
the yummy smell in the house. She'd been cooking. Again.

"Mm-hmm." Brianna nodded. "But you're going to make me fat."

"Please. You could stand to put a little meat on your bones. You're skinny as a rail.
Sometimes I think you have a hollow leg."

Brianna chuckled. She loved her grandmother's funny sayings. Still, it was a
miracle she'd maintained her college weight, what with the great meals placed
before her. Not that she would turn any of them down. To do so would be highly
insulting to the one person she loved above all others. And, besides, all of this
cooking gave her grandmother something to do. It kept her busy.

"Come on into the kitchen, then." Gran-Gran led the way, and within minutes
they sat together at the table, enjoying bowls of hearty vegetable soup, made from
the leftovers of last night's pot roast. And the chocolate cake looked divine!

"How was your day?" Brianna asked between mouthfuls.

Gran-Gran's brow wrinkled a bit, and concern filled her eyes. Brianna couldn't
help but wonder what had put that look on her grandmother's usually cheery
face.

"It's that new fella next door." Gran-Gran sighed, and a sad look registered.
"Mr. Campbell."

"What about him?" Immediately Brianna's gotta-take-care-of-Gran-Gran
antennae elevated.

"Well. . ." Her grandmother reached for her napkin and twisted it a couple of
times. "He's just such a. . .a nuisance."

"Nuisance? He just moved in this morning."

"Yes, but what a day! I've hardly rested since he arrived. He kept that stereo
blasting all day long. Hurt my ears something awful. And that dog of his. . ."

"Oh? He has a dog?"

Gran-Gran nodded. "Must be huge. He barked like a maniac all afternoon."

"That's so strange. I haven't heard him." Brianna took another spoonful of the
soup as she thought about it. She would need to do something about this if the
situation didn't improve. She hated to intrude on a new neighbor, particularly
one as handsome as the fellow she'd caught a glimpse of this evening. But with
Gran-Gran rattled, someone needed to get involved. And the sooner the better.

"I've lived in this duplex for thirty years and haven't had a minute's trouble
with any of my neighbors," her grandmother noted. "Not once. And you know
I'm not one to complain about such things."

"Of course not." In fact, Brianna couldn't remember a time when her grand-mother had ever spoken a word against anyone in the neighborhood, so this must be very serious. With Gran-Gran's blood pressure running a little on the high side, it wouldn't take much to send it soaring into the danger zone. This rowdy stranger would have to mind his p's and q's if he wanted to go on living next door under peaceable terms.

The wrinkles in her grandmother's forehead deepened further. "I do hope my heart can take the intrusion, Bree."

It didn't take any more than that to convince Brianna. She would take care of this, even if it meant confronting a handsome stranger. Gran-Gran was worth it.

Chapter 5

The following morning Brianna marched across the lawn and rapped on the stranger's door. When he didn't answer after a minute or so, she turned to double-check something. Yep. Car in the driveway. Likely he'd seen her coming and decided to hide out inside the house. He must suspect an impending confrontation. Or maybe he was still sleeping. It was Saturday morning, after all.

Well, she wouldn't back down. Not that easily.

Brianna knocked again, a little louder this time. She half-expected to hear his dog barking in response. Instead the door swung open, and she found Mr. Trouble with a capital T himself standing on the other side. Wow. He was a lot taller than she'd guessed—at least six feet four—and wider than she might've imagined, too.

No. *Wider* wasn't the right word. He certainly wasn't chubby. Just. . .solid. Especially around the shoulders and upper arms. Did he lift weights? *Man.* She gave him another quick once-over, trying not to be too obvious. Yep. Solid.

Mr. Campbell's face lit into a smile, and she couldn't help but notice his deep, well-placed dimples. And that dark, wavy hair really suited him, too. She blinked hard and gave him a curt nod as she struggled to stay focused.

His opening line caught her off guard. "You're Bree!"

Okay. So he had what turned out to be the richest velvety voice she'd ever heard; so what? She wouldn't let that distract her. Other charmers had tried to get to her in the past, but she had seen beyond them, hadn't she?

"I'm Brady Campbell. It's great to finally meet you." His emerald green eyes seemed to come alive with excitement as he reached for her hand, and as she took it Brianna suddenly couldn't remember why she'd stopped by in the first place.

"Yes, well. . . ," she managed, as she tried to collect her thoughts.

"I feel like I already know you."

"You do?"

"Yes, though I half expected you to be Abbey, bringing me a slice of chocolate cake."

How did he know Gran-Gran had baked a cake?

They stood there for a few seconds, his hand, large and calloused, dwarfing her own. Finally she pulled free from his welcoming gesture and attempted to compose herself.

"I, um, really need to talk with you, Mr. Campbell. It's pretty important."

His expression changed immediately. "Of course. Come on in." He gestured for her to join him inside. Did she dare?

She took a tentative step inside. Though his home was the mirror image of her own, the decor was the polar opposite. No knickknacks or doilies. In fact, there didn't appear to be much of anything on the walls, at least not yet. Just a jumbo-sized television set in the corner and a couple of leather sofas.

So. Mr. Trouble with a capital T is a minimalist. Maybe he just couldn't be bothered with decorating.

Just then Brianna noticed the stereo, situated on the wall joining their two houses. Bingo. She looked around for signs of the dog but couldn't find any. Likely he had crated the beast upstairs. Or . . . , her mind wandered. Maybe the mongrel had taken to roaming around the tiny fenced backyard, digging holes under the fence and scaring children in nearby houses. Regardless, the offending canine would have to be kept under control if he wanted to live in this neighborhood.

Brianna focused on the matter at hand. "Look, Mr. Campbell—"

"Please. Call me Brady." He gave her an inviting smile. She shifted her gaze to the floor, unsure what to make of him.

"Brady. I know you've only just moved in, but I need to talk with you about my grandmother."

A look of concern registered in his eyes. "She's okay, isn't she?"

"Well, physically, yes."

"That's a relief. You had me scared for a minute." He motioned for her to take a seat on the larger of the two brown sofas, which she did. Then he joined her, gazing intently into her eyes as he spoke. "I just love that grandmother of yours. She's completely amazing. Quite a little spitfire for being eighty-four. And a great cook, too—but then again you probably already knew that."

"Well, yes, but—"

"That pot roast was the best I've had in years. And she bakes a mean apple pie."

"Oh? She brought you pie?"

"Yes. Even gave me the recipe. I didn't have the heart to tell her I can't bake my way out of a paper bag." His boyish laugh reverberated around the room, and Brianna couldn't help but smile. "Still," he continued, "those yeast rolls were my favorite. I've never tasted anything like them. Never."

"Yeast rolls?" Hmm. Why hadn't Gran-Gran mentioned any of this?

"Yeah. They were manna straight from heaven." He shrugged. "But I guess I'm giving you the wrong impression. I don't want you to think the food was what drew me in. Abbey has the best personality in town. It's her strong suit, for sure."

"R–right."

"And her stories." He chuckled. "To be honest, she had me laughing till my sides hurt. I could probably tell you anything you wanted to know about almost everyone in your family, right down to naming names on your family tree."

Okay, this was weird. Gran-Gran had talked about one brief visit with Brady Campbell, nothing more. Maybe she'd been trying to butter him up. Regardless, this fellow, kind or not, needed to know what a nuisance he had become.

"She's really won me over," he continued. "And the best part is, she's agreed to pray for me, and I really need that."

"Yes, well, look—I hate to bring this up," she started. "But my grandmother is—"

"Say no more." He jumped up and sprinted to the kitchen, then returned with a pie plate in his hands. "She's missing this, I know. I promised to bring it back to her last night but forgot."

"No, I didn't come about a plate." Brianna shook her head, growing more confused by the moment. "In fact, I didn't even know you and Gran-Gran were this . . .acquainted. I actually came because she seems to be a bit put off by you right now."

"Put off?" He gave her a confused look.

"Perturbed might be a better word," she explained. "And I don't really blame her."

"You don't?" His eyes reflected genuine concern.

Why do they have to be such a great shade of green? Focus, Brianna—focus.

"I'll get right to the point." She stared him straight in the eye, to make sure he understood the severity of her words. "My grandmother's blood pressure has always been a little high. But yesterday, with that stereo of yours blaring—"

"Stereo?"

"And that dog barking nonstop—"

"Dog?"

"All the noise is wearing her out. She can't take it anymore. And since I'm the one responsible for her care, I need you to understand that whatever concerns her concerns me. So if she's upset by the noise coming from your place, I'm upset, too."

"Well, that would be understandable if—"

Brianna interrupted him by raising her hand. "Look. I don't want to cause unnecessary trouble. That's the last thing I want or need. Gran-Gran and I are great neighbors. Always have been. Ask anyone on the block."

"Well, I never said—"

"I can't remember a time when I've had a run-in of any sort with anyone in the neighborhood, but my grandmother means everything in the world to me, and I'm going to rush to her defense if she's wounded in any way. If anything were to happen to her. . ." Brianna's eyes filled with tears, and she used the back of her hand to swipe them away. After a deep breath, she finished her sentence. "If anything were to happen to her, I don't know what I'd do."

He gave her a blank stare, and she had to wonder at his coldness. Did he not care that her elderly grandmother had been inconvenienced? Was a frail senior citizen's health of no concern to him whatsoever? How could that be, after all the kind things he had said about her? What sort of man was this, anyway?

"So. . ." She rose to her feet and took a couple of steps toward the door. "I've said what I came to say."

"Well, I can see that, but. . ." His eyes, once bright, had darkened with concern.

"No apologies, then?" She stared him down, hoping he would do the right thing.

"I, uh. . .I'm sorry about this. . .misunderstanding."

Misunderstanding?

He handed her the pie plate and muttered a quiet "Please give my regards to Abbey."

Brianna took it from him and turned to walk out the door. The look of sadness on his face almost caused her to turn back at the last minute.

Almost.

୨ଈ

Brady pulled back the blinds and peered out the front window as Brianna shot across his lawn, pie plate in hand. She moved away from his house like a woman possessed.

"What was *that* all about?"

He raked his fingers through his hair with his free hand as he thought back over her accusations. Not one of them had been true, though she clearly believed them to be. The only time he'd turned on his stereo since moving into the duplex was late yesterday afternoon when Abbey stopped by for a second time. She'd insisted he play his Frank Sinatra CD for her. Track 3, if memory served him correctly.

Brady smiled as the memory registered. Abbey had waltzed around his living room like a prom queen—alone at first—and then she'd gestured for him to join her.

Okay, so he'd felt awkward whirling around the room, too. In the beginning. But she'd won his heart and eventually his feet.

So why the accusation? And what was all that about a dog? He hadn't owned a dog since junior high school.

At that moment something occurred to Brady, something that almost made

147

him sick to his stomach.

Was it possible. . .could it be. . .that Abbey suffered from delusional thinking? Dementia? That would certainly shed light on her apparent on-again, off-again behavior. Childish and carefree one moment. Frustrated and accusing the next. And it would more than explain Brianna's possessiveness where her grandmother was concerned.

"No way." He shook his head as he contemplated the idea. It would certainly explain a lot, wouldn't it?

As the potential reality set in, Brady released his grip on the blinds. They fell back into place.

If only he could've said the same thing about his heart.

Chapter 6

L ess than an hour after the visit from his neighbor, Brady received the call he'd been waiting for, with news of the all-important press conference.

"We'll make the announcement this afternoon," Coach Carter said. "So be prepared for a media blitz."

"I've had a couple of calls already," Brady acknowledged. "One from a local paper, and another from a cable sports affiliate."

Carter sighed. "You know how this goes. News always leaks out. What did you tell 'em?"

"Just said 'no comment' and hung up."

"Perfect. Just keep it up till after we make the announcement, okay?"

"Of course, Coach."

"Those reporters will get all their questions answered in a few hours anyway," Carter explained. "I hope you're up to the attention."

"I'll manage. Where should I meet you?"

"At the stadium in the press room." Carter went on to explain that Alex Mandel, the team's owner, would be there, as well as Mack Burroughs, general manager. "Be there by 2:15," Carter instructed. "We'll need time to prep and to get you into your new jersey. How does the number seven sound to you?"

"Perfect."

"Great." Carter switched gears. "Did you get the playbook I sent over?"

"Got it."

"Memorize it. Only two days till your first game."

"Yes, sir."

The coach's voice softened slightly. "And Campbell?"

"Yes, Coach?"

"Welcome to Pittsburgh, son."

Brady noticed the cell phone trembled in his hands as he stammered, "Thanks, Coach," then ended the call.

He plopped down on the sofa and began to pray. Words of thanksgiving escaped his lips. They weren't planned or rehearsed but rather flowed out of a heart filled with gratitude. Opportunities like this didn't come along often; he knew that. He would not take this one for granted. And he would use every chance he had to thank God. . .publicly.

A peal of thunder caught his attention, and Brady rose to look out the window. Great. An incoming storm. Well, no problem. He didn't need to leave for a couple of hours.

Minutes later he sorted through his closet in search of something to wear. As he dressed he tried to imagine how the afternoon would go. He could hear it all now. . .the clicking of the cameras, the stirring of the reporters, as the general manager stood and approached the microphone.

"Ladies and gentlemen, I'd like to present the newest member of our team," Mack Burroughs would say. "Number *seven*, Brady Campbell."

Reporters would interrupt with questions, likely wanting to know details of his trek from Tampa to Pittsburgh. They would criticize some of his past plays. Then the real chaos would begin. Those hoping to elevate their ratings would likely stir up old rumors about his wild past and possibly even start a few new ones.

He shuddered as he thought about it. A heaviness filled his chest as he contemplated the past—the man he used to be, the one reporters had chased from bar to bar in Tampa less than a year ago. Rumors—some true and others not so true—had almost destroyed his career and his personal life.

B.C. Before Christ.

Those same initials once represented *his* name—Brady Campbell—but had quickly been replaced with a name far greater. A wave of relief washed over him as he remembered. . .the past was truly in the past.

He hoped Pittsburgh's reporters would leave it there.

Brady showered quickly then dressed for the press conference, careful to look as presentable as possible. Then he called his mother to tell her about the upcoming meeting.

She answered on the third ring, and he opened with the question that always seemed to stir up trouble. "How would you feel about living in Pittsburgh, Mom?"

"It's cold up there."

"Well, yes, but I hear it's beautiful in the winter. And you'll love the bridges."

"It's cold up there," she repeated.

"Yes, but you'll be plenty warm in that new house I'm going to buy for you," he coaxed.

"I'm perfectly happy in my mobile home," she said with a hint of laughter in her voice. "How many times do I have to tell you that? I'd get lost in a big house. Give me something small and quaint any day."

"Still. . ." He hoped to convince her she could learn to love it in Pennsylvania, in spite of her Tuesday canasta group and her Monday/Wednesday date at the YMCA for water aerobics.

He jumped into an explanation of the press conference he would soon attend, and the pride in her voice let him know she cared deeply about all he was going through. As the conversation drew to a close, she offered to pray for him.

"Of course," he agreed.

Not that he could've stopped her. His mama had been known to stop a crowd in a supermarket for a prayer meeting.

Oh, how he missed his mama.

After she wrapped up the prayer, Brady ended the call with the same words he always did: "Love you, Mom."

"I love you, too, Brady. But remember—"

"I know, I know. . ."

They said the words in unison, as always: "It's cold up there."

He snapped his cell phone shut and smiled. One way or another, he would talk her into it.

At one thirty Brady could wait no longer. The storm appeared to have passed, though the roads were plenty wet. And even though the roads weren't likely to be crowded on a Saturday, he still wanted to leave early.

He grabbed an umbrella and shot out the front door. As he made his way toward the driveway, something—or rather someone—next door caught his eye.

Abbey.

He nodded and smiled but hoped she wouldn't wave him over for a chat. He didn't want to hurt her feelings, but he had no time to visit today.

Hmm. Not that she seemed to notice or care. No, she seemed intent on reaching her mailbox. . .a woman on a mission. Abbey clutched her umbrella in one hand and waved with the other as she made her way toward the metal box at the end of the drive.

Brady climbed into his car and backed out of the driveway. He'd gone no more than a dozen feet or so when he noticed something. He brought the car to a halt and looked around but saw nothing. Abbey had disappeared from view.

He scrambled out, fearing the worst. Right away, he caught a glimpse of Abbey on the ground, her umbrella bouncing across the lawn as the wind picked it up.

Brady sprinted in her direction, rain pelting down and soaking him to the bone. He knew, even before he drew close, that she was in dire straits. Her gut-wrenching cries broke his heart.

"Abbey. I'm here." He knelt down beside her on the driveway, his slacks now soaked. Her left leg appeared to be twisted beneath her in an awkward position, but he knew better than to move her, at least not yet.

She looked up with pain in her eyes. "Oh, Brady!" she cried out. "Look what I've gone and done. I'm such a clumsy old lady!"

"No, you're not. The driveway is slick. It could have happened to anyone. Where does it hurt?"

"My h–hip." Her hands trembled violently, likely as much from fear as pain. Though, from the looks of things, she was clearly in tremendous pain.

"I'm not going to try to move you just yet," he explained. "But if you can, hold on a minute while I get your umbrella."

After locating it and securing it over her, he flipped open his cell phone and dialed 9-1-1. Within seconds an operator came on. He explained their predicament, and the operator assured him help would arrive shortly. In the meantime, she instructed him to keep the patient calm and still.

Not an easy task in the rain or when the patient was in such pain.

All the while he thought about Coach Carter and about Mr. Burroughs. Should he call to say he would be late? Brady glanced at his watch. One forty-five. Surely he could wait until the paramedics arrived and still make it in plenty of time.

"Bree's at the dry cleaners," Abbey said as they waited on the ambulance. "Let me give you her cell number."

Brady entered the number in his phone, then made the call. He quickly explained the situation, and she began to cry at once. "W–where are they t–taking her?"

"Allegheny General, wherever that is."

"I know where it is," Brianna said. "I'll meet you there." She hung up before he could tell her that he couldn't possibly—under any circumstances—meet her there.

Several minutes later the ambulance arrived. The paramedics lifted Abbey, whose face was white with pain, onto a stretcher then placed her into the back of the ambulance.

"We're headed to Allegheny General!" the older one called out to Brady. "We'll meet you in the ER."

"No, I. . . See. . ." He glanced at Abbey's tear-filled eyes and heard her cries.

He sighed as he looked at his watch. One fifty-five. Maybe if he timed this right, he could swing by the hospital on his way to the team headquarters. It was on the way, after all. He hoped.

He followed the ambulance out onto the highway and trailed it into town. They arrived at the emergency room door at exactly 2:03. He hoped Brianna was already here and would take over. Surely she would understand.

❧

Brianna fought the blinding rain as she made her way toward Allegheny General Hospital. The very thing she feared most had actually happened.

"Gran-Gran." Tears filled her eyes, blurring her vision even more. She whispered a prayer—her fifth or sixth since getting in the car.

Brianna swiped at her eyes, determined to remain focused. Her grandmother needed her. A lump rose in her throat as she contemplated the truth of it. *I'm the only one Gran-Gran has.*

Well, unless you counted Brady Campbell.

Hmm. He *had* been kind enough to call the paramedics, then stay with her all the way to the hospital. Maybe he wasn't the ogre she had made him out to be.

Well, no time to think about that right now. With the hospital fully in view, Brianna had only one thing on her mind—getting to her grandmother—and the sooner the better.

Chapter 7

At five minutes after two Brady snapped open his cell phone to make the dreaded call.

"Coach Carter, this is Brady."

"Where are you?" Carter bellowed. "We're expecting the media anytime now. Can't do this without you, son."

Brady did his best to explain, but his words were met with hostility.

"What do you mean, you're going to be late? This is your day, Campbell. *Your* day. If you're not here, there *is* no day."

I'm having a day, all right. "You see, sir—"

The team's general manager must have taken the phone away from Carter. "I've already called your agent, Campbell," Burroughs interrupted in a huff. "So if you're holding out for more money—if this is some kind of ploy—"

Brady let out a groan. "No, sir, that's not it at all. This is a true emergency." He went on to tell the story of what had happened to Abbey, hoping against hope Burroughs would find it in his heart to be compassionate. Surely he had a mother or grandmother out there—somewhere.

"You've only been in town a couple of days, and you want me to believe you've already befriended an old woman?" Burroughs snorted. "Just tell me what's really going on here, Campbell. How much more money are you thinking you can weasel out of us?"

Brady drew in a deep breath before answering. "I'm telling you the truth. I was backing out of the driveway in the rain, with every intention of heading toward the stadium, when I saw her fall. No one else was there, so I had to stop."

"Humph." After a pause Burroughs's tone of voice changed. "So you're saying this is weather-related, then."

"Well, yes, I suppose you could say—"

"Where are you now?"

"The emergency room at Allegheny General Hospital."

"Hmm." Burroughs seemed to soften a bit. "Can't exactly do a press conference there, now, can we?"

"No, sir."

"Okay, then here's what we're going to do. We'll tell the press we've filled the empty spot on the line, and, of course, speculations will begin." Here his voice became very business-like. "We'll delay the announcement—tell them our new player was unavoidably detained because of the weather."

"B–but—"

"No buts. And we'll play up the do-gooder thing later, once the story has broken. In the meantime we'll get rid of the media and reschedule for tomorrow—same time, same place."

"Yes, sir."

"Keep a low profile, son. They're going to be on the lookout for you. Just lay low."

"Of course."

"And don't make me come looking for you," Burroughs groused. "I'm going to have a doozy of a time smoothing this one over, as it is. And Campbell—"

"Sir?"

"I'm sending a car for you—tomorrow at one o'clock. You *will* be here, understand?"

"Yes, sir."

Brady clicked off, feeling absolutely sick to his stomach. How could this have happened? And yet. . .he peeked inside Abbey's room, saw the pain in her eyes, and asked himself, *What else could I have done?*

સ

Brianna entered the hospital, breathless and terrified. She approached the nurse at the front desk.

"I'm looking for my grandmother. She was brought in about a half hour ago. Her name is Abbey Nichols."

The woman glanced at the computer screen then looked up. "She's in room 3, just through that door," she said, pointing down the hall.

Brianna raced through the double doors and down the hallway until she found the door with the number 3 outside. It was slightly ajar, and she almost pushed it open. Almost. Instead, she came to a grinding halt as she heard Gran-Gran's voice.

"I have a confession to make, Brady." Her grandmother's words were strained. Brianna leaned in with a huge lump in her throat, terrified but not wanting to interrupt.

"What is it, Abbey?" Brady's tender voice took Brianna by surprise.

"I–I've been playing a little prank on Bree."

What?

Gran-Gran giggled, and Brianna almost bolted through the door. Instead she stood as still as a mouse to hear the confession in question. What was her grandmother up to?

"I've been fibbing," Gran-Gran said with a sigh. "I told Bree some things about you that weren't—weren't true."

Oh, dear.

"I had a feeling," Brady responded. "But why?" Brianna could hear the concern in his voice, and remorse suddenly flooded over her for the things she'd said to him just this morning.

"Well. . ." Another giggle erupted from Gran-Gran. "I was trying to be clever, trying to think of a reason to send her over to your place for a visit. I knew from the moment I met you, you two were perfect for each other."

No!

"Oh, you did, did you?" Brady laughed.

"I wanted her to get to know you."

Tell me you didn't!

"Aha." Now Brady was the one chuckling. "Well, I have to admit, I'm relieved. After she paid me a visit, I racked my brain trying to figure out why you would've told her those things. She thinks I have a dog!"

I don't believe this.

"Sorry, Charlie!" Gran-Gran's giggles took over from there. "But if it will make you feel better, I'll get you one. I have friends at the ASPCA."

"Um, no, thanks."

Brianna decided to break up the party. She cleared her throat. Loudly. She wanted to make an entrance but certainly didn't want them to know she'd heard a word.

"Anyone here?" she called out.

Suddenly Gran-Gran let out an exaggerated whisper, clearly meant for Brady. "It's Bree!" After another second or two she used a much different voice to call, "I'm here, sweet girl! Come in—come in."

Brianna walked in and found her grandmother in the hospital bed. Brady stood at her side, clasping her hand. Though tempted to give Gran-Gran a piece of her mind, she stopped short when she saw the heart monitor and IV drip. That, along with the look of pain on her grandmother's face, was enough to cause her to drop the speech she'd been formulating. She rushed to the bedside and ran her fingers through Gran-Gran's thin wisps of hair.

"What happened?" she managed over the lump in her throat.

"Don't ask me. I was just headed out to get the mail, like always, and the next thing you knew I was belly-up on the driveway."

"Oh, no." Brianna reached to take her grandmother's free hand in her own, then looked over at Brady. He wore a look of true concern on his face.

"Thank the Lord for Brady," Gran-Gran said, then rested her head back against the pillow. "If he hadn't been there, if he hadn't seen the whole thing— turns out he's a knight in shining armor."

"Um, not exactly." Brady looked embarrassed.

"An angel, then," Gran-Gran said.

At this Brady let out a laugh. "Don't go polishing my halo just yet."

Brianna looked up at their neighbor with newfound compassion. She had been wrong about him in every respect.

"Thank you," she whispered.

He shrugged then looked back at Abbey. "I'm just glad I happened to be there. God put me in the right place at the right time."

Kindhearted *and* a believer? Was it possible?

"I think I saw stars when I hit the ground," Gran-Gran acknowledged. "Then I looked up, and Brady was standing over me. And then I remember seeing the umbrella bouncing down the driveway. Crazy thing had a mind of its own. I think I said something foolhardy to Brady. Something about being a clumsy old woman."

"You're not clumsy," Brianna and Brady spoke in unison, then looked at each other and laughed.

"You just think you're indestructible," Brianna added. "That's all."

Gran-Gran shrugged but then let out a groan as she tried to shift her position in the bed. "I don't feel so indestructible now. I feel like a broken china doll."

"I'm sorry." Brianna gave her a kiss on the forehead, then looked her in the eye. "What have they done for you?"

Brady quickly explained. "They took her back to radiology for a series of X-rays and then started her on an IV drip—antibiotics, as a preventative, and something for the pain."

That would explain the slurred speech and the impromptu giggles.

"But they've got you on a monitor," Brianna noted. "What's up with that?"

"Oh, something about my blood pressure," Gran-Gran said with the wave of a hand. "I guess they were worried about my heart or something. I told 'em to focus on my hip, not my heart."

"Still. . ." Brianna's eyes filled once more. If this episode brought about too much strain, her grandmother's heart could very well be affected. Oh, thank God Brady had been there to take care of her and to make sure she made it to the hospital safely.

"You're going to do exactly as the doctors say, Gran-Gran," Brianna said sternly.

"What are my other options?" Her grandmother managed a weak smile.

Just then the doctor entered the room and introduced himself as Lloyd Peters, an orthopedist. "It looks like you've got quite a break, Mrs. Nichols." He pulled out the X-rays to show them the proof. "Your hip is broken in two places. We're going to have to pin you back together."

"Pin her together?" Brianna and Brady spoke in unison again.

"It's not as bad as it sounds," Dr. Peters explained. "And I've done this surgery dozens of times before. But I do need to make you aware of the risks before we go to the OR."

Gran-Gran nodded, watching him closely.

"Your bones are more brittle than most, due to the osteoporosis," Dr. Peters explained. "But we'll be able to get you fixed up. I'll start by making a surgical incision; then I'll apply metal screws to hold you together while you heal."

He went on to explain things that could go wrong, but Brianna hardly heard a word. Instead everything kind of faded to gray.

Gran-Gran would require surgery. Then a hospital stay for a couple of weeks. Then she would be transferred to a rehab facility to learn to walk again.

Everything inside Brianna wanted to scream. Instead she kept the most hopeful look on her face she could manage, for her grandmother's sake. She needed to play it cool, needed to act as if all of this would turn out just fine.

But would it?

She tried to swallow the lump in her throat and looked away for a moment. *Oh, God, please take care of her. Don't let anything go wrong in the operating room, please.*

After a thorough explanation from the doctor, she headed out into the hallway to chat with the doctor in private. Once there he explained the risks a little more thoroughly.

"Even with surgery the hip might not heal properly. If the nerves or blood vessels leading to the bone were significantly injured during the break, the bone could die."

"W–what can I do for her?"

"She'll be in the hospital for some time, as I said. She will need that lengthy period of bedrest to help the bone heal."

Brianna swallowed hard and nodded. She would make sure Gran-Gran was taken care of. Somehow.

"After that she will be transferred to rehab. Once she's there you will need to encourage her to get up and around. As I mentioned, rehabilitation will be critical to her recovery, so make sure she cooperates."

The doctor wrapped up his instructions then turned, leaving Brianna in stunned silence.

Grief overtook her, and she leaned against the wall, tears streaming. At that very moment she felt a strong arm reach around her shoulders, drawing her into an awkward embrace. She leaned her face into Brady's chest and wept, silently at first, then with unashamed abandon.

When she calmed down she closed her eyes and shook her head. "What am

I going to do?"

"We're going to do exactly what she needs us to do," he explained. "Starting with going back in there to spend a few minutes with her before they prep her for surgery. Then we're going to pray." He looked into her eyes. "You heard what the doctor said, Bree. She's going to be okay."

Brianna nodded but didn't feel the same assurance in her heart. Whenever she thought about losing Gran-Gran, fear gripped her. She didn't know how she would make it if—

"Let's go back in the room." Brady interrupted her thoughts. "She's probably missing us by now."

They entered the room to find Gran-Gran with the remote in hand. Her eyes, once filled with pain, now twinkled with delight. "You're never going to believe this!" she said as she turned to look at Brianna.

"What, Gran-Gran?"

"They've got cable TV! I'm watching the sports channel."

Brianna dropped into a chair. "Of all things."

"And get this," Gran-Gran continued with a frustrated look on her face. "All that stuff about a press conference today at three o'clock? Baloney! It's been canceled."

Brianna noticed Brady's gaze shift to the floor.

Her grandmother forged ahead, clearly upset about something having to do with a new player. "The fact that he didn't show up for the press conference just confirms what I've been saying all week. In fact, Rena and I argued about this very thing last night. All of this frenzy is a hoax to give fans false hope. We're not getting a new quarterback. All of this media attention is just to sell tickets."

Brianna turned to look at Brady to see if he could make any sense out of Gran-Gran's words. Maybe he understood a little something about football. Clearly she didn't.

As she opened her mouth to ask for his opinion, she glimpsed his face.

For whatever reason, the man looked like a deer caught in the headlights.

Chapter 8

Brady paced the tiny OR waiting room with a cup of coffee in his hand. He passed the desk, which sat empty. Off in the distance a wall-hung television flashed photos of a car accident on one of the local highways. No one in the room seemed to be paying much attention to the news. Most were gathered together in huddles, worried looks on their faces. A few sat slumped over in chairs, dozing.

Brady shuddered as he remembered another time, years ago, when he and his mother had gathered with his older siblings in a similar hospital waiting room in Florida. His father had been whisked away into surgery to repair a clogged artery in his neck. Just a minimal procedure, according to the doctors. No big deal.

How long had they waited in the room together, hunkered down, like so many of these folks—two hours? three?—before the doctors came to give them the grim news. Unexpected and horrifying news.

Massive stroke.

Another shiver ran down Brady's spine as he remembered the series of events that followed.

Coma, little hope.

Days of waiting, praying.

His older brother—distant and removed—acting like nothing was wrong.

An ever-present mob of his mother's church friends.

The morning to end all mornings.

Casseroles.

Everything after that one awful day had involved casseroles and older women with white hair moving back and forth in a steady stream from the house, tending to his mother's every need.

Ironically his father had tended to his mother's every need also, even before passing on. Turned out his organizational skills had worked to everyone's advantage. Brady smiled as he remembered the day his mother had pulled out the paperwork. His father had taken care of every detail in advance, right down to writing his own eulogy and obituary and planning the order of service. He'd left nothing to chance, even naming his favorite hymns and selecting a suit to be buried in.

No, James Campbell had left nothing for his wife to deal with after the fact—nothing other than mourning the only man she'd ever loved.

Brady glanced back up at the television and sighed. He hoped today's surgery would in no way be reminiscent of all that. He shook off the memories and turned toward Brianna. She seemed to be holding up pretty well, all things considered. Her tears still flowed intermittently, but who could blame her? She was her grandmother's caregiver, after all, and her love for Abbey was. . .what was that expression Abbey always used? Ah, yes. Sure and certain. Brianna's love for Abbey was sure and certain.

Brady gave Brianna a closer look. Her beauty had been apparent from the get-go, but seeing her here, in this situation—seeing the compassion in her eyes and the concern etched across her brow—made her all the more appealing. This was a girl you could take home to Mama.

Whoa. Slow down. What are you thinking? You just met her.

"Brady?" Brianna interrupted his thoughts as she stood. "I'm going to the gift shop for a few minutes."

"Can I come with you?"

When she nodded, he followed on her heels down the corridor in search of the gift shop. They wound their way through a maze of hallways, observing the signs, until they arrived at the tiny, crammed shop.

Brianna at once began to search for a gift. Her brow wrinkled in concern after just a couple of minutes. "What should I get for her?"

"What does she like?"

Brianna rolled her eyes. "Trust me—they won't have what she *really* likes in here."

Brady wondered at that but didn't ask. "Maybe flowers?" he tried. When Brianna shrugged, he suggested something else. "Candy?"

"I don't know if the doctor will have her on a special diet or not," Brianna said with a sigh.

"Hmm. I see your point." He looked around the room, and his gaze finally came to rest on a bouquet of Mylar balloons. "Hey, what about those?"

As Brianna looked up, a smile lit her face. "Yeah. That's perfect." She made her way to the counter where she ordered a half dozen GET WELL and YOU ARE LOVED balloons in a variety of colors and shapes.

As the clerk filled the balloons and then rang up her total, Brady found himself distracted by the greeting cards. One in particular caught his eye. It was funny—witty, really—just like Abbey. It even had a dog on front. He carried it to the cash register and paid for it with a grin. "I think she'll like this."

As they left the shop he handed the card to Brianna. As their hands touched, her cheeks flushed, and he grinned. Something about the touch of her hand, even for a moment, felt good. Felt right.

And completely odd. Nothing like this had ever happened to him before.

Brianna took the card and read it, giving him a funny look as she spied the dog, then laughed aloud. She handed it back to him with an admiring gaze. "You really *do* know her well, don't you?"

He shrugged. "Well, I feel like I do. In so many ways she reminds me of my mother. Older, of course. But my mom's no spring chicken. I'm the youngest of four kids, and my siblings are considerably older than I am. I was born when my mom was forty-two."

"You were a surprise package?"

"What?"

Brianna smiled. "That's what my mom always called my younger brother—her little surprise package. He came along years after I did."

Brady nodded. "I guess that about sums it up." He paused for a moment to gather his thoughts. "My parents were ten—maybe even fifteen—years older than my friends' parents, but they were young-acting." He smiled. "My mom is still young at heart. She has a terrific sense of humor, just like Abbey. Even cooks like her."

"Does she live in Pittsburgh?"

"Nope. But I'm working on that. She lives in Florida, but I'm hoping she'll move here before long. My older siblings aren't great at taking care of her. She really depends on me. It's always been like that."

Brianna flashed him a smile. "Did you say you're from Florida?" When he nodded, she delved into a lengthy explanation of how much she missed the beach. "I'm from L.A.," she added.

"Yes, I know—"

"Abbey told you," she finished for him.

When he nodded, Brianna laughed. "If I didn't know any better, I'd have to say my grandmother has been up to some tricks."

"Oh?" He didn't dare reveal any of the things Abbey had shared with him in the emergency room. Instead he glanced over at Brianna to gauge her expression. As he did he noted a hint of a smile on her face. It warmed his heart.

In fact, everything about this girl warmed his heart.

❧

Brianna fought the grogginess that seemed to consume her as the hours ticked by in the waiting room. Many times she glanced over at Brady, wondering how long he planned to stay. He'd come in his own car, after all, and could go whenever he liked.

Still, he seemed satisfied to sit next to her, staring at the muted television and occasionally striking up a conversation.

She peeked at him out of the corner of her eye. Surely Brady Campbell had something better to do on a Saturday night than sit around a dreary hospital, waiting for news about a woman he barely knew. But he looked content. Strange.

Why had she disliked him so much? Ah, yes. Because of Gran-Gran.

She grinned as she replayed the conversation she'd overheard between her grandmother and Brady earlier in the day. Funny how one little thing could change her mind so completely.

"What are you smiling about?"

"W–what?" Brianna looked up into Brady's laughing green eyes. *Who has eyes that gorgeous?* She was embarrassed at having been caught so deep in her thoughts, particularly when most of those thoughts concerned him. "Oh, I—"

"You're smiling," he said.

"Oh? Well. . .I was. . .thinking of Gran-Gran." It wasn't a lie. She had been thinking of her, hadn't she? And Brady, too, of course, though she wouldn't mention that part.

"I can see why you're smiling," Brady said with a nod. "I'm glad you're feeling better about her surgery. I'm sure she's going to come through this with flying colors."

Brianna nodded. "I know you're right. She's tough as nails most of the time, so it'll be interesting to see how she fares under stress. I'd imagine she'll be a lot of fun to care for. She should be fine, at least on Monday nights."

"Monday nights?" He gave her a curious look.

"Yes, she's quite a football nut. Turn on the game and she's as happy as a lark."

"Oh, really." His eyes lit up, and for a moment she half expected him to jump into an animated play-by-play of last week's game, like almost every other guy she knew. Instead he offered a weak shrug and turned back to the television.

Maybe there was hope for this guy.

Seconds later Dr. Peters entered the room. He looked exhausted but was smiling. "She came through fine," he said. "She's in the recovery room now. We'll be moving her to a private room when she wakes up."

"She—she's going to be okay?" Brianna asked.

The doctor gave her a confident nod. "I have every reason to think she'll do just fine. She's a feisty one, for sure, but that will work to her advantage. She seems to have an indomitable spirit."

"Yes, she does," Brianna agreed.

After a few words of instruction from the doctor, they were escorted to the recovery room, where they found Abbey waking up. She seemed frightened and disoriented. Brianna did her best to soothe and comfort her grandmother, but it took a good hour before she seemed to come around.

A short time later Brianna and Brady followed along behind the rolling bed as they made their way into a tiny private room at the east end of the hospital. The nurse came to check Gran-Gran's vital signs, then gave her some medication for pain. Within minutes she dozed off into a fitful sleep. Brianna kissed her on the forehead and settled into a nearby chair.

"Aren't you going home?" Brady whispered.

She looked up, confused. "Home?"

"You're not going to stay here all night, are you?"

"Well, yes. That's my plan anyway."

He shook his head. "You need your rest if you're going to take care of her."

Brianna shrugged. "I'll sleep here in the chair."

"This is just my opinion," Brady pointed out, "but I think you'll do a better job of caring for your grandmother if you've had a good night's sleep."

"He's right, you know," Gran-Gran mumbled in a groggy voice.

Brianna groaned and gave Brady an accusing look. "You're saying I should go home? Leave her here?"

"Nurses are on call around the clock," Brady said. "She'll be well taken care of. But if it will make you feel better, you can talk to the head nurse and ask her to call you if there's a problem."

A yawn escaped Brianna's lips. Maybe he was right. Maybe a good night's sleep was in order. Tomorrow was Sunday. She could come back in the morning and stay all day.

"Go home, Bree," Gran-Gran whispered through her medicated fog. "I need my rest. . .and I won't sleep a wink. . .if I know you're sitting over there worrying."

"Fine." Brianna stood up and reached for her jacket. "I'm going home, then."

"Let me drive you," Brady offered.

"Oh, I have my car."

"Leave it. I'll take you home, then follow you back up here in the morning." Her eyes widened, and he added, "I won't be able to stay long tomorrow, but I want to come for a while before heading off to. . .work."

He works on Sunday? What does he do?

"You're a good boy," Gran-Gran muttered in a slurred voice.

Brianna giggled. "I think she's got something there." She looked at Brady with growing admiration. "And I think I'll take you up on your offer. I'm too tired to drive right now anyway."

"All right then."

He leaned over to brush a soft kiss across Gran-Gran's cheek, and she whispered, "You two go on now. Leave me be," in a hoarse voice.

As they walked through the door, Brianna, with tears in her eyes, looked back at her grandmother. She whispered a silent prayer that Gran-Gran would make it through the night without pain, then she stopped at the nurse's station to leave her phone number.

Then, with exhaustion eking from every pore, she followed Brady toward the parking garage.

Chapter 9

The next morning Brady awoke with a smile on his face. Might've had something to do with the fact that he'd dreamed about Brianna. In his dream she'd been sitting on the sidelines at the game while he scored a touchdown. The electric lights celebrated his victory, and the roar from the crowd made him feel welcome. Brianna had rushed to his side at the end of the game, slipping easily into his arms. Her kiss had caused more excitement than the touchdown.

Yep. Definitely a dream. But what a nice one.

Brady lingered in bed for a few minutes, praying. He lifted up his mother's name as always. Next he covered his siblings, though praying for his older brother still proved to be a challenge, all things considered. Afterward he prayed for Abbey—for her healing and for her psychological state.

Finally he turned to Brianna.

Hmm. He tried to stay focused on the prayer time but found himself slightly distracted as he remembered the look of pain in her eyes last night at the hospital. How wonderful it had felt to wrap her in his arms, to offer comfort. Something in him wanted to protect her, to kiss away every tear, to tell her everything would be all right.

Best to get back to praying.

He took a few minutes to pray about today's press conference, adding a special request: "Please let Burroughs forgive me for what happened yesterday." If everyone came into today's events with a good attitude, the media would surely pick up on that. Being the new kid in town, he wanted to put his best foot forward.

A short time later Brady climbed out of bed and padded downstairs to the kitchen, where he switched on the coffeemaker. Wouldn't take long for the pot to fill. In the meantime he needed a shower and a shave. As he did that, he laid out a plan of action for the day. What was it Burroughs had said? Ah, yes. "I'll send a car for you at one o'clock."

Brady would be waiting at the house. Of course, that meant his visit with Abbey would have to be brief.

He chuckled, thinking of his elderly neighbor. Even heavily medicated, her matchmaking skills were still intact. "You two go on now." Was that what she had said? Surely she'd meant, "You two spend a little more time together. It'll do my heart good."

Not that he minded. No, he'd be happy to spend as much time as possible with Brianna. She did *his* heart good.

Brady headed off to the kitchen, where he popped a slice of bread into the toaster and poured a cup of coffee. As he settled down at the table, he tried to envision Brianna next door, doing the same. For whatever reason he started to chuckle, thinking about the fact that she'd accused him of having a dog—a noisy one, at that. Maybe he should set the record straight today—tell her the dog was nonexistent and the stereo had only been used at Abbey's insistence.

On the other hand, if he shared that little tidbit, she would know Abbey had made up the stories in the first place. From there she would likely guess her grandmother had ulterior motives. *Nope, I won't tell her today.* He didn't want to create a stir, especially not with Abbey in such a fragile state.

Brady glanced down at his watch and realized he'd daydreamed away nearly twenty minutes. He'd promised to meet Brianna at her place at nine o'clock. Better get on the ball.

≥●

As soon as Brianna heard the knock on the door, her heart leaped into her throat. *Brady.* She glanced in the mirror, checking her makeup one last time. Not too bad. The eye shadow on her left eye was a bit heavier than the right, but who would really notice?

She paused to grab a sweater from the closet, then sprinted down the stairs to the door. She answered in a somewhat breathless state. "Good morning." Brianna ushered him inside. "Are you hungry?"

"Well, I, uh. . ." He gave her a puzzled look. "Do we have time?"

"Gran-Gran spent much of yesterday morning baking, so the kitchen is filled with breakfast goodies needing to be eaten. And, besides, we always do a big breakfast on Sunday mornings. It's tradition. So follow me."

She led him down the hallway, chatting all the way. When she didn't hear a response she turned back, stunned to find him still standing in the living room, gazing at her grandmother's spoon collection. She took a few steps back in his direction. He looked around the room, eyes wide.

"I don't believe it," he said.

"Believe what?"

"Well, for one thing, this spoon collection. My mom has one just like it. And the knickknacks. It's just like—like home."

"Ah. Well, it *is* home." She flashed him a warm smile.

"Yes, but how odd that I'd come all the way from Florida to Pittsburgh only to feel so completely at home again." He shrugged. "You know, I'm convinced my mom and Abbey would be good friends. They'd keep each other busy; that's for sure. My mom takes all sorts of classes to stay active."

"Internet courses?"

"Yes, and others, too. Like water aerobics. Arts and crafts. That kind of thing." He chuckled. "She's a real go-getter. And her taste in decorating is pretty much the same, too." He gestured to the sofa. "Let me guess. Abbey has had that couch since the '80s, right?"

"Seventy-nine, according to Gran-Gran," Brianna said with a nod. "And the recliner has been here longer than that. My grandpa used to sit in it every day after work." She grew silent as she thought about it. How long had it been since she'd mentioned her grandfather? He'd died years before she moved to Pittsburgh, leaving Abbey alone—and Brianna with a host of questions about what he must've been like. She'd barely known him, though her grandmother had tried to tell her a little.

She shook off the memory and invited Brady again to join her in the kitchen. There she served up a steaming mug of coffee with French vanilla creamer and sugar. He eyed the large coffee cake in the center of the dinette table. "You weren't kidding. This looks great."

"You should see the cinnamon rolls." She opened the microwave and pulled out a plate of the warm, gooey rolls, covered in frosting.

"How do you eat like this all the time and stay so—?" He didn't finish his sentence. His cheeks reddened and he muttered, "Sorry."

"No, it's okay." She shrugged. "My job is really active. I'm on my feet much of the time. And I take a lot of walks with my grandmother when the weather cooperates. In other words, I burn off all the calories." She smiled. "I'm always telling Gran-Gran to cut back on the shortening and sugar, but the more I tell her, the more she bakes. It's useless."

"Do you cook?"

Brianna shrugged. "I try, but there's no comparison. Gran-Gran got all of the cooking skills in the family. It's kind of a—a gift."

His eyebrows elevated playfully. "One we *all* get to share."

"Yep." As they settled down at the table to enjoy a quick bite to eat, Brianna looked into his eyes—eyes filled with goodness and compassion. How had she missed that the first time around?

"Tell me about your life in L.A.," he coaxed.

"Ah." She drew in a deep breath, wondering where to begin. "My mom is great. She and I have always been close ever since I was little. And my younger brother is a hoot. I think you'd like him. He's a lot younger than I am, so we didn't have a lot in common."

"What about your dad?"

She was quiet for a moment. "My dad and I haven't always seen eye-to-eye," she finally said. "We had a falling-out of sorts when I was eighteen. He did something. . . ." She didn't finish. No point in weighing the conversation down with that. "Anyway, when the time came to make a decision about college, I needed to get away, to clear my head. I opted to come here to live with my grandmother. It opened a world of possibilities to me, and I've never been sorry."

"How are things with your dad now?" Brady asked.

"Oh. . .I don't know," she said with a sigh. "He's just kind of. . .absent. Always has been. He has his priorities, and family is pretty far down on the list."

"I'm sorry to hear that." His gaze shifted downward. "I lost my dad awhile back. It's been really hard without him. I miss him so much."

Ouch.

She drew in a deep breath. "I'm so sorry, Brady. And I don't mean to give you the wrong impression. I love my dad, and I'm working on the relationship with him. I just keep praying and trying."

"That's all the Lord would ask you to do," he said.

"He's not as bad as I've made him out to be, I guess," she said. "And sometimes it's hard to believe he's Gran-Gran's son. They're so opposite." *Well, except for their love of the game.* "She's as soft as butter and loves me as I've never been loved before."

"That's one way to put it." He grinned, then gave her a reflective look.

"What about you?" she asked. "You're a self-proclaimed mama's boy, right?"

His gaze shifted downward, and she had to wonder what was going through his mind.

Just then her cell phone rang, creating a distraction. She reached to open it, startled to hear Gran-Gran's voice on the other end of the line.

"Bree, can you bring me my bathrobe? And my denture case. I had a doozy of a time finding my teeth this morning."

Brianna chuckled. "Of course. Anything else?"

"Well, they've told me I can eat anything I like," her grandmother said. "And I'm missing my Sunday morning feast, so bring some of those cinnamon rolls. And I want my own coffee. Can you bring me a thermos filled to the top?"

"As long as you're sure the doctor won't mind."

"Oh, don't worry about the doctor. He won't mind, but even if he did, I'd tell you to bring it anyway."

"Yes, but I wouldn't—because I love you and care about your health."

Gran-Gran sighed. "You're a good girl, Bree."

Brianna glanced across the table at Brady, and he warmed her heart with his boyish grin. "Is everything okay?" he asked.

"Yeah. She's found her teeth and wants some cinnamon rolls."

"Um, okay." He laughed. "I guess that makes sense in the grand scheme of things. Is she anxious to see you?"

"More anxious to see *you*, I'd be willing to bet."

His eyes twinkled. "Me?"

"Yeah. She's a sucker for a Steelers' fan."

"Steelers' fan?" He looked down at his T-shirt and realized it bore his new team's logo. "Ah."

"Just wait and see," she said with a wink. "Just wait and see."

Chapter 10

Brady looked across the hospital room at Abbey, who lay in the bed with a more-serious-than-usual look on her face.

"Everything okay?"

She glanced his way, her eyes filling with tears. At once he stood and joined her at the bedside. "Should I go and find Brianna?"

"No, I'm glad she's stepped out for a minute. I don't want her to see me like this."

"I understand. Would you feel better if I left you alone for a few minutes?" He glanced down at his watch. Eleven forty five. He'd have to leave soon anyway.

"No, please don't go. Pull your chair a little closer so we can chat."

He did as instructed but was still a little startled when Abbey reached for his hand. He offered it willingly.

"Do you pray, Brady?" she asked.

"I do. I've been praying for you. Just this morning, in fact."

"Humph." She shook her head. "I'm just fine. Might make more sense for you to pray for our political leaders or the country's economic situation."

"Well, I do that, too."

"I've walked with God a mighty long time," she said with a sigh. "We're like two old friends—God and me, sitting together on the couch, talking."

"I can see that." He gave her hand a squeeze. "It shows that you spend time with Him."

"I might be spending time with Him face-to-face soon," she said softly.

Her words took him by surprise, but he tried not to overreact. Instead he opted for an easygoing approach. "Are you looking forward to that?"

"I'm looking forward to eternity," she said with a smile. "When the time is right. Getting to see my husband, Norman, again. And Katie."

"Katie?"

"My baby girl." She reached up with her fingertips to brush away a loose tear from her lashes. "She passed away when she was only three. Nearly broke my heart in two."

"Oh, I'm so sorry. I didn't know."

Abbey smiled. "Bree was the spitting image of Katie when she was little. And when I look at Bree. . .well, I kind of imagine that's what Katie might've looked

170

like if she'd lived to her twenties. But that's not how things turned out." Her voice softened. "Sometimes things don't go the way you expect them to."

"Right." He couldn't think of anything else to say. He wanted to tell her about his father, how he'd been snatched away too soon, but didn't want to interrupt. This was her time.

"I have so many regrets." Abbey's eyes filled once again.

Brady spoke with tenderness. "What kind of regrets?"

Her lip quivered, and she didn't answer for a moment.

"My son—Bree's father—we've never been very close. I wish I could change that."

Her revelation seemed to match Brianna's earlier description of her "absent" father.

"Maybe he'll come around," Brady encouraged. "Just keep praying."

"He's so much like his father that it hurts," she said. "My husband, Norman, was distant, not around much. When he did come home, he seemed set on getting his own way most of the time." She paused and shook her head. "Really *all* of the time. He didn't like to take no for an answer. And when Glen came along I could see they were two peas in a pod, which made for a bit of head-butting when Glen reached his teens."

"I'll bet."

"Glen wasn't a bad boy. He worked extra hard to please his father, but things became so strained between them that Glen went off and joined the military right out of high school."

Brady observed the pain in her eyes as she spoke.

"Being in the marines was good for Glen," Abbey continued. "But in some ways it only seemed to harden him more than before. When he came back, he and his father barely spoke. Glen married his wife, Mary, and took a coaching job at a high school in Southern California. We rarely saw him after that."

"Then Brianna was born," Brady added.

"Yes, she was their firstborn." Abbey's face lit in a smile. "I flew out to L.A. to spend a week with Glen and Mary when Bree came. She was a precious little thing." Abbey's eyes clouded over. "But I could tell Glen wouldn't make the best father, even then. He was so disconnected and"—she paused before she whispered the word—"uncaring. He wasn't the sort to gather a child in his arms and kiss away the tears, if you know what I mean. He was always more interested in whatever team he happened to be coaching than in his own family. Broke my heart."

Brady had to stretch his imagination to understand a man like that. His own father had always bent over backward to show love and compassion, even when Brady hadn't deserved it. Why did Brianna, beautiful girl that she was, have to grow up in a household with such a distant father? Some things just didn't make sense.

"I guess Bree was in sixth grade, maybe seventh, when her little brother, Kyle, was born," Abbey explained. "Kyle's always had a heart of gold."

"Ah." Another interesting twist. If only his own brother had a heart of gold instead of a heart of stone, maybe they'd get along better, have an actual relationship instead of strained conversations.

Abbey paused, and her eyes filled with tears. "That next year, when Bree was just fourteen, something awful happened." She shook her head. "One morning my husband, Norman, wouldn't wake up. I tried and tried to wake him, but"—tears slipped down her wrinkled cheeks, and she didn't even bother to brush them away—"there was nothing I could do."

"I'm so sorry, Abbey," Brady said softly. He knew what it felt like to lose a loved one.

"Doctors said it was an aneurysm. He passed away in his sleep," she whispered. "I guess I should be grateful he didn't suffer. That would be the Christian thing, wouldn't it? To be happy Norman was in the arms of his Maker, safe and sound? That he hadn't struggled in his last few days, like so many?"

Brady nodded but didn't know what to say.

"I had to call Glen and tell him what had happened," Abbey continued. "I knew he'd just been transferred to a new school that fall, a new team, and I didn't know how he would respond. But I wasn't prepared for him to say his team had made it to the play-offs, and he wouldn't be able to come at all."

"Oh, Abbey." He gave her hand a squeeze.

"I—I—had to plan Norman's funeral by myself. There was no one to help me. Just a couple of the ladies from my little church, God bless them, and Pastor Meyers, of course. At the last minute Bree showed up with her mother and Kyle. They were wonderful. But I missed my son. I *needed* my son."

Whoa. What an opposite picture to what his mother had faced. People had swept in around her on every side.

Abbey gazed up into his eyes. "Then"—she started to smile—"a miracle happened."

"A miracle?"

"Bree." Her face came alive as she mentioned her granddaughter's name. "I fell in love with her during that visit, and vice versa. I told her about the university here, and she agreed to look into it when the time came. All those years I prayed, and when she graduated from high school I got the word—she was coming to Pittsburgh! I can tell you there was never a happier day in my life than the day that beautiful girl came marching into my house."

"I can imagine." It all made sense now, why Brianna took such good care of her grandmother, and Abbey of her granddaughter. They had needed one another pretty desperately back then. And now.

"I felt bad for little Kyle back at home. I knew he'd probably not get much fathering. Still, there was little I could do but pray." She shook her head. "But that's a story for another day. I think I've worn out your ears already."

"No, of course not. I wish I had time for more."

Just then Brady's cell phone rang. He looked down at it, fear kicking in. So much for the No CELL PHONES hospital policy. "I forgot to turn this off. Sorry." He quickly shut it off.

"Didn't you need to take that call?" Abbey asked.

He shrugged. "It was just my agent. I'll call him back when I get to the car."

"Your agent?"

"Yeah." Brady glanced down at his watch, startled to see the time: 12:20. "I hate to tell you this," he said with a sigh. "But I have to leave now. I wish I could wait till Brianna gets back, but I just can't."

"Are you going to turn into a pumpkin if you don't leave by a certain time?" Abbey asked.

"I guess you could say that." He stood and pushed his chair back to its original place near the window.

"Wait." Abbey extended her hand. "I know you're in a hurry, but do you have just a minute to pray with me before you go? I'd feel so much better if you would."

"Of course." He walked to the side of the bed and, with love framing every word, began to pray.

ॐ

Brianna stood at the door of the room, overhearing yet another conversation between her grandmother and Brady. Funny, this one—the tail end of it anyway—seemed to be about her father.

Ironic, considering the fact that she'd spent the last fifteen minutes on the phone with him, begging him to come to Pittsburgh ahead of schedule. To see his mother right away.

He'd argued, of course. The start of the new season and all. Nothing unfamiliar about that story. But by the end of the call she'd convinced him at least to consider the possibility.

"You don't know how long she'll be with us, Dad."

Had she really said those words aloud?

Now, as she stood at the door of her grandmother's room, eavesdropping, she saw the picture from Gran-Gran's point of view. How sad she sounded and how much she needed and wanted her son to be a part of her life.

Determination took over, and Brianna settled the issue in her heart. If her father wouldn't do the right thing, she would. His lack simply made her want to do more. She would pour out love and affection on Gran-Gran at every available opportunity. What was it the Bible said? "But encourage one another daily, as long as it is called Today."

Yes, she would continue to pour herself out on her grandmother's behalf.

Even if it meant putting off things at work. She would call her boss and ask for vacation time for the next couple of weeks. Whatever it took to keep Gran-Gran's spirits up.

Just then the sound of Brady's voice raised in prayer distracted her. What a great guy he'd turned out to be—in no way like the man she'd first pictured. As she listened in, he prayed for Abbey's healing and then started praying for her family—every member. Brianna wondered at the depth of his words. This was clearly a man familiar with spending time on his knees.

As he finished, she pushed open the door to the room and slipped inside. "Sorry, I didn't mean to interrupt you," she whispered.

"No, it's okay." He flashed her an inviting smile. "We were just wrapping up. I have to leave."

"Do you?" She gave an exaggerated pout, and he laughed.

"I do, but I'll try to come back by later tonight, if you like."

"*I* like." Gran-Gran smiled. "And while you're at it, why don't you stop off at the store and pick up a deck of cards so I can play solitaire?"

"I'm sure they sell cards in the gift shop," Brianna said. She looked at Brady. "So don't you worry about that."

"Well, I'm happy to do it," he said. "But don't count on solitaire. I'll pick up a couple of decks, and we can play hearts. How does that sound?"

"Heavenly!"

Brianna chuckled. Gran-Gran had this guy eating out of her hand. Then again. . .she looked at Brady. He didn't seem to mind a bit. In fact, he appeared to want a reason to return.

He said his good-byes and slipped out of the room, leaving Brianna alone with her grandmother. She pulled a chair close to the bed and sat.

"I, uh. . .I heard what you said."

"You did? Which part?"

"The part about Dad. All of it."

"Ah." Gran-Gran's cheeks reddened. "I sure didn't mean for you to hear all of that—an old woman rambling about her regrets."

"But you were willing to tell Brady."

"That's different."

"Oh?"

"I guess I should have talked to you about all this stuff years ago," Gran-Gran said with a shrug. "But I know you can't control what your father does any more than I can. I just know"—her lip started to quiver—"that when you get to be my age, you wish you could do a few things over."

Brianna tried to swallow the lump in her throat and nodded. She decided a change of subject was in order. "Well," she said with a smile, "looks like you didn't mind pouring out your heart to our handsome neighbor. If I didn't know any better, I'd say you have a crush on him."

"What?" Her grandmother appeared stunned. "That's just plain silly. But"—she gave Brianna an inquisitive look—"I wouldn't say it's out of the question for *you* to have a crush on him by now."

"M–me? I hardly know the man."

"But what you see you like, right?"

"Gran-Gran, don't."

Her grandmother leaned back and rested her head on the pillows. "I'm just saying, the Lord clearly brought him to Pittsburgh for a reason, and maybe that reason—at least in part—is you."

Brianna stood and began to fuss with her grandmother's covers, straightening them. "That's just silly. I have no idea why he moved to Pittsburgh, but I'm sure it wasn't to meet a woman. Likely it was business related."

"Maybe. And I have some idea of what business he's in, thanks to a little slip on his part today." Her grandmother's eyes glistened as they always did when she had a secret aching to be shared.

"Oh? What's that?" Brianna asked.

"I think he's an actor," Gran-Gran said with a nod.

"An actor?"

"Yes. You said you overheard our conversation. Did you miss the part where he said his agent called?"

Brianna thought about that a moment. "Yeah, I heard. Guess it slipped right by me." She paused to think about it. "But it doesn't make sense. If he's an actor, what's he doing in Pittsburgh? Why isn't he in L.A. or New York?"

"I don't know, but I'm sure we'll find out. Maybe he's filming a movie here or something. I wouldn't be a bit surprised to find out it was something like that." A few seconds later Gran-Gran's eyelids fluttered shut, and Brianna realized the medication had kicked in.

"Pleasant dreams," she whispered.

"Mm-hmm."

Brianna walked over to the window and looked down onto the parking garage. Somewhere down there Brady was getting into his car and heading off to. . .who knew where?

Funny. She hadn't given much thought to what he did or why he'd come to Pittsburgh. Maybe it didn't matter.

Maybe she was just supposed to settle back and enjoy the fact that he had arrived.

Chapter 11

Brady stopped off at the house, changed clothes, then rode in the back of a plush limousine to the stadium. He arrived with nearly an hour to spare. As he made his way to the media room, he found himself distracted, pondering the fact that he would soon be playing ball right here in this very place. The thing he had hoped and prayed for for years had come to pass. In spite of his past fumbles.

"There's our star player." Burroughs looked over with a nod as he came through the door. "Glad you could join us."

Brady gave him an I'm-sorry smile. "Yeah. Thanks so much for yesterday. I'm really sorry."

"How's the lady? The one who took the fall?"

"My neighbor? Abbey? Her hip was broken, but the doctors pinned her back together," he explained. "I was at the hospital till late last night with her, uh, family."

"*That* story will go to print in a few days," Burroughs said. "STAR QUARTERBACK RUSHES IN TO SAVE THE DAY FOR LOCAL WOMAN. We'll go on to tell them how much you love Pittsburgh, so much so that you'd stop the clock to care for a neighbor in need."

"I, uh, I really don't think that's necessary, sir."

"Why not?" Burroughs slapped him on the back. "It'll make for a good story, and a good story translates into ticket sales. Not hard to figure that one out. We play up every opportunity we can get."

"Hmm." Brady wasn't sure how Abbey would react if she read her name in the paper. Or Brianna. He shuddered, thinking about it. What would she say? Would she feel taken advantage of?

He would find some way to smooth this over. Or talk Burroughs out of leaking the story.

Coach Carter entered the room with a jersey in his hands, which he tossed to Brady. "You've got your work cut out for you between now and tomorrow night. Hope your memorization skills are as good as your plays."

"Thanks." Brady slipped on the jersey, loving the way it felt.

Minutes later a stocky man with a thick mustache entered the room. Brady stood at once. "Mr. Mandel." He extended his hand toward the team's owner, who shook it with vigor.

"Glad to meet you, son." Mandel patted Brady on the back. "We're counting on you to pull us out of a slump."

"Yes, sir. I'll give it my best shot."

"I know you will."

Brady swallowed hard and sat back down, and the room slowly filled with reporters, no doubt armed and ready to snag their story.

At three o'clock straight up, Burroughs approached the microphone with Mandel at his side. Brady watched it all, his excitement building. The reporters—who till now had been talking loudly among themselves and snapping an occasional photograph—grew silent. The clicking of cameras filled the room.

"Thank you all for coming," Mandel said with a nod. "The news today is good. As you know, Harper's out of the game. That left us with a hole in our line. We've had our feelers out, and I'm proud to announce today that Pittsburgh has a new starting quarterback, Brady Campbell."

He motioned to Brady, who smiled broadly. At once the cameras shifted his way. He nodded.

Mandel continued on with a look of confidence. "Brady is more than going to fill Harper's shoes, starting tomorrow night. We're looking forward to our best season ever."

The reporters tried to toss out a couple of questions, but Burroughs interrupted them. "Coach Carter will speak for a few minutes, and then you can ask your questions."

Carter stood and approached the podium. He started a rapid-fire dissertation of Brady's skills, homing in on his successes in Tampa over the past two years. Afterward he gestured for Brady to join him at the microphone.

Brady trembled as he opened his mouth to speak. "First, let me say how excited I am to be here. I had two great years in Tampa. Great years. Got my start in the league there. For a while it looked as if I might be watching the game from the sofa this year. But coming here to Pittsburgh, to be part of this franchise, is a dream come true for me. To lead this football team is"—he stumbled over the words as the lump in his throat made it difficult to speak—"to lead this team is nothing short of a miracle."

Mandel slipped into the spot behind him and put his arm over his shoulders. "You know how I feel, folks. Winning is about growing. Getting better. We're committed to getting better, and adding Campbell to our family of players does just that—makes the whole team better. I truly believe this is going to be the best year ever for our fans." At this point Mandel opened the floor to questions.

"How are you adjusting to life without beaches?" one reporter asked.

Brady laughed. "That's an easy one. I didn't get to the beach much. The field was my beach."

"Yeah, but you know it snows here," another reporter added. "Even on the field." They all erupted in laughter, obviously aimed at Brady.

"That's what I hear."

"Have you ever played in snow before, Campbell?" the reporter asked with a smirk. "For that matter, have you ever *seen* snow before?"

"Seen it." Brady looked at the coach for reassurance before admitting, "Played on it a couple of times over the years." He tried to think of something clever. A smile rose to his lips. "But I plan to move so fast that it melts underneath me, so I doubt it will be a problem."

Another round of laughter rang out, this time in his support.

"Why didn't Tampa renew your contract this season?" one reporter asked.

Brady cleared his throat, then spoke with as much confidence as he could muster. "I leave the negotiations to my agent, and he leaves the passing and throwing to me."

"Any reason why you weren't picked up by another team?" another reporter called out.

Brady shrugged. "Just wasn't God's plan, I guess."

"God?" A couple of the guys chuckled. "So are you saying God led you here—to Pittsburgh?"

Brady noticed the look of surprise in Burroughs's eyes but forged ahead. "Well, I guess you could put it that way."

"He's here now, and that's what matters," Burroughs interjected. "And we're happy to have him. We know the fans will be, too."

"Especially the women!" one reporter threw in. "Are you still a ladies' man, Campbell?"

Brady felt his cheeks flush and simply shrugged to avoid the dreaded subject. *Lord, please don't let this story go any further.*

"I'm not the man I was back in Tampa; let's just leave it at that."

The time came to pose for a few photos. Brady put on a winning smile and stood alongside his new coach and manager. With the cameras in his face and the jersey on his back, he was ready—ready to run for the goal.

> ❧

Brianna thought back to her last bit of time at the hospital as she pulled away in her car. At ten minutes till three Gran-Gran had announced her need to watch the news conference, which gave Brianna the perfect opportunity to slip away for a couple of hours.

"I have some grocery shopping to do," she said. "But I'll be back later tonight if that's okay with you."

"Of course, of course!" Her grandmother had waved her away, turning to the television, and Brianna slipped out the door, content for some time alone to plan for the days ahead.

Now, as she made her way north, she found her thoughts drifting to Brady. Despite her earlier thoughts, Gran-Gran was right. What she saw she liked. A lot.

But did he like her, too? Would it be presumptuous to think so after such a short time? Interesting to think about it.

On the other hand, she needed to shake off this childish fantasy and stay focused on her grandmother. She would have plenty of time in the future for romance. Right now Gran-Gran needed her, and she came first.

Brianna whipped the car into the parking lot of the grocery store and got busy making her purchases. By the time her grandmother returned home in a few weeks, Brianna would be ready with some of her favorite foods. She would spend the weeks learning.

And Brady. . .

Maybe she would invite him over for dinner. Let him know she had acquired at least a bit of her grandmother's talent in the kitchen.

Brianna left the grocery store with a smile on her face. Once she got home and put the groceries away, she would rest a few minutes then head back up to the hospital.

Hmm. Maybe she'd better call Gran-Gran before leaving the house, just in case she wanted or needed anything from home.

Lost in her thoughts, Brianna made her way toward the duplex. When she pulled onto the street, she almost didn't recognize it as her own. A mob of television vans lined each side, as well as cars and vans bearing the logos of prominent radio stations. They seemed to be centered in front of her house.

Or were they? How could she tell through the traffic?

She honked at a fellow with a television camera in his hand as she attempted to pull her car into the driveway. *What?* He pointed the camera in her direction, and for a moment she wanted to jump out of her car and smack the guy. He had some nerve!

With her pulse racing, she drove slowly up the driveway toward the garage. The second she stepped out of the car, a mob of reporters surrounded her on every side, many of them shoving cameras in her face. She couldn't make heads or tails out of what they were saying.

At first.

But then one name rang through, clear as a bell: Brady Campbell.

"B–Brady?" she stammered. "W–what about him?"

A female reporter who introduced herself as a sportscaster for a cable affiliate started a round of questioning. "Can you confirm that Brady Campbell lives next door? If so, can you tell us anything about him?"

"Well, I, uh, he's a great guy," Brianna managed to say. "But why do you want to know?"

A laugh went up from the crowd. "Why do we want to know?" one male reporter jeered. "That's priceless."

"So tell me," the female reporter continued, "how does it feel living next door to the man who's going to take our team to the Super Bowl this year?"

"What?" For a minute there Brianna thought the woman said Super Bowl.

"We hear Brady was quite a ladies' man back in Florida," another reporter threw out. "A woman on each arm and a party that never ended."

A woman on each arm? Parties? They had to have the wrong guy. Surely.

"Would you say Pittsburgh has changed him much?" the female reporter asked. "Or are old habits hard to break?"

"Yeah, is he throwing any passes your way?" another man hollered out.

A roar of laughter went up from the crowd, and Brianna turned to face the man, anger rising to the surface. Enough was enough.

"Look," she said. "I don't know what you're talking about—any of you—but this much I do know. You're trespassing on private property. You are going to get off my lawn, or I'll call the police and have you removed."

Several of them backed off right away, and a few of the ones who remained gave her the oddest looks she'd ever seen. As if she'd just spoken to them in a foreign language.

"Lady, are you kidding?" one asked.

"We thought you'd be thrilled to tell us about Brady," someone else said with a shrug. "No harm intended."

He and the others trekked across the lawn to Brady's driveway, where one or two began to photograph and videotape his side of the duplex. Brianna stood in stunned silence as she attempted to figure out what had just transpired.

She raced back through the tidbits of conversation in an attempt to make sense of things. Surely the woman hadn't said Super Bowl? Brady was an actor, right?

An idea began to emerge, one she couldn't shake. Maybe the paparazzi had followed him here. Maybe all that stuff about women and parties was part of a gag, something his agent had cooked up to draw publicity for a movie or something.

Still. . . Even at that, something about all this just felt wrong.

Brianna grabbed her bags of groceries and shot inside the house, ignoring her phone, which was ringing nonstop. Once inside the safety of the kitchen, she looked down to discover she'd missed three calls.

From Gran-Gran.

She called back right away, amazed at the emotion in her grandmother's voice as she cried out, "Bree!"

"Y–yes?"

"You're not going to believe it!" Gran-Gran let out a squeal. "Brady Campbell—the one and only Brady Campbell—*our* Brady Campbell—"

"Y–yes?"

"He's our new quarterback!" Her grandmother began an animated conversation about all she had seen and heard during the press conference, but Brianna never heard a word. Everything was starting to spin out of control.

Was it possible? Could it be? Mr. Trouble with a capital T was just that—trouble. Only a different kind from what she'd expected.

With Gran-Gran still chattering away, Brianna snuck a peek out of the kitchen window, staring in horrified awe at the crowd of people on Brady's lawn. The news teams clearly wanted to meet him face-to-face—drill him full of questions about his past and his future.

A wave of nausea came over Brianna, and she dropped down into a chair. Her hands trembled as the grim reality set in. She'd done it again—fallen for a guy whose first love was the game. Only one problem this time. . .

This guy didn't *love* football.

This guy *was* football.

Chapter 12

After the press conference Brady decided to swing back by the house to send a few e-mails before going to the hospital. He arrived home to an unexpected mob scene. As the limo driver eased the car down the road, the press met them on every side. They started pounding on his car windows before he ever hit the driveway, shouting questions at him through the tinted glass.

You've got to be kidding me.

The driver managed to pull up to the curb, and Brady mumbled a thank-you, then wrangled his way out of the backseat, hands up in the air. "Easy, fellas!" he said, as one guy almost hit him in the head with a microphone on an extended boom stand. "I'd like to live to play my first game if you don't mind."

They began to barrage him with questions, many of which he was able to answer without trouble. He only stumbled when they got to the part about his last year in Tampa.

"So you spent some time in a twelve-step program," one of them jabbed. "What was that like? Are you clean and sober now?"

"I, um. . ." He raked his fingers through his hair, embarrassed, yet knowing this was a question he couldn't avoid. "I haven't touched a drink in months. In fact, my whole life has changed—every aspect of it."

"Would you like to elaborate?" a female reporter asked.

"I–I'm a different man. I'm not the old Brady Campbell anymore. I'm the new, improved version."

"Same throwing arm?" one of the guys jeered.

"Yeah, same arm. Just different. . .heart."

On and on they went, pounding him with questions and asking about his new team members. And the one who'd preceded him.

"What's your opinion of Harper?" the female reporter asked. "Do you feel like you can fill his shoes?"

"Harper's great," Brady acknowledged. "One of the best players in the game today. I wish him the best with his recovery, and I'm honored to take up where he left off. But I am *not* Harper. I'm Brady Campbell. So don't look for me to lead the team in exactly the same way, okay?"

Just then something caught Brady's eye. Brianna, in the next driveway, slipping into her car. She glanced his way with an odd look. He could read the pain in her eyes, but why? What was up with that?

Ah. She was probably a little confused. He hadn't exactly prepared her for this, had he? Then again he couldn't have. Keeping everything under wraps had been critical. But now he could tell her everything. And she would not only understand, but he hoped she would also celebrate alongside him, as would Abbey.

If he could just get to her through this crowd.

Brady managed to shake off the reporters, promising to give them all interviews at a later date. As they dispersed, he watched Brianna pull away. He wanted to run after her, but she seemed intent on leaving.

Well, no problem. He would catch up with her later. . .at the hospital. Surely by then the frenzy would be behind him.

He hoped.

❧

Brianna pulled up a chair next to her grandmother's bed and did her best to ignore the zeal in the reporter's voice from the television across the room.

"Listen, Bree—they're talking about Brady again."

"Uh-huh." She refused to look. Let them talk. Why should she care?

"Well, listen to this—why don't you—?"

The reporter's interview covered Brady's past plays on the field and off. In a clip at the end Brady added a few lines, insisting he wasn't the man he used to be.

Whatever.

As the report came to an end, Brianna turned toward her grandmother, who couldn't seem to say enough about Brady.

"I just knew there was something special about that boy. I knew it."

"But you heard what those reporters said," Brianna argued. "He's got a—a past."

Gran-Gran gave her a scrutinizing look. "We've all got a past, Bree. That's why we need Christ so much."

"Well, I know, but this is different. He's going around talking like he's a Christian, and then every news channel flashes photos of him in bars. With women."

"But you heard what he said in that last interview," her grandmother scolded. "He said he's a different man now. His heart is different. And you know what that means. You've spent time with him. It's clear to see that his sins have been washed away—just like yours—just like mine."

Brianna let out a lingering sigh. "Well, if it's true he's a different man, and I'm not so sure it is, then he should have warned us about this football thing. Should have told us why he'd come to town in the first place."

"Why? Why should he have told us?"

"Well, I don't know. He just should have. It would've been polite."

"Bree, I don't expect you to understand this," Gran-Gran said in a sympathetic voice. "But I'm sure they had him under a gag order. He couldn't breathe a word. But now that this press conference is behind him, I'd imagine he'll show up ready to talk. And when he does—"

At that exact moment a rap on the door interrupted her grandmother's sentence. Brianna looked across the room, startled to see Brady standing there with a fistful of pink roses. Tea roses, no less. Her grandmother's favorite.

"For the lady of honor," Brady said as he took a step in their direction.

Brianna wasn't sure whose hand he was going to place the roses in. Just in case, she turned her head and shifted her gaze out the window. *I will not, under any circumstances, let that man think I would expect—or even take—those flowers from him.*

She turned back in time to see him pass the roses to Gran-Gran, who took them with a squeal.

"You're the best, Brady." She gestured for him to sit—which he did upon her command—then gave him a motherly look. "But as tickled as I am, I still think you need a good spanking."

Brady's gaze shifted to the floor. "Yeah, I'm really sorry, but I couldn't say anything. They wouldn't let me."

"See, Bree. I *told* you!" Gran-Gran crossed her arms in front of her, as if that settled the whole thing. Brianna shrugged, as though it didn't matter. But what she really wanted to do was give Mr. Campbell a piece of her mind.

She glanced at her watch then bounded from her chair. "I, um, I really need to leave."

"Leave?" Gran-Gran and Brady spoke in unison.

"Um, yeah. I'm really tired. Didn't get much sleep last night. And I'm kind of hungry, too."

"Well, let me take you to get some food." Brady rose to his feet.

"I really think I just need some rest," she explained. "So if you don't mind. . ." She made her way to the edge of the bed and gave Gran-Gran a kiss on the cheek. "By the way," she said, "I called Pastor Meyers early this morning before the service started. Apologized for not being there and told him why. He and his wife are coming by to see you later this evening."

"Well, bless you for that. And bless them, too."

Brianna nodded and turned to leave. As she did, she noticed the pleading look in Brady's eyes.

Well, let him plead. She didn't feel like talking right now.

Maybe another day.

Chapter 13

Brady looked at Abbey, stunned. "What's up with that? She's not speaking to me?"

"I guess not."

"Because I didn't tell her who I was?" he asked. "Is that it, or is there more to it?"

A look of pain crossed Abbey's face as she shifted her position in the bed. "There's more to it than that. I know this might not make much sense, but Bree is a little sensitive about football."

"Football *players*, or the game in general?"

"The game in general. It all goes back to something that happened with her father when she was in high school, but I'm not the one to tell that tale," Abbey said. "Besides, I think it will do Bree good to get it off her chest." She added, "I have a feeling you might be just the one to win her over."

"To the sport?" he asked.

With a twinkle in her eyes Abbey answered, "Among other things."

"Humph. That would require her actually staying in the same room with me for more than five seconds."

"She will," Abbey said with a nod. "I know that girl better than I know myself." Her eyes lit up. "So why don't you go after her?"

Brady shook his head, confused. "I don't even know where she's going."

"Oh, I do. Every time she gets frustrated, she goes to the same place. I'll be happy to give you directions." She pointed to the tablet and pen on her bedside table, and Brady scribbled down the details.

"Are you sure?" he asked.

"Sure as I'm living and breathing." Abbey clamped her hand over her mouth as soon as the words escaped. "Maybe I should've phrased that another way." She gave him a wink to let him know she was teasing.

Brady said good-bye and turned to leave. Just as he reached the door, Abbey called to him. "Hey, Brady?"

"Yes?" He faced her.

More wrinkles than usual etched her brow as she whispered, "Ask her about Daniel."

Brady paused then shrugged. "Okay."

Just as he attempted to walk through the door, two elderly women met him

185

head-on. They took one look at him, and exaggerated squealing began.

"Hush, ladies," Abbey insisted. "Or the nurse will toss you out on your ears!"

After a minute or so of whispered glee, one of them appeared to hyperventilate. Her red orange curls bounced up and down as she tried to catch her breath. For a second Brady wasn't sure if she was *really* struggling to breathe or simply acting.

Yep. Acting.

The woman extended her hand with a sly grin and introduced herself. "I'm Lora Patterson," she said, "and you're—you're—Brady Campbell."

"Yes. Good to meet you."

He extended his hand, and she took it but refused to let go. When he finally managed to break free, she clutched her hand to her chest with a dreamy-eyed look on her face. "I'm never washing this hand as long as I live!"

From the bed Abbey let out a grunt. "Then don't count on coming back to my house for dinner."

"Oh, hush, Abbey." Lora's cheeks flushed as she made her way to the side of the bed. "Let me have some fun."

"Well, that's a fine how-do-you-do after all I've been through," Abbey said with a pout.

Brady wanted to slip out before they engaged him in conversation, but the woman left standing in the doorway was, well, a bit on the wide side. And she didn't appear to be moving anytime soon. Instead she stared at him in bug-eyed silence with her mouth hanging open.

"Move out of the way, Rena," Abbey scolded. "Brady was just leaving."

"D–do you have to?" The woman looked as if she might cry.

"I'm sorry, but I was just—"

"He's going after *Bree*," Abbey explained. "So scoot, Rena. Let the man pass."

"B–but I wanted to ask for his autograph," Rena stammered. She reached into her purse and came up with a grocery store receipt and an ink pen. "Sorry, but it's the best I can do," she said as she shoved them both in Brady's direction.

He gave her a warm smile and quickly scribbled his name.

"How ironic is that!" she said, as she pointed to the paper. "You signed your name right on top of the word *honey*."

Abbey rolled her eyes. "Rena, stop flirting."

"I'm not flirting." The woman batted her eyelashes and gave a girlish giggle.

"Excuse her, Brady," Lora said. "She doesn't get out much."

"Yeah," Rena acknowledged with a wistful smile. "My back goes out more than I do."

All three women erupted in laughter. Brady joined in—for a minute. But he couldn't stay there forever. He needed to catch up with Brianna. He nodded in the direction of the women—"Happy to meet you both"—then shot out of the door while the shooting was good.

Minutes later he found himself on the highway, headed toward his destination. What he would say when he got there was a mystery. Still, if he didn't follow her, if he didn't let her know he cared about what she was thinking, feeling. . .

Hmm.

He *cared* about what she was thinking and feeling.

The revelation hit him hard. How long had it been since he'd cared—*really* cared—about what someone else thought about him? Years probably. Something about sobering up brought back his ability to care. To genuinely care.

And this was a girl worth caring about.

He pulled into the parking lot of the tiny strip mall, just a few blocks from home. Where was it? Ah, yes. On the end. Steel City Scoop-a-Rama—Pittsburgh's premiere ice cream eatery, according to Abbey. And Bree's favorite spot for drowning her sorrows.

Brady entered the store and walked up behind her. He listened with a smile as she ordered a deluxe double scoop of white chocolate mocha with an extra serving of candy bar "mixin's" stirred in. The fellow behind the counter placed the scoops of ice cream on a marble slab and began to mash the bits of crunchy chocolate candy into it. Then he pressed the whole conglomeration into a large waffle cone, also coated in chocolate.

"Sprinkles on top?" he asked.

Brianna leaned her elbows on the countertop and stared at the cone. "Mm-hmm. Yeah. Lots of 'em."

Wow. When this girl drowned her sorrows, she drowned her sorrows. Likely she'd be up all night on a sugar high, if he didn't step in and do something about it.

The clerk handed her the cone and rang up her total. Six dollars and forty-nine cents? That was a high price to pay for an emotional breakdown, even a well-deserved one.

Brady remained behind her, still and silent, as Brianna fumbled around in her purse with her free hand for the money. Her moves grew more frantic. "I—I can't find my wallet."

"Excuse me?" The young clerk gave her a suspicious glare, and she started looking again, nearly tipping the cone over in the process.

"Maybe I left it in the car. Or maybe. . ." She looked at the fellow again, her voice quivering. "I know what I did. I left my wallet at the hospital. I'd taken it out to get some change to buy a soda, and I must've forgotten to put it back in." She stared at the cone as ice cream dribbled down the sides. "What should I do?"

The kid let out an exasperated sigh, then reached out to take the cone from her hand.

And Brady, quiet until now, pulled out his wallet.

ја

Brianna saw the hand reach around from behind her and heard the credit card slap down on the counter. She turned, half horrified and half grateful. When she saw Brady's face, her stomach knotted. What was he doing here?

She shook her head. "I can't let you do that."

"You can and you will," he said. "Because you're going to share it with me. If we can get to it before it melts into a puddle." He reached to take it from her hand, then licked it around the edges.

How gross is that? Brianna let out a groan, more for effect than anything else. "Now you're going to have to eat the whole thing."

"No, I'm not."

Unbelievable.

Then again, he *was* paying for her ice cream. Once again he'd swept in and saved the day. How many times was he going to do that?

The kid behind the counter swiped Brady's card and waited on the machine to respond.

"How did you know I was here?" Brianna asked. Then, knowing the answer in her heart, added a quick, "Never mind. Skip that."

"It was right of her to tell me," Brady answered, taking a nibble from the edge of the cone. "I know you're upset at me, and I want to get to the bottom of it."

She crossed her arms. "I never said I was upset."

"You didn't have to."

The clerk started to hand Brady his credit card. But then he glanced down at the name on the card and back up again into Brady's face.

"Hey, you're Brady Campbell."

"Uh. . .yeah." Brady took the card and shoved it into his wallet then handed the cone to Brianna.

"Our new starting quarterback. From Tampa."

Brianna groaned. Would it always be like this when Brady was around?

"I saw the press conference. My name is Kevin Nelson. I play for North Hills High School."

"That's great," Brady said with a smile.

He gestured to a table across the room, and Brianna, grateful to be away from the kid behind the counter, headed over to it. She sat down and began to lick the edges of the cone to keep the drips from landing in her lap.

In spite of an incoming crowd of teenagers, the kid who'd waited on them seemed intent on staring. Even from across the room she saw him pull out his cell phone. Was he making a call? Brianna tried to ignore him, but he seemed to have the crazy thing pointed straight at them.

She jabbed Brady in the arm. "What is he doing?"

Brady turned around, and the clerk pressed a button on his cell phone. A camera.

She slapped herself in the head. "I can't take you anywhere."

"Things will simmer down soon. Once the dust settles from the media hype, I'll just be an average Joe."

"Somehow I doubt that."

"Can you tell me why you're suddenly so upset at me? Is it because I didn't tell you who I was?"

A wave of guilt washed over Brianna as she saw the confused look in his eyes. What had he done to her? And yet she must say something; otherwise, he might go on staring her down for the rest of the night.

"I just have an aversion to football—that's all. Long story."

"Is it the thing about your dad being a coach? The stuff you told me earlier?"

"That and a lot more." She shifted in her seat, uncomfortable with the direction of the conversation.

"I'm here if you want to talk."

She wanted to open up, wanted to tell him the whole story. How much she'd loved Daniel. How he'd been the star player on her father's team their senior year in high school. How he'd already received a scholarship to play for UCLA the next year. How her father had destroyed all of that with one thoughtless decision.

"I'll let you know when I'm ready," she said finally.

"I understand." Brady paused then surprised her with his next words. "One reason I wanted to see you was to tell you something. All those news stories about what I was like back in Tampa. . ."

She drew in a deep breath before answering. "Those television reporters didn't paint a very rosy picture of you."

"That was the old me." He gave her an imploring look. "You have to trust me. The old Brady Campbell is dead and gone. Those things I used to do—they felt good for a season. But that season is over. God has given me a fresh start."

"I understand fresh starts. I do."

"Can I ask you a question?"

She shrugged. "Sure. Go ahead."

"Who is Daniel?"

Brianna nearly choked on her ice cream. "Daniel? How did you know about him?" He opened his mouth to answer, but she stopped him. "Let me guess." *Gran-Gran, this is too much. You shouldn't have opened that door.*

"I'm sorry," he began. "I didn't mean to—"

"Forget it." Just then the kid who'd waited on them drew near to their table, cell phone open wide. What was he up to? "I have to go." Brianna stood, anxious to escape.

"But why? Because of what I said?" Brady reached to touch her arm—a gesture of kindness, she knew—but she shook him off.

"I just need to get away for a while by myself to think."

And with no other explanation than that, she left him sitting at the Steel City Scoop-a-Rama. Alone.

Chapter 14

A s Brady settled down on the sofa to read the local paper early Monday morning, he was horrified to discover the whole saga of how he had helped Abbey on the day of her accident, plastered on the front page. The headline read, QUARTERBACK RIDES INTO TOWN ON WHITE HORSE.

"Oh, no. Please, no."

Surely Mack Burroughs was to blame for this. But why? After a lengthy discussion by phone late Sunday night, Burroughs had promised to do the right thing. Brady assumed that meant *not* running the story.

Then again, maybe Burroughs thought exposure for one of his key players *was* the right thing. Who knew? But, as Brady scanned the article, a sickening feeling came over him.

For the most part, the story had the facts straight. But it made him out to be some kind of superhero. What would Abbey and Brianna do when they read this slanted write-up? Would they come after him with a spatula in hand and run him out of town?

No telling.

Brady tried to put together a plan of action for what he would say to them tomorrow when he made another visit to the hospital, but he couldn't think clearly. Tonight's game—and that intensive playbook—had him preoccupied.

Instinctively Brady flipped to the sports section of the paper for a glance-through before his morning shower. He almost fell off the couch when he came across several photos of him and Brianna, obviously taken by the kid at the Scoop-a-Rama. One showed Brady holding a dripping ice cream cone, licking the edges as Brianna looked on in interest. The caption underneath read, QUARTERBACK MAKES GOOD ON CLAIM TO MELT ICE.

Brady groaned as he noticed another photo—a shot of Brianna with her finger pointed toward him and an angry look on her face. The caption underneath proclaimed, LOCAL WOMAN RESISTS CAMPBELL'S CHARMS. The article went on to tell the whole story of his problems in Tampa. It was all in there—his issues with women and drinking and his claims of recovery. Everything.

Brady laid the paper on the coffee table and leaned his head into his hands. He wanted to pray—wanted to see this remedied—and quickly—but hardly knew where to begin. He was no longer worried about simply offending Brianna. Now he worried that she and Abbey might never speak to him again. How had he managed to drag them into this? And what could he do to undrag them?

He thought about it as he showered and then dressed for the day. He pondered it as he drove to the practice. He prayed about it as he geared up for the game. And he agonized over it as the lights on the field came alive, revealing thousands upon thousands of screaming fans.

If he could just get through tonight's game. . .he would make everything okay again.

Somehow.

❧

Brianna paced the hallway of the hospital, avoiding her grandmother's room at all costs. Inside Rena and Lora sat on either side of the bed, waving their pennants as always and shouting craziness to the television.

"Use your hospital voices, ladies!" Brianna had encouraged them. Not that it appeared to matter. Folks in nearly every room seemed to be watching the game, and a rousing cheer went up from the whole floor as Brady led the team to victory.

The whole thing proved to be more than irritating; it was downright annoying, particularly in light of today's events.

She fumed as she went back over the newspaper articles in her mind. How could Brady have used the incident with her grandmother to promote himself? Did he not realize Gran-Gran would be hurt?

Okay, so she wasn't really hurt. And, yes, she'd actually enjoyed the story, claiming it cemented her as the Steelers' biggest fan. But, really, what right did Brady have to tell the press about her grandmother in the first place? Would he do anything to get a story, even at the expense of others?

She continued to pace long after the game ended. Finally, when she could wait no longer, Brianna made her way back into the room and pretended to busy herself with a magazine.

"Brady Campbell is the best thing that ever happened to us," Gran-Gran declared with a satisfied look on her face. "Handsome—and a great player to boot! And he got me my first-ever write-up in the paper. Eighty-four years I've lived and have never seen my name in the paper once. Till now. Gotta give the boy a hand for that and for leading us to victory tonight!"

At that she let out a whoop, and the other ladies followed suit. Brianna rolled her eyes. Obviously they didn't see Brady as a problem.

Hmm. If they didn't, why did she?

Well, never mind all that right now. She needed to shoo her grandmother's visitors out of the room. She did so with the wave of a hand.

"Ladies, I think it's time for Gran-Gran to get her beauty sleep. Doctor's orders."

"Aw, do they hafta leave?" her grandmother asked with a pout. "I'm in the mood for a slumber party."

"No sleepovers tonight," Brianna scolded.

Lora stood, and Rena tried to follow suit. She let out an exaggerated groan as she finally made her way to her feet, followed by a winsome "If I'd known I was gonna live this long, I would've taken better care of myself."

After a bit more grumbling, the two older women headed out of the room, singing Brady's praises all the way. They waved their good-byes at the door but never stopped the chatter for a minute.

Gran-Gran settled back against the pillow and yawned. "You missed a great game, Bree," she said. "You have no idea how good Brady is."

"It's more likely we have no idea how *bad* he is," she muttered in response.

"Careful now, girl," Gran-Gran said with a frown. She turned back to the television. "Oh, look—the news is on!" She reached for the remote to turn up the sound. The television reporter was giving an animated play-by-play of the game. From the background clips Brianna could see Brady truly was a great player, maybe better than most she'd seen. But that didn't make him a good person, did it?

The story ended, and she'd just reached down to give Gran-Gran a good-night kiss on the cheek when the lead for an upcoming story grabbed her attention. What was that the news reporter said? Something about Brady and an ice-cream video?

She turned to face the television, her jaw dropping as she watched a rough, unedited video clip. *Oh, no!*

It was all there, the two of them seated together at the Steel City Scoop-a-Rama, talking. Brady taking her by the arm when she tried to leave. Oh, dear. How did that crazy kid videotape this? Was that even possible on a cell phone?

As the news clip ended, her grandmother gave her an inquisitive look, then spoke softly. "It was obvious he didn't want you to leave. He wanted you to stay with him."

"I guess." She exhaled a sigh as she replayed the look on Brady's face over and over again. Maybe he *hadn't* wanted her to leave, but that hadn't stopped her, had it?

"Are you sure you can't give him one more chance, honey?" Gran-Gran reached over and stroked her arm. "He's a great guy."

Brianna shrugged and reached for her purse. "I'll pray about it," she promised. "That's about all I can offer at this point."

"Well, then!" Her grandmother's smile lit the room. "Don't be surprised if the Lord grabs hold of that prayer and does something with it, something re-markable."

"Trust me—nothing would surprise me at this point." Brianna kissed Gran-

Gran on the cheek once more and headed for the door. She stopped just as she reached it and turned back. "But answer this one question for me."

"Yes?"

"Are you gonna go on matchmaking forever?"

A serious look came over her grandmother's face before she answered. "Well, on *this* side of forever anyway. Don't likely know as I'll go on doing it from the *other* side." She gave Bree a playful wink.

"You're a pill. You know that?"

"Yeah, I know," Gran-Gran said as she fussed with the sheets. "But you love me."

"More than life itself." Brianna blew her grandmother a kiss and headed off on her way home.

Chapter 15

Brady spent the next few weeks fending off reporters and practicing with the team. A cool front hovered over Pittsburgh, and it seemed to have affected Brianna's heart. He'd noticed it nearly every time he visited with Abbey at the hospital and then the rehab facility, but that hadn't kept him from trying. A couple of times he'd gone knocking at Brianna's door, thinking she was holed up inside the house. Not once had she answered the door.

One Friday morning, as he sat reading the paper, Brady noticed some movement through the open blinds at his living room window. He eased his way toward it and watched Brianna pull her car into the driveway next door. So Abbey was home at last. He would rest much easier knowing that.

He headed out the front door right away with a smile on his face, ready to be of assistance. He made it over to Brianna's car in seconds and helped her pull the walker from the trunk. She nodded her appreciation. Then he went to the passenger side and opened the front door for Abbey.

"Glad you're home!" he said with a wink as he extended his hand.

With his help she managed to stand. Then, with Brianna's support, Abbey gripped the walker and took a couple of steps.

"Would you mind getting those?" Brianna gestured to two small suitcases and a plastic bag with the hospital's name on it.

"I'd be happy to." Brady walked along behind them until they reached the front porch. Once there Brianna handed him the house key, and he opened the aging wooden door with a grin. "Welcome home!"

He followed the ladies into the living room, startled to see a twin bed where the love seat used to sit. Abbey made her way over to it with a look of chagrin on her face.

Brady gave Brianna an inquisitive look.

"Had to," she whispered. "Doctor's orders."

"I might be old, but I'm not deaf," Abbey interjected. "Besides, you won't hurt my feelings by speaking up. I'm not ready to climb those stairs just yet. Not for another week or so."

"How did you get the bed down here?" he asked Brianna.

"Pastor Meyers helped," she said with a shrug. "We put the love seat in the garage for now. It's just temporary."

A sense of disappointment came over Brady as he realized Brianna hadn't come to him for help.

Brianna helped her grandmother get situated in the bed, and Brady made himself busy putting the walker in the front hall closet. He looked around the room again, stunned at how different it looked. Its hospital-like decor made him a little uncomfortable.

"Gran-Gran, I need to get your prescriptions filled," Brianna said, reaching for her purse.

"Would you like for me to sit with her while you're gone?" Brady offered.

"You, um, don't mind?"

"No. Not at all."

After Brianna left, Abbey gave Brady a woeful shrug. "Kind of sad that I need a sitter, don't you think?"

"Of course not! I'm just a friend here for a visit. That's all."

She sighed as she looked around the room. "I don't think I'm going to enjoy sleeping in here; that's sure and certain. The sun comes in through that window in the morning." Her brow wrinkled in concern. "But I guess I'll manage, regardless. It's only for a week or so."

"Well, you do as the doctor says," Brady encouraged her. "No stair climbing until he says it's okay. Don't go trying to be a hero."

"No, *you're* the hero," she said. "You're the best player we've seen in years. I've been watching you, you know."

"Hardly the best." He paused then gave a more detailed apology than the one he'd given her at the hospital for the ongoing news stories, along with a lengthy description of what had really happened, including the part about his troubles back in Florida. He ended by telling her about his conversion to Christ, focusing on the role his mother had played in leading him to the Lord.

"She sounds like someone I would like," Abbey said.

"Oh, you'd love her." He paused then said, "And I know she knows I'm solid in my relationship with the Lord, so I'm not sure why I worry so much about what other people think. I guess, because I'm in the limelight, I just want to be careful—I don't want to give God a bad name." He let out an exaggerated sigh.

"You're worried for nothing, Brady," Abbey said. "When I watch those news stories, all I see is a man who's no longer what he used to be. A man who wants a second chance. Just like all of us at one point or another."

"Thank you." He smiled.

"And besides," she added, "there's hardly a person mentioned in the Bible who didn't give the Lord a bad name. David was a murderer but went on to be called a man after God's own heart. And Paul, before he came to the Lord, put Christian converts to death. Several of the great men of faith, like Abraham, for example, got ahead of the Lord and created their own plans. Peter, one of Jesus' disciples, denied Him several times over but still went on to do great exploits for Him. Shall I go on?"

"Nah. No point." Brady felt relief wash over him as she spoke. Somehow, talking to Abbey always made things better. She seemed to feel the words, as if she'd lived them personally.

"Good. Now let's talk about Bree," Abbey said, looking rather stern.

"What about her?"

"Well, it's clear to me God has brought you here to Pittsburgh for a reason—other than just playing football, I mean—and I'm convinced it's to marry my granddaughter."

"O-oh?" For a second Brady was stunned. "What makes you so sure?"

"I just know in my knower. And trust me—my knower's been around long enough to get it right much of the time."

"I see. So what do you suggest I do about this?"

"Well, we've lost several weeks, what with me being in the hospital and all. We've got to make up for lost time. First order of business will be to watch and pray. Time will be the thing that wins her over. That and a few more winning games from you."

"Brianna cares about football scores?"

"Well, no. . ." Abbey's gaze shifted, and he noticed a smile. "But a few winning games would continue to win *me* over, and that's very important if you're going to develop a relationship with her."

"Aha. I see. Well, I wouldn't want to lose your favor, that's for sure." He smiled, then looked out the window as he thought about Brianna. It would likely take more than time to win her over. But to start the ball rolling, he had to know more about her.

Some things, of course, were obvious. Clearly she was a strong Christian, vastly different from most of the women he had known. But would a girl who had followed the Lord most of her life give a guy like him a second glance? Did she question his relationship with the Lord? He wouldn't blame her. She only had the news reports to go on, and they appeared to contradict it. But what could he do about that? Seemed a bit futile even to ponder the idea of winning her heart.

And what was up with the football thing? So her dad was into the game. Neglected the family. Was that really enough to keep her from developing a friendship with someone involved in the sport? Maybe this would be a good time to ask the big question.

"I, um, I tried to ask her about Daniel that night at the ice cream shop," he started.

"Oh?"

"She shut me down. I could tell that was a closed door."

"Well, it's about time it opened." Abbey's eyes glistened, and for a moment he thought she might cry. "I was hoping she would tell you herself—thought it would be good for her to talk about it—but I don't mind spilling the beans."

"Are you sure?"

"Yes." She paused then started the story. "Daniel was Bree's sweetheart in high school. He was a quarterback on the team her father coached—their senior year."

"Wow. I would think having a player for a boyfriend would have endeared her to the game, not pushed her away."

"Well. . ." Abbey fiddled with the sheets then sighed. "From what I've been able to gather, my son has always been a tough coach. The players respect him, but he demands a lot from them. And everything came to a head during one particular game."

"Oh?"

"Mind you, I wasn't there that night. I only know what I've been told. Daniel was playing really well, and they were leading. In fact, they were far enough ahead that the first-string should've been pulled."

"Right."

"Glen was trying to prove some sort of point to the opposing coach by running up the score, so he kept them in the game—well beyond the exhaustion point."

"Yikes. Dangerous."

"Right. From what I've been told, they were worn out by the fourth quarter. Daniel took a dirty hit late in the game, and they thought—at least at first—he'd broken his neck. Praise God, that wasn't the case. Several cracked vertebrae. But you know as well as I do what that meant for his career."

Brady knew, all right. All it would take was one more hit to a neck already damaged and the guy could be paralyzed for life.

"Daniel never played again. Never went to UCLA."

"Man, that had to be tough."

"Bree was devastated," Abbey added. "And Daniel was never the same after that, either. He pushed her away. I think he might've blamed her dad, and—from what I've been able to pick up—she did, too." Abbey's eyes misted over. "Her real issue has always been with her father, not football. It's funny how she has the two linked together in her mind."

A stirring at the back door startled them both.

"Bree," Abbey whispered then put her finger to her lips to bring the conversation to an abrupt halt. "She's home. I'll have to finish later."

"Okay."

Seconds later Brianna entered the room with three prescription bottles in her hand. She looked at Brady and offered him a curt nod. "Thanks for keeping an eye on things so I could do this. It put my mind at ease to know you were here."

"Sure. We had a great time."

"Brady's really lifted my spirits," Abbey added. "I was happy to have him. And I'm hoping he'll stay for lunch."

Brady looked at his watch, stunned to see so much time had passed. "Oh, I'm sorry, but I can't. The game calls."

"Then you must answer," Abbey said in a more-than-serious tone. "We can't have our star quarterback late for practice, now can we?"

He flinched at the words *star quarterback* but didn't argue. To do so would only add more attention to it, and that wouldn't bode well for him right now.

He nodded at Brianna as he made his way toward the front door. He wanted to pause, to take her by the hand and talk with her, to draw her into a quiet conversation, like the one they'd had at the hospital that day.

He couldn't seem to take his gaze off her, but she seemed distracted, distant, so he settled on a quick good-bye. "You ladies have a great day," he said with a smile.

Brianna offered a polite nod, and Abbey said, "Go get 'em, tiger!" then gave him a thumbs-up sign.

He swallowed the temptation to laugh and shot out the door, ready to face the rest of the day.

&

The weekend passed uneventfully. Brianna fixed a couple of great meals, which Gran-Gran seemed to love. Several ladies from the church brought food, too, including Mitzi Meyers, the pastor's wife, who stopped by after church on Sunday. She prayed for Abbey and told her how much she'd been missed by everyone at Calvary Community.

On Monday morning, with Lora stepping in to care for her grandmother, Brianna finally felt free to return to work.

"Promise me you'll call if you need me for anything," she urged.

"Oh, go on now," Gran-Gran said. "It'll be good for you to get back to work. Besides, Lora's been itching to get into my kitchen to cook for me."

"I have?" Lora's eyes grew large. "You know I'm no cook, Abbey."

"Exactly. Which is why you need the practice. And I'll be here to guide you every step of the way."

Lora let out a groan, and Brianna giggled as she gazed at the two older women. She hoped when she reached their age she would have as much spunk.

A short time later, after weaving through morning traffic, she arrived at AB&D, where her bosses met her with a dozen questions and a collection of cards for her grandmother. She responded to more than forty e-mails and several phone messages, though it took a couple of hours to do so.

At lunchtime her boss Roger appeared at her office door.

"Hey, Roger. What's up?"

"Just wondered if you wanted to grab lunch. Several of us are going out for Italian food."

"Ah. I wish." She leaned back in her chair and groaned. "But I'm so far behind on my work. And we have some pending accounts I might be able to acquire for the company if I play my cards right. *If* I move quickly, which means I'd better stay put."

"Okay." His gaze shifted to the ground, which struck her as mighty suspicious.

"All right, Roger," she said, looking him in the eye. "Out with it. Why do you really want me to go to lunch with you and the other guys? And be honest."

"Oh, well, we were just thinking. . . ." He squirmed a bit then shrugged. "We were kind of thinking you might want to share some info about Brady Campbell. He's lived next door to you for a few weeks now." His voice grew more animated, and his eyes lit up. "We all saw the articles in the paper and heard the story on TV, so we're dying to know what's up. We figured you had the inside scoop on the guy—that's all."

Brianna let out a groan. "I might've known this had something to do with football."

"Well, it doesn't *have* to be about that. But. . ."

"What?"

"Well, we were thinking—since you live next door to the guy and all—that you might throw a party or something and invite us over. To meet him."

"Are you serious?"

"Sure. Why not? And besides"—he gave her a serious look—"rumor has it he's thinking about buying a house in town in the spring, down in the Riverparc area or maybe even Firstside."

"Where did you hear that?"

"Read it in the paper. We're talking about a guy with lots of money here, Brianna. He's going to want a mega-house. Or condo. And we were thinking—"

"I could coerce him into becoming a client?" She crossed her arms in front of her and gave him her best I-don't-think-so look. "Is that it?"

"Well, what would it hurt to let him know you're in the construction business?" Roger asked. "Really?"

"You're shameless."

"Look—you know how important it is to acquire new clientele, especially before the winter sets in. If he buys one of the older houses near town, he'll need a major remodeling job, maybe even an addition. And if he buys a condo he's likely to need upgrades. So who better to serve his needs than AB&D?"

"Uh-huh." *So that's what this is about.*

"If we can get his endorsement for the company, business would soar through the roof," Roger argued. "And it's not like we'd be using the guy, not really. We'd do quality work, work we'd all be proud of, as we always do."

"Roger, tell me you don't mean it. You would *not* put me in this position. Surely not."

"Just tell him about our competitive prices and focus on the quality craftsmanship. I can put together a list of satisfied customers from our existing clients." On and on he went, singing the company's praises.

She finally worked up the courage to interrupt him. "Roger."

He backed out of the door, his hands in the air. "Just think about it. That's all I'm asking."

Brianna shook her head and looked down at the papers on her desk. She would not give Roger an inch on this one. If she did, he might take a mile.

After he left, she plunged into her work with a vengeance. His words fueled her, giving her an added motivation to work hard—to put this whole Brady Campbell thing out of her mind.

Moments later, however, she sat staring at the computer, unable to work. She gnawed on the end of a pencil until the eraser was nearly gone. She thought back over her earlier conversations with Brady, how she'd been swept in by his beautiful green eyes and his broad smile—not to mention his broad shoulders.

"I'm just like one of those cheerleader-type groupies of his," she acknowledged to the empty room. "I'm pathetic."

For a second—just a second—she let herself think about the possibilities of getting involved with someone like Brady. He had been great to—and for—her grandmother, hadn't he? And their prior conversations, particularly those at the hospital on the day of Gran-Gran's accident, had been very sweet, hadn't they? Surely he was just a normal guy, in spite of the media frenzy.

Just as quickly she remembered the newspaper articles, the stories of where he'd come from, the man he used to be.

Was Gran-Gran right? Had he really changed, or was he simply taking advantage of the media to make himself look good?

Hmm.

Maybe, in spite of all outward signs, he was just a man longing to begin again. And maybe she should keep her opinions to herself. . .and let him do just that.

Chapter 16

Several weeks went by, and Brady settled into a routine of daily practices and football games. Playing well became a top priority. After all, Pittsburgh was known for its quarterbacks, and Mack Burroughs seemed intent on adding Brady's name to the ever-growing list of greats.

"Pittsburgh is the Cradle of Quarterbacks, Campbell," Burroughs reminded him daily. "Some of the greatest men who ever played the game came out of the City of Champions, and you're going to be no different. You're going to shine like a star."

The idea of shining like a star held little appeal, but playing well did, so Brady spent hours each week perfecting plays, poring over the playbook, and working out with his trainer in the weight room. Between practices and games, of course. And all in an attempt to better himself. To make his new team proud. He nearly wore himself out in the process, but he knew it would be worth it in the end.

As for the players, most of the guys were fun-loving and easy to get along with. A couple ran on the arrogant side, but that would pass with time. This he knew from his own history. And four of the guys on the team were strong Christians. One of them—Gary Scoggins—even invited him to church. Brady visited a few Sundays, then tried a couple of others, including Abbey and Brianna's church, which he loved. On those visits Brianna had been gracious enough to offer him the spot next to her.

One thing about going to church proved difficult. Thanks to the recent media coverage, folks tended to greet him like royalty. One awestruck pastor even pointed him out to the congregation. Awkward. How he wished he could blend in for a change. Maybe with time.

Somewhere in the mix of all he had to do, Brady found time to slip over to Abbey's a couple of times a week for a gab session. And food. Always food. He enjoyed long conversations with her and kept a watchful eye on her healing process. The mending came slowly, but, thanks to physical therapy and lots of prayer, she seemed to be moving a little better. Surely by midwinter she would be back to her old self again. Maybe then he could invite her to a game and make sure she had one of the best private boxes in the stadium, where she could entertain her friends.

The weather in the Pittsburgh area shifted rather abruptly in late October, and by early November he experienced his first-ever snowfall. That same week he received a call from his mother. He predicted her opening line.

"I know, Mom," he said with a groan. "It's cold up there." They spoke the words in unison, but for once he didn't let them get to him. Undaunted by his mother's lack of zeal for his new home, he went on to sing Pittsburgh's praises. And he didn't have to exaggerate. In spite of the weather, he'd fallen in love with the city already, so much so that his desire to bring his mother there intensified with each passing week. The more he got to know Abbey, the more he felt sure she and his mom would be fast friends. Add Rena and Lora to the mix, and his mother would *have* to fall in love with Pittsburgh, cold or not.

"Let's see how you do this season," his mother finally agreed. "If it looks like you're going to be staying in Pennsylvania for more than one season, I'll agree to pray about it. But I'm telling you now—"

He didn't mean to interrupt her, but his response just slipped out. "Mom, I plan to be here for the rest of my career." Where the words came from, he had no idea. To be honest, as much as he loved his coaches and fellow players, he'd never really thought about living there for years to come. Most in his profession were usually itching to move on after a couple of seasons.

Still, it would be great to have his mother there, and he reiterated that point as he ended the call. He could see himself settled down with a wife and a couple of children, with his mom and Abbey nearby to watch over them.

Abbey?

Hmm. If he moved to Riverparc, like so many of the other players, he probably wouldn't see much of Abbey.

Or Brianna.

His heart grew heavy as he thought about her. For weeks she'd given him little more than a polite nod or a wave. Even when Abbey had invited him for dinner, Brianna had been noticeably quiet. He prayed she would let go of any pain from the past and give him a chance.

Truth be told, he cared about her. And he wished—he wished she cared for him, too.

The revelation had come over time as he'd watched the way she fretted over Abbey. As he'd heard her laugh with Rena and Lora. As she'd shoveled snow from the driveway.

As she had reached to touch his hand that day in the hospital.

Brady peeked out of his living room window and sighed as he saw the snow-packed front yard. His mom was right. It *was* cold up here. And, as he glanced toward Brianna's duplex, he realized. . .it was even colder. . .over there.

&

By mid-December, Brady Campbell had drawn more attention to the team than any other player over the past three years. Brianna tried not to focus on the newscasts, tried to avoid the in-office drama associated with all of the hype. But she had to admit, he had proven to be a great player.

This she noticed as she watched the games in secret in her bedroom.

Between practices he came and went from the duplex, though she had it on good authority—Gran-Gran—that he would soon be listing his duplex with a Realtor. For some reason, the thought of him moving away caused a tightening in her chest, one she couldn't seem to shake.

Gran-Gran would miss his visits, to be sure. She counted on his great stories and hearty laughter. And Rena and Lora would be devastated, too. If Brady moved away, they'd lose their claim to fame.

Brianna tried not to think about it. She also tried not to think about the rumors going around that local women now found him to be Pittsburgh's latest hot bachelor. With all the attention, would he slip back into his old ways? Brianna couldn't be sure why this bothered her so much. Likely because of his friendship with Gran-Gran.

Right?

She prayed about this very thing as she made her way to the airport the week before Christmas to meet her parents and her brother. She also prayed about her relationship with her father, asking the Lord to give her the right words to say in his presence and to relieve the feeling of pressure she felt in her chest every time he was around.

Brianna met her family in the baggage claim area with a squeal of glee. Her mother wrapped her in a warm embrace. So did Kyle. Her father seemed to be a little travel-weary but offered a loose hug. Maybe he was softening with time.

They arrived back at the duplex, where her mother scurried into action, pouring her attentions into helping Abbey and cooking dinner. Both Kyle and her father seemed intent on meeting Brady, so Brianna slipped next door to see if he would be willing to stop by for a visit. Unfortunately he wasn't home. Then again, the Steelers were in the play-offs. Likely he was at practice.

She plodded back home, the bearer of bad news. Kyle seemed to take it well, but her dad looked disappointed. Still, he made polite conversation during dinner, asking Brianna about her job and telling Gran-Gran he would hire someone to paint her house once the spring came. Overall, things seemed to go a lot smoother than Brianna had expected. In fact, by the time the meal ended she felt a renewed hope that God could restore her relationship with her dad.

After polishing off some homemade banana pudding, she ventured into the living room ahead of the others to plug in the lights on the Christmas tree. The whole room seemed to come alive with color. This put Brianna in the mood for Christmas music, so she turned on the radio.

As the vibrant melody of "Carol of the Bells" filled the room, she found herself glancing out the window, looking toward Brady's place with a sense of longing. Had he even come home?

Nope. No car in the driveway. He was gone. For some reason she felt a twinge of disappointment. She had looked forward to introducing him to her family. Maybe she would catch him later in the week.

She sighed as she realized the truth of it. She missed him. Missed his funny jokes. Missed the way he always made Gran-Gran smile. Missed the way she felt whenever he was around, the fluttering in her chest, the sense of anticipation whenever he spoke, the glimmer in his beautiful eyes.

Brianna snapped back to reality when she heard Kyle's voice nearby. "Let me ask you a question."

"Um. . .okay." She turned to face him.

"You're interested in Campbell, aren't you?"

"W–what?" She tried not to let her expression give her away. "Why would you ask that?"

Kyle shrugged and smiled. "Well, Gran-Gran said a few things on the sly, and the rest I figured out on my own."

"There's nothing to figure out," she snapped.

"Mm-hmm."

He planted a kiss on her cheek. "I believe you. 'Course, I used to believe in Santa Claus, too. And the tooth fairy. But what things *appear* to be and what they turn out to be are often two different things, aren't they?"

She reached over and gave him a sisterly slap.

"Hey, what's up with that?" he grumbled.

"Just watch yourself, oh, brother of mine." She flashed a warning look. "I've already got Gran-Gran trying to plant thoughts into my head. I don't need you doing it, too."

"Who, me? Plant thoughts in your head?" He chuckled then slipped his arm around her shoulder and pulled her into a warm hug.

Just then her mother called out, "Coffee, anyone?"

Brianna turned to see her parents entering the room. Her mom carried a tray of filled coffee cups, and her father followed along behind, holding the sugar and creamer. Gran-Gran brought up the rear, smiling as she inched her way along. Brianna couldn't remember when she'd ever seen her look happier.

As they settled in front of the tree, Brianna leaned back against the sofa and looked around the room.

" 'Tis the season," she whispered.

The season to begin again.

Chapter 17

The day before Christmas, weather forecasters predicted incoming bad weather. As much as Brianna hated for her family to leave early, she knew catching a flight before the storm hit was crucial. They said goodbye at the airport. Her mother held her in a lengthy embrace, and Kyle gave her a brotherly hug.

Ironically, her father glanced down at her with what looked like tears in his eyes. "I miss you, Bree," he whispered then planted a kiss on her cheek. She swallowed back the lump in her throat and told him she missed him, too. Then she slipped her arm around him and gave him a tight squeeze.

She pondered her father's actions for the rest of the day. Had she been wrong to hold him at arm's length for so long, to somehow pay him back for what had happened to Daniel? Was she still harboring unforgiveness, even after all the times she'd dealt with her feelings?

She fell asleep that night, thinking of the years they had missed, wishing she could make up the lost time.

The following morning she awoke to a white Christmas. Brianna and her grandmother opened gifts together mid-morning. A light snow covered the lawn, just perfect for Christmas Day. "That's one thing they never had in L.A.," Brianna said, pointing toward the window.

"Pretty, isn't it?"

"Mm-hmm."

They sat for a moment before Brianna remembered she had a turkey roasting in the oven. She scooted off to tend to their meal. After all, Rena and Lora would be here within the hour.

And Brady.

Why he had accepted her grandmother's last-minute invitation was a mystery. Now that he'd become the city's star player he could have had Christmas dinner with almost anyone. But Brady had chosen to spend this special day with them . . .for whatever reason.

A few minutes later Gran-Gran pulled Brianna into the living room. Her face wore a worrisome look, one Brianna didn't know quite how to interpret.

"Sit for a minute, and let's have a chat."

Brianna sat on the sofa and pulled a blanket over her feet. "What's up, Gran-Gran?"

Her grandmother's brows knitted, and her lips grew tight. "You know I'm quite a talker."

"Clearly." Brianna nodded with a smile.

"So I'd imagine that for me to say I'm going to have a little trouble sharing this story will put things in perspective for you," Gran-Gran said.

"Definitely."

"There's something I've been wanting to tell you," her grandmother whispered. "Had to wait till just the right time."

"And this is it? Christmas?"

"Well, Christmas, yes. And something else, too." Her grandmother's eyes took on a faraway look. "It has a little something to do with the fact that your father was just here. I've been praying the Lord will restore our relationship. Maybe this trip provided a start for that; it almost felt like it."

"I agree," Brianna said. "I felt the same way. So is that what you wanted to talk about? Dad?"

"Well, it's kind of a story that leads up to your father," Gran-Gran explained. "And I have to go backward in time to another Christmas season years ago. Do you have a few minutes to listen to an old woman ramble?"

"Don't be silly." Brianna snuggled in close. "I love your stories."

"Hmm. Well, this one begins in December 1941, just after the attack on Pearl Harbor."

"Wow. This is a *history* story."

"I guess you could call it that. It's the history of our family." Gran-Gran paused a moment then started. "I was just out of high school, and I'd fallen in love with a boy named Tommy. He was handsome, that boy."

Brianna giggled. "I don't think I've ever heard you talk about him."

"No, you wouldn't. Tommy was the first boy I ever loved, and I thought he hung the moon. I adored him. We dated the last two years of high school."

"Whatever happened to him?"

"Ah. He was drafted just out of high school. Went off to fight in the Pacific."

"Wow."

Gran-Gran's eyes misted over. "I loved that boy so much, and when he left it nearly broke my heart in two. We wrote letters the first few weeks, until. . ."Tears rose to cover her lower lashes, and she brushed them away with her fingertip.

"What, Gran-Gran? What happened?" Even before she got her answer, Brianna's heart grew heavy. This would not be a happily-ever-after kind of story.

"Bree, I'm not proud of what I did." Her grandmother spoke in a hushed voice. "I was just a girl in love. So in love I couldn't see straight."

"I'm not sure I know what you mean," Brianna said, reaching to squeeze her hand. "What did you do?"

Her grandmother's gaze shifted to the floor. "When Tommy had been gone about two months I knew something was wrong. I could feel it. I didn't know anyone who had ever had a baby before, but I just knew. . . ."

Brianna's heart felt as if a vise grip had taken hold of it. "Oh, Gran!"

"I was a foolish girl, and I let my heart lead me into something that was wrong. Very wrong." She began to tremble at this point, and Brianna clutched Gran's hand as if her life depended on it. "Back in those days. . .well, it wasn't like it is today. Once a girl was found to be. . ." She didn't say the word, but she didn't have to. "Anyway, I waited as long as I could to tell my mother. She was devastated."

"I'm so sorry," Brianna whispered. "I'm sure it was a terrible time for both of you."

"Worse than you know." Gran-Gran shook her head, and a lone tear slipped down her cheek. "We got the news about Tommy when I was only four months along. He was. . .he was. . ." She covered her face with her hands and cried softly for a few moments then whispered, "He was killed in Bataan, along with thousands of other American soldiers."

"Oh, Gran, I'm so sorry! I'm so sorry." Brianna wrapped her grandmother in her arms. They sat together for what seemed like an eternity before she finally spoke. "W–what happened? What happened to you—and to the baby?"

"My parents didn't want anyone to know," she said. "So they sent me to stay with my aunt Nadine out in the country. She was my mom's youngest sister, not much older than I was, but happily married with a couple of kids of her own. Other than Nadine and the children, I didn't know anyone there," her grandmother explained. "It was a horrible, lonely time for me. Nadine and her husband wouldn't let me go anyplace, except to the tiny church they attended. But even there the lies were thick. She got a little wedding band out of a Cracker Jack box and put it on my finger—made me tell her friends and her pastor that my husband had died."

Brianna shook her head. "That's awful," she whispered.

"But then Katie came." Gran-Gran's face lit up at once.

"Katie." Brianna nodded. "I've heard you talk about her." She also remembered the photo on Gran-Gran's bedside table of the little cupie-doll girl with wispy curls and a winsome smile.

Her grandmother shook her head, and her hands trembled. "My parents wouldn't let me keep her. They told me I had to. . .to let her. . .go." The tears began again. "They made me leave her with Nadine to raise. I couldn't hold her, couldn't kiss her pretty little face, couldn't even let her know she was my own."

"But—" None of this made sense. "Everyone there knew you were the mother."

"Yes, but they went on believing the stories Nadine told them. She and my mother came up with what they thought was a foolproof plan. Nadine told her church friends I was too frail to care for the baby, too emotionally insecure. And, of course, my friends back home didn't know the difference. They didn't even know there *was* a baby. They just knew I'd gone to visit my aunt for a few months."

Gran-Gran paused and looked out the window as she whispered, "But *I* knew.

I knew my baby girl had been stolen from me, and I prayed for her every single night." She paused, and some of the life returned to her eyes. "Nadine seemed to soften a bit over the next few years and even sent me pictures of the baby. She was gorgeous, a cherub, if I ever saw one. A real angel. I would hide those pictures under my pillow and cry myself to sleep. Then one day. . ."

A sinking feeling came over Brianna as her grandmother began to cry.

"We g–got the c–call on a Wednesday. Katie was just three and a half years old, not even old enough for school. She'd been out in the field with my uncle, and there was an accident. . . ."

Brianna squeezed her eyes shut, then let her own tears fall as her grandmother finished.

"She was riding the tractor with my uncle Raymond. She loved to ride up there. Loved it. But that day she. . .she slipped and fell and. . ."

Gran-Gran wept while Brianna held her close. She knew the rest already. No more needed to be said. Her grandmother had suffered enough already, and getting this story out had likely been the hardest thing she'd ever done.

After a few minutes of quiet mourning, her grandmother finally looked up at her.

"So now you know," she whispered. "You know—"

"That we've both faced terrible pain in the past?" Brianna spoke over the lump in her throat. "That we've both needed—and received—God's forgiveness? That we've been able to forgive others, in spite of our pain?"

Gran-Gran nodded then reached for her hand. " 'All have sinned and fall short of the glory of God,' " she said quietly. "I can't tell you how many times I've quoted that scripture. And my other favorite one—the one about being cleaned as white as snow—"

" 'Cleanse me with hyssop,' " Brianna started.

" 'And I will be clean,' " Gran-Gran added. " 'Wash me, and I will be whiter than snow.' "

Yes, she knew that scripture well.

Something at the window caught Brianna's eye. Through the thin curtain she could see the sky, heavy and white. The bits of snow fluttered softly, slowly to the ground. She thought about them in light of everything her grandmother had said.

Whiter than snow.

She turned back with a smile on her face. Suddenly she could hardly wait to see Brady.

❧

Brady arrived at Abbey's house at exactly twelve thirty on Christmas Day—the appointed time. Brianna answered the door with a broad smile.

"Merry Christmas," he greeted her.

"Same to you. Come on in out of the cold." Oh, those words! They almost felt symbolic, as if Brianna were somehow declaring a truce, tearing down the wall that had risen between them.

She swung wide the door and ushered him inside. He shrugged off his coat, then managed to sneak a peek at Brianna out of the corner of his eye as he hung his coat in the closet. She looked especially pretty in that blue sweater. It really went well with her blond hair, which she'd swept up into a loose ponytail. And he liked her without makeup. No pretense.

"Well, hello there, Brady!" a trio of voices greeted him as he made his way into the kitchen. There his three biggest fans sat at the kitchen table, smiling.

"We're so glad you could make it," Abbey started. "How marvelous you didn't have a game today!"

"Amen to that." Brady chuckled at their enthusiasm. "And thank you for having me."

"Shame you couldn't go home to see your mama for Christmas," Rena said with a sympathetic shrug.

"Just before the play-offs?" Abbey exclaimed. "Are you kidding me?" She turned to face Brady. "Still, a good boy would've offered to fly his mama up for a visit at Christmastime."

Brianna chuckled from across the room.

"Oh, trust me." He raised his hands in the air for emphasis. "I've tried again and again to get her here, but I finally decided I should wait till spring. You'll just have to trust me on this." He paused then rubbed his belly. "Something smells mighty good."

Brady could hardly understand a word after that. All of the women began to talk at the same time, each giving a dissertation on the food items she'd prepared.

Only Brianna, who'd started to slice the turkey, remained silent. He looked at her as she lifted the knife and gave her a warm smile.

When she returned the gesture, he walked over to her and took the knife from her hand.

"Allow me," he said with a wink.

She took a step back and shrugged. "Sure." Her cheeks flushed pink. "And thanks."

"You're welcome."

He went to work, carving like a pro. All the while he watched her out of the corner of his eye as she finished up the other dishes. At one point he almost got so distracted, the knife slipped.

Better watch what you're doing, Campbell. Don't want to lose a finger.

He gave Brianna another look, then turned back to his work, determined to stay focused.

Nope. Better not lose a finger. Not when he'd already lost his heart.

Chapter 18

January blew in with a vengeance, bringing a northeaster with it. Brady watched, astounded, as a blanket of white covered the whole city of Pittsburgh on the Saturday morning of a critical play-off game. He drove through heavy snow squalls, doing his best to maneuver the car on slick, ice-packed roads on his way to the stadium. Tree limbs, broken from the weight of clinging ice, littered the roadways. Even the rooftops seemed heavy with snow.

He half expected another one of those it's-cold-up-there calls from his mother, but he was thankful she held back.

Good thing, too. He would've had a hard time convincing her that this whole playing-in-a-storm thing was a piece of cake. In truth he was worried, not just about the journey to town, but today's play-off game against Denver, as well. Though he'd managed a couple of games on a muddy, snow-caked field, there was something to be said for indoor stadiums.

Still, he would give it his all.

By late morning, Brady arrived at the stadium and found the field to be mushy and white. He couldn't shake a stuffy nose and a lingering headache he'd had since practice, but he suited up as always. He went through the usual motions, even prayed with the guys before heading out of the locker room. As he jogged out onto the field with his teammates, the near-white field almost blinded him. The field wasn't just hard to see; it was particularly difficult to maneuver. Brady looked up at the skies and willed the snow to stop.

Moments later he stood on the sidelines, waiting for the game to begin. Even with the warmers in his jersey, he couldn't stop shivering. Was it just the weather, or was he really sick? Regardless, he hoped the biting cold would dull to a chill once he started playing.

"You doing okay, Campbell?" Coach Carter asked.

"Yeah." He pressed his gloved hands together and worked them back and forth, back and forth.

"Careful with that." Carter gestured to Brady's fingers. "Don't rub your hands together between plays, even if you're cold. You'll lose your ability to coordinate them well later on."

"Ah." Brady had no idea what Coach meant but immediately stopped the rubbing.

"I see it happen all the time," Carter continued. "Players end up jamming fingers or getting stepped on." He slapped Brady on the back. "Just one more trick to playing in the cold. But you'll learn."

Yes." Brady nodded then looked up at the skies overhead. "I guess this would be a perfect opportunity to make good on that promise to melt the snow underneath my feet."

"Looks like it," Carter agreed. "Just do your best, son."

He nodded, and once he took the field, the roar of the crowd motivated him to jump in the game, regardless of the weather or the numbing headache.

The first quarter passed uneventfully. Whether it was the snow or a lack of the usual motivation, neither team managed to score.

By halftime the score was 6-3, with Denver taking the lead. The players drifted back to the locker room, clearly discouraged. Brady would have been, too, but by now the dull ache in his head had magnified. He pulled off his helmet and rubbed at his forehead to try to relieve the pain.

The coach sat the team members down and gave them a stern lecture. He focused on his offensive players, asking them to go the extra mile.

And that's just what Brady determined to do. He headed back out to the field at the start of the third quarter and played like a champ, headache or not.

Unfortunately Denver rose to the challenge as well. By the end of the third quarter, the score was tied, 21-21.

Coach Carter sent his men back out onto the field at the beginning of the fourth quarter with a rousing cheer and an insistence that they bring this one home. Less than five minutes later the snow began to fall in sheets. Brady could hardly see his hand in front of his face, let alone the ball flying through the air. He somehow lost his bearings at one point, jarred by the movement of a fellow player.

He felt disjointed, uncoordinated. It seemed the cold had a grip on his spine, causing his back to lock up.

"Not now," he grumbled. If he played his cards right, he still had one good play left in him this afternoon, one last chance to score. Then his team would end up on top and advance to play another game.

He shook off the headache as best he could and took advantage of an unexpected opportunity as they neared the end of the quarter.

Hurry, Brady—hurry.

He managed to snag the ball, then faced the monumental decision of passing it off to someone else or running it over the goal line himself.

With the torrent of white snow blinding him, he ran toward the goal, dodging opposing players at every turn.

At first.

He remembered every second of the play—his labored breaths, painful from the cold. His lungs, feeling as if they would explode. His head, feeling hot and heavy. Nearing the goal line with the ball clutched in his hands. Hearing the hopeful cheers from the crowd. Trying to slow his gait.

Everything after that seemed to move in slow motion.

Brady remembered colliding with another player. Heard the splintering sound of the impact. Felt a horrible jarring in his neck. Pondered why a jolt of electricity shot through him. Sensed his legs go numb. Wondered why the world began to spin.

After that everything faded to sepia tones. The rush of other players surrounding him brought a strange comfort. The appearance of the team doctor added a degree of curiosity. But the look of terror in Coach Carter's eyes threw everything into a tailspin.

Brady felt the oddest sensation of being the center of attention as paramedics rushed onto the field. He couldn't seem to get the shivering under control. He'd never felt such cold.

Through the fog Brady wondered, *Did I cross the goal line? Did I score?*

He also found himself wondering what his mother might be thinking. Was she watching the game?

"It's cold up there."

The shivering grew more exaggerated—from fear or the cold, he could not be sure. The pain in Brady's head intensified, and he tried to figure out why his legs felt like electricity still coursed through them. After a moment or two the pain dissipated, and he seemed to completely lose feeling in both legs.

"Son, can you hear me?" The paramedic looked at him intently, even snapping his fingers in Brady's face.

"S–sorry?" The roar of the crowd seemed deafening. Or was it whisper-quiet? He couldn't tell.

"Can you move your legs?" The paramedic shouted to be heard above the crowd.

"I—I. . ." Brady did his best to lift his right foot, but it refused to cooperate. Frustrated, he opted for his left.

Nothing.

The sting of tears in his eyes further blurred his vision. He shot out a prayer, not caring who heard. "Oh, God! Help me!"

He lay shivering for what seemed like an eternity before they placed him on a stretcher and loaded him into the ambulance.

Ambulance?

After that, everything faded to black.

❧

Brianna heard the scream from the bathroom and ran out into the living room to see what had Gran-Gran and her friends so worked up. Her grandmother sat on the edge of her seat, and Lora paced the room, wringing her hands.

"What happened?"

Gran-Gran looked up with tears in her eyes and shook her head.

Brianna glanced at Rena, who appeared to be the only one in the room not falling apart. "*What* happened?"

"It's Brady," Rena whispered. "He's been..." She pointed at the television set, and Brianna dropped onto the sofa next to her grandmother to watch. What she saw took her breath away. Brady lay in the midst of a snow-covered field, completely still. A team of paramedics worked on him feverishly, though she couldn't make heads or tails out of his injuries.

Right away her hands began to shake. Bree grabbed one of the throw pillows from the sofa and gripped it as tears filled her eyes. She found herself caught up in a memory of the night Daniel had been injured. Her sobs had been deafening, even more than the ladies' were now.

And she had known. Known Daniel would never play again. Known her dad had been responsible. Known...

This is why! This is why I can't stand the game. Why does this always seem to happen to the people I love? Why do they always end up hurt?

She drew in a deep breath and tried to remain calm as the truth settled in her spirit. Daniel had recovered from his injuries—internally and externally. He'd gone on to live a normal, healthy life. Surely the Lord would do the same for Brady. Wouldn't He?

Brianna turned her attention back to the television set, watching as the paramedics lifted Brady onto the stretcher and carried him away in the ambulance. Her heart felt broken in two, and she reflected on her earlier thoughts: *Why does this always seem to happen to the people I love? Why do they always end up hurt?*

The *people* I love? *They?*

So this wasn't just about Daniel anymore.

This was about her love for Brady, too.

How had she pushed down the feelings that now consumed her? How had she gone this many weeks—months—and not been honest with herself about how she felt about him? Why did it take something this catastrophic to convince Brianna that her feelings for him were deeper than she'd dared dream?

Oh, God, please touch him. Heal him. Protect him.

Brianna covered her face with her hands and wept. Gran-Gran reached to take her hand. "I know, honey."

Just three words. But they said it all.

Chapter 19

The next day Brady lay in the bed, unable to think clearly. Results of the initial tests, CT scans, and MRIs were inconclusive. But after sixteen hours the feeling had returned to his legs. Thank the Lord. Brady didn't know when he'd ever been as shaken. Both his faith and his body had taken a tumble over the past day or so.

And all for a losing game.

He couldn't throw off the fact that he'd come so close—*so* close.

And yet so far.

The doctor—a fellow who had introduced himself as David Grant—entered the room with a nod and a hint of a smile.

"Good news, I take it?" Coach Carter asked from his chair next to the bed.

"Well, no breaks. Nothing permanent. What we're looking at here is what's commonly referred to as a stinger injury."

Brady nodded and remembered a fellow player in Tampa who'd been off his feet for days with a stinger injury.

"The nerves that give feeling to the arms and hands start out in the neck area." Dr. Grant reached to a spot at the back of Brady's neck. "Nerve injury often happens when the athlete makes a hard hit using his shoulder. The direct blow to the top of the shoulder drives it down and causes the neck to bend toward the opposite side."

"I felt it when it happened," Brady said.

"No doubt. We're talking about a motion that does a whopper of a job stretching or compressing the nerves, to the point where it triggers a pretty intense discharge of electricity. For a few seconds the electricity shoots down the nerves to the tips of the fingers."

"Felt that, too. Just after the impact."

"In your case," Dr. Grant said, "the spinal cord in your neck was bruised during the impact, causing your whole body to be affected from the neck down, not just your arms. We see this occasionally, though it always gives the patient and the doctor quite a scare."

Carter stood and began to pace the room.

Brady watched his coach out of the corner of his eye as he propped himself up in the bed. He still fought a lingering headache. "But this isn't permanent,

215

right?" he asked. He just needed to hear it again, to assure himself.

"Well, your symptoms—pain and tingling in both arms and legs—have passed," Dr. Grant explained. "There are no cracks. No breaks. Nothing like that. Once we have determined that your sense of feeling, strength, neck motion, and reflexes have returned to normal, you will likely be able to return to the game next season."

"Likely?" Carter and Brady spoke in unison.

"Look." Dr. Grant pulled up a chair next to the bed and took a seat. "I've seen this before—where an athlete has a stinger injury—then doesn't wait until he's completely healed before jumping back into the game. The goal here is to prevent a recurrent stinger. If you take another hit, your injuries will likely be more severe. We could even be talking permanent nerve damage if you're not careful. So no practices, nothing like that, for a while. We want to err on the side of caution. And I mean that."

"Right." Carter nodded. "And we put these guys through an exercise regimen at the beginning of each season to develop full range of motion in those muscles. We'll keep a close eye on him, I promise."

"Good." Dr. Grant turned back to Brady. "In the meantime I'm referring you to an orthopedic doctor, and he'll perform a thorough evaluation of your neck, shoulders, and nerves."

"Here? In the hospital?"

"Nah. No need for that. Oh, and by the way—"

"Yes?"

"You have a low-grade fever. Have you not been feeling well?"

"I had a terrible headache last night," Brady said. "Felt a little woozy. And I've been kind of stuffy. I wondered if the shivering was from the cold or something else."

"Ah. Well, we've seen a lot of flu-type symptoms going around, so I'll put you on a decongestant for that. Could be that's what had you so off balance in the first place."

"Thanks," Brady said. Then with a sigh he leaned back against the pillows.

"Just so you know," Dr. Grant said with a sympathetic smile, "you've played great all season. Everyone in this city is proud of you. And right now they're just rooting for you to get better so you can come back next season."

"He's right, Brady," Coach Carter said with a nod. "That's the important thing here—getting you better. And not *just* because of the game."

Brady smiled his thanks.

"Okay." The doctor nodded. "I'm releasing you. Just make sure you have someone with you over the next few days. Head and neck injuries are nothing to ignore. You'll need to be watched."

"We'll make sure of that," Carter said.

"Okay, well, be looking for a nurse to show up in about an hour or so with your discharge papers. You can go ahead and get dressed if you like." He walked out of the room, saying something about writing a prescription for pain.

Carter gave him an inquisitive look. "You okay, son?"

"Yeah."

"I wanted to let you know the mayor called this morning to check up on you."

"He did?"

"Yes, and someone from the governor's office, too. They're all rooting for you."

"Wow." Brady shook his head at the thought of it.

"Of course, a dozen or so reporters are hanging around in the lobby of the hospital, so we'll have to make a statement on the way out. Just wanted to get you psychologically prepared for that."

"It'll be fine." Brady smiled.

"Great." Carter glanced at his watch. "I'm going downstairs and make a couple of calls before we leave. Just call my cell when they've discharged you, and I'll meet you downstairs to take you home. And don't worry—I'll make sure you get back and forth to your doctor's appointments, that sort of thing. We'll take care of everything. You just rest easy."

"Yes, sir."

Seconds later Brady found himself alone in the room—alone with his thoughts. He felt torn between being thankful God had spared him from a more serious injury and regretting that he'd fallen short of the goal line. He hadn't led his team to victory. For whatever reason, that brought on a nagging feeling of guilt. He couldn't shake it.

Then again, guilt seemed to be his middle name.

Maybe it had something to do with the call from his mother late last night. She'd been in quite a state, and he couldn't blame her. He knew how desperately she wanted to come, but he'd insisted she not fly up there with the weather so bad. Besides, he'd told her, he would recover within days. By the time she could travel, he'd be feeling great.

She promised to come in the spring, as soon as the snows cleared. He hoped the weather would cooperate; otherwise, he'd never live it down.

He thought about that for a while. Maybe he placed too much stock in what people thought, even people he cared about deeply. Maybe that's where the guilt came from—caring too much.

Or maybe he could blame it on the look in Brianna's eyes when she'd come by for an unexpected visit this morning. Just the idea that she'd forged through the storm to visit him had brought a sense of hope. . .expectation.

Brady closed his eyes and reflected on the pain in her expression. Looking at those eyes had convinced him of one thing.

She cared about him.

She didn't have to say it. Not yet, anyway. But he knew, as Abbey had said, in his knower. He knew Brianna had come to see him because she cared.

And soon enough, if the Lord continued to work in such a miraculous way, he would be ready to tell her how much he cared, too.

Brady smiled as he thought about their visit. So many good things had come out of it. For the first time in weeks they'd talked. Really talked. She had even shared a few tears and an apology.

He reflected on that part—how she'd finally told him her reasons for hating the sport. She explained about Daniel's terrible injury and the forgiveness she'd finally been able to offer her father after so many years of holding a grudge.

Her tears had flowed as she shared about her past and the changes she'd been through in recent weeks. Brady's favorite part was her embarrassed confession—what fun!—that she'd finally started watching the games—in spite of her fears that someone, like him, for example, might be hurt.

The look in her eyes as she'd gazed at him made every bit of the pain worthwhile.

Oh, how wonderful it had been to spend an hour with her, just talking—about their hopes and dreams. Their pasts. Their futures.

Brady's eyes opened, and he half expected to see her standing there beside him, her hand clutched tightly in his own.

If the Lord responded favorably to his prayers, one day she would be.

❧

On the day after Brady returned home from the hospital, Brianna took a meal to his home. She stood at his front door, bundled in her heaviest coat and clutching a plate of food in her hand. It contained several of his favorites—meat loaf, fried bread, and the creamiest mashed potatoes in town—and she was happy to deliver it. In fact, everything about being with Brady made her happy, and she was finally ready to admit it.

After a couple of knocks the door opened. Brianna gasped as she saw both of his eyes completely blackened.

"Oh! You look worse than you did in the hospital."

"Humph. I don't know whether to thank you or be offended," he said with a weak smile. He gestured for her to enter the house, which she did with a shiver.

"Hungry?"

"Always!" He took the plate from her and led the way to the kitchen, where he pulled back the plastic wrap, then looked up with a big smile. "Thank you so much."

He set the plate on the table and pulled out a chair for her. Brianna hardly knew how to react. How long had it been since a man had offered this gesture of kindness and chivalry? Ah, yes. Christmas Day. Brady had done the same thing when they'd shared Christmas dinner together. It had felt good then, and it felt even better now that they were actually alone together. She slipped into the chair, feeling more comfortable around him today than ever.

Brady took a seat next to her and looked back down at the food, his eyes lit. "A couple of the guys from the team stopped by with take-out last night," he said. "But it's not the same as Abbey's great cooking. This is certainly worth thanking God for." And he did. His prayer was simple and heartfelt. Afterward he took a bite of the meat loaf then sat back with a sigh. "Ah, yes. She's a pro. Gotta give her that."

Brianna finally worked up the courage to tell him something. "Actually I, um"—she did her best not to blush—"I made the food this time."

"Really?" He gave her an admiring smile. "Well, you've acquired her talent; that's for sure."

"You think so?" She watched him as he took another bite and nodded. "I've been working at it."

"It's great."

As he continued to eat, Brianna took silent assessment of his injury, at least the part visible to the eye. She wondered how deep the wounds went, psychologically speaking. This must be quite a blow, especially knowing he'd have to take it easy for a while. Should she ask him about it? With more sighs coming forth from him, she opted for Plan B: food and chitchat.

She would give her questions to the Lord as she lifted Brady's name in prayer each day. And she would also ask the Lord something else, too.

She would ask Him if He would give her the desires of her heart.

Chapter 20

The following Sunday morning, after a week of snow, the city of Pittsburgh remained blanketed in white. Brianna wouldn't have gone to church, even if the weather had cooperated. She called the pastor's wife early in the morning to explain their predicament. Gran-Gran was sick. Really sick. She'd been fighting a cold for days, and it seemed to have settled into her bronchial tubes.

Mitzi prayed over the phone and let her know others would be praying. A second telephone call, this one to the doctor, relieved Brianna's mind a little. He'd been happy to call in some antibiotics to the pharmacy, but he cautioned her to keep a close watch on her grandmother. And that's just what she did.

Under other circumstances Gran-Gran would've laughed it off. She always managed to remain positive and upbeat, even in times of sickness. But this time she kept herself quiet and still under the bedcovers, coughing and trembling as the fever peaked. Brianna made sure she administered the medication every four hours, along with aspirin.

As she did she prayed fervently that the sickness wouldn't develop into pneumonia. She found herself given over to that concern, however, on more than one occasion. What would she do if she needed to get Gran-Gran to the doctor's office or the hospital in a hurry? The roads were in such a mess. Would she have to call for an ambulance?

About ten thirty in the morning, Brianna went into her grandmother's bedroom to check on her. She found her tossing and turning in the bed, clearly uncomfortable.

"Is there anything I can get for you, Gran?"

"Hmm? Oh, Bree, is that you?" Her grandmother looked up with glazed eyes. "I think I was dozing."

"You look a little restless to me," Brianna observed. "Can I get you something from the kitchen? Do you need some hot tea? Or maybe you're ready for some chicken soup? I've been downstairs cooking all morning."

"In a few minutes, maybe." Her grandmother sat up in the bed, and a coughing fit erupted. When she finally finished, she looked at Brianna and sighed. "I'm not having much fun with this."

"I hear ya. I've been praying. I know Brady is, too."

"Brady." Gran-Gran's eyes lit up for the first time that day. "How is that boy?"

"Oh, he's recovering slowly," Brianna said with a shrug. "I've been over to his house off and on, taking food."

"Caring for two invalids at once is a lot to ask from one girl," Gran-Gran said. "And you're a doll to do it. I know we're both grateful." She paused a minute and shook her head. "It's Sunday, right?"

"Right."

"I don't even know if I feel up to watching the next play-off game, to be honest."

"Whoa." Brianna sat on the edge of the bed and placed her palm against her grandmother's forehead. "You really are sick, aren't you?"

Gran-Gran nodded then looked toward the window. "Is it still snowing out?"

"No. Nothing since last night. But I watched the forecast on television this morning, and they're asking folks to stay put in their houses." Brianna glanced over at her grandmother's bedside table, her gaze falling on a tiny, framed black-and-white photo. She'd seen it hundreds of times before, naturally, but this time it seemed to affect her in a different way.

"You're looking at Katie." Gran-Gran's weak voice took her by surprise, and for a minute Brianna felt like a kid caught with her hand in the cookie jar.

"She was really pretty."

"You looked just like that when you were three," her grandmother said with a nod.

"I did?"

Her grandmother reached to pick up the tiny frame, which trembled in her hand. "I always imagined she would've turned out just like you if she'd lived. I just know she would have. And so many times. . ." She got choked up.

"What, Gran?"

"So many times I've thanked God for sending you here to me. He gave me a second chance with a little girl."

Brianna laughed. "Well, I wasn't exactly a little girl when I came to you, was I?"

A serious look came into her grandmother's eyes. "You were on the inside. You were a hurt little girl, needing someone to reach out to love her."

A lump filled Brianna's throat as she thought about that. As always, Gran-Gran had hit the nail right on the head, though this one carried a bit of a sting.

"I told you on Christmas Day that I've been praying the Lord will restore my relationship with your father," her grandmother said with a slight sigh.

"Yes."

"I've been praying the same thing for you, too—that God will restore *your* relationship with your father."

Brianna stood and began to pace the room. "It's not so bad. I mean, we're civil and all. You saw how it was when he was here. We didn't argue or anything. I think we're making progress."

"Right." Her grandmother paused for a moment before responding. "But a relationship—a real one—is more than distant, guarded conversations. A relationship is—"

"It's what *we* have." Brianna sat once again and took her grandmother's hand in her own, as tears dampened the edges of her lashes. "And, to be honest, my relationship with you has been the healthiest one of my life. You're my best friend, Gran."

"Same here, pretty girl." Her grandmother's hand trembled in her own. "But that doesn't keep me from longing for the same with my son. In fact, it makes me want it more—for both of us."

Brianna thought about that before saying anything. "What can we do?" she asked.

"Hmm. I've been thinking on that a lot. Prayer, of course. We'll continue to pray. But in order to achieve a genuine breakthrough, I think I need to ask your father for forgiveness."

"Forgiveness? For what?"

A single tear slipped down her grandmother's cheek, breaking Brianna's heart. What could Gran-Gran possibly need to ask forgiveness for?

"I started telling you a story on Christmas Day."

"Started?"

"Yes. Remember I told you I'd leave the rest for another day?"

"Ah." Brianna nodded as the memory surfaced. "I remember now. You did say that." She gave her grandmother an inquisitive look. "What's the rest of the story, Gran?"

"The part I left out was this." Her grandmother's eyes filled with pain. "After I lost Tommy and the baby, I was the emptiest, most brokenhearted girl I knew. I couldn't seem to relate to the other girls. They were silly and flighty and had never been through anything like what I'd been through." She sighed deeply. "And the worst part was, I couldn't even tell any of them. I cried myself to sleep every night. It was the only relief I was afforded. That, and of course forgiveness from the Lord, which came many years later when I finally gave my heart to Him."

Brianna reached to squeeze her hand.

"I want to tell you about how I came to be courted by your grandpa Norman," Gran-Gran said with a smile. "He was tall, dark, and handsome, just like you read about in books. Worked at the filling station."

"I never knew that."

"It's true." Gran-Gran's eyes lit with pleasure. "I'd go over there with my dad to gas up the car and buy a soda pop or candy bar, that sort of thing."

"So Grandpa was really handsome?" Brianna asked with a grin. She had a hard time imagining such a thing but didn't say so.

"Like a movie star," Gran-Gran insisted with a nod. "And for whatever reason he seemed to take a liking to me. I knew my papa liked that notion. He wanted me to marry. I think he felt sorry for me, though he never came out and said so."

"Oh, I'm sure he did."

"Norman was a nice man and had lived in our little town forever. He was just the right kind of boy for me, kindhearted and stable. From a nice family. We all went to the same church, attended the same functions, had so many things in common."

"So he asked you to marry him?"

Her grandmother smiled. "Well, after a proper courtship. We married in the spring of '47. Things were really good those first few years. But when you enter into a relationship with an untold secret like the one I carried, it's only a matter of time before things get sticky."

"So you didn't tell him about Tommy?"

"Oh, he knew about Tommy," Gran-Gran explained. "They'd been friends. . . schoolmates. Norman didn't know about—"

"Oh." The baby.

She closed her eyes. "I wanted to tell him. I can't tell you how many times I started to. Especially after we'd been married a couple of years or so. He wanted a child, and I"—her voice broke—"I just didn't know if I could handle the idea. But I couldn't tell him why."

Brianna shook her head, trying to imagine how hard that must have been—for both of them.

"Your father was born in 1951," she explained. "He was a handsome boy, the spitting image of his father. And in my heart I loved him so much. But. . ." She shook her head. "I don't know how to explain it, but I just couldn't seem to get close to him." Her eyes flooded with tears, and Brianna's heart nearly broke in two.

"That's not unusual after losing a child, Gran," she whispered. "It's hard to show affection to the next one. I've heard about that."

"But it wasn't fair to him—or to your grandfather." Gran-Gran began to cry and then started coughing again. When she finally calmed down, she explained. "I loved your grandpa, even if it wasn't quite the same kind of love I'd had for Tommy. I was a wonderful wife. Did all the right things. Thought he would never find out, but. . ." She closed her eyes while more tears fell.

Brianna watched in silence, whispering a prayer that the Lord would get her grandmother through this. Somehow she knew cleansing would come with the telling of this story. And understanding. And hope for the future—for their family.

"It happened when your father was just a toddler," Gran-Gran whispered. "Your grandpa Norman was searching through the drawers in our dresser for a savings bond. He stumbled across my photo of Katie, the one my aunt Nadine had sent. I. . .I. . ." She shook her head, and for a moment Brianna thought she wouldn't be able to go on. "I thought about lying to him. I knew my mother would expect me to. And my aunt, though she had softened. But I couldn't do it. I took one look at that photo in his hands and told him everything."

"W–what happened?"

Gran-Gran bit her lip and didn't say anything for a minute. Finally she said, "He handed the picture back to me, told me to destroy it. Said we'd never mention it again to another living soul. I couldn't tear up the photo, so I hid it away. But from that day on, things were never the same between us. He became angry, distant. We went through the motions of being a married couple, but in reality we were both so far apart."

Brianna could hardly imagine her grandmother living through such pain.

"It was all so sad." Gran-Gran drew in a deep breath. "Funny thing is, I really loved the man. Loved him till the day he died. And you can blame him for my love of football." A hint of a smile graced her lips. "It was the one thing we had in common those last few years. We'd sit together and watch the games, and for just a few hours we were close. We could talk together and laugh. When the game was on I almost felt like all was right with the world—that nothing had ever happened to pull us apart. And I think he felt it, too. In fact, I'm sure he did."

She leaned back against the pillows and closed her eyes.

"Do you need to stop for a while, Gran-Gran?" Brianna asked.

"Just one last thing I need to tell you," her grandmother whispered. "Your father. . ."

"Yes?"

"He never knew."

"About Katie?"

"That's right. He never knew about her."

Confusion filled Brianna. "But you've kept her picture out for everyone to see."

"No. Only here at the house. And he rarely comes here. When he does he never seems to notice—least he's never asked about it. I've needed to tell him for years. I really want him to know. I feel like I need to ask his forgiveness for not being the kind of mother he needed, for pushing him away as a youngster when I should have drawn him close. The Lord has forgiven me"—her voice broke—"but I need the forgiveness of my son. I need it something awful."

Brianna tried to think of something to say, but no words would come. So many things swirled through her head at once, and her heart seemed to be caught up in the confusion. Just when she thought she couldn't absorb one more thing, Gran-Gran's eyes fluttered open once again.

"Was there something else, Gran?" she managed.

"I was just thinking of Brady."

"What about him?"

Her grandmother let out a lingering sigh. "I know he has a rocky past, and I can certainly relate to that. I also see how much he regrets his mistakes. I'm sure he wishes he could do it all over again. I see regret written on his face every time someone brings up his days in Tampa."

Brianna's heart twisted inside her at these words. She had been so hard on Brady in the beginning. How she regretted that now.

"But when I consider the two of you together as a couple," her grandmother continued with a smile, "I feel so hopeful. You've already opened up and shared about your issues with your dad, and he's told you his mistakes and failures. You've both come clean. There are no untold stories, no lingering secrets."

Brianna nodded. "Right."

"That's the best way to start a relationship, honey. The only way. With honesty. Each of you coming into it healed and whole, completely forgiven. Knowing without a doubt that God loves you and has washed you clean—as individuals. When you do that, you stand the best chance for a long, happy life together, with God at the center of your union."

"Union?" Brianna whispered the word. "Do you think—?"

Gran-Gran smiled. "I've spent a lot of time with the Lord in the past few weeks, and I sense what He's up to. I'm just so glad to know He's already done a healing work in you—and in Brady. The hardest part is truly behind you."

"Mm-hmm."

The only thing Brianna could think of was the scripture her grandmother had reminded her of on Christmas Day—the one about being as white as snow, about being washed, made clean. She wanted to remind Gran-Gran of that but couldn't seem to speak.

She wanted something else, too.

For the first time in a long while Brianna wanted to pick up the phone and call her dad.

❧

Brady paced around the house late Sunday morning, restless. Every time he thought about today's play-off game between Denver and Cincinnati, he felt ill. *We should have been the ones playing today. I should have led my team to victory.*

He began to pour out his heart to the Lord, all the while circling the living room like a caged tiger, leaving track marks in the carpet. On and on he went, emptying himself of the frustration and eventually receiving much-needed peace in its place.

When he finally reached the point where he could think clearly, Brady picked up the telephone to call Brianna.

If he couldn't play the game, he would at least watch it—with the woman he loved.

Chapter 21

Brianna took extra time getting ready for Brady's arrival. She planned to wear her pink sweater and jeans and put on the tiniest bit of makeup. Then she would warm up the chicken soup and rolls, just in case he hadn't eaten lunch. All of this she did with a renewed sense of anticipation. And a few butterflies. She hadn't felt this way since. . .

Hmm. She didn't recall ever feeling this way. But she certainly liked the way she felt.

With Gran-Gran sleeping upstairs, she and Brady would have a chance to settle down on the sofa side by side and watch the game. Of course, she was still on a learning curve where the plays were concerned, but surely he wouldn't mind that. He might even be grateful for the chance to share his expertise.

Just about the time she climbed out of the shower, the doorbell rang. "What?" He was early. Almost an hour, in fact. She scrambled into a robe, wrapped her hair in a towel, and sprinted down the stairs. When she inched the front door open enough to ask him to give her a few minutes, she came face-to-face with Rena instead.

"Afternoon, Bree!" Rena pushed the door open and gasped. "Oh, my! You're in your robe." She quickly shut the door behind her, almost dropping the Crock-Pot she held in her hands.

"What's that?" Brianna asked. She certainly hadn't been expecting a food delivery today. Perhaps Gran-Gran had arranged it without telling her.

"Beef stew. Thought it might make Abbey feel better."

"Well, I made—"

"I just know she loves my beef stew," Rena added. "And with the big game coming, she needs to keep up her strength in order to cheer with the rest of us."

Rest of us? "Oh, well, she's not going to watch the game," Brianna explained. "She's sleeping."

"What?" Rena's stunned expression spoke volumes. "I don't believe it. Abbey? Miss a play-off game? Impossible!"

"She's really sick," Brianna said. "And it's probably not a good idea for you to be here. Likely she's contagious."

"Oh, pooh. I've had my flu shot. And I never get sick anyway. I have the strongest constitution in town. It's all that starch I eat. Gives me a backbone.

226

Now just let me get this off to the kitchen, and then I'll stay and watch the game with you."

"Well, I—" Brianna never had the chance to finish her sentence. Rena disappeared into the kitchen.

Brianna had just turned to sprint back up the stairs when the front doorbell rang again. She let out a groan, then inched the door open once more. This time she found Lora on the other side, clutching a large pan in her hands.

With a sigh Brianna swung the door open and ushered the woman inside. "What have we here?" she asked, though the smell gave it away.

"Corned beef and cabbage," Lora responded. "Best thing in the world for opening up the sinuses. Abbey will be well in no time."

No doubt. "Rena's already in the kitchen. I'm headed upstairs to get dressed. Brady's going to be here—"

A knock at the door interrupted her sentence.

"Would you get that?" Brianna whispered. "I have to get dressed."

"Of course, of course." Lora set the pan down on the coffee table then turned to open the door just as Brianna disappeared up the stairwell. Her heart thumped like mad all the way up the stairs. She could hear Brady's voice as he and Lora shared their hellos. His boisterous laugh rang out through the house, and Brianna felt a wave of relief wash over her. Apparently he didn't mind that two elderly women would be joining them today.

Make that three.

Just as she neared the upstairs bathroom, Gran-Gran made an appearance in the hallway, dressed in her robe, her hair piled all topsy-turvy on her head.

"What are you doing up?" Brianna scolded.

Her grandmother gave her a puzzled look. "I heard voices. Woke me up. Thought maybe it was a heavenly choir. Gave me a bit of a jolt."

"Very funny."

"Who's here? And why?"

"Everyone and their brother." Brianna let out a sigh. "And they've come to watch the game."

"Ah." Gran-Gran nodded. "I forgot to uninvite the ladies. They always see a game as a standing invitation. Are you upset?"

"Nah. I suppose it just wouldn't be right without them." Brianna gave her grandmother a motherly look. "But none of this explains why you're up and about. You should be in bed."

Gran-Gran shrugged. "I'm feeling better. My fever broke, and that decongestant you gave me really worked wonders."

"Uh-huh. Sure it did." Brianna stood in the doorway of the bathroom, gazing into the red-rimmed eyes of the woman she loved more than almost anyone else in the world. She wouldn't argue with her about something as silly as a football game. If her grandmother wanted to watch the game, she would watch the game, no arguments.

"Kickoff is in twenty minutes."

"I know." Brianna laughed. "I'm trying to get dressed, but no one will let me."

"Please." Her grandmother gestured toward the bathroom. "Be my guest." She gave her a wink. "And while you're at it, wear your blue sweater."

"Blue sweater? Why?"

Gran-Gran gave a little giggle then added, "I have it on good authority someone thinks it brings out the color of your eyes."

"Aha." Her cheeks warmed, and she closed the bathroom door to avoid any further embarrassment.

Brianna spent the next ten minutes slipping into her clothes, blow-drying and styling her hair, and applying a bit of lip gloss. All the while she thought about Brady.

Hmm.

Maybe she'd better not think *too* much about him while trying to apply mascara. The trembling in her hands made for a messy application.

Still—she gazed at herself in the mirror. Could he ever really love someone like her?

Love. Hmm.

She stared at her reflection, noticing the peaceful expression in her eyes. Oh, how wonderful it felt. Then with a happy heart she descended the stairs. Brady met her at the bottom step, his eyes growing wide as he saw her.

"You look great," he whispered. "That blue sweater is—"

He didn't finish the sentence, but she didn't care. The look on his face told her everything she needed to know. She managed to whisper a gentle thank-you and found herself unable to look into his eyes without blushing. *I feel like a schoolkid.*

Oh, well. There were worse things.

Brady took her by the hand, a gentlemanly gesture, for sure, and helped her down the last stair. She took hold of his hand as if she wouldn't have made it otherwise.

"Where are the ladies?" she asked.

"In the kitchen, warming up the food." He laughed but never let go of her hand. "I peeked. We're going to have a, uh, rather unusual meal."

"I think the corned beef and cabbage threw us over the edge," she agreed. "But don't feel as if you have to eat any or all of it. They think you're pretty special whether you eat their food or not."

His fingers gently intertwined hers, and he gazed into her eyes. "What about you?"

Her breath caught in her throat as she pondered his question. Did he want to know if she thought he was special or—?

"What did you cook?" he asked with a wink.

"Ah." She grinned. "Chicken soup."

"Ironic."

"Oh?"

"I have a hankering for chicken soup today. Call it a coincidence."

"Mm-hmm. Sure."

Just then something distracted them. The sound of three elderly women coming down the hallway toward the living room, chattering all the way.

"D–did you h–hear that?" Rena asked, breathless. "We're missing the k–kickoff."

"Oh?" Brianna pulled her hand out of Brady's, but not before her grandmother took note of it. The look of pure joy in her eyes was worth any amount of embarrassment. "Seems we have a game to watch," Brianna said, gazing up into his eyes. "Are you ready?"

"I'm ready." He reached once more for her hand, and together they walked into the living room to join the others.

❧

Brady sat on the love seat next to Brianna for most of the game. Most of it. Part of the time he paced the room, talking to the television screen. Not that anyone outside of this living room could hear him, but it did make him feel better. And the women seemed to get a kick out of it. Once Lora even leaped into position, pretending to catch the ball in midair. He smiled.

He wanted Denver to win, naturally. Needed them to win. What good would it do for the team that had taken them down to turn around and lose to someone else?

Midway into the fourth quarter, with Denver lagging behind, something occurred to Brady. What did it matter in the grand scheme of things? A game won. A game lost. Wasn't God in control, and wouldn't He work it all together for His good?

As the game came to its woeful conclusion, the four women sat with stunned looks on their faces. Most stared Brady's way, likely waiting for a comment. For a moment not a sound was heard in the place.

Well, unless Rena chomping on potato chips counted. "Well, that's that." She stood and folded up the bag, closing it with a chip clip. "C'mon, everyone. Let's go into the kitchen and have some apple pie," she suggested. "It just came out of the oven and looks delicious. I'll even dish up some ice cream to put on top."

"In this weather?" Lora argued. "You want ice cream?"

"Of course! What good would apple pie be without it?"

"Rena," Abbey scolded, "you told me just this week that you were starting a diet."

"Yeah, I thought about it," Rena said with a shrug. "But I've decided the older you get, the tougher it is to lose weight. By then your body and your fat are really good friends. And I've never been one to break up a friendship. You know that."

Brady tried not to laugh but couldn't hold it back for long. He was glad that within seconds everyone else joined in, even Rena.

"Well, you can't say I didn't give it some thought," she said with a shrug. "Now come on. Let's go get that pie."

Brianna and Brady followed the women into the kitchen where they all sat together at the table. Rena set the pie in the middle of the table and began to slice hefty triangles.

After swallowing down several bites of the warm cinnamony stuff topped with vanilla ice cream, an idea occurred to Brady, one he had to act on. He turned to Brianna. "Wanna go for a walk?"

"What? It's freezing outside. Are you sure? You've been sick."

"I've been well for days," he argued. "But if it makes you feel better, we'll bundle up. I just really need to get outside and walk."

"In the snow?" Rena said with a snort.

"Rena, leave them alone," Abbey instructed. She looked Brady's way and gave him a wink. "You kids go on now and take a walk. Don't mind us. We've got things to do."

"We do?" Lora asked.

"Yes." Abbey rose from her chair and grabbed some pens and stationery. "We're writing letters to every player on the Pittsburgh team, congratulating them on such a good season." She looked up at Brady with a big smile. "Will you make sure they get them?"

"I will." He nodded, then followed Brianna as she rose from the table and headed toward the coat closet. Once there she slipped on a heavy winter coat, gloves, a scarf, and a hat. He did the same, and within minutes they found themselves out on the sidewalk, easing their way through the white drifts that threatened to end their walk even before it began.

Finally they settled into an easy stride, only occasionally pausing to step over a patch of ice. Brianna pointed to the western sky. "I always think the sunset is prettier when the ground is covered in white."

Brady paused to look at it then nodded. The whole yard seemed to reflect the red-orange glow of the setting sun. He glanced back into Brianna's eyes, and she gave him a warm smile.

An invitation perhaps?

He reached for her hand, and she took it willingly. Even with gloves on he still felt the connection, still marveled at the fact that they had finally reached this point—where they knew they were falling in love.

They enjoyed a comfortable silence for a while before Brianna asked him a question. "How are you really feeling about everything that's happened over the past couple of weeks? And be honest."

"Well. . ." He paused to think about it. "Every player dreams of making it to the Super Bowl. But not every team can win every time. That's just the way it goes. It doesn't mean the Lord has suddenly stopped blessing my team when we lose a game; at least that's the way I look at it. I think maybe some of the guys on the other team just needed a boost."

She stopped walking and gave him an admiring look. "You're taking this really well."

He gazed into her eyes. "I have everything a man could ask for and more."

"Oh?"

He nodded. "I feel like the most blessed man on the planet this evening—championship or no championship." He gave her hand a squeeze, and she gazed up into his eyes with a hint of a smile on her face.

"Do you really mean that?" she whispered.

As he nodded, a light wind pulled a loose hair into her face. They both reached up at the same time to brush it aside. As their gloved hands met, Brady felt a rush of joy, sensing what was coming. He ran his fingertip lightly across her cheek, and she leaned into his palm and closed her eyes.

A cold wind blew around them then, and Brady remembered his mom's words: "*It's cold up there.*"

But as he leaned in to kiss Brianna, to whisper words of love into her ear, he had to conclude—there was nothing cold about it.

Chapter 22

On a Tuesday in late April, Brady drove to the airport with anticipation mounting. How long had he waited for this day? Months! Finally, finally, his mom was coming for a visit.

He met her inside at the baggage claim area. Brady laughed as he saw her approaching in her heavy winter coat, wool scarf, and mittens. The hot-pink hat topped off the ensemble. He gave her a bear hug, lifting her off her feet as he often did. "It's about time. I'm so glad you're here!"

"Brady, put me down. People are watching."

"Aw, what do we care?" In truth he'd gotten used to people snapping his photograph in public places, so if any paparazzi happened to be hanging about, they could snap their cameras at will. He truly didn't mind.

Then again maybe his mama did. He loosened her from the embrace and looked at her with a smile.

They gathered her bags then headed out to the parking garage. She gave the blue skies an accusing look and yanked the scarf from around her neck. "Well," she grumbled. "It's downright warm here."

"It's nearly May. What were you expecting?" Brady laughed as he pulled her two rolling suitcases in the direction of the car. Once they were settled inside, his mom pulled off her hat and gloves. She spent a few minutes catching him up on life in Florida, especially concerning his older brother.

"God has been doing a real work in Patrick's life over the past couple of weeks," she said.

"Oh?"

"I think we're seeing a real turnaround. And he's been calling me—a lot."

"It's all those prayers you've prayed," Brady said. "They're powerful."

"They are indeed." She gazed out of the window with a look of wonder on her face. Finally, for some unknown reason, she turned and punched Brady in the arm.

"W–what was that for?" he stammered.

"Flowers are blooming on the side of the highway."

"Uh, okay."

"Flowers."

He wasn't sure what that had to do with anything.

"Just like we have in Florida. And look at that—" She pointed off in the distance at the hills. "Why, that's about the prettiest thing I've ever seen. This place isn't at all like you made it out to be."

"What *I* made it out to be?" Brady erupted in laughter. "Mom, you're a hoot. A hoot. But I love you."

She looked at him with an admiring smile. "Yeah. I love you, too, kid. I don't think I tell you that enough." She paused, and then she was all business. "Now tell me—have you made up your mind how you're going to do it?"

"Yep." Brady nodded. "We're going to her office."

"You're proposing at her office?"

Brady's heart swelled at the word *proposing*. From the minute he'd made the decision, he hadn't been able to wipe the smile off his face. And he had the perfect plan for how to go about it. Oh, sure, his buddies had suggested waiting till the new season—flashing Brianna, Will You Marry Me? up on the scoreboard. But he had something a little more private in mind.

Hmm. Maybe *private* wasn't the best word, considering all the people who'd be there. He looked at his mom with a smile. "I'm not actually going to propose at the office. It's just that she's expecting me there for a meeting. I've hired her firm to renovate my new place. They're upgrading the kitchen and bathrooms and replacing all the light fixtures, that sort of thing."

"Ah. So we're picking her up and going over there?"

"Yes." He smiled. "But I've already been there. All morning, in fact. I fixed up the balcony with candles, roses, music. It's gorgeous. And I have the prettiest view, so it just seemed like the perfect place. If she says yes."

"If?" His mom gave him a reassuring look. "She'll say yes. If she's half the woman you say she is."

"Oh, trust me—she's probably double the woman I say she is." Brady grinned. "I don't think the dictionary has enough words to describe how wonderful she is."

"Well, then, I feel better about letting her have you. I couldn't have parted with you to just anyone, you know."

"I know. But, Mom, you're going to love her. I know you are." He thought back to what he'd been saying before. "If she says yes, I'm hoping we can get married in the summer, right after the renovations are finished on my new place."

He could see them there—married. Raising a family.

With all his heart he could see it.

પ્ર

Roger Stevenson appeared at Brianna's door with a smile on his face. "Hey."

"Well, hey to you, too." She yawned and leaned back in her chair. "What's up?"

"Oh, nothing much. Just wanted to make sure you remembered we're all going over to Brady's condominium to make some decisions about additional design features. He wants your input."

"Right." She smiled as she thought about Brady's inexperience with home remodeling and his insistence that she play a major role in all the selections, right down to the granite countertops and stone floor in the kitchen. "He's on his way here now to pick me up."

She'd no sooner said the words than Brady appeared behind Roger. Her boss shook his hand, then agreed to meet them in the lobby in ten minutes.

Brianna stood and gave Brady a warm hug as he entered the office. "Hi there."

"Hello to you, too." He gave her a tender kiss, one now so familiar that she didn't know how she'd ever lived without it.

Brady flashed a suspicious smile. "I want you to meet someone." He stepped back outside the door and reentered with an older—very tanned—woman in a bright pink T-shirt and jeans. She looked oddly familiar. Hmm. Might be the emerald green eyes. They matched Brady's exactly. Unless the crinkles around the edges counted. And the wide smile was familiar, too.

"You're—you're—" Brianna couldn't seem to get the words out.

The woman pushed her way past Brady and grabbed Brianna like a long-lost child. "You're Bree!" she squealed. "I've heard your name a thousand times if I've heard it once."

"And you're Cora." *Why didn't Brady tell me you were coming?*

"I am." The woman took Brianna by the hands, then stepped back to look her over from head to toe. "So you're the little darling my boy has fallen in love with."

Brianna felt her cheeks flush but nodded anyway. *I love him, too. More than anyone will ever know.*

"Well, let me tell you a thing or two about him," Cora said. "For instance, did you know he snores?"

"Mom." Brady crossed his arms and gave his mom a pretend warning look.

She waved him away then added with a whisper, "Like a freight train. And he leaves his socks on the floor."

Brady slapped himself on the head. "What are you trying to do, drive her away?"

"And," his mom continued with a gleam in her eye, "he's notorious for remembering people's birthdays and also for showing up unexpectedly with flowers in his hand for no good reason."

Brianna laughed. "So I've discovered. But I think I can live with that one."

Cora wrapped her in a motherly embrace, which she returned with a smile.

She loved this woman already. But why was she here? And why didn't Brady tell her she was coming?

Brianna glanced up at the clock on the wall, then reached for her purse. "Roger's probably already headed down to the lobby. Are you ready to go?"

"Oh, I'm ready, all right." Brady gave her a wide smile, and the sparkle in his eyes stopped her.

Yes, he appeared ready.

But she wasn't quite sure for what.

Chapter 23

Brady's mind reeled as he drove toward the condominium with both of the ladies chattering away. They didn't seem to notice his nervous condition. Good thing. He put his hand on his pocket for the hundredth time to make sure the box hadn't fallen out.

Nope. Still there. Just like the last time he'd checked. And the time before.

He went over the plan of action in his head, strategizing about how he would call her out onto the balcony to talk about patio furniture or some such thing. How he would drop to one knee and take her hand. How she would look down at him with a look of astonishment on her face.

His heart beat double-time as he thought about the suggestions his team members had made for what to say first.

"Tell her she's your first draft pick."

"Write *Will You Marry Me?* on a football and toss it to her."

"Ask her if she'll wear your jersey. . .for the rest of her life."

Brady chuckled, almost forgetting where he was.

"Everything okay?" Brianna looked at him.

He smiled and nodded. "Just thinking."

"Well, a penny for your thoughts then. I want to smile like that."

I hope you will. Soon.

He was thankful his mother—God bless her—swept Brianna up in yet another conversation. He would have to remember to thank her later.

In the meantime he'd better get back to making plans.

And quick.

❧

So many things about this day just didn't make sense.

Why Brady's mom showed up unannounced.

Why John and Roger Stevenson both insisted upon following them to the condominium to oversee the changes. They rarely got this involved.

Why Brady couldn't seem to stop smiling.

Why she had the uncanny sense something huge was about to happen.

They arrived at the condominium, and Cora chatted like a schoolgirl as they made their way to the front door where they were greeted by—Gran-Gran and her friends?

Okay, this is weird. Brianna turned to give Brady a questioning look. "What's going on?"

He shrugged. "I wanted them to meet my mom."

Hmm. Well, that *almost* made sense, though they certainly could have met later—at the duplex.

As they stood outside the front door, the proper introductions were made. Brianna could tell right away that her grandmother and Cora would be fast friends. They started an animated conversation, one she couldn't keep up with if she tried.

Even on a normal day. When things weren't so out of kilter.

Brady's hand appeared to be trembling, and he fumbled with the key in the lock.

"You okay?" she whispered.

He nodded, but his pale complexion said otherwise.

"Are you sick?"

"No, I, um. . .come on in." He ushered everyone inside, but Brianna remained behind with him.

"Brady, I'm worried about you. You're not telling me something."

"What makes you think that?"

"Well, for one thing, the fact that you look as if you're about to lose your breakfast. And for another—" Just then she glimpsed the inside of the condo. "Wow. They've already started working. I didn't realize." She swept past him and went to examine the kitchen, which was nearly finished. "How—?"

Roger entered, followed by his brother. "Brady wanted a rush job, so we've been on it for days."

"But I thought"—she turned to look at Brady—"I thought we were here to finish choosing materials today."

"Actually we're here because there's something I need to ask you."

"About the condo?"

"No." He gave her a faint smile and took her by the hand.

Why is his hand shaking?

Brady led her up the stairs and through the master bedroom, where he drew back the vertical blinds covering the sliding glass door that led to the balcony. Brianna gasped. The roses. The candles. The twinkling lights. They could mean only one thing.

"Brady," she whispered, then turned with tears in her eyes.

He slid open the door and ushered her outside. "After you." He gave her an impish smile, then looked out across the city. "I have the best view in town."

"Yes." She could hardly keep her emotions under control. "You're right about that."

"I can see myself out here in the morning with a cup of coffee."

"Mm-hmm."

"With you by my side."

"What?"

She turned to discover he had dropped to one knee. Tears rose to cover her lashes. "Oh, Brady."

"I love you, Bree," he said softly, taking her hand. "You're the best thing that's ever happened to me. And I know you're the reason God brought me here to Pittsburgh."

She tried to speak but couldn't. The lump in her throat wouldn't allow it.

He gazed up into her eyes and smiled. "I told you I have the best view in town, and I do. It's right here in front of me. If I could spend every morning of my life waking up to that smile—those eyes—that beautiful heart—I'd be the happiest man in town."

She nodded and managed to whisper, "I love you, Brady."

His eyes filled with tears, and he reached into his pocket, drawing out a tiny box. Her heart beat faster as he popped it open to reveal a large, exquisite marquise diamond in a white gold setting. Could this really be happening?

"I love you, Bree. I think I've loved you from the first day I saw you outside the duplex. And I've loved you more with every passing day. The more I get to know you, the more there is to love. You're the most giving, caring person I've ever known."

No, you are.

He grinned and gave her an innocent pleading look as he stammered the rest. "Will you—would you do me the honor of marrying me?"

She hardly remembered saying yes, barely remembered the feel of the ring as he slipped it on her finger.

What *would* stay with her—for the rest of her life—was the cheer that went up from the other side of the open sliding glass door.

Epilogue

On a Saturday afternoon in mid-July Brady suited up—not in his football uniform, but a tuxedo. He turned to Gary Scoggins, football player turned groomsman, for assistance. As always he was full of sage advice.

"Shake off the nerves, Campbell," Scoggins instructed. "No point in getting tensed up before the big game." He laughed as he realized his mistake. "I, uh, I mean big *day*."

"Okay." Brady went through a couple of his usual warm-up routines, though it proved to be difficult in a tux. His heart swelled with joy as he thought about all the Lord had done over the past several months. Seemed as if he'd lived in Pittsburgh forever.

His heart raced at the thought of marrying Brianna. *Why have You blessed me so much, Lord? You know my history. You know where I've come from. What did I ever do to deserve her?*

The answer came in the form of a gentle reminder that he was not the man he used to be. Not even close.

He glanced up at a sign on the wall, one he'd read dozens of times during the season: THE GAME OF LIFE IS A LOT LIKE FOOTBALL. YOU HAVE TO TACKLE YOUR PROBLEMS, BLOCK YOUR FEARS, AND SCORE YOUR POINTS WHEN YOU GET THE OPPORTUNITY.

Ironic. Especially when he considered the fact that they were getting married on the fifty-yard line.

A rap on the locker room door caused him to turn around. Brady's mouth dropped open when he saw his older brother standing there, looking spiffy in his black tux. Their mother stood at his side.

"I don't believe it!" Brady exclaimed. "I thought you said you couldn't come."

Patrick shrugged as he entered the room. He sauntered Brady's way and extended his hand. Brady took it. For a second. Then he grabbed his big brother and gave him a bear hug.

"I'm so glad you're here. It means so much to me."

"Well, I heard you needed a best man."

"You heard right." Brady glanced over at his mother, who looked stunning in her light blue dress. She moved in his direction, and he leaned down to whisper, "Thanks." Then he gave her a soft kiss on the cheek.

"No, I'm the one who's thankful," she whispered back. "You've done so much for me."

"Done so much?" What had he done, after all? Introduced her to three of the goofiest women he'd ever met? Watched as she'd fallen in love with the church—and the city? Moved her into his old duplex? Spiffed up the place to suit her taste? Created an opening between her side and Abbey's since they spent nearly every waking moment together anyway?

"Just one thing, Brady," she said, as she stepped back to give him a once-over. "What's that?"

She pulled a paper fan out of her purse and waved it back and forth in front of her face. "Why didn't you tell me it was so hot in Pittsburgh?"

The laughter that followed was probably heard out on the field.

⁊⁊

Brianna primped in front of the full-length mirror, amazed at the fairy-tale-like quality of the white gown and tiara. She truly felt like a princess. Her mother leaned over to insert another bobby pin to hold the veil in place.

Brianna heard a sniffle and turned to see who had walked into the room. She looked up into her father's tear-filled eyes and smiled, not just because he'd flown from L.A. to Pittsburgh to walk her down the aisle, but because the Lord had done such a marvelous work in their relationship over the past few months. Their weekly calls had progressed from awkward to genuine and heartfelt. And the fact that they had openly discussed the past—asking for and receiving forgiveness from one another—had sealed the deal.

Well, that and the fact that she'd fallen in love with a football player. Her father was more than a little happy to be getting a quarterback for a son-in-law, though he never came out and said so.

Not that Brianna minded. Her days of football angst were definitely behind her. No twinges of doubt left. She would start the new season as Pittsburgh's biggest fan.

A strain of music drifted in from outside, and Brianna looked up, startled. "Is it time already?"

"They told us to listen for the Vivaldi piece," her mom said. "So I'd better go take my seat. I'll see you in a few minutes!" She leaned over and gave Brianna a kiss on the cheek. "I love you, babe. And I'm so proud of you."

Brianna looked around the locker room, suddenly alarmed. "Where's Gran?" She couldn't get married without her matron of honor, now could she?

"I think she's disappeared on us," Brianna's father said.

Her grandmother appeared, right on cue. "Sorry, sorry! I had to make one more trip to the little girls' room, just in case. Thanks for waiting." She let out a giggle. "Nerves, I guess. I've waited all my life to step onto this field, but I never dreamed it would be for a wedding."

Brianna laughed. Leave it to her grandmother to make this entertaining.

"Do you think I look okay?" Gran-Gran asked as she joined her at the mirror.

"You're prettier than the bride," Brianna said.

"Oh, posh. Now that's just ridiculous." Her grandmother stepped up for a closer look, dabbing at her lipstick. "But I do look pretty good if I do say so myself."

"Yes, you do." In fact, she looked amazing in her sky blue dress. But there was something more. Gran-Gran glowed with both an inner beauty and an outer one. Now that was something one couldn't buy in a bottle or spread on with an applicator. No, this was a true-to-the-heart kind of beauty.

They stood, side by side, gazing into the mirror. In so many ways, Brianna saw herself in her grandmother's reflection, and vice versa. That revelation almost brought tears to her eyes. She couldn't think of anyone she'd rather be like than the woman who had poured so much into her.

Gran-Gran yanked up her skirt a few inches and fought with her slip. "Crazy thing," she muttered. "Hope it stays in place."

Brianna chuckled. "I certainly hope so, too. I can see the headlines now."

"Oh?" Her grandmother looked up, intrigued. "Do you think I'll make the papers again?"

"Well, not for *that*, I hope," Brianna said with a smile.

A shift in the music let them know the time had come. Abbey led the way, and Brianna followed behind on her father's arm. They made their way out of the locker room and onto the ball field, where rows of chairs had been strategically placed facing the fifty-yard line.

Even from quite a distance she could see Brady standing next to Pastor Meyers, waiting for her at the center of the field. A man who looked suspiciously like him stood to his left.

So Patrick came, after all.

Surely Cora had a hand in that. But how wonderful that Brady was finally able to communicate with his brother again.

She squeezed her dad's arm, and he glanced her way. "Doing okay?" he whispered.

Her eyes filled with tears, but she nodded anyway. When she thought back to that wounded young woman who'd boarded the plane to Pittsburgh years ago—when she reflected on how far she'd come—she couldn't help but cry.

She brushed back the tears and watched as Gran-Gran made the trip up the aisle on Gary Scoggins's arm. Sure, she moved a little slow, but everyone in attendance seemed quite taken with her, something Brianna knew she loved. As her grandmother took her place at the front on the pastor's right, Brianna's gaze landed on Brady. He looked stunned as he saw her for the first time in her wedding gown.

The bridal march began, and the moment she had waited for all her life arrived at last.

"Are you ready?" her father whispered.

She nodded, and they started the rehearsed march toward the fifty-yard line. Right, together. Left, together. Right, together. Left, together.

Oh, forget that.

"Can we pick up the pace?" she asked her dad with a wink.

When he nodded, she hiked her skirt up a couple of inches and sprinted—sprinted toward the goal.

OUT OF THE BLUE

Dedication

To my sisters, Connie. How wonderful it must be,
living so near those breathtaking Amish farms!
Thanks for that fun trip to Lancaster Country last spring.
I had a great time, and it was even more special
because I got to share it with you and Mom.

Prologue

Paradise, Pennsylvania

Stand still, Katie, or I might accidentally stick you with a pin."

Katie Walken stopped her twisting and turning long enough for her mother to finish pinning up the carefully measured hem of her new dress. She let out an exaggerated sigh, wishing she could be anywhere but here. Why Mamm and Aunt Emma had chosen Friday, her busiest day at the store, to finish a simple sewing project was beyond her.

She glanced down at the navy blue broadcloth and sighed. It hung heavy on her, like a weight, a burden in need of lifting. Oh, how she wished she could wear a pair of jeans and a T-shirt, like so many of the English girls who came into the store. And if only she could cut her cumbersome mane of brown hair into one of those trendy styles, tossing her white kapp for good. . . Then she would be happy.

The last few weeks had been filled with such longings. Katie pushed them aside at first, remembering her obligations, her strict Amish upbringing. But now, as the summertime crowd of tourists made their way through Lancaster County, as the outside world merged with her own once again, she could avoid the inevitable no longer. Katie ached for what she could not have—the life of an Englisher. One free of pointless restrictions.

Like this ridiculous blue dress.

The rocker in the corner creaked as her aunt Emma eased her weight back and forth, back and forth. "I wore that same shade of blue on my wedding day," she said with a smile. "I was just eighteen, like you."

"I'm not quite eighteen yet," Katie replied as she gave one of the sleeves a tug. "And I'm not altogether sure I will ever marry, in this dress or any other." She continued to pull at the fabric, wondering why it seemed to stifle her breathing.

"Of course you will!" Her mother eased another pin into the sturdy cloth. "Karl Borg will ask you to be his as soon as you turn eighteen." She gave Katie a little wink. "That boy has been smitten with you for as long as I can remember."

"Everyone in Paradise knows the two of you will marry in the fall," Aunt Emma concurred.

245

Katie did her best not to groan. Karl was her best friend, to be sure. Their mutual affection had started in childhood and lingered still. She'd watched his sparkling blue eyes twinkle with mischief many times over the years as they'd played together. But marriage?

Mamm reached for another pin. "Your father says Karl has already come to him, asking for permission. Why do you think we must hurry with the dress?"

Hearing this news almost knocked the breath out of Katie. Right away, her hands began to tremble. "What did Datt say?"

"He will give his permission as soon as you are baptized and join the church." Her mother's eyes watered. "And I will wait for that day with a joyful heart. To think, my daughter will be happily married before the year's end."

She dove into a lengthy conversation about the many benefits of a godly marriage, but Katie found herself lost in the words. All she could think about—all she would ever again be able to think about—was Karl Borg's visit to her father. . .and what she could do to stop this wedding from ever taking place.

Chapter 1

Doylestown, Pennsylvania, twelve years later

Katie leaned back in her chair and glanced at the calendar on the wall. Friday. Funny how she could never keep one day straight from another. With such a hectic schedule, remembering the names of her clients—and the addresses of her listings—took all of her energy. She couldn't be expected to remember the day of the week on top of everything else, could she?

Not that she minded the busyness, really. Filling the days with work certainly beat the alternative: quiet solitude. Too much time to think, especially about the past, wasn't a good thing.

For a moment, she allowed her mind to slip back to the farm, to a quieter, simpler life. It seemed like a hundred years had passed between then and now. Had she really left all of that peacefulness behind, swapping it out for a chaotic lifestyle, one she could barely keep up with?

For a moment, she allowed her thoughts to go there. To Paradise. Just as quickly, she shifted back to reality. In an attempt to distract herself, Katie gazed around her office, taking in the beautiful decor. She couldn't help but wonder what her parents would think if they saw all of this, especially the framed artwork on the walls. Such luxuries were forbidden among the Amish.

But the furniture would hold some appeal, especially to her father. The mahogany bookshelves. The matching credenza. The fabulous desk with its glass top. Such beautiful craftsmanship. Then again, Katie wouldn't have it any other way. These furnishings—which she had chosen with great care—made her feel at home.

The blinking of the cursor on the computer screen beckoned, and Katie shifted gears. She spent a few minutes entering some necessary information and uploading a few photos of an exquisite lakefront property she'd just listed, one complete with a spacious five-bedroom house. She also chose a new photo of herself, one recently taken, to replace her old one on the company's site.

She stared at it for a moment. The woman in the picture smiled back at her with a white-toothed smile, her green eyes sparkling, her yellow linen suit freshly pressed, and her shoulder-length hair styled in the latest fashion. Yes, she looked quite professional. And why not? You had to put your best foot forward in real estate if you wanted to garner the top clientele.

After finishing up on the Internet, Katie checked her voice mail. Only six messages this time. Three pressing. Two not so pressing. One from a former client, asking for a date. Nothing new there. He'd been at it for several weeks. How long she could continue putting him off was yet to be seen.

"Hey, girl!"

A voice at the door distracted Katie from the phone. She glanced up to discover her coworker Aimee Riley. The petite blond looked especially pretty today in dark slacks and a sky blue blouse. Katie couldn't help but wonder what Aunt Emma would think of that particular shade of blue.

"Hey, I'm surprised to see you here." Katie turned her attentions back to her friend. "Did you skip lunch?"

"Yeah, I was busy," Aimee said with a shrug. "Had about a dozen calls to make. I'm following a couple of pretty good leads."

"I've been busy, too." Katie grinned. "Just uploaded some new photos to our Web site. You'll have to sign online in a few minutes and check them out."

"I heard." Her coworker gave an approving nod. "Congratulations on your new listing. I hear that's a million-dollar property you just signed."

"A million *two*." Katie corrected her with a playful wink.

Aimee dropped into the wingback chair in the corner and sighed. "Must be nice."

"Yes." Katie closed the laptop and gazed into her friend's eyes. "It's a great place, Aimee, and I'm so blessed to get it. There's the most amazing house on multiple acres of land. On the lake. And here's the thing—with the market so hot right now, I'm convinced it'll pull in more than the asking price. I'm hoping for at least another hundred thousand before all is said and done."

"Man." Aimee shook her head. "I wouldn't mind taking home 6 percent of a million three."

Katie chuckled. "Well, get busy! Find me a buyer, and we'll split the commission." She reached into the desk drawer and came up with a tube of lip gloss, which she liberally applied to her parched lips.

"You've got a deal. I'll give it my best shot, anyway." Aimee paused and glanced down the hallway before asking, "Does Hannah know?"

"Are you kidding?" Katie put the lip gloss away. "Of course. She's always the first to know everything around here."

"That cousin of yours is a real pistol," Aimee said. "Ever since she made office manager, she. . ."

"I what, Aimee?" Hannah appeared in the doorway with an inquisitive look on her face. The slightly overweight thirty-something folded her arms at her chest, lips pursed.

"Um, you've turned this whole company around," Aimee said with a nod.

"That's more like it." Hannah's frown eased its way into a smile.

Katie couldn't help but smile, too. In spite of her cousin's tough exterior, Hannah really had done a great job of getting Bucks County Realty back on its feet. Excellent at keeping things—and people—in order, Hannah made a top-notch manager. If only the same positive comments could be made concerning her rowdy children and messy home.

Aunt Emma would surely cluck her tongue in disapproval at her oldest daughter's habits. Then again, the conservative older woman would likely disapprove of a great many things that went on in Hannah's house—like fast food for dinner, piles of laundry on the floor, excessive television watching, and children who talked back to their parents when they didn't get what they wanted.

"I just came in to tell you that a new client is on his way." Hannah's words drew Katie back to the present. "An investor, looking to buy up several farms in the area."

"An investor?" Katie drew in a deep breath. "What is he going to do with all of those properties?" She dreaded hearing the answer. For months now, investors had been sweeping in, buying up prime farmland to build apartments, housing developments, and so forth. Parking lots now reigned supreme, taking the place of the quaint farms of the past.

For that matter, many things from Katie's past had been replaced, hadn't they?

She shrugged off her sadness and turned back to her cousin with a strained smile.

"I don't have a clue." Hannah shrugged. "I just know he's interested in the Chandler place, and that's worth a pretty penny. He also mentioned something about that piece of property off on Wilcox, as well as a couple of others."

Katie's eyes widened. "Are you serious?"

"I'm serious." Hannah looked back and forth between the two Realtors. "So, which of you ladies wants to court this gentleman?"

There was something about the word "court" that didn't sit well with Katie. She made a quick decision to step aside and let her coworker take this one. "I just got that new listing," she explained with an easy lilt to her voice. "Why don't you take this guy, Aimee? The Chandler place is yours, anyway."

Her friend's eyes lit up and excitement laced her words. "Are you sure?"

"Yes. I'm going to have my hands full trying to sweep buyers off their feet with this new lakefront property."

"If you say so." Aimee turned back toward the door, almost tripping over her own feet. She looked over at Hannah and asked, "When is he coming in?"

"I told him to be here at four."

"That's less than an hour." With a flustered look on her face, Aimee headed out into the hallway then circled around to pose one more question. "Oh. I forgot to ask. . . .What's the guy's name?"

Hannah glanced down at the papers in her hand. "I'm pretty sure he said his last name is Borg," she said. "I wrote it down. Hang on." She looked a little closer at the paper, and her eyes grew wide.

"What is it, Hannah?" Aimee asked.

Hannah looked over at Katie, her face turning pale. "I just realized why this name sounded so familiar." After a brief pause, she stammered, "It–it's Karl. Karl Borg."

Karl Borg? Katie's stomach twisted in knots the moment she heard the familiar name. Could it possibly be the same man?

Regardless, she found herself wanting to run—to leave the building before he arrived. She'd managed it twelve years ago, hadn't she? Slipping out of her bedroom window in the cool of night had been her mode of operation then.

Avoiding him today might prove to be a little trickier. The windows at Bucks County Realty were far too small—and she might mess up her designer suit.

❧

Karl exited his sports car just outside the office of Bucks County Realty with his briefcase in hand. Slipping away from his law office midafternoon had been a challenge, but he'd finally managed to get here, albeit five minutes late. He paused as he caught a glimpse of his reflection in the glass front door. The wind had done quite a number on his hair. Setting his briefcase on the ground, Karl ran his fingers through the choppy strands then straightened his tie.

Seconds later, he entered the foyer of the Realtor's office. Once inside, he approached the receptionist at the front desk and asked to speak to Aimee Riley, the woman he'd been referred to. He hoped he had landed with just the right agent. Several pieces of property interested him at the moment, and he prayed he would get the best possible deal on each of them. He would need a savvy Realtor to accomplish that.

As he waited, the receptionist offered him a cup of coffee, which he willingly accepted. He added a couple of packets of sugar then gave it a stir. After a busy day and no lunch break, he certainly needed the caffeine.

One sip, however, convinced him otherwise. The murky liquid tasted burnt. Ironic, since it wasn't even warm. Unsure of what to do with it, he set it on a small end table and continued to wait. Moments later, a pretty blond appeared in the lobby with a broad smile on her face. "Mr. Borg, I'm Aimee Riley." She extended her hand, and he shook it. "Please, follow me to my office."

He grabbed his briefcase then pondered his dilemma as he looked at the cup of coffee. If he refused it, the receptionist's feelings might be hurt. If he took it, he might actually have to drink it. With his free hand, he reached to snatch it up then trailed the Realtor down a long, narrow hallway.

They entered her office, and Karl looked around in awe. He placed the cup of coffee on the edge of the glass-topped desk and gestured to the artwork on the walls. "This is really nice," he said. "Reminds me of home."

"Oh? Do you collect Keller's paintings, too?" she asked.

"No." He couldn't help but smile. "I grew up in a house that looked like that." He pointed to the farmhouse in one of the paintings.

"Oh, I see." She gave him a nod. "Well, I'm glad you like it. We'll take that as a confirmation that you've chosen the right Realtor." She sat at her desk and gestured for him to take the seat across from her. "I just hung the pictures a couple of weeks ago. It was pretty plain in here before that."

Plain.

As he sat, Karl drew in a deep breath, forcing images from his past behind. All memories of life on the farm brought back painful recollections of the day his world had changed forever. The day the woman he thought he would marry had sprinted out of his life, leaving him in the dust. He shook off the memory and placed his briefcase in the empty chair to his right.

With determination eking from every pore, he focused on the task set before him. "I'm here to talk with you about several pieces of property I'm interested in purchasing. I am particularly interested in the listing on Chandler," he explained. "It's a beautiful piece of farmland, but it's been on the market more than ninety days."

"Right."

"I plan to make an offer, but it will be far below the asking price."

He reached for the coffee cup, forgetting it was undrinkable until he'd swallowed a mouthful of the nasty stuff. He tried not to let it show on his face as he put the cup back down once again.

"Ah." She nodded. "I took a couple of clients out there just last week. I think the asking price is a bit high, and I'm sure the owners—an older couple—will come down if pressed. They're running behind on their mortgage, so if we move quickly, we might be able to make them an offer they can't refuse."

His heart lurched as the news of the late mortgage registered. "If no one buys, will they lose the place to foreclosure?"

"Likely." She shrugged. "But who knows. These farmers are up one minute, down the next, depending on the weather."

"And a host of other things," he interjected.

His mind took him back to that awful day, just weeks after his parents' deaths. As an only child, selling the farm had been his only real option. Karl had sprinted from Paradise—almost as fast as Katie.

"I listed the property several months ago, and there haven't been many showings." Aimee continued on, clearly oblivious to his thoughts. "So the goal here is to get it sold at a price everyone can live with."

They wrapped up their meeting in short order, and Karl stood to shake Aimee's hand. "You've been very helpful." He offered her a warm smile.

"I hope things end as well as they've started," she responded. "You never know what's going to happen in real estate. A situation can look like it's all wrapped up one minute, then be up in the air the next."

Her statement left him feeling a little discombobulated. Isn't that just what had happened in his life? His whole life in Paradise felt completely "wrapped up" as she had said. And then, in one swift move, it had all come crashing down.

With a sigh, Karl leaned down to pick up his briefcase with one hand. Noticing the still-full cup of cold coffee, he reached to grab it, as well. He could always toss it when he got outside.

Aimee ushered him out into the hallway, and just as they neared the lobby, another woman entered the narrow space, papers in hand. He couldn't really get a good look at the brunette's face. She appeared to be focused on the documents she carried, not paying a bit of attention to her surroundings. Karl tried to shift to the right at the last moment, realizing she was going to hit him head-on if he didn't dodge her.

Unfortunately, he didn't quite make it.

The clipboard in her hand turned out to be just the right height to take out his cup of coffee. The Styrofoam cup shot from his hand, straight up into the air, then back down again.

Landing right on top of her head.

Chapter 2

Katie let out a screech as the cold, sticky liquid oozed its way down her face and all over her expensive yellow suit. "Why don't you look where you're—" She looked up into the eyes of the stranger and realized. . .he wasn't a stranger at all.

Karl.

She watched his expression change—from one of embarrassment to shock. Or was it horror? She couldn't be quite sure. Either way, he looked like he wanted to bolt. Just like she'd done all those years ago.

If Katie could have avoided this day for the rest of her life, she would have. She had managed for twelve years, hadn't she?

Hoping to distract herself, she dropped to her knees to rescue the papers, which now lined the hallway. The coffee had done a number on those, too. They trembled in her hand as she fetched them.

Within seconds, Karl bent to his knees to offer assistance. "Katie, I. . .I'm so sorry."

"No, it's my fault." She looked into his beautiful blue eyes and instantly felt herself transported back in time twelve years. No, further than that. These were the same mischievous eyes that had drawn her in as a young girl, had wooed her to befriend a pesky neighbor boy who loved nothing more than to tease and torment her with frogs and lizards.

Hmm. He didn't appear to be hiding any of those in his pockets today, did he?

No, she had to admit. Looking at him now, tall and solidly built with his tailored suit and stylish haircut, he looked to be quite the professional. Clearly, he had left the old ways behind, as well. But when? And why? Had her impulsive actions resulted in that, too?

With his help, she managed to gather up the soggy papers and then stand. His hand—the same hand that had reached to take hers as they crossed the narrow bridge over Pequea Creek all those years ago—steadied her now as she rose to her feet.

"Thank you," she managed. The heat in her cheeks alarmed her, but not as much as the thought of what she must look like right now. She reached up to touch her hair then groaned. "I. . .I have to go take care of this. I look. . ."

"Amazing," he whispered. Then his cheeks reddened. He raked his fingers through his blond hair, and his gaze shifted to the ground.

Katie turned toward the ladies' room.

Aimee followed on her heels. "Katie? Want me to come with you?"

"No, I'm fine."

As she rounded the corner, she had to admit. . .she wasn't fine. In fact, after looking into Karl Borg's striking blue eyes, Katie wondered if she would ever be fine again.

ȥ

Karl paced the foyer of Bucks County Realty, his mind reeling. For years he had attempted to push all thoughts of Katie Walken out of his mind. He'd done a pretty good job, too. Karl had nearly forgotten how pretty she looked when she got riled up. How the sunlight played with the fine strands of blond in her brunette hair. How the early summer sun gave rise to a smattering of freckles on the end of her nose.

But now, seeing those green eyes, hearing the sound of her voice, feeling the touch of her hand in his. . . Surely he would have to work overtime to rid himself of these new feelings that flooded over him.

In all the scenarios he had imagined in his mind, he'd never come close to this. His Katie—once tall and slim with brunette hair pulled back under her kapp— now wore perfectly applied eyeliner and mascara. Her cheeks, once sun-kissed, now shimmered with a store-bought blush, and her full lips, the same lips he had dreamed of kissing for years, were covered in a soft pink gloss.

And that outfit! How she carried herself in it, like a woman, not a girl. Karl didn't remember her curves being quite so pronounced, but then again, under the straight dresses she'd always worn back in Lancaster County, he wouldn't have.

He closed his eyes and tried to remember what she used to look like then opened them again to merge the two images in his brain. Nope. It wouldn't compute.

And yet he'd seen it with his own eyes. Katie Walken—all grown up and looking like something straight off the pages of a fashion magazine.

Aimee interrupted his thoughts. "Mr. Borg, would you like another cup of coffee?"

"No thanks." He continued to pace, trying to make sense out of this. Katie worked in a realty office. She sold property. He bought property. It was inevitable they would eventually meet, right? Surely this was all just some crazy coincidence.

On the other hand, he didn't really believe in coincidences, did he? Most of the coincidental things in his life had proven to be God-incidences, after all. Karl pondered that possibility. Had the Lord moved him to Doylestown to find Katie again? And if so, did she even *want* to be found?

He took a seat in one of the large wingback chairs and tapped his fingers on the end table, trying to figure out what, if anything, to do.

"I'm sure Katie will be fine," Aimee said with a reassuring smile. "There's really no reason for you to stay."

"I have to."

"Oh. . .okay." She gave him a curious look then shrugged. "I have some work to do. If you don't mind. . ."

"No, go ahead. But, please, would you let Katie know that I'm not leaving until I talk to her? I'll sit here all day if I have to."

"Um, sure." Aimee shrugged. "Whatever you say."

As she rounded the corner, Karl called out, "Aimee?"

She returned right away. "Yes?"

"There wouldn't happen to be a window in that bathroom, would there?" He began to rap his fingers on the end table once again as his nerves kicked in.

"Well, yes, I think so," she said, looking confused. "Why?"

"Oh, no reason." He leaned back against the chair and drew in a deep sigh. "No reason at all."

à.

Katie stood in front of the bathroom mirror and worked feverishly to get the stains out of her jacket. Not that it mattered. Even if she got it back in shape, she could do little about her hair.

Gazing at her reflection, she groaned. She wouldn't want to be seen by anyone in this condition, especially not Karl.

Tears sprang to her eyes, and she dabbed them away with a piece of toilet paper. No point in getting emotional. It certainly wouldn't make things any better, would it? And besides, the past was in the past.

Giving up on the jacket, she took a paper towel and tried to dab at her hair. Hanging her head upside down might be her best choice. She flung her hair forward and tipped over, then took the paper towel and began to work it through the matted strands in an attempt to soak up some of the moisture.

Just then, she heard a rap on the door.

"Katie?" Aimee stepped inside the room and closed the door behind her.

"Aimee, I'll explain later." Katie continued on in her upside-down position, hoping her friend would give her some time alone to get her thoughts straight—to figure out why the Lord had suddenly dropped Karl back into her life once again, after all these years.

"I just wanted to tell you that Mr. Borg is waiting up front for you."

Katie groaned and stood upright. "Maybe he'll go away if I stay in here long enough." She began to work her hair into place with her fingers, but it didn't want to cooperate.

"He's not going anywhere," Aimee explained, her brow still wrinkled in concern. "He said he would sit out there all day if he had to."

Another groan escaped Katie's lips. So, Karl hadn't changed. He'd always had the patience of a saint. Just one more area where they were polar opposites.

Her thoughts slipped back in time to another day when he had waited on her for hours. They were supposed to meet at the edge of the creek to go fishing at seven in the morning. Katie's mother had given her more chores than usual that morning, and she didn't make it until ten thirty. But there he sat, hat on his head, pole in his hand, legs slung over the edge of the creek, as if he had nothing better to do than spend three and a half hours waiting on her.

On the other hand, he'd managed to catch quite a few fish in her absence that day.

Still, with the sharp business suit he now wore, he likely had far more to do than sit in the front lobby of Bucks County Realty waiting on an old flame.

Hmm. Maybe flame wasn't the right word. They'd never even kissed, after all.

She tried to avoid her friend's expression, but Aimee made it difficult. Her penetrating gaze was tough to ignore.

"So, are you going to tell me what's going on, or am I going to have to guess?"

"He. . .he's just someone I used to know." Katie took another glance in the mirror. "From my former life."

"Ah. Well, he's certainly got you all shook up. There's got to be a reason why."

"I'm just embarrassed, is all. It's not every day I bathe in coffee."

"I'll admit the whole thing was plenty embarrassing." Aimee folded her arms at her chest and shook her head. "But there's more to it than that. Did you used to date this guy?"

"I can say in all honesty that I *never* dated Karl Borg." No lying there. Teens in her conservative Amish community hadn't dated, at least not in the traditional sense. Unless you called a buggy ride a date. Or a quiet walk after a barn raising.

"Hmm." Aimee reached over and straightened the back of Katie's collar, then stepped back to give her a once-over. "You never dated him, and yet your eyes lit up the moment you recognized him. Very suspicious."

My eyes lit up? Katie pondered that for a second. There had been a moment of recognition but nothing more. Except, perhaps, fear.

After drawing in a deep breath, she turned to face her friend, ready to deal with the obvious. "I'm going out there."

"I wish I could come, too. I would pay money to hear this conversation."

"I'll fill you in later. I promise." Katie reached to open the bathroom door then took a tentative step into the hall. Then another. And another. All the way to the lobby, she debated what she would say once she saw him.

Maybe it would be better not to plan anything out—just let nature take its course when the moment came.

On the other hand. . .as she rounded the corner into the lobby and took one look at Karl with that boyish face of his, only one thing came to mind. She wanted to give him her hand and let him guide her across the bridge at Pequea Creek one more time, for old time's sake. Surely once would be enough to stop this crazy pounding in her heart.

Chapter 3

Karl stood the moment Katie entered the room. He tried to squelch the anxiety that rushed over him as he stared into her beautiful face. She had changed in so many ways, and yet underneath that polished, coffee-coated exterior, the old Katie remained. Driven. Excited about life. Ready to take on the world.

As she drew near, Karl tried to figure out what to do. Should he embrace her? After all, they were old friends. Old friends met with a hug, didn't they? At least among the Englishers. She reached out first, slipping an arm around his waist. He drew her close, and they remained, if only for a second.

Katie stepped back all too quickly, and he noticed the fear in her eyes. Would she find an excuse to shoot out of the front door or give him a few moments to ask the questions that had been nagging at him for years?

"I. . .um. . .was just about to leave for the day." She glanced up at the clock on the wall, and he followed her gaze. 5:24.

"I can't just leave without talking to you." He gave her his best pleading look. "Couldn't we please go out for—" He started to say "a cup of coffee" but stopped himself after thinking better of it. She'd already had enough coffee for one day. "Maybe a bite to eat?"

"I don't know." Katie paused and ran her fingers through her hair. "I look like a wreck."

"You look wonderful," he managed.

Her cheeks flushed pink, just as they had done a hundred times as a little girl when he'd teased her. Only now, she didn't seem to mind his comments. In fact, she seemed to soften more as time went on.

"Just a few minutes to talk?" He tried again.

As she nodded, a wave of relief washed over him. Maybe he would get the answers he had been seeking, after all.

"Let me just run back to my office and grab my purse," she said. "I'll have to shut down my computer and turn out the lights, so it might take a couple of minutes."

"I'll wait."

"Or you could come with." She gestured toward the hall, and he followed along behind her like a puppy dog.

His eyes grew large as they entered her spacious office. "This is amazing,

Katie." He approached the mahogany bookshelf unit. "The craftsmanship on this piece is beautiful."

She smiled and her cheeks turned pink. "I've always wondered what you might think of it. Your woodworking skills were the best in Lancaster County."

"Hardly." He laughed. "But I could definitely see myself working on something like this." He drew in a deep breath and added, "In another life, I mean."

"I hear ya." She reached over to turn off her computer, and the room fell silent. Karl tried to cover up the awkwardness by looking at the pictures on the bookshelf. His heart nearly shifted to his toes as he came across a photo of three small children. Strange. He'd never thought to look at Katie's left hand for a ring. If she had children, surely she had to be married.

Thankfully, she took note of his interest in the photograph and offered up a more palatable explanation. "What do you think of my cousin's children? Aren't they cute?"

Karl tried not to the let the relief show in his eyes as he turned back toward her. "They're a nice-looking crew. The little girl reminds me of you at that age." He looked again at the photograph, realizing the child wore modern English clothes and had a stylish haircut. "Except for a few obvious things." He turned to give Katie a warm smile. "She does have the same batch of freckles on the end of her nose, just like you."

Katie groaned as she reached for her purse. "I always hated those freckles."

"I didn't. I used to count them."

Her gaze shifted down to some papers on the desk, which she rearranged. "The little girl's name is Madison. She's the spitting image of her mother." Katie looked up, locking eyes with him. "You remember my cousin Hannah, right? Aunt Emma's daughter?"

"The one who ran away when she was eighteen and married the English boy?" he asked. Karl wished he could take the words back as quickly as they were spoken, but there was no swallowing them now that they were out.

"Yes. She met him during her *rumspringa*, while visiting friends in Doylestown," Katie explained. "And tried to fight her feelings for him. I think she must have convinced herself she could overcome her love for him, because she was baptized as soon as she returned home, made her commitment to the church."

Karl knew what that meant of course. Once an Amish teen made the decision to be baptized, it was a public covenant to the Amish way of life. . .forever. To leave after making such a declaration would result in only one thing, at least in their Order.

"Less than a month after her joining the church, Matt showed up, completely brokenhearted. Told her that he couldn't live without her." Katie sighed. "I remember how torn she was over the decision. Despite her attempts to the contrary, her love for him proved to be very strong. And yet she knew if she left after joining the church, she would be—"

"Shunned."

"Yes, and it's so sad," Katie explained, "because Matt's a great guy, and he really loves the Lord. I think the decision to leave Paradise nearly killed Hannah, but she did it out of love for him."

"I understand that kind of love." His gaze shifted downward as soon as the words slipped out. Though he had not planned to convey such feelings, they obviously could not be held back. After a few seconds, he garnered the courage to look back up into Katie's eyes.

"Love is a powerful thing," she continued.

"And it often calls for sacrifice," he added. *At least from my experience.*

"Yes, well. . .Hannah did sacrifice a lot. She had to give up one family to gain another."

"Sad."

"Well, most of the story is happy. She and Matt got married and settled in Doylestown, near his family. They're both great people, very active in their local church. I've just always hated it that they can't go back home to see her family. I know she's thinking about it. From what I hear, many of the Amish are softening their stance on shunning. I've heard of a great many Amish teens leaving after their baptism then being welcomed back at weddings and funerals and so forth."

"I've heard the same." He had always balked at the idea of shunning those who left the community but had kept his opinions to himself. Secretly, he had been relieved that Katie had sneaked away before her baptism, realizing it left the door open for her return. She could go back if she wanted to.

Not that it looked like she wanted to.

He thought back to the events surrounding her leaving. Getting the news early in the morning. Hoping, praying, it was some sort of joke on her part. Waiting for days to hear something, anything. Finally getting the message about her trek to Doylestown to stay with extended family members.

Oh, how he had prayed during those days and weeks following her abrupt exit from Paradise. How he had fought the urge to run after her, to plead with her to come back—not just to him, but to the quiet, simple life they would live together.

As he gazed into her eyes now, Karl had to admit she seemed better suited to this fast-paced lifestyle. Perhaps she had found her niche, after all.

Maybe she'd found someone to love, as well.

He gave the bookshelf unit a quick glance, in search of another photo. Thankfully, he found nothing but real estate books and knickknacks. He looked at her left hand, praying he would not find a ring.

No ring.

Just then, Katie crossed the room in his direction to turn off the light. For a moment, she and Karl stood quite close in the semidarkened room, almost close enough to reach out and touch one another. He struggled with the feelings that gripped him at her nearness.

With resolve building, he took a step backward, giving her the space she needed to close up the room. Maybe that was all she had ever needed. . .space.

❧

Katie pulled off her jacket before entering the restaurant. The white blouse underneath was free of coffee stains. Besides, she felt constricted in the jacket, especially on a warm June evening like this.

Karl met her at the door of her car, a smile lighting his face. "Are you hungry?"

"Always."

"That's the girl I remember."

Katie couldn't help but laugh as their eyes met. Just as quickly, she stopped. No matter how comfortable she felt around Karl, she did not want to give him the wrong impression. She didn't want to give *any* man the wrong impression, for that matter.

They walked together toward the restaurant with Karl making stilted conversation about the weather. She played along, not sure what else to do. Likely once they got inside, the tough conversation would begin—the one she'd avoided for twelve years.

The hostess took their names and within minutes led the way to a table near the back of the room. Karl put his hand on the small of Katie's back and guided her through the crowd. His touch offered a sense of security. She'd almost forgotten how safe she felt around him. How protected.

After they had ordered their food, she could put off the inevitable no longer. "I have to get this out," she said, looking him in the eye. "I need to tell you how sorry I am that I left like I did." Katie noticed his eyes glistened with moisture as she continued. "I know you probably think it was because of you. Because I didn't want to—"

"To marry me."

She drew in a deep breath and gazed at the table. "I'll admit I wasn't ready to get married. I had so many things I wanted to do, so many places I wanted to go. I knew if I got married, those things would never happen."

"Not necessarily."

"Still, the chances were slim." She gazed into his eyes, hoping to make him understand. "The more time I've spent away from Paradise, the more I've come to realize—it wasn't *you* I ran away from. It was the lifestyle. The constraints. I'm convinced I was born for. . ."

"Bigger things?"

She sighed—partly out of relief at the fact that he understood and partly because she realized how pompous that sounded. "It seems so ugly when you say it like that," she said. "And so. . .worldly. I'm not a worldly girl, Karl. Not really. I still have a very strong faith, probably stronger than it was back then. I just wanted to think in broader terms, travel in wider circles."

"I understand."

"And I certainly wasn't hoping for bigger things in a husband. In fact"—she gave him a shrug—"I wasn't *hoping* for a husband at all. That was the problem. I wanted to get out and see things for myself. I wanted an opportunity to spread my wings and fly a little, to see what I could become on my own. Without—"

"A man holding you back."

Another sigh slipped out, but she didn't answer right away because the waitress appeared at their table with water glasses in hand.

"Not everyone is meant to marry," Katie offered, after the waitress left. "There were plenty of spinsters in our community, remember? They cared for other people's children and took in laundry to earn a living. That would never have suited me."

"You were never meant to be a spinster." He reached across the table to take her hand. "But I do get your point. I know what it feels like to be trapped, to think there's no way out."

"You do?"

"Yes." He paused and withdrew his hand, looking a bit uncomfortable all of a sudden. "It's possible you've already heard this, but about two years after you left, my parents were both killed in a fire."

Katie's eyes filled with tears right away. "I did hear, though it was some time after, and I'm so sorry." She didn't add that she'd tried to track him down after getting the news. Tried to send a card. But by then, he'd already moved away from Paradise.

Now his eyes filled with tears. "The house burned to the ground after being struck by lightning. I lost more than my parents that day. I lost. . .my whole life. My existence. My place in the community."

"What do you mean?"

He shrugged. "I'm an only child, as you know, and not a child, at that. But to rebuild after such a tragedy just felt. . .overwhelming. I can honestly say I've never felt more alone in my life." He paused for a moment then added, "Don't misunderstand me. I knew the Lord was with me. I felt His presence daily. But I guess I needed the reassurance of someone who could help guide me. Advise me."

A thousand things went through Katie's mind at once as she took note of the woeful look on his face. If she had stayed in Paradise and married Karl, they would have rebuilt the farm. . .together. He never would have faced those things alone.

"I heard you sold the farm to Ike Biden," she said.

"Yes." Karl's face lit in a smile. "Ike was always such a good friend. He built a fine home on it, one now filled with half a dozen children and a wonderful wife. And I moved on to Harrisburg."

"Harrisburg?" She took a sip of water and then leaned back in her chair.

Karl nodded. "I had an uncle there. My father's brother. He convinced me I had what it took to become an attorney."

Katie's eyes widened. "An attorney? But the Amish are opposed to that occupation, aren't they?"

"My uncle was an Englisher. And it didn't take him long to convince me that I could actually do some good if I got the proper training. So, he pointed me in the right direction. I got my GED. My test scores were really high, actually."

"Same here." She couldn't help but smile. "Guess that small classroom environment really paid off."

"Yeah." He smiled. "After that, I went to college then on to law school."

"Turning you into a lawyer makes perfect sense to me." Katie chuckled. "You were always great at debating me on every little thing."

Karl laughed. "I can debate with the best of them, I guess. Least, that's what my uncle said. So off to law school I went. After I passed the bar, I worked at his firm in Harrisburg. Then, about a year ago, I was offered an opportunity to practice real estate law in Doylestown. I couldn't turn it down."

"I see." She paused and gave him an admiring look. "You've really made something of yourself, Karl. I'm so proud of you."

He shook his head. "There's a part of me that wishes I could go back. This new life is so. . .crazy. Hectic. Sometimes I miss the old days, working with my hands, sitting out by the creek with a fishing pole in my hands. It's different now."

"No kidding."

"What about you?" he asked. "Did you go to college?"

Katie released a sigh. "My story is a little different. For all of my bravery—slipping out of that window and running away—I have to admit I was pretty scared. . .of everything. I can't tell you how many times I wanted to run back home those first couple of years. But, instead, I stayed with Hannah. Listened to her talk about her dream of becoming a Realtor. She'd been bitten by the real estate bug."

"She's a broker now, right?" he asked.

"Yes." Katie grinned. "But it took awhile. She wanted a home, a family, and a job. Doing all of that takes a lot of work."

"I'm sure she had a lot of help from you." Karl gave her a warm smile.

Katie shrugged. "Helping out with the kids—once they started coming along—was easier than facing the real world. But somewhere along the way I overcame my fears. Went to junior college for a couple of years. Got my associate's degree. Then"—she paused, remembering—"I guess it was watching Hannah that did it. She'd get so excited about the houses she'd sold. It wasn't just the money. . .it was the whole thing. Realizing she could balance a job and a family." Katie shrugged. "She's the true modern-day woman. Sort of the polar opposite of the ideal wife and mother we grew up with."

"And you wanted to be like that?"

"Well, I wanted to try my hand at a career, and Hannah was willing to walk me through the process," Katie explained. "I took the classes, got my license, and she set me up at Bucks County Realty." She looked over at Karl with a shrug. "The rest, as they say, is history."

The waitress made her appearance with their food, and Karl offered to pray. As they bowed their heads, Katie heard the same passion in his voice for the Lord that she had loved as a youngster. Surely leaving the Amish country hadn't diminished his faith. If anything, it seemed stronger now than ever.

As they began to eat, Karl dove into a discussion of particular interest to Katie, one near to her heart, in fact.

"Practicing real estate law has really opened my eyes to some of the atrocities taking place in the industry," he said. "I've never seen so many get-rich-quick schemes in my life. And I can't tell you how many clients have been taken advantage of—both buyers and sellers."

"I hear you," Katie concurred. "I've seen more than a few scams since I started in this business myself. Everything from overpricing houses to mortgage fraud. It's shameful."

Karl nodded. "I've seen a lot of other things that break my heart, too. Like all of the farms being bought up right and left by people who have no interest in the land itself. They just see it as a potential apartment complex or strip mall."

Katie's eyes grew wide as she listened. How interesting that their feelings were so similar, and on such a sensitive subject. "I feel the same. It seems like every day some investor sweeps in and buys up farmland, turning it into a parking lot or shopping center."

"I'm doing what I can to prevent that."

He spent the next fifteen minutes explaining his plan of action to save the farms in the area, and Katie listened with genuine interest. So. . .his love for the land hadn't died after all. In fact, he seemed more passionate about it than ever.

His faith had grown.

His love for the land had grown.

His desire to do the right thing had grown.

Clearly, Karl had entered the world of the English without letting it consume him. He was living proof that one could be in the world but not of it.

As she nibbled at her salad, troubling thoughts rolled through Katie's mind, and she had to wonder, despite her earlier comments to the contrary, could the same thing be said of her?

Chapter 4

The following morning, Katie received a telephone call that shook her to the core. Her mother's tremulous voice conveyed the bad news. Her father had suffered a massive heart attack. He refused to be taken to the hospital. Would Katie come home right away?

She flew into action, packing a small bag and then telephoning Hannah. "I don't know how long I'll be," she explained. "But I want to stay as long as they need me. And it must be bad, Hannah. Otherwise, Mamm would never have used the telephone."

Hannah cried. Something she rarely did these days. "Tell your parents I love them and I'm praying. And tell my mamm. . ." Her voice trailed off.

Katie finished the sentence for her. "I will tell her that you love her and miss her."

"Thank you."

She made another quick call—this one to Aimee. Though she hated to think about business on a day like today, she needed to make sure someone took her calls and covered any potential showings. Saturday was a busy day for Realtors, after all.

Aimee listened to her explanation then responded with deep concern in her voice. "I'm here for you, Katie. Anything you need. And I'm praying for your father."

Katie pushed back the lump in her throat as she thanked her for being such a good friend. Then she ended the call.

The journey to Paradise was made with only the sound of a worship CD playing in the background. Katie offered up prayer after prayer for her father, pleading with the Lord to spare his life. Surely he would recover and go on to live many more healthy years. Right?

She contemplated many things as she wound through the familiar back roads of Lancaster County. Her father's condition. The sound of fear in her mother's voice. The fact that she'd only been home a handful of times over the years. Oh, her family had always welcomed her back with open arms, but she felt like an outsider every time. It seemed the trips back to Paradise were fewer and further between. Staying away was just. . .easier. A shiver ran up her spine as she contemplated today's trip. Surely it would cause her two worlds to collide once again. Was she ready for the collision?

Katie's thoughts drifted to her older brothers, Daniel and Amos. They were both happily married with children. As was often the case in Amish households, they had built their homes on the Walken property to be close to the family.

Katie smiled as she thought about her younger sisters, Emily and Sara. They were both married, as well, and Sara was expecting a baby in a few short weeks. Of course, the girls and their husbands lived inside the main house with Mamm and Datt. What would *that* be like—to be a newlywed living in your parents' home?

More curious still, what would it be like for Katie to spend quality time with all of her family members again, and under such sad circumstances? Would they still feel connected, even after all this time—and distance?

Her sisters' days were filled with washing clothes, sewing, scrubbing floors, cooking, and other such household chores. Hers were filled with clients, meetings, and bidding wars. Her sisters knew nothing about the crazy, fast-paced world of real estate. Would they have anything in common at all, or would their conversations be strained, painful?

Thinking of the stark contrast between the two worlds reminded her of Karl and the conversation they had shared last night over dinner. She contemplated his apparent love for the Lord and his ability to live in the world without letting it consume him. And, after a bit of thought, she decided the same could be said of her.

I'm doing a pretty good job with that, too, she reasoned. After all, her love for material things hadn't gone too far. Sure, she loved great clothes. And having nice things in her office was a given. She had clients to impress, after all. But, as for letting her possessions mean too much to her, had she reached that point? She hoped not. She *prayed* not.

The appearance of a farm market and several small roadside stands let Katie know she would soon be home. She glanced down at the speedometer and slowed her pace as she drew near.

Off in the distance, a particular piece of property nearly took her breath away. The lush rolling pastures—greener than she remembered—seemed to be endless, and the white wood-framed farmhouse had a familiar feel to it. However, the For Sale sign out front told a different story. How sad to think the owners would have to leave such a lovely piece of land.

On the other hand, how wonderful for the Realtor to list an amazing property.

Katie was reminded at once of her recent lakefront listing and offered up a quick prayer that it would sell for the best possible price. Still, pretty as it was, it could hardly compare with the breathtaking beauty of Lancaster County's Amish farmland.

As she took it all in, Katie couldn't help but see the glaring irony. What were all of her possessions in comparison to the beauty of God's creation? Had she really traded this for a condo in the city? Sure, she'd filled it with great furnishings and artwork, but nothing would ever compare to the simple beauty found here, in the very place where she had started.

Odd, now that she thought about it. All of those years living in this breathtaking place, and she had missed the beauty all around her. Now she had replaced it with other things—also beautiful—but in a different way.

Hmm. Maybe her possessions had grown to mean too much to her, despite her earlier thoughts on the matter.

As Katie drew near her parents' home, she took a few moments to pray. Maybe, in the midst of the chaos and the busyness, she had set her sights on more worldly things. Getting her priorities straight might be in line, after all. She asked the Lord to forgive her and to redirect her thinking. *Take me back to the place where I don't care so much what people think—about how I look, what I own, where I work.*

Katie arrived at the farm around noon, her thoughts shifting at once to her father. As she contemplated his heart issues, she couldn't help but offer up another prayer on his behalf.

Pulling her car into the driveway felt odd. Of course, she had driven up the driveway many times as a teen—in a buggy. Often with Karl at her side. But only a few times in her adult life had she returned to the scene of the crime, the place where she had stolen away. Her gaze shifted at once to the window—the corridor she had slipped through into another life.

A shiver ran down her spine as she thought back to that cool summer night. The moon had been full, casting a more-than-adequate amount of light on the area outside her bedroom window. She had taken a small bag—not much bigger than the one she carried today. After easing the window open, she had tossed the bag out first then climbed through the small opening and out onto the lawn.

A trip to town on foot had proven difficult, in spite of the moonlight. She'd hidden out behind the store, knowing the place well and feeling safe there. When the sun had risen, she'd slipped into a telephone booth to make the collect call to Hannah. Her cousin had agreed to come and fetch her but insisted she leave a letter for her parents. Katie had mailed it that same morning.

Oh, but how she had missed her parents and her brothers and sisters those first few days. How she wanted to turn around and run right back to the safety of their arms. To the farm, the only life she'd ever known.

And now, as she eased her way from the driver's seat, as she made her way toward the front porch of the house where she'd grown up, Katie longed, once again, to run into the safety of her father's arms. Overwhelming guilt took hold, and she almost stopped in her tracks. Would she ever be able to do that again?

A few more moments of reflection might very well have sent her running in the opposite direction, but ironically, she was distracted by a golden retriever leaping up to greet her and licking her in the face.

"You must be a new one." Katie gave the pup a scratch behind the ears.

Just then, the front door of the house opened and her mother came running toward her. "Katie, oh, Katie!"

Mamm shooed the dog away then stopped short, possibly confused by Katie's appearance. After all, she had changed a lot since the last visit. A new haircut. A change in wardrobe. A different approach to makeup. Yes, she continued to morph into quite the city girl, no denying that.

"Mamm." Katie wrapped her arms around her mother and gave her a warm hug. "How is he?"

Her mother shook her head and her eyes watered. "Not good. The doctor just left. He says it's in the Lord's hands."

"And Datt refuses to go to the hospital?"

"Yes. He wishes to be here, with his family. We cannot change his mind."

"The boys?"

"Your brothers are working in the fields today. We will send for them if we need them."

"Emily and Sara?"

"They have stayed close to the house, though Emily has just taken the buggy to town to fetch some items from the store. Sara is resting. This has been difficult on her."

Katie swallowed hard at that last comment. Had she been here, perhaps her sister's load would have been lifted. Once inside the house, Katie greeted her younger sister with a smile. Sara glowed with maternal happiness, and her extended belly showed that her time would not be long.

"You look wonderful," Katie gushed.

Sara put her hand on her stomach and shook her head. "Hardly. But thank you."

They embraced in a warm hug, and then Katie turned her attentions to the reason for her visit. After a few more brief questions about her father's condition, she drew in a deep breath and followed her mother to the bedroom.

There she found her father lying still in the bed. "Datt?"

"Katie?" His eyes fluttered open, and his trembling hand reached for hers. She sat on the edge of the bed, doing all she could to prevent the tears as she wrapped her healthy hand around his frail one. Oh, how the tables had turned. How many times had he reached for her with strong hands, held her safe?

What could she offer him in exchange?

⁂

Karl paced the living room of his small house and prayed. All afternoon he had waited for word about the Chandler place. His original offer had been countered by the owners. He offered a bit more, in the hopes that they would accept quickly.

Surely Aimee should know something by now. He picked up his cell phone and punched in her number. She answered on the third ring.

"No word yet, Karl." Her opening line drew a sigh out of him.

"Let me know the minute you hear something?"

"I will." She laughed. "If I didn't know better, I would think you were anxious about this one."

"Not anxious, really," he said. "I've just heard rumors that other investors have been looking to build a new subdivision out there, and I'd hate to see that. The property is some of the best farmland in the area and could be productive with the right owner."

"Are you a farmer, Mr. Borg?" Aimee asked.

Karl paused a moment before answering. "I used to be. But I'm not buying the property for myself. I have a list of clients who are interested in keeping Pennsylvania farmlands alive and well."

Aimee conveyed her satisfaction at his answer then shifted the conversation. "Before I let you go," she said, "I heard from Katie awhile ago. Her father is very ill."

"Oh?" The news startled Karl. He had only known Katie's father to be a healthy, sturdy man—one in love with the land and with his family.

"Yes. Apparently he had a heart attack, and the prognosis is pretty grim."

"That's awful." Karl felt the pain acutely. Mr. Walken had treated him like a son, after all. "Thank you so much for telling me. I'll give her a call right away."

Without so much as a pause, Karl pulled Katie's business card from his wallet and dialed her cell number. She answered on the third ring.

"Katie?"

"Karl, is that you?"

He heard the catch in her voice and knew she'd been crying. "Yes, it's me. I just talked to Aimee. How is your father?"

"Oh, Karl, he's not good at all. The doctor has been here off and on all day because Datt won't go to the hospital. He says he wants to be here, with his family. But his heart is so weak, and Doc Yoder says he might not have long."

"I'm glad you're there. He needs you now, Katie."

"But. . .I need him, too." She began to cry in earnest now. "I don't know what

I'd do if he. . ."

"I'll be praying," Karl said. "And I'll put in a call to my church so that others will be praying, too. In the meantime, I wonder how you would feel if I came out there. I could spend the night at Ike Biden's place. I think he would have me."

"You would do that?" Katie asked. "Drive all the way out here?"

"Your father has always been so wonderful to me," Karl said. "And I want to be there for him." He swallowed hard and added, "And for you."

Her quiet "Thank you" warmed his heart.

"I should be there by nightfall." He hung up the phone and threw some clothes in a bag, then settled into his car for the ride, praying all the way.

Going back to Paradise wouldn't be easy—not after all he'd been through. But going back, at least for now, certainly felt like the right thing to do.

Chapter 5

Katie spent the first night at her parents' house at her father's bedside. She didn't want to leave him, even for a moment. He had rarely awakened since her arrival, though at times his eyelids fluttered and his lips would move as he recognized her voice. His breathing remained labored throughout the night, giving her great cause for concern. According to Doc Yoder, her father's heart and lungs were slowly shutting down.

If only she could talk Datt into going to the hospital, perhaps the doctors could do something to help him. But he would not be persuaded. Katie knew his decision to remain at home had nothing to do with rules and regulations. The Amish had no problem receiving medical care. No, her father's logic came from someplace else. She could sense it as the hours wore on. He knew his time was near.

And she knew it, too.

Many times Katie had heard people speak of death, how they could sense it in a room. She could almost taste it in the air, here in her parents' bedroom, but it did not frighten her. On the contrary, she found herself surprised at its gentleness. A lulling of sorts took over—like a mother rocking a child to sleep. Was this how God called His children home? Did He woo them with His love, urging them to let go of their pain and suffering and ease their way into His arms? Was death, like so many other things in life, a matter of releasing hold and giving God total control?

Katie vacillated between praying for her father's healing and giving in to what appeared to be inevitable. Her heart ached at the idea of releasing him. She hadn't spent enough time with Datt, and now she regretted it as never before. Her days had been consumed with work, busyness. Why hadn't she come home more? Why hadn't she taken the time to sit and talk with her father more frequently, as she'd done so many years ago?

As the hours passed, regret gave way to exhaustion. Katie finally managed to doze in the rocking chair, though fitful dreams took hold—images from the past merged with scenes from her current life.

All too soon, the early morning sun peeked through the bedroom curtains, rousing her from her agitated slumber. She rose from the chair and approached the bedside.

"Datt?" She leaned down to give him a gentle kiss on the cheek. "It's morning."

He seemed to come awake, at least to some extent. His lips began to move, and she eased her way closer in to better hear what he had to say.

His words were strained and difficult to understand. "I. . .I'm so glad you've come h–home, Katydid. It. . .means the world to me."

A lump rose in her throat as he called her by the pet name she hadn't heard in years.

"I'm happy to be here," she managed. "I love you, Datt, and I'm praying for you." She gave his hand a little squeeze.

"I've prayed for you, as well." He spoke in a strained whisper. "I need to know . . .that all is well with you."

Katie gripped his hand, understanding his full meaning. "I am well, Datt, in every respect. I have a strong faith in God. Stronger than ever. I want you to be assured of that. But please get some rest. We want you to get better."

"My focus is not on this world, Katydid. It is on the next." His eyes drifted shut, and she could almost see him slipping away into a dreamland, where heaven opened its doors to him and bade him come inside. His breathing grew more labored, and he drifted back off to sleep.

She leaned down to kiss him on his whiskery cheek. As she did, her mother entered the room, her face pale and drawn.

"Has he wakened?" she asked, drawing near.

"For a moment." Katie looked into her mother's tired eyes. "Mamm, you need to sit down. You look exhausted."

"I am fine."

"You've been up all night."

Her mother's treks in and out of the room through the night had been many. Katie knew Mamm had spent much of the night tending not just to her husband but to the needs of the others in the house. Nothing had changed there. Her mother had always put everyone else first, even in the hardest of times.

"I slept for a couple of hours on the sofa," her mother said.

"Aunt Emma said she would come back this morning. She will take over the household chores for you. Please rest."

Brushing the tears aside, Katie stood and walked toward her mother. She eased into the comfort of those familiar arms and began to weep. After a moment or two, her mother joined in, and before long, a quiet chorus of grief filled the room.

❧

Karl arrived at the Walken farm around eight in the morning, praying he was not too late. A fitful night's sleep at the Bidens' had left him feeling exhausted, but he chose to come anyway. Hopefully, they would be happy to see him.

As he made his way up the front steps of the house and onto the porch, he reflected on the hundreds of times he'd been here before. As a teen, he had arrived—a clean-shaven boy with butterflies in his stomach—to see Katie. To spend time with the girl he would one day marry.

Today, as he approached the front door, a different feeling washed over him. Karl knew that this visit would be far more somber. In fact, he couldn't help but feel it would change his life forever.

No sooner had the idea settled in his spirit than a large dog leaped up to greet him, placing its muddy paws on his chest and covering his face with slobbery kisses. Karl managed to get the mongrel under control, even managed to get him to sit obediently at his feet.

He gave the front door a gentle rap, then stepped back and waited. The door swung wide and a beautiful young woman greeted him, one who looked remarkably like Katie had in her late teens. This girl wore the traditional Amish garb, though it appeared to stretch over an extended belly. It took a moment to register. Ah. This must be. . . "Sara." He smiled and extended his hand.

She stepped out onto the porch, her face lighting into a smile. "Karl Borg! It's been so long." She gave his hand a squeeze and ushered him into the house. "Katie told us you were coming. We're so glad to have you."

"I'm happy to be here."

"Come and see the others."

Once inside, the other family members greeted him, and all concerns about how they would receive him were pushed aside. Karl recognized Daniel and Amos, Katie's older brothers. And Emily, the youngest of the Walken girls. But he had never met the spouses and children, and they were many.

After making introductions, Sara slipped off to fetch Katie. He hated to disturb her, especially if she was spending time with her father.

As soon as she entered the living room, Karl could tell Katie had barely slept. Her eyes had a hollowed-out look to them, and what he guessed had once been near-perfect makeup was now smudged and faded. He wanted to sweep her into his arms, to tell her everything would be all right. Strange how his first desire was to protect her. That hadn't changed, in spite of everything.

"Karl." She approached with tears in her eyes, extending her hand. "I'm. . .we're so glad you could come."

He took her hand and gave it a squeeze. "I can think of no place I'd rather be than here." He glanced around the room. "With all of you."

At once, Mrs. Walken drew near and wrapped him in a warm embrace. "I know it will mean so much to Elam that you've come. Would you like to see him now?"

"If I may."

She led him into the bedroom, and he gazed in silence at the man whose head rested on the white pillowcase. Katie's father had aged considerably in the years Karl had been away, that much could not be denied. His beard, once salt-and-pepper in color, was a soft white now. His hair, once thick and dark, had thinned and lightened.

The thing that surprised Karl most, however, wasn't what he saw, but what he smelled. Though the room appeared to be spotless, an undeniable scent lingered all around him. He had heard of this before, of course, but never experienced it firsthand. Death had entered the room and had brought with it a compelling odor, one that almost made his head swim.

Karl reached over to take Katie's hand as she stepped into place beside him. He knew it would not be long. And, from the look on her face, she knew it, too.

Standing there, with Katie's hand in his, staring into the face of a man who had loved him as one of his own, Karl could not hold his emotion inside. He tried to swallow the lump that grew up in his throat, but it would not be squelched. Instead, he gripped Katie's hand a bit tighter, as if to say, "I am here for you. We will get through this."

She squeezed back, silent tears falling down her cheeks.

Standing hand in hand, they faced the inevitable. . .together.

Chapter 6

An undeniable holiness permeated the room at the moment her father slipped into the arms of Jesus, an overpowering sensation she had never before experienced. She could genuinely feel the presence of God in a real and remarkable way. And yet, she had to admit, she could also feel the gut-wrenching pain of loss, a pain so deep that it seared her heart, cut her to the quick.

The moment her father's last breath was drawn, Katie wondered if she might ever be able to catch her own breath again. It didn't seem right—or fair—that she should be allowed to breathe. To carry on. That any of them should be allowed to carry on. How could they, when the man responsible for their existence had been taken from them?

And yet he hadn't been responsible, had he? Surely the Lord had been the one to give life to everyone in the room, and surely the Lord had seen fit to take her father home. And though she disagreed with both God's timing and method, Katie could not change the fact that her father's time on this earth had drawn to an end.

The mourning among those in the room took on varied forms. Katie's older brothers swooped in around her mother, making her their primary focus. Her younger sisters had privately confided their pain and grief but never openly. . . like this. Today, as they gathered around Datt's bed to say their good-byes, every broken heart risked exposure.

Katie's reverie did not last long, however. She watched in awe as her mother began the necessary work related to his passing. *Always working, Mamm. Always working.* Even in a situation such as this, her labors never ended.

Her mother insisted on a few moments alone in the room to wash Datt's body before the undertaker arrived. Aunt Emma ushered the children off onto the front porch, where they sat together in near silence. Every now and again, someone would interject with a story about Datt, and then the tears would start again. Other than that, the only noise came from Buddy, the golden retriever, who let out an obligatory bark anytime someone came or went from the house.

Out of the corner of her eye, Katie watched Karl. He had been so good to come. And clearly, he belonged here. He really was like family, after all. Hadn't he always been?

Even now, in the midst of so much grief, Katie marveled at his ability to fit in so well with the other young men, to speak with them as if they were old friends. She appreciated his goodness to her family and would have to remember to tell him so later, when things were back to normal.

Normal.

She thought about the word with a sharp pain working its way through her heart. Would anything ever be normal again?

The funeral director, an older man named Mr. Slagel, arrived at the house within the hour, offering his condolences. He came in the familiar horse-drawn hearse, which Katie had seen many times during her childhood. She listened closely to all he had to say, though she knew, of course, what the next few hours and days would be like.

Her father would be taken to the funeral home and prepared for burial in a simple, basic coffin. Someone from the family would provide the lining, as was the custom in Amish households. Datt's body would be returned to the house in that same coffin, where it would remain until the day of the funeral. On the day before the service, friends and family members would come by to pay their last respects.

She had been down this road many times before, just never with someone in her own family. The whole thing seemed strangely surreal, as if it were happening to someone else. And yet it wasn't happening to someone else. This was very real...and horribly painful.

Mamm continued on, doing what she always did—working. She made arrangements for Datt's white pants, vest, and shirt to be sent with Mr. Slagel. Though Amish tradition dictated burying the deceased in white, Katie couldn't help but smile at the thought of her father in anything but the dark straight-cut suit he always wore. After years of seeing him working the fields in his traditional clothing, she wondered if he might be recognizable to her.

She paused for a moment to think about that. In spite of her haircut, makeup, and new clothes, Datt had recognized her the moment she walked in the room. He had sensed her presence even before his eyes had opened. Real love could clearly see beyond the external.

She spent the next few minutes pondering this, almost forgetting the goings-on inside the house. Only when several of the local men arrived to assist the undertaker did she shake herself back to reality.

A short time later, Katie stood off in the distance, watching with silent tears as Mr. Slagel and the minister lifted her father's body and carried it out to the hearse. The clip-clopping of the horses' hooves against the dirt-packed driveway provided a reminiscent sound, one she recognized from years of traveling by buggy.

But never had she watched a parent being led away in such fashion. And never had she anticipated the day she might.

Yet that day had come, whether she'd prepared for it or not.

After they left, she excused herself to the field behind the house, hoping for a time to release her emotions. Surely everyone would give her a bit of space without asking too many questions.

She eased her way through the crowd, noticing the questioning look in Karl's eyes. He seemed to ask, "Can I come with you?"

She did not respond. For now, she simply wanted time by herself. Time to mourn in private. Katie walked around the side of the house alone. Well, almost alone. Buddy insisted on joining her, his tail tucked between his legs as if sensing her pain.

Together they approached the back of the house. As her gaze landed on the beautiful green pasture behind the home, she was swept back to her younger years. How many times had she taken off running through the ribbons of green grass when her heart ached?

For a moment, she tried to convince herself that no proper young woman would do such a thing. But then, as the pain settled in and the grief took over, she kicked off her shoes and began to run. She made it past the doghouse and out into the clearing. On she ran, until her lungs cried out for relief. Katie could hear Buddy's pants as he moved alongside her. Funny how the rhythm of his steady gait kept her going.

She finally drew to a stop, breathing in great gulps of air. The tears came freely now, and the dog, perhaps in an attempt to bring comfort, lifted his front paws onto her chest. Katie gave him a rub behind the ears, and he nuzzled up against her.

She thought about Datt and all of the years she'd worked alongside him in the fields. She remembered the gleam in his eye as he'd taught her to drive a buggy. The look of sheer joy on his face as they sat across the dinner table from one another telling funny stories. Oh, how she wished she could go back, just once more. To have just five more minutes with him. Was that too much to ask?

After a period of true mourning, Katie finally dried her eyes. She looked back to see just how far she'd come and discovered the house was quite a distance away. This time, instead of running, she walked with slow, steady steps. Buddy, as always, kept his place beside her, a faithful companion. When she reached the back door, Katie dropped onto the porch step, exhausted.

She was greeted by Sara, who had a concerned look in her eyes. "Still running, Katie?"

"W—what?"

"I'm sorry." Sara bowed her head, cheeks turning red. "I didn't mean that the way it sounded. It's just that you were always so fast when you were a little girl, moving ahead out of the pack. Remember when we were young and you would challenge us to race from the front door to the street?"

"Oh yes. I thought you meant. . ." Katie's thoughts shifted back, once again, to the night she ran away from home.

Are you still running, Katie?

She took a seat on the porch step and tried to steady the trembling in her hands.

"I hate to bring this up," Sara said, taking a seat next to her. "But we need to let people know. Mamm has asked that someone write an obituary for the paper."

"Would Datt have wanted that?"

"He wouldn't want us gushing over him or making him look better than others," Sara said, "but I think it's important to spread the word to others in the community. An obituary is not inappropriate."

"I see."

"Would you mind writing it, Katie? Your writing is the strongest in the family."

"I don't know if I can," she whispered.

Just then, Karl appeared at the door. "Do you ladies need anything?" he asked. "A glass of lemonade? Water?" He gave them a please-let-me-help look, and Katie smiled at his kindness. She shook her head, and he added, "May I join you?" with a tentative look in his eyes.

"Sure." Sara gestured for him to sit on the step next to them, and Karl eased his way down to a sitting position.

"We were just talking about the obituary," Sara explained. "I think Katie should write it."

Katie sighed, not saying anything for a moment. Then suddenly something occurred to her. "Wait a minute." She turned to look at Karl. "You were the best writer in our class."

"What?"

"Yes, and I'll bet you do a lot of writing in your line of work." She gave him an imploring look. "Would you help me, Karl? Please?"

❧

Karl looked into Katie's tear-filled eyes, and his heart felt as if it would come out of his chest. Of course he would help her. He would do whatever she needed.

Minutes later, with half the family crowded around him at the dining room table, he began the task of putting together a carefully constructed obituary, covering the most basic things about Elam Walken's life. He knew better than to praise the man, as this was frowned upon among the Amish. No, plain and simple would do. *Just the facts, ma'am,* went through his head.

And so he listed the facts. On the surface they might appear rather ordinary—at least to those who didn't know Elam. Husband. Father. Church member. Farmer. Neighbor. But those who truly knew and loved the man would read between the lines. Elam's dedication to his wife and children was beyond compare. And his love for those in the community and the church could not be questioned. Best of all, his steady faith in the Lord resounded in every detail of his life. Karl did his best to insert these things in a subtler way.

After completing the piece, Sara insisted Karl read it aloud to everyone in the room. He did so hesitantly, hoping he'd done the man justice and yet hoping he hadn't gone too far. When he finished reading, tears filled every eye.

"You got it just right," Mrs. Walken said. She drew close and gave him a hug.

"Yes, you've done a wonderful job." Sara dabbed at her eyes.

The others in the family added their thoughts on the matter, all positive. Still, there was one who had not commented, and he longed to hear what she had to say. Karl looked into Katie's beautiful green eyes, wishing he could kiss away the tears he found there. He wanted to wrap her in his arms, to tell her everything would be okay. Instead, he waited in silence until she nodded and whispered, "It's beautiful, Karl."

He gave a simple nod in response then, realizing they couldn't fax the obituary to the local newspaper, offered to drive it into town and hand-deliver it.

Again, Katie looked at him with a look of genuine gratitude, mouthing a silent, "Thank you."

"Are you sure you don't mind?" Emily asked.

Karl rose to his feet. "Of course not." He would drive to town, no problem. In fact, he would willingly drive halfway across the country if he thought it would ease Katie's pain. With the piece of paper folded in his hand, Karl headed for the door.

Chapter 7

Katie marveled that the morning of her father's funeral turned out to be so sunny and bright. It hardly seemed fair, in light of the family's great loss. The sky overhead beckoned with a brilliant blue—the very color she'd avoided for years. She couldn't overlook the irony, no matter how hard she tried. Across the broad expanse of the back yard, wildflowers bloomed in colorful display, a vivid message that life, no matter how painful, would go on.

The unquestionable beauty of the surroundings kept Katie's tears at bay. As she stepped out onto the back porch, a gentle breeze wrapped her in its embrace, bringing comfort. Surely the Lord Himself leaned in to whisper in her ear as the winds drifted by.

She glanced down at her plain brown dress, one she had borrowed from Emily. She wore it both out of respect for her family and out of a desire not to draw attention to herself. With so many from the community in attendance, she simply wanted to blend in. This day was all about Datt, not an opportunity to make a fashion statement.

People from all over the county arrived by buggy for the simple service inside the Walken home, led by Jonas Stutzman, the local bishop. After everyone gathered in the living room—with some spilling out onto the porch—the bishop stood near the coffin to address the congregation. Katie knew that he would not speak of her father. Most Amish ministers did not mention the deceased at a funeral, choosing, instead, to speak from the story of creation.

"'Earth to earth, ashes to ashes, dust to dust,'" Jonas read from his prayer book. "'From dust man was created and to dust he returns—in sure and certain hope of the resurrection into eternal life.'"

He then spoke to the crowd from the Gospel of John, the fifth chapter, referring often to the resurrection of the dead. Katie closed her eyes and tried to picture it. The image of her father working in the fields came to mind, and in her daydream state, she could almost imagine him being snatched up, raised to the pale blue skies out of the green fields below to meet the Lord face-to-face.

She opened her eyes once again, trying to stay focused. Across the room, Karl stood with his old friend, Ike Biden. A feeling of peace enveloped her as she caught him looking her way. His actions over the past few days had more than proven one thing—his loyalty to her family had not wavered, in spite of her actions all those years ago.

In so many ways, Karl's loyalty reminded Katie of her father's steadfastness. Never had she met a man so dedicated to family as Datt, so selfless, so willing to give of himself to others, even at his own expense. She had never heard him complain. Not once. Her thoughts shifted to her work at the realty office. How many times a day did she whine about this little thing or that? Dozens likely.

If I could be half the person he was, I'd be doing well.

After the brief ceremony, the crowd of people shifted out-of-doors, to prepare for the ride to the cemetery. Each buggy received a number, designating the order in which it would proceed. Katie stood alongside her sisters, watching as Datt's coffin was placed in the hearse, a boxlike enclosed carriage drawn by a horse. Then she glanced down at the long line of buggies heading to the cemetery. They presented a solemn, impressive sight.

It took a considerable length of time to make it to the cemetery, what with the whole caravan of buggies, but Katie didn't mind. She wanted to put off the inevitable as long as possible. When they finally arrived, Karl appeared next to their carriage, ready to offer a hand to the women in the Walken family. He greeted her mother with a look of genuine caring and then helped Sara next. Finally, he reached out to take Katie's hand. She held on to his as she stepped down onto the ground—ground that would soon swallow up the wooden box that held her father's body.

Katie didn't realize that she still gripped Karl's hand until they arrived at the gravesite. With embarrassment taking hold, she loosened her grip and focused on the task ahead. She took one look at the chasm in the ground, however, and her heart lurched. If anything, she wanted to reach for Karl's arm once more, to steady herself. Instead, she brushed away a loose tear and planted her feet firmly on the ground, determined to remain strong for her mother and siblings.

As was the custom with Amish funerals, no songs were sung during the burial service. Instead, Bishop Stutzman read the words to an old familiar hymn as the pallbearers lowered the coffin into the grave. Afterward, the whole group silently prayed the Lord's Prayer. Katie thanked the Lord for the opportunity to close her eyes, to shut out the reality of what took place directly in front of her. She half wished the whole thing had been a dream, that she could open her eyes to discover Datt standing beside her, arm around her shoulder, offering comfort.

At some point during the prayer the tears came in force. Only then did she feel a hand slip into her own—a strong hand with a gentle touch. A hand with a tissue in it. She would have to remember to thank Karl later for his kindness.

Following the burial, friends and family members gathered around to console the family. Katie watched as her mother received embrace after embrace and tried to imagine what it would feel like to lose the only person you had ever loved. It surely left her mother's heart with a gaping hole inside, one only the Lord would be able to fill over the following months and years.

After the crowd thinned, Sara drew close for a quiet conversation. "Several of the ladies have brought food to the house, so we're going back for lunch." She looked over at Karl, who remained nearby, and added, "We hope you will join us."

"Of course." He nodded then looked at Katie, perhaps in an effort to get her opinion on the matter. She offered up a warm smile and a nod. Of course he could stay for lunch.

Having Karl here, beside her, felt so right, so normal.

Katie couldn't help but wonder, *Why did it feel so wrong all those years ago?*

❧

Karl kept a watchful eye on Katie throughout the afternoon. The exhaustion in her eyes grew more apparent with each step she took. In spite of his best attempts to slow her down, she insisted on scurrying around the room, tending to the needs of others. Working with great zeal, she filled plates and helped out in the kitchen. He couldn't get her to sit, no matter how hard he tried. In that respect, she was much like her mother. Perhaps too much.

Karl pondered that for a moment. The Amish work ethic had always been drilled into him, from childhood on. How many times while growing up had he heard the words "Be wary of idle hands"?

The Walken family members were the hardest workers in the community, and Katie appeared to have inherited a double dose of their energy. She never seemed to slow her pace, even during the hardest of times. He thought back to their childhoods, remembering the many times she had taken on extra chores around the farm, as if to prove she could outwork anyone else in the family. And then as a teen, her lengthy hours at the store had always concerned him.

Karl was reminded of his recent visit to her posh office at Bucks County Realty. Beneath the polished exterior, he'd noticed stacks of papers on her desk and a very full calendar with dozens of appointments penciled in. Surely she had taken on the challenge of hard work with a vengeance. No one could deny that. But when did she rest? She seemed to run full throttle day and night.

Running.

She'd been running for as long as he could remember, now that he thought about it. And if she didn't slow down soon, she would eventually burn herself out.

Unable to control the protective feelings that flooded over him as he watched her, Karl decided a change of focus was in order. He sat next to Amos, Katie's oldest brother, and engaged him in conversation. They talked about the future and the efforts Daniel and Amos would continue to put into the farm.

"We love this land," Amos explained. "And we will work hard to keep things going, as Datt taught us."

Karl knew the Walken farm remained in good hands but had to wonder how Elam's sons would manage without their father's expertise. The man had been a brilliant farmer, always producing the best crops in the county. And his dairy cows were among the heartiest, as well. Karl hoped Elam's sons and sons-in-law would take over where Elam had left off.

Later that afternoon, the crowd thinned and Karl finally managed to get Katie to himself. They sat together in adjoining wicker rockers, and she kicked off her shoes, grumbling about her aching feet. No doubt they ached. She'd been on them all day.

She closed her eyes for a minute or so, but when they opened, he noticed the glistening of tears. He longed to reach out and take her hand but didn't dare—not here in the house, anyway.

"You've had a hard day," he managed.

She nodded.

"Is there anything I can do?"

Katie let out a lingering sigh. "Not unless you have the ability to go back and change some of the mistakes I made in the past."

Karl smiled. "Trust me, if I could do that, I'd start with my own mistakes."

Her momentary silence bothered him, but not as much as what she said after. "You've never been prone to mistakes, Karl. I'm talking about the big stuff. The kinds of things I've done that hurt my family. And you."

He wanted to quote a Bible verse—to remind her that everyone sinned, everyone fell short of the glory of God—but didn't. Instead, he simply listened as she bared her soul.

"I know there's really no way to undo the past," Katie said with a wistful look in her eye. "I know that. But if I could, I'd go back and do so many things differently."

Karl wondered which things, specifically, she referred to but did not ask. "Life is filled with 'could haves' and 'would haves.'" He shrugged. "The only thing I can suggest is that you forgive yourself for the things you regret and thank God that every day is a brand-new beginning."

"Mmm-hmm." Katie took a nibble of coffee cake and then leaned back against her chair. After a few seconds of neither of them speaking, she finally broke the silence. "It's just hard to picture tomorrow as a new beginning after what we've been through." She shook her head. "I can't even imagine what my mother will do without Datt. And my brothers and sisters—they have so much work ahead of them with the farm, the house, the store. It's going to be a lot to handle without my father here to lead the way."

Ah. So she's worried about their workload. Feeling guilty about not being here to help. Somehow that didn't surprise him.

"What are you thinking?" he asked finally. "Are you contemplating coming back—to live?"

Her face paled. "Oh, Karl, I. . .I can't imagine it." Her voice lowered to a whisper. "Can you?"

He shook his head. "I've thought about it hundreds of times, but I truly feel the Lord has given me my marching orders. I don't think I'll ever go back to the Old Order again, to be honest."

"Me either." She shook her head. "But I won't be much help to my mother from Doylestown, will I?"

"I know you well enough to know you will stay in touch with her. And you can always visit," he said. "It's just a couple of hours, after all."

"True." She leaned back and closed her eyes once more, and he wondered if she might doze off. Instead, she whispered, "I never thought my dad would die. He just seemed. . ."

"Immortal?"

She nodded. "I know we're all going to die eventually, but I never really spent much time thinking about it, at least as it pertained to my family. And my dad, of all people! He was. . ."

"Invincible?"

She opened her eyes and gazed at him with a nod. "Yes. That's the word. He was the strongest man I've ever known. And he lived such a wonderful life."

Karl looked into her eyes, his heart swelling as he remembered something his father had always said. "Life is a gift," he said, repeating his datt's familiar words, "and death is a given."

"You're really wise," Katie said with a sigh. "Has anyone ever told you that?"

"Hardly." He laughed. "Though some of the attorneys in my office come to me for advice on occasion. And some of the kids in my youth group at church, as well."

"I can see why." She gave him a pensive look, and for a moment he wanted to slip his arm over her shoulder, to draw her close.

Unfortunately, his cell phone chose that very moment to ring. He'd meant to silence it earlier in the day, out of respect for the family. Somehow, he must've forgotten. Thank goodness it hadn't rung during the service.

With a sigh, Karl glanced down at the number then reacted rather quickly to what he saw. "It's Aimee," he whispered, rising to his feet, "hopefully calling about the Chandler property. I'll take it out on the porch."

With a spring in his step, he bounded for the door.

Chapter 8

The morning after the funeral, Karl approached the Walken house with a fishing pole in his hand. The idea had come to him in the night. At first he had pushed it off, wondering if Katie would think it inappropriate. Then, after wrestling with the sheets for a couple of hours, he had settled on the idea that a visit to the Pequea Creek would be therapeutic for both of them.

Besides, he would be leaving for Doylestown later in the day to sign a final contract on the Chandler place. If everything went as planned, he would close on the property by month's end. A second call, this one from his office, had filled him in on a host of other work-related things that awaited him back at home.

Home. Hmm.

He sighed as he thought about it. As much as he wanted to get back to work, leaving Paradise seemed wrong, at least if Katie remained behind. Still, he could do little about it. Work called, and he must answer. If possible, he would spend his final hours here with her. Surely that would ease the pain of leaving.

Karl pondered that for a moment. Despite his best attempts, his heart still remained tied to Katie. Sure, he'd dated other girls over the years, tried to care about one or two of them in the same way he'd care for her. But nothing felt the same.

Why those age-old feelings returned with such a vengeance now, he could not say. After all, he had done his best to squelch them. Hadn't he? And surely she had shown no particular interest in him beyond friendship.

Thankfully, Katie answered the door. The weariness in her eyes stunned him.

"You could use a break." He lifted the pole for her to see. "What would you think about a little fishing trip?"

"Fishing trip?" She looked stunned. "I can't leave Mamm here alone with so much to be done."

"You go on, Katydid," her mother said, appearing behind her. "Aunt Emma is coming by to help me, and your brothers will be by later, as well. They will tend to whatever needs I have. Besides, I'm plenty tired. I might just lie down and take a nap this morning."

"Are you sure?"

"Yes." Her mother yawned then walked back into the house.

And so, in spite of her argument to the contrary, Katie agreed to join Karl along the banks of Pequea Creek for a morning of fishing, just like the old days. His heart swelled with joy at the thought of it. They would have one last morning together before. . .well, before normal life kicked in again.

As they walked along, Katie seemed preoccupied with their surroundings. "I can't believe these wildflowers." She pointed to a cluster of pink impatiens. "Were they always this colorful?"

"They were."

"And the grass." She pointed out across the pastures. "I honestly think it's greener since I left."

"Your leaving turned the grass greener?" He couldn't help but laugh. "That's pretty humorous, you have to admit."

"I'm just saying I don't remember things being this. . .beautiful. How was I raised in all of this without actually seeing it for what it was? The Amish country is the prettiest land I've ever seen, and I've traveled extensively over the years."

"Agreed," Karl said. "And I've thought about the irony many times."

"Irony?"

"We both left Paradise to enter the outside world."

"Ah"—she sighed—"I see what you mean. That is ironic, especially when you see how pretty it is."

They arrived at the edge of the creek, and Karl stood spellbound by the sight. Somehow he remembered the creek as being larger. Wider. But today it seemed a narrow slit across the land, just a trickle of water in comparison to the picture he'd locked in his memory.

In spite of this, he still wanted to fish, if for no other reason than to be with the woman who now captivated both his heart and his thoughts. He located the perfect spot for Katie to sit then joined her. After a few minutes spent baiting their hooks and tossing them out into the water, he felt compelled to finish the conversation they had started earlier.

"About what I said before—I didn't mean to imply that leaving the Amish life was a mistake," Karl said. "I don't think I could have stayed, in fact, and not just because of losing my parents. Still, something about being here in this part of Pennsylvania felt right." He leaned back against the trunk of the elm tree and tossed his fishing line into the water, adding, "Not just comfortable, either."

"It is serene here," Katie agreed. "Things are just more peaceful away from. . . well, the world."

Karl laughed. "It's interesting you should put it like that. I keep thinking about Adam and Eve in the Garden of Eden. They had everything they could've ever wanted right in front of them, and still they wanted more."

"I've thought about that myself. Several times, in fact. I suppose the same could be said of me, at a younger age anyway. Now that I've tasted and seen what the world has to offer, I'm not convinced it's all better."

"Yeah." He leaned back against the tree and listened to the rippling of the water against the rocks.

"Don't get me wrong," she said with a hint of laughter in her voice. "There are a lot of things I'd have a tough time doing without."

"Like?"

"Hmm." She paused for a moment. "Well, fast food, for one. And pedicures."

"Pedicures?"

She flashed an impish grin then shrugged. "Yeah. Once you've had one, it's impossible to turn back." After a moment's pause, she added, "I'd have the hardest time doing without my car. It's hard to imagine getting around Doylestown without it."

"Sometimes I wonder how we managed out here at all," he agreed. "Then I come back and I'm reminded of how simple, how peaceful life used to be."

For a moment, neither of them said anything. He closed his eyes and remembered back to a time when the two of them had sat together, listening to the same sounds, feeling the same early morning summer breeze. A time before either of them had owned a car or television or fancy clothes.

"What do you miss most about living here?" she asked.

"Hmm." He smiled. "I miss the sense of community. I mean, I go to a great church and I have a lot of great people around me, but it's not quite the same. People don't seem to have the same investment in one another. As children, we knew that people in our community would come rushing in if we needed something. Sometimes folks in churches get overlooked when they're going through troubled times. That always frustrates me."

"It is sad." She dipped her toes in the water and wiggled them around. "At my church they have committees for that sort of thing."

"Still, people are often passed over. We were never passed over as children, were we?"

"No," she said, "but I'm not naive enough to think I will ever have that same sense of family I experienced as a youngster. Not without moving back for good, I mean."

He shrugged. "You never know."

"What else do you miss?" she asked.

"I miss the barn raisings. And the buggy rides." He started laughing. "Remember that time we got stuck in the mud coming back from town? That older woman stopped to help us then offered us a ride back to your house in her car?"

"Mmm-hmm." Katie's eyes grew wide. "I remember how much I wanted to climb in that beautiful car and ride all the way back." A sigh escaped her lips. "Then I pictured the look on my mother's face if I'd come cruising up the driveway in a luxury sedan."

They both erupted in laughter, and Karl's heart seemed to come alive. Perhaps they weren't living in Paradise anymore. But sitting here, with Katie at his side, was the closest he'd come in years.

❧

Katie spent the better part of the morning trying to accomplish two things: catch a fish before Karl did and quiet the crazy beating in her heart every time he looked her way. For whatever reason, she felt like a jabbering schoolgirl whenever he tried to engage her in conversation. Only this time, her feelings were different than they had been as a teen. Stronger. Unavoidable, really.

Perhaps, as a young woman, she had managed to push aside any feelings for Karl in her quest to escape the lifestyle. But now, having tasted the things of the world, she suddenly found herself far more captivated by the gentleness of the man sitting next to her.

Surely the beauty of the Amish countryside wasn't the only thing she'd taken for granted as a child. Had Karl always been this good, this kind? And had she really not noticed how well their hands fit together? How beautifully they finished each other's sentences?

These things and more she pondered. . .until she felt a tug on her line. "Ooo! I've got one!"

She pulled up a smallmouth bass, and Karl whistled. "That's a beauty. Looks like someone's having fish for supper."

"Datt would've loved this." She sighed as she thought about the many times her father had fished alongside her and the gleam in his eye every time he hooked a prize catch.

Together, Katie and Karl worked to ease the frantic bass from the hook and into a bucket filled with creek water. She stared down at him in wonder, noting the beauty of his rich green color. He looked up at her with sad eyes, as if to say, "Release me, please."

In an impulsive decision, she lifted the bucket and carried it to the edge of the creek.

"What are you doing?" Karl gave her an incredulous look. "You just caught—"

He never had a chance to finish his sentence. Katie leaned down and tipped the bucket over, allowing the fish to slither back into the waters of Pequea Creek. She glanced over at Karl with a shrug. "Sorry. I just didn't have it in me."

He stared at her in disbelief. She wanted to explain but wasn't sure where to begin. The little guy just wanted to be free. In many ways, she was reminded of herself as a teen, wanting to be released out of her tiny bucket—the Amish community—into a bigger stream. She had escaped from the bucket back then. Tipped it over herself and climbed out. But this poor bass needed help, needed someone to assist him.

Clearly, Karl didn't get it. He continued to stare at her with a look of genuine confusion on his face.

"I have a confession to make," Katie said, after sitting once again.

"A confession?" Karl wiped the perspiration from his brow and gave her an inquisitive look.

"Yeah." She brushed the dust from her hands. "When I slipped out of the window all those years ago, I made myself a promise."

"Oh?"

"Yeah. It might sound crazy, but. . .I've never worn blue since I left Lancaster County."

"Are you serious?"

A wave of relief washed over her as she told the story, one she'd never before told a soul, not even Hannah. "I grew up wearing mostly navy blue or brown dresses," she explained. "The night I slipped out of the window, I was wearing a blue one. My mother and Aunt Emma had just sewn it for me. For. . ."

"For our wedding day."

"Yes." She let her gaze shift to the ground. "It was the last time I ever wore blue."

"How in the world do you manage? Half my wardrobe is blue," Karl said.

"It would be a tragedy for you to avoid that color. Your eyes are the prettiest shade of blue I've ever seen." Katie clamped her hand over her mouth the minute the words were out, not quite believing she'd actually said such a thing out loud.

Karl laughed. "Well, thank you."

"To answer your question," Katie continued, "I do wear jeans. That's my only compromise. But no blue blouses or dresses, anything like that. I don't even own a blue nightgown." She laughed. "I can't believe no one has ever noticed I avoid the color."

"Probably because your eyes are green," Karl said with a wink. "You do wear green, I see." He gestured to her blouse.

"I do." Katie laughed and then remembered a story she wanted to tell. "When Hannah and Matt got married a few years after I moved to Doylestown, I was in quite a fix. She'd chosen blue for her bridesmaids' dresses."

"What did you do?"

"Convinced her that blue wasn't trendy. Talked her into lavender." She smiled, remembering. "She was fine with that, actually, so I didn't feel too bad. And I think she figured out what I was up to. She was raised alongside me, after all."

"That she was."

Just then a shout in the distance caught their attention. Katie looked up to discover Emily approaching, breathless and red-cheeked.

"You have to come back to the house," her sister managed between pants.

"What's happened?" Katie scrambled to her feet.

"It's Sara. The baby is coming."

"The b—baby?" Katie gave her sister a wide-eyed stare, hoping she didn't mean what she thought she meant. "But Sara's not due for four weeks."

"Someone needs to tell that to the baby."

"Jacob will take her to town in the buggy," Emily explained. "To the birthing center. But Sara is asking for you. She wants you there."

"The buggy?" Katie gave her younger sister a curious look. "Wouldn't it be better if I took them in my car?"

Emily shrugged. "We will let Sara determine that. She likely has enough time to get there in the buggy. But it's possible she will want one of you to call ahead to let the midwife know she's on her way. I would go myself, but Mamm isn't feeling well, and I think I should stay with her."

"Of course."

"Should I wait here?" Karl reached for his fishing pole.

Emily shook her head. "No, you should go, too. Jacob will need menfolk to gather around him, no doubt. Having you there will help keep him calm until the baby is born."

Katie gave Karl an imploring look. "Yes, please ride with me."

"I'll do one better than that," Karl said, rising to his feet. "I'll drive you there myself."

Relief washed over her as she nodded. How many times had he stepped in over the past few days, bringing comfort? Like an umbrella, he had shielded her from a multitude of storms.

And, from what she could tell, the rain was about to start up again.

Chapter 9

Karl eased his car out onto the road behind Jacob and Sara's buggy, ready to tail them all the way to town. He glanced at Katie, who appeared to be a nervous wreck.

"You okay?"

"Mmm-hmm." Just then Katie leaned over and pressed the horn. "Did you see that?" She pointed out to the road. "The guy in that SUV nearly hit Sara's buggy. If he had any idea there was a pregnant woman inside. . ."

She continued to rant as Karl watched her in amusement. In truth, the car hadn't come near the buggy at all, though he would certainly never say so. No, at this point it would be far better just to let sleeping dogs lie. Or. . .ranting women rant.

He felt like a snail crawling along behind the buggy. If only they'd been able to talk Sara and Jacob into joining them in the car; surely they would have been there by now. He'd seen the flash of panic in Jacob's eyes back in the house, but Sara insisted they would do just fine going to town in the usual way, reminding him that first babies rarely came quickly.

However, no more than a mile from the Walken home, the buggy came to an abrupt halt. Karl pulled his car off the road behind them and leaped from the seat to see what had happened. He found Jacob wide-eyed, seemingly frozen in place.

"Everything okay?" Karl asked.

Katie appeared on the other side of the rig, ready to be of assistance to her sister.

Sara's eyes grew huge as she panted. "I. . .don't. . .think. . .I'm. . .going. . .to . . .make. . .it."

Katie took one look at Sara's face and made a pronouncement. "Everyone into the car. We're driving you the rest of the way."

"But the rig, the horses. . ." Jacob scrambled out of the buggy in a dither.

"Don't worry about them." Karl tossed his car keys to Katie, who caught them with ease. "Katie will drive you to town in my car, and I'll follow with the buggy."

"Are you sure?" Jacob had relief written all over his face.

"Of course. Now go on. Don't wait on me. No time to waste."

Karl waited until the car pulled out onto the road before climbing into the rig. Once inside, he took the reins in his hands and drew in a deep breath. He spoke a handful of words aloud, more to convince himself than the horses, "It's been awhile, boys, but I think I've still got it in me." With a snap of the reins, he was on his way.

The midday traffic breezed by. Several cars beeped their horns, trying to push him out of the way. Karl stayed as far to the right as possible but couldn't seem to calm the drivers down. The horses were a bit skittish, as well. Thankfully, he managed to keep them under control.

Just a mile or so outside of town, some tourists obviously took Karl for a true Amish man as the car slowed and one of them snapped his picture. No doubt they would get quite a jolt when they took a closer look at the photo and realized he wore jeans and a T-shirt. He wanted to shout, "Hey, cut that out!" but didn't. Most Englishers didn't realize the Amish frowned at picture taking. So Karl bit his lip and continued to plod along, easing his way down the highway toward the birthing center.

Only one problem. He had no idea where the birthing center was.

Ah, his cell phone. He did have that, though he'd kept it turned off since Aimee's call. Karl used one hand to hold the reins and another to punch in Katie's number. All the while, he couldn't help but laugh. What would the curious tourists think now if one snapped a photo of the Amish man with a cell phone in his hand?

Katie paced the halls of the birthing center and prayed. From what the midwife had said, it wouldn't be long. Sara's water had broken while in the buggy, and the baby's appearance was imminent. There seemed to be some concern about Sara's blood pressure, which was running on the high side, so the midwife ushered Katie out of the room. Of course, there had also been the issue of the baby coming early.

With so many variables factored in, Katie had been instructed to wait in the hall—and to pray. And that's exactly what she did.

Until her cell phone rang.

She fumbled around in her purse for it, surprised to hear Karl's voice when she answered.

"Is everything okay?" she asked.

"Mmm, yeah. I'm just a little lost."

She proceeded to give him directions then conveyed her fears about her sister's condition. To her great relief, Karl offered to pray. She continued to pace the hall as his comforting voice took over. His appeal to the Almighty for a safe and healthy delivery of the baby eased her troubled mind.

As he finished with an "amen," Katie was struck with the realization that he'd telephoned her from inside the buggy. She tried to envision what he looked like plodding through the center of town in the rig with a cell phone in hand, praying aloud as he went. Must be quite a sight, especially for curious onlookers.

Just about that time, she heard a cry from the other side of the door and realized the little darling had arrived. "We have a baby!"

Karl responded with a whoop, which nearly deafened her. "I have the birthing center in sight," he said. "I'll be there within minutes."

No sooner had he arrived than the midwife emerged from Sara's delivery room with a broad smile. "You can go inside now," she told them.

Katie took a step toward the door, but Karl's feet remained planted on the hall floor.

"You go ahead," he encouraged her.

She tiptoed into the room, her heart swelling with pride as she saw Sara sitting up in the bed with the little bundle in her arms. Her sister's hair hung down in long, beautiful tresses around her shoulders. Katie hardly recognized her without her kapp.

Sara gestured for her to draw near. "Come and see your niece."

"She's a. . .it's a girl?"

"Yes, and she wants to meet her aunt Katie."

Katie took a couple of tentative steps in her sister's direction. The little bundle in Sara's arms wiggled and let out a squeal. Glancing down, Katie noticed the squinted eyes and pink face. Wrapped up in a soft white blanket, she looked like a perfect little baby doll. Tiny, to be sure, but perfect.

"She's beautiful, Sara!" At once she wanted to scoop the little darling in her arms but kept her distance, not wanting to intrude.

"Thank you." Sara looked up at Jacob with a warm smile. "I wouldn't have made it without him. He was such a help to me."

"I'm sure he was." Katie reached over to give him a hug. "Congratulations, Datt."

Even as the word was spoken, everyone in the room grew eerily silent. The truth registered at once. *The Lord giveth and the Lord taketh away.* The scripture had never felt so personal, so. . .real.

"What will you call her?" Katie whispered, brushing away a tear.

With a smile, Sara gave her answer. "We've settled on Rachel." She gazed down at her daughter. "I think she looks like a Rachel, don't you?"

Katie peered down at the wriggly bundle. "I do."

"She's only five and a half pounds," Sara explained, "but we've been told she's healthy enough to take home."

"When?"

"By nightfall, I would imagine."

"Are you serious?" Katie could hardly believe it.

"Yes, we will give Sara a few hours to rest; then I will take her back to the house." Jacob looked toward the door with a curious look on his face. "That reminds me. . .did Karl make it here with the buggy?"

"He did." Katie resisted the urge to tell them about his adventures along the way. "He's just outside the door."

"Oh, invite him in." Sara gave an imploring look.

"Ah. . .are you sure?"

"Yes." Sara fussed with the covers to make herself more presentable.

It took a bit of wooing to get Karl into the room, but when he saw the baby, his face came alive at once. "Oh, Sara, she's amazing." He went into a lengthy discussion about her beautiful features, and Katie couldn't help but smile. The Amish weren't prone to accept flattery, but her sister didn't seem to mind the glowing report about her daughter.

After a brief visit with Karl, Sara nodded off to sleep. Jacob followed Katie and Karl out into the hallway. "It would be good if you could take the car and go back to the house to tell the others," he explained. "I'm sure Sara's mamm is anxious to hear the news, and Emily, too."

"Will you be okay if we leave?" Katie asked.

Jacob smiled. "We will be fine. And, as we said, we will return home by nightfall, anyway."

Katie sneaked back into the birthing room once more for a quick peek at her tiny niece. She reached down with her index finger and ran it along Rachel's cheek. "Happy birthday, baby girl," she whispered. "Now, sleep tight."

Minutes later, Katie settled into the car with Karl behind the wheel. She leaned her head back against the seat, trying to take in all of the day's events. For whatever reason, her eyes began to water.

"You okay?" Karl looked over at her in concern.

"Yes." She used a fingertip to brush away a tear. "I just find it interesting that the baby was born today, the day after we buried Datt. It's almost like the Lord wanted to prove that life would go on in spite of our pain."

"Amen." Karl reached to give her hand a squeeze, and they sat that way for some time.

"One life ends and another begins," she whispered. "Though"—the tears began in earnest—"I can't help but wonder what Datt would've thought of the baby. He was always so wonderful with the little ones."

"Your father was a man who really knew how to live—and love," Karl said. "I used to watch him with his animals and marvel at how he treated them with such tenderness."

"Yes." Katie smiled as the memories flooded over her.

"And I can remember one night when I was about seventeen," Karl continued "your datt and I were standing out on your front porch looking at the sunset I was ready to go back in the house as the sun dipped off to the west, but he wanted to linger a few minutes more. It might sound strange, but I learned a lot from him, how he paused to take in every precious second of a sunset. He told me to stop, to be patient. That I would miss the best part if I hurried away."

Before responding, Katie thought about the many times she had hurried away from things. And people. "What did you do?"

Karl chuckled. "I stood there, of course. And within minutes, the colors all kind of merged together—red, orange, gold, pink. They slipped away behind huge white clouds. It was like the outer edges of the clouds were suddenly broadcast in Technicolor display, like something you'd see in a rare photograph. And I almost missed it. But your datt—"

"He never missed a thing," Katie said thoughtfully. She paused as she pondered that, finally adding, "Until now."

Karl pulled his hand away and reached to start the car. "Oh, I don't know. I'd like to think he was looking on today, observing from above."

"Observing *which* part?" Katie turned to Karl and chuckled. "The part where his granddaughter entered the world or the part where a young man he once trusted enough to marry his daughter chatted on a cell phone while driving his buggy?"

Karl erupted in laughter as he slipped the car into gear. "Okay, you've got me there. Maybe it's better to assume he was distracted getting the Walken family mansion ready instead of keeping an eye on us."

Katie thought about Karl's words all the way back to the house. It did bring her some comfort to know her father had led the way. Perhaps he'd already discovered a patch of farmland in heaven, ready to be plowed. Or maybe he'd stumbled upon a creek stocked full of smallmouth bass, ready to be caught.

At any rate, he was sure to be enjoying every sight, every sound.

Katie glanced out of the car window at the beautiful countryside and, with a wistful sigh, committed to do the same.

Chapter 10

Katie paid particular attention to the exquisite colors of the Pennsylvania sunset that night. Perhaps it had something to do with Karl's story about her father. Or maybe it had a little something to do with the fact that Karl pulled away from the farm at the very time the sun slipped off the edge of the horizon to the west.

Regardless, she stood quite still on the front porch of the house she'd grown up in and paid extra-special attention to the mesmerizing details as they unfolded, minute by minute. Sure enough, what started out as a blazing yellow ball in the sky eventually morphed into shimmering shades of orange and then fiery red. The whole thing seemed to happen in stages, and she didn't want to miss even one.

Funny. Watching the progression made her think of Karl—how her relationship with him had moved along in varying stages over the years, changing colors at each point. Her heart twisted a bit at the revelation. To know that she'd hurt him all those years ago brought such pain. And guilt.

Tonight, just before he pulled away, Katie had taken a few moments to beg for his forgiveness, something she should have done years ago. Karl, in his usual gracious way, had told her there was nothing to forgive, that God had already mended any wounds she might have inflicted, intentional or otherwise. Clearly, he had forgiven her years ago. And truly the Lord had forgiven her as well. How many times had she poured out her heart, asking God to wash away any pain she might have caused her friends and family as a thrill-seeking young woman?

But now, as she stood staring at the sunset, Katie had to wonder, had she forgiven herself? If so, why did this gripping sensation grab hold of her every time she remembered what she'd done? Perhaps this would be just the time to take care of that.

As the red in the skies above faded to a soft bluish pink, Katie took a moment to release herself from the overwhelming guilt. To set herself free. Within seconds, the weight she'd been carrying began to lift, and she literally felt better. Now she could truly look to the future.

A sudden gust of wind whipped through the trees in the front yard, startling her. Katie discovered a hummingbird swooping down upon its feeder above, its tiny wings whirring with anticipation. Oh, to be that carefree! Did the little creature have a worry in the world?

After dipping his beak into the sweet liquid, the angelic creature flew away apparently in a rush to move on. As he lifted off and disappeared from view, Katie's burden seemed to fly away with him, heading off to the vastness of the horizon. "As far as the east is from the west." She quoted the familiar scripture.

She thought about her relationship with her family and how like that little hummingbird she'd become over the years—touching down only when she felt like it. Her parents had sugared the water many times, trying to woo her back home. Still, she had remained distant.

Katie turned in curiosity as the hinges on the screen door let out a squeak. She smiled as her gaze landed on Emily, who appeared on the porch with a concerned look on her face.

"Ah, here you are. We've been looking for you. Mamm has made supper."

"She should be resting."

Emily shrugged. "Still, she's made supper and won't start until you join us. You know we never sit to eat until everyone is there."

Yes, Katie certainly knew the family's time-honored traditions.

She followed her sister into the house and joined the others at the table for what looked to be quite a feast. Surely her mother had not cooked all of this food today. No, much of it had to have come from women in the community.

As she took her seat at the table, Katie glanced over at her mother. Mamm's face carried a weary expression; the wrinkles around her eyes had deepened over the past few days. However, she never stopped working, not for a second. Katie wondered if her mother secretly longed for a different kind of life—one that would allow for an evening of Chinese takeout with an old movie on television afterward. If anyone deserved a rest, Mamm did.

Observing her surroundings, Katie had to admit her mother clearly liked things as they were. Everything in the home had a practical purpose. Each item had its use. If Mamm quietly longed for beautiful things—jewelry, clothes, and so forth—it certainly didn't show. Likely she'd never considered it.

These things Katie contemplated as she filled her plate with amazing foods—corn chowder, beef and noodles, cabbage, beets, and more. The smells wafted upward, tantalizing her, taking her back in time to when this kind of meal was commonplace. Diving into the familiar fare, Katie wondered if she would ever get used to her regular food routine again.

The conversation around the dinner table proved to be considerably quieter tonight. Her older brothers, she knew, were working up the courage to talk to Mamm about the work that needed to be done on the property. She'd heard them quietly talking earlier in the day, trying to iron out details. They had a good plan, but Katie secretly hoped they would pick another night to discuss such things. Tonight, all of them needed to rest both their bodies and their minds.

Thankfully, the meal passed quickly. As they nibbled at generous slices of shoofly pie afterward, the sound of Buddy's barking from outside the house startled them. Katie rose from the table and went into the living room, looking out the window to discover Sara and Jacob had returned in the buggy.

"They're home, Mamm!" Katie hollered out, and the room filled with people. They all waited at the front door until Jacob and Sara appeared, with the baby in her mother's arms.

"Let me see that little one." Mamm reached out her arms, and Sara willingly complied by handing the infant to her own mother.

Katie watched from a distance as her mother's silent tears flowed. She knew, of course, the thoughts that must be rolling through Mamm's head, the same words that had gone through her own, just hours before: *The Lord giveth and the Lord taketh away.*

"This precious child is blessed of God," Mamm said as she gave the little one a tender kiss on the forehead. "And will follow Him all the days of her life."

A resounding "amen" echoed around the room as their mother gave such an anointed blessing. Katie couldn't help but hear Datt's voice among the others. Surely he would have prayed over Rachel himself had he been here.

In her usual way, Mamm quickly handed the baby back to tend to her work. There were dishes to be done, after all, and floors to be swept. Idle hands were the devil's tools. Katie could practically hear the words rolling around in her mother's head, even now.

All pitched in, and before long they were able to enjoy a few moments together on the front porch. Katie gazed up into the sky, wondering if Karl had made it back to Doylestown okay. She wanted to call him, but several things prevented her from picking up the cell phone. To do so on her mother's front porch would be a direct insult, and. . .well, to call Karl so quickly after his leaving might make her look anxious.

Was she anxious?

Buddy came and sat at her feet, placing his head on her knees. Katie gave him a good rub behind the ears. "What are you looking for, sweet puppy—more attention?"

He nuzzled against her and let out a soft moan.

Emily chuckled. "He's just missing his wife, is all."

"His wife?"

"We have a beautiful female retriever in the barn. Looks just like him, only a bit smaller. Her name is Honey."

"I can't believe I haven't seen her running around," Katie said as she gave Buddy another affectionate rub.

"There's a reason for that. She's nursing eight puppies."

"Eight?" No wonder the poor thing hadn't been out for a visit.

"I'll take you to see them in the morning," Emily said with a yawn. "In the meantime, I think we're going to turn in for the night."

Katie watched as her sister and brother-in-law disappeared into the house hand in hand. How wonderful it must be to have someone walk you through such a difficult time, to hold your hand and tell you everything was going to be all right. And how wonderful to know that same person would still be there, day after day, holding you close as you grew old together.

With a sigh on her lips, Katie resolved to shift her thoughts to something else, something a little less painful. She wondered how things were going at the office and promised herself she'd call Hannah in the morning before heading back to Doylestown.

Thinking of the realty office reminded Katie of the property she'd recently listed—the one near the lake. She hoped there had been some showings, despite her absence. She smiled as she thought about it. The lake. The house. The acreage. It was the closest thing to heaven she'd seen in a while.

On the other hand. . .as she glanced around the Walken farm as the evening skies kissed it good night, Katie was suddenly aware of the truth. No other piece of property on planet earth could begin to compare with the one in front of her right now.

⁂

As Karl made the drive home, he remembered to turn his cell phone back on. Checking the messages, he noted four from the law office, including one that sounded fairly urgent. He would have to take care of that one quickly. He also found a message from Aimee at Bucks County Realty regarding the Chandler property. Finally, Karl was surprised to hear a somewhat lengthy message from a young woman at his church who worked in the children's ministry, asking if he would consider assisting in kid's church one Sunday morning a month.

As he flipped the phone shut, he took a moment to let that one sink in. Help with the children's ministry? He'd never worked with children before. Well, unless he counted all those years ago when he wasn't much more than a child himself. But even then, caring for little ones hadn't come naturally to him. On the other hand, just one glimpse at Jacob and Sara's newborn had melted him like butter. Maybe he had loved children all along and just didn't know it.

Still, he had to wonder about this particular young woman's request that he help out in the children's ministry. Karl had it on good authority—his best friend and pastor, Jay Ludlow—that DeeAnn Miller had her eye on him. And not just for ministry.

What any woman would see in him, Karl had no idea. For the most part, his workload kept him too busy for a relationship. And when he did think about spending time with a woman—which wasn't often—he had a hard time not comparing her to the only woman he'd ever loved.

Karl arrived back at his house, his stomach rumbling. *I'm going to miss the food from Paradise, that's for sure.* He reached into the refrigerator and pulled out a bottle of water and an apple. Settling down onto the sofa, he let his mind wander. For whatever reason, the only thing he could think about—the only *person* he could think about—was Katie. He wondered what she was doing right now at her mother's house. Had she turned in for the night?

He glanced at the clock. 8:45.

They were probably just winding down for the day. Maybe Sara and Jacob had arrived home with the baby.

In many ways, Karl envied Jacob. A caring wife. A healthy child. A beautiful home on some of the greenest land in all of Lancaster County. A simple life, and yet. . .

Life in the Amish country hadn't all been simple, had it?

No, after Katie had left, nothing had ever been simple again. In fact, the hole she'd left in his heart when she slipped out of the window had only grown larger over time. And when his parents died. . .

He remembered back to that day with a chill running down his spine. It had truly been the worst day of his life, one he did his best to put behind him.

Why now, after all these years, had it come back to haunt him? Likely, visiting Paradise had done that. And seeing the property now—with his own eyes—and how the land had been restored and a new home built only intensified the pain.

Karl pondered that for a moment, finally realizing the truth of it. He'd forgiven Katie for running away all those years ago. And strange as it might sound, he'd even forgiven his parents for leaving him behind as they'd ventured on to heaven ahead of him. The only One he might not have forgiven, now that he thought about it, was the One who could have prevented it all from happening in the first place.

The revelation nearly drove Karl to his knees. Had he been harboring unforgiveness. . .against God? Was such a thing really possible?

He settled onto the sofa to spend some time thinking through the matter. After a few minutes, he came to the conclusion that he had, albeit subconsciously, held the Lord responsible for the emptiness in his heart. With determination settling in, he opted to release that blame—once and for all.

Chapter 11

There was something rather magical about an early summer morning on a Pennsylvania farm. Perhaps it could be blamed on the green leaves of the oak trees as the soft breeze moved them back and forth. Or maybe it had more to do with the misty dew on the grass, which put Katie in mind of those majestic summer mornings as a child.

The summers had been her favorite time, after all. How many times had she pulled off her shoes and run barefoot through the fields, hidden behind majestic stalks of wheat? And how many times had Datt come running after her, his resounding laughter riding along the breeze?

Now, as midsummer inched its way over her parents' farm, one thing remained abundantly clear—the seasons of Katie's life had changed. She could smell it in the air, like a much-anticipated rainstorm. She wasn't quite sure what it meant, but a shift was definitely coming. She could no more control it than she could control summer turning to fall, or fall to winter.

Katie leaned back in her rocking chair, happy for a few additional minutes of solitude as the morning settled in around her. If only she could capture this feeling and bottle it! How wonderful it would be to take it back to the city.

The rhythmic creaking of the rockers against the aging wooden slats of the front porch lulled her into a dreamlike state. After a few carefree moments, however, the time came to say good-bye, not just to the morning but to the farm. And her family. And that precious new baby. She had to return home. Her work could wait no longer.

Less than an hour later, Katie loaded her suitcase into the back of her car. She paused to look up as she heard Emily's voice ring out. "Katie, before you leave, you have to come to the barn to see the puppies."

She closed the back door of the car and turned to her sister with a forced stern look. "Okay, but promise me you won't try to pawn one off on me. I don't have any room in my condo for a golden retriever, trust me." She couldn't even imagine such a thing, no matter how hard she tried.

"I promise." Emily grinned. "But they're the most precious little things. You've really got to see for yourself." She shifted into a lengthy discussion about the breed, focusing on their loyalty to owners and uncanny ability to adapt to life in a variety of settings. Katie tried not to respond, biting her tongue till it nearly bled. She would not be swept in, no matter how hard Emily tried.

Katie plodded along across the yard behind her sister until they drew near to the barn. Her heart ached as she stepped inside, remembering back to the day when friends from the community had come to help Datt raise the spacious white building. What fun they'd had helping Mamm and the other ladies prepare food and serve it to all the menfolk. The day had been joyous, from beginning to end.

Katie especially remembered Karl—the look of contentment on his face as she handed him a glass of lemonade. How his blue eyes had sparkled.

Why could she see so clearly now what she'd managed to overlook all those years ago?

Katie looked around the inside of the barn, noticing it seemed bigger than ever. . .and emptier than ever without Datt here to fill it with his love and laughter. He'd always managed to make work enjoyable. His fun-loving personality, larger than that of most men in their small community, had been his strength. And his weakness. Many had whispered in private that Elam Walken tried to draw attention to himself by making others laugh. Katie had always tightened her fists at such a suggestion.

Strange. She found her fists tightened now, too. Thankfully, the sound of whimpering pups off to her right offered a nice distraction from the bittersweet memories. Katie followed the sound until she stood directly in front of the mama dog and her puppies. The little darlings tussled about, pawing each other and yipping. The mama dog, God bless her, looked exhausted. Katie reached down to scratch her behind the ears. "You're a brave girl," she whispered.

Emily knelt down in the hay and bade Katie to do the same. She did so reluctantly, having already dressed for her trip back to Doylestown. It certainly wouldn't look very good to show up at the office with hay, and who knew what else, all over her knees.

Still, the puppies were awfully cute, and one in particular seemed to call out to her. She reached down to pick it up, cradling it close to her heart. Suddenly Katie's nice clothes didn't matter. The puppy nuzzled its cold black nose against her neck, and she giggled, breathing in that soft puppy scent she remembered from childhood.

"We call that one Miracle," Emily said. "She's the runt. We almost lost her at birth. I doubt anyone's going to want to buy her."

"Are you serious?" Katie pulled the pup back for a scrutinizing look. "Why not? She's gorgeous."

"Still, she's small. And very attached to her mama. She's just the kind to think she was born for indoor life, not outdoor."

Katie held the pup a second longer—until she realized what her sister was trying to do. "Oh no you don't," she said, putting the puppy back down. "You're not getting to me that easily."

"What?" Emily gave her an innocent look. "What did I do?"

"You know very well." Katie stood and brushed the hay from her knees. She looked down at her brown silk blouse and sighed as she saw the blond dog hair Miracle had left behind.

"Golden retrievers don't shed," Emily interjected.

"Sure they don't." Katie did her best to remove the hairs with her fingertips, but they clung stubbornly to the silk.

Emily rose to her feet and gave Katie the saddest look. "You're really leaving, aren't you?"

"Yes. Did you think. . .?"

Emily shrugged. "I've been hoping you would change your mind and stay here, with us." She gave a little pout.

Katie took her sister by the hand. "When I'm not here, I miss you so much. All of you. I hope you know that. And, in case you doubt it, I love you as much now as ever. I do wish I could see you more. I'm just so—"

"Busy."

"Yeah. But I promise I'll come back more often. I won't wait so long next time." She wanted to add, *And if you just had Internet access, I could stay in touch. I would write you every day. Send you funny e-mail forwards to make you laugh. Talk to you over Instant Messenger.*

Instead, she said nothing.

Katie gave the puppy another glance then looked at her watch. "I've got to go soon, but there's another baby I need to see first." In fact, she could hardly wait to hold Sara's little daughter in her arms one last time before making the drive back home.

Home. Hmm.

She quickly made her way out of the barn and across the property to the main house, where she found Sara helping Mamm with the canning in the spotless kitchen.

"Shouldn't you be resting?" Katie scolded as she washed her hands at the kitchen sink.

"I'm fine. Fit as a fiddle," her sister responded. "No point in pampering me just because I've had a baby."

"Still." Katie shook her head and decided not to argue, though she would certainly hope for a bit of pampering if she'd been the one to have the baby. Instead, she walked over to the cradle and reached down to scoop up her niece in her arms and rock her back and forth.

"I just got her to sleep!" Sara pretended to look irritated.

"I'll put her right back down. I promise." Katie gave Rachel a half dozen little kisses all over her wisps of hair and pink little cheeks. "Don't you miss your auntie too much, little girl," she whispered. "And you do everything your mamm tells you."

A twinge took hold of her heart as she said the word "mamm." No matter how much she tried to convince herself otherwise, Katie longed to be a mother, too, to have a darling baby girl to call her own. She'd known it from the day Hannah's first child was born, though she'd pushed the feelings aside. But now, as she stared into this precious newborn's face, she could deny it no longer.

Katie placed the infant back down with a sigh, making sure she was wrapped snugly in the little blanket. Plain white, of course. No frills for this child. No ruffled bonnets or darling pink outfits. Nothing to draw attention to—or exaggerate—the baby's beauty. No, this little one would be raised with far simpler attire than most newborns these days.

"I don't think I could do it," Katie whispered. "I'd want to dress you up like the baby doll that you are!"

She looked over at her mother and sister as they worked alongside one another. They'd never known the thrill of dressing in fancy clothes, either, and had probably never missed it. No, they seemed more than content to keep things as they were. And to stay busy. Always busy.

Just watching her mother made Katie tired. Mamm had a quiet inner strength, born out of trusting God, even in the hardest of times. A strength that gave her the tenacity to keep going, keep working. This Katie knew from years of careful observation. Mamm would work her way through the pain and the grief and would do it out of love for her children and her God.

As Katie watched her family members working together, her heart ached. What would it be like to work side by side with those you loved, sharing nearly every moment together? Would you giggle over the sweet things and cry over the sad ones?

She thought at once of Hannah and the work they did together at the office. As much as she loved her cousin, it just didn't feel the same. Perhaps with a little effort it could. She would work on it, and things would improve.

For now, the inevitable was upon her. Katie moved in her mother's direction, arms extended. "I. . .I have to go, Mamm."

Her mother turned, brushing tears from her lashes. Katie could almost read the message in those weary eyes. They cried out, "We miss you, Katydid. Come back to us."

For a moment, she almost resisted. Then she remembered the workload awaiting her back at Bucks County Realty and knew she could hesitate no longer.

After a tearful good-bye, Katie climbed into her car and headed out on her way. She thought about that tiny hummingbird lighting down upon its feeder only to lift off and fly away once again, and a niggling feeling of guilt crept over her. How she wanted to dip her beak in that sweet water once more before taking flight.

Katie tried not to look back as she pulled away from the farm but couldn't resist. As her gaze fell on the barn, she thought once again of her datt, and the tears flowed freely. For the first several miles out of Paradise, she grieved the loss of her father. She'd never felt pain so deep.

Then, as her thoughts shifted, Katie cried because of that sweet little puppy, Miracle. Silly, she knew. But she couldn't stop the tears from flowing every time she remembered the feel of that little angel's fur against her neck and the scent of puppy breath against her cheek.

Katie finally managed to get things under control about the time she hit the turnpike. She tried to convince herself that her life, though chaotic and somewhat disconnected, fulfilled her on nearly every level.

And she did everything in her power to force that crazy image of the hummingbird out of her mind—once and for all.

❧

Karl hung up the phone after talking to his pastor and sighed. Sometimes he wished he'd chosen another profession, something simple like ditchdigging. Or brain surgery. Anything would be better than real estate law, at least today.

What was it with friends and relatives? Why did they feel that asking for free legal advice was okay? He'd dished out far too much of it over the years. And on a day like this, with so much already going on, he hardly had time for other people's problems. Right?

With a heavy heart, Karl quickly repented for his frustrations. He didn't really mind offering advice where his pastor was concerned. No, he would gladly share his expertise with Jay. Only one problem this time—his good friend appeared to be dealing with something complex, something that might not end well for the church unless Karl got involved personally. And, if he had to be completely honest about it, Karl didn't *want* to get involved personally.

For a moment he thought about Katie, how she'd climbed out of her bedroom window and run away from a seemingly unavoidable situation. Karl's gaze shifted across the room to the large window, and he had to laugh. As much as he'd like to avoid getting involved in the church's situation, climbing out of this window would be impossible. He was on the third floor, after all. Still, the temptation did present an issue.

Karl yawned and stretched in an attempt to stay awake. Nothing seemed to help. Maybe a ten-minute power nap would help. He closed his eyes and reflected on his time at Pequea Creek. He couldn't stop thinking about atie—how she'd tossed that bass back into the water. Crazy. Still, there had een a look in her eyes, something he couldn't quite determine. Almost as if he'd understood the fish's plight. Didn't make a bit of sense to him, regardless.

He drifted off to sleep, and the dreams came in dizzying array. He fancied himself a fish, swimming upstream in Pequea Creek, trying to avoid being caught. Off in the distance he saw what appeared to be a slender, iridescent worm, slithring through the water. He opened his mouth to snag it, quickly discovering e'd been caught on a cleverly disguised hook.

He felt his body being pulled, pulled, pulled—out of the water and into the air. Gasping for breath, he stared directly into the wide green eyes of Katie Walken.

Even in his dreamlike state, Karl knew enough not to resist. However, he ound himself devastated when she pulled him from the hook. . .

. . .and tossed him back into the water.

Chapter 12

Katie arrived back in Doylestown late in the afternoon. She rushed to meet all of her appointments and return all of her phone calls, stunned at how much work had piled up. Thankfully, one of those calls was from a woman named Debbie Morrison, a California transplant wanting to look at the property Katie had just listed. The big one.

Katie whispered a prayer that tomorrow's showing would go well and that the Morrison family would fall in love with the place. And make an offer, of course. She quickly did the math. If they bought the house at the asking price—a million two—her commission would be seventy-two thousand dollars, more or less. Yes, she could certainly make do with that.

A thousand ideas swept through her mind at once. With that kind of money she could make a hefty donation to her church and give a good deal of money to missions besides. She could send a check to Mamm monthly to help with expenses. Katie's mind reeled as she considered all of the possibilities. How she would love to bless her mother, especially now. Seventy-two thousand dollars would spread a long way.

Her thoughts shifted to the condo. For years, she'd wanted to renovate, to add wood floors throughout. That might be possible now. If she went with wood floors, she might be able to consider a small dog as a companion. Right?

With such grandiose plans in mind, Katie allowed her thoughts to soar further. Maybe she could eventually update the appliances in the kitchen, something she'd wanted to do for years. The seal on the refrigerator had been giving her fits, and one of the knobs on the stove was broken. Wouldn't it be wonderful to replace them both with brand-new things?

Yes, there were a great many things she could do with funds of that magnitude. Again, Katie whispered a prayer for God's will to be done. She didn't want to get ahead of Him, by any stretch.

She finally made it home from the office about the time the sun fell past the horizon. Though she longed to look up in the sky and see the same beautiful colors she'd noticed back in Paradise, the high-rise across the street blocked her view. She stood in the parking lot a moment and closed her eyes, trying to remember last night's sunset.

Had it really only been twenty-four hours? Strange. It seemed she'd been back

306

or ages. Perhaps this had something to do with the uncanny amount of work he'd accomplished in such a short time.

Katie opened her eyes and sighed, trying to make the best of things. She picked up her pace as she made her way into the condo. Once inside, she placed her laptop, cell phone, and purse on the kitchen counter and headed off to the bedroom to change into her most comfortable pj's.

Once settled, she looked in the fridge for something to eat. Nothing much grabbed her attention; likely eating at her mother's table once again had convinced her tastebuds they deserved more than the usual after-work fare. Regardless, she ended up reaching for a frozen dinner, something rather bland looking with pasta and chicken. She popped it in the microwave and leaned against the countertop to wait for the beep.

In the meantime, Katie opened her laptop, waiting a moment for it to boot up. By the time her food was ready to come out of the microwave, her high-speed wireless Internet access had kicked in and she scrolled through her e-mails to see if Karl had written. She knew he was busy—he'd said as much—but she still hoped he would write. Or call.

When Katie realized her e-mail box held nothing from him, she reached for her cell phone to check for missed calls. One from Hannah. Another from Aimee. Nothing else.

For whatever reason, her heart twisted at the idea that Karl hadn't tried to contact her yet. Why it mattered so much, she could not be sure. Until a week ago, she hadn't given him another thought. *Why do I feel like this? Why do I even care? Surely if he wanted to stay in touch, he would. Right?* Then again, maybe she had imagined the look in his eyes yesterday at the creek. Maybe the security of his hand in hers had been something she'd made too much of in her girlish daydreams.

Or maybe the busyness of his schedule prevented it for now. In the hours since she had arrived back in Doylestown, Katie had barely had time to catch up. Chaos reigned. Nothing new there. Perhaps Karl was dealing with the same thing on his end.

The microwave beeped again, and Katie reached to grab the instant meal. After pulling back the half-melted cover, the steam from the food inside burned her fingers. She almost dropped the hot plastic container but managed to get it under control. Then she carried it to the table with the laptop carefully balanced in her other hand. Surely she could catch up on some work while she ate. Nothing wrong with that, right? After all, idle hands were the devil's tools.

Katie's thoughts wandered to her life as a teen, when her greatest exposure to the world had been the store where she waited on curious tourists. Things had changed considerably over the years. If she still lived in Paradise, she certainly wouldn't be using the Internet tonight.

On the other hand, if she still lived in Paradise, she'd probably be happi married to Karl Borg and have half a dozen kids by now. And a dog. They'd b eating fish for dinner—fish that she'd caught in Pequea Creek. And shoofly pi for dessert.

As she nibbled on the somewhat mushy pasta and flavorless chicken, an in stant message came through. Katie smiled as she saw Karl's words:

"Are you there?"

"I'm here," she typed in response.

"I'm still at work."

"No way." She took another bite of her food, nearly burning her tongue. Kati wished she'd grabbed a diet soda out of the fridge before sitting down but didn dare budge now. She didn't want to miss anything. "What are you working on?

"Helping my church unwind itself from a legal mess."

"Whoa. Care to elaborate?"

"Maybe later," he sent. "Right now I'm worn out."

"Me too." She took another bite of her food and thumbed through the file she'd brought home from work. "But good things are happening on this end. might have an opportunity to make a sale. A really big one."

"With a smile like yours, who wouldn't buy a house from you?"

A girlish giggle slipped out as Katie thought about his words. Looked like their issues from the past were truly behind them. Better yet, it looked like thei present—and their future—was brighter than ever. Especially if he kept saying things like that.

If they could just manage to spend a little time together. . .

"I wish things would slow down," Karl sent. "I would ask you out to dinner."

Katie smiled as she responded. "I would accept."

"In that case. . .tomorrow night?"

"Sorry. I have a meeting." She took another nibble of her meal, realizing i tasted a bit more like school paste than pasta.

"Friday then?"

Katie sighed as she typed, "I promised Hannah I'd help with her daughter's birthday party."

"Looks like I'm never going to see you again."

As Katie stared at the screen, she realized just how painful it would be never to see him again. Perhaps the twinge she now felt was a small taste of what he had experienced the first few years after she left Paradise. Maybe she had it coming to her.

Or maybe God could use this opportunity to turn the tables.

"Want to come to a nine-year-old's pizza party?" she typed. Katie leaned back against her chair and waited. Likely he would think she was nuts.

She couldn't help but laugh when he responded with, "Pepperoni?"

"Sure. Whatever you like. Call me on Friday afternoon, and I'll give you the specifics. In the meantime, I'll be praying about your church situation."

"Thanks. And I'll be praying you make that big sale. Then you can take me out for a steak dinner to celebrate. With cheesecake for dessert."

"Mmm." *Nearly as good as shoofly pie.* "You've got a deal."

"G'night, Katie."

"G'night."

As she signed off, Katie leaned back in her chair and closed her eyes. Funny, even with them shut, she could still see Karl so clearly in her imagination. His sturdy build. His blond hair. Those amazing blue eyes. His heart for others.

"Thank You, Lord, for showing me what I missed years ago. And thank You—a hundred times over—for giving me a second chance. And now, Lord, a special request. . .please. . .help me not to blow it."

Karl tossed a load of laundry into the washing machine and poured in the detergent. As he did, he reminded himself to take his gray suit to the dry cleaners tomorrow morning, along with several dress shirts. For now, he was happy to wear shorts and a T-shirt—his usual after-work attire.

Closing the lid of the washer, he looked around the basement with a sigh. So many things needed to be done around the house, but he rarely had time. Still, he couldn't stand the idea of things being in disarray. Every night as he laid his head on the pillow, Karl promised himself: *Tomorrow. Tomorrow I'll get organized.*

Unfortunately, with his workload so high, tomorrow never seemed to come. Maybe one day he would hire one of those home organizers to come and help him put everything in its place. Someone who had an eye for such things and time to accomplish them.

Karl's thoughts shifted to the farm where he'd grown up. Everything was always in its place in his father's shed. Every tool taken care of. Every square inch of the house in perfect order at all times.

Karl sighed. Seemed that no matter how hard he worked, he could never keep up with things, though not for lack of trying.

Don't be so hard on yourself.

Where the words came from, he couldn't be sure. Had the Lord dropped them into his heart, or were they his own? Regardless, Karl made a quick decision to pay special attention to the message. As long as he gave every situation his best, he had no reason to scold himself for the things that remained undone, right?

And speaking of things that were undone. . .

He smiled as he thought back over his instant message with Katie. Their back and forth bantering had been fun, but he hated to read too much into it. Once before, he had given his heart to her only to be disappointed. Was she just toying with his emotions this time around, or had a spark really ignited between them?

Karl offered up a prayer, asking the Lord for a second chance. He dared to hope for what had once seemed impossible. And once again he opened his heart, making himself completely vulnerable.

Surely this time around nothing would go wrong.

He prayed.

As exhaustion set in, Karl was reminded of Katie's invitation to her niece's birthday party. He could hardly wait. And who knew? Maybe a pizza party with a bunch of nine-year-olds would be fun. He enjoyed being around kids. Certainly, getting to see Katie once again would make his day.

If only he could keep his heart in his chest from now till Friday, he would be just fine.

Chapter 13

The following day, Katie showed the million-dollar property to the Morrison family from Southern California. They were particularly drawn to the land around the house, and why not? Surely it was some of the prettiest in the county. Green rolling farmland beckoned, and the spacious yard was dotted with colorful flower beds. The house, a sprawling five-bedroom, proved to be more than big enough for their feisty brood of four children.

Katie fell in love with the youngsters right away, especially the tiniest girl, who, ironically, shared her new niece's name: Rachel. The youngster—probably no older than four or five—held Katie's hand as they wound their way through the many rooms of the house. The little girl oohed and aahed over many of the home's upgraded features, as did others in the family.

And who could blame them? The beautiful two-story, five-bedroom home sat on some of the prettiest acreage in Bucks County. And being this close to the lake was a plus, especially for a family used to living along the Pacific. Mr. Morrison told countless stories about his boat, and Mrs. Morrison raved over the spacious kitchen with its updated cabinets and granite countertops.

All the while, Katie kept her cool and answered their questions. She didn't want to do anything to sway them one way or the other. If the Lord intended them to have this house, they would have it. In the meantime, she would simply enjoy being with them. She could imagine herself a part of a family like this one day. A sprawling house. A handful of kids. A husband who talked about his boat.

Maybe. Someday.

A couple of hours later, she received the call. The Morrisons wanted the house. And the best news of all. . .she now represented both the buyer and the seller. That meant the full 6 percent commission.

Katie contacted the owner on his cell phone. He answered on the third ring.

"Mr. Hamilton?" She tried to contain her excitement so as not to give away the surprise.

"Yes?"

"Katie Walken from Bucks County Realty."

"Calling with good news, I hope."

"Very good news. We have an offer on the property—full asking price."

"Well, I want to move forward, but I, um. . ." Here he hesitated, albeit slightly. "I guess I should tell you that I have a few wrinkles to iron out first."

"Wrinkles?"

"I'm dealing with a probate issue related to the property."

"What?" Katie felt her stomach twist in knots. "Are you saying the house is still tied up in probate? That it's not technically yours?"

"Well, I think I told you this was my mother's property before she passed. She left it to me. I'm an only child and the executor of her will."

"Yes"—she tried to maintain her cool—"but I had no idea it was still in probate. I would *never* have listed it. That's. . .unethical."

"You'll have to forgive me, Ms. Walken. I've never been in this position before. I'm sure you heard the part where I said I lost my mother."

"Yes." She swallowed hard, memories of Datt surfacing. How would she feel if someone confronted her on something related to his death, after all? She tried to soften her approach. "I'm sorry. Really I am."

"I've never been down this road before," he explained. "I went ahead and contacted a Realtor because I'd been told it was just a matter of time before the property would be released to me. To be quite honest, I didn't think we'd receive an offer so soon. You're really good at what you do."

Katie opted to let his flattery slide right by her. She needed to stay focused on the issue at hand.

"I figured the whole thing would be settled before the first showing. Turns out, settling the estate is a bit more complicated than I thought, especially without a probate attorney. Guess I should've hired one."

Oh no. Please don't tell me this.

Brian Hamilton continued on, his voice never wavering. "A savvy lawyer could take care of this in no time, I'm sure. I hate to think it's come to that, but I might have to hire an attorney to get the whole thing squared away."

"Oh!" As she reached to look at her cell phone to get Karl's number, a wave of relief washed over her. "I happen to know an excellent real estate attorney, and I'm sure he's familiar with probate issues. He could probably get this settled quickly."

"Great!"

"In the meantime, we're going to have to stop the process. You know that, right?"

He dove into an argument, claiming that the whole thing would be dealt with by the time they went to closing, but Katie knew better. She would have to pull the listing, at least for now. She didn't want to alarm her potential buyers. But surely they would wait a few weeks longer to officially make an offer if they really wanted the house badly enough.

Katie committed the whole thing to prayer. God had brought this amazing property to her, hadn't He? Surely He would see fit to help her with its sale, no matter what road bumps might get in the way.

❧

Karl approached the pastor's office a little unnerved. From what Jay had told him over the phone, the church was about to be embroiled in a serious legal mess. And, from the looks of things, Karl would likely end up smack dab in the middle of it. He didn't have to get involved, but with so much at risk for his church family, he needed to make himself available, even if it took him away from his other work.

After rapping on the door, he heard Jay's familiar voice call out, "Come on in, Karl. It's open."

He entered the small office, sensing the tension in the air. Looking beyond the stacks of books and papers on the cluttered desk, Karl took note of the concern etched into the forehead of his good friend.

"You look terrible," he offered.

"Thanks." Jay sighed. "I know what the Bible says about not worrying, but I'm having a hard time with this one." He shook his head and looked Karl in the eye. "I wouldn't tell that to just anyone, you know."

"I know. But who could blame you?" Karl opened his briefcase and pulled out his digital recorder. "Do you mind if I record our conversation? No one will ever hear this but me. I just like to go back over things when I get home, and that's tougher to do with handwritten notes because I don't always catch everything."

"Sure, I've got nothing to hide."

"I only know what you told me on the phone," Karl said as he fumbled with the recorder in an attempt to get it to come on. "When Mildred Hamilton passed away, she left the church a piece of property out on the lake."

"Yes."

Karl smiled as he remembered the elderly Mrs. Hamilton. She always had an impish grin on her face and a finger in every pie. The four-foot-eleven dynamo had headed up everything from the benevolence ministry to the prayer team over her many decades at Grace Fellowship. The only thing church leaders hadn't let her do was drive the church bus. And since her passing a few months ago, she had been sorely missed by all.

Jay let out a sigh. "I know how much this meant to her—making sure the church had the property for our new facility. We discussed it at length. It had always been her plan to leave it to the church. She figured the house could be used for a parsonage. In fact, it's large enough that it could be used for both a parsonage and a retreat center for missionaries on furlough. There are acres and acres of prime land that would be perfect for the new sanctuary, parking lot, gym . . . everything."

"And now someone in the family is trying to sell it out from underneath you?"

"Her son." Jay shook his head. "He's a nice enough guy. Lives in Texas. Doesn't have any plans to move onto the property himself, so it's not an emotional issue for him. From what I understand, he and his mother were distant. Not really estranged, but he rarely showed up to help her, even toward the end."

"So he just wants the funds from the sale."

"Looks that way." Jay shrugged. "Though it's not my place to say. I certainly don't know his heart. But it seems mighty strange that he's shown up now, after her death, and not before."

"You're sure the property isn't already in his name? Maybe she was just living there but didn't own it outright?"

"Oh, the house was definitely in Mildred's name." Jay sighed and raked his fingers through his hair. "And the donation of the property is clearly stated in her will. I have a copy. But her son claims to have a different will, one that names him as the beneficiary of the land."

"Have you seen his version?" Karl asked.

"I haven't." Jay drew in a deep breath. "And I suppose it's possible that Mildred drew up another one I knew nothing about, though she talked about that new facility right up until the day she passed away. So the whole thing just smells—"

Karl almost envisioned the smallmouth bass Katie had tossed back into the creek as he responded with, "Fishy?"

"Yes. And here's the thing. Let's say the will her son has in his possession *is* older than the one we have. Even then we're going to have problems, because this guy intimated that Mildred was coerced into making the donation to the church, and that she wasn't in her right mind when she made it."

Karl couldn't help but laugh at that. Mildred had been in her right mind, to be sure—and happy to give folks a piece of it, which she did regularly.

He pulled out a pen and paper, preparing to hear more. "Surely there were witnesses to the version of the will that the church has in its possession?"

"Yes, but all three were church members, and from what I've been told, that's not going to look very good. I wish we'd thought of it at the time." Jay went off on a tangent, expressing his many regrets over that particular decision.

Karl did his best to calm his friend. "Still, those individuals aren't direct beneficiaries, so it shouldn't be an issue."

"Well, that's good. I guess." Jay rubbed his brow with his palm, but the wrinkles only deepened.

After pausing to think things through, Karl prepared to get to work. "Okay. I need you to be more specific now. I need names. Facts. Dates. Details. And I'll need to see a copy of the will, if you have it handy. And Jay. . ."

"Yes?"

"Most estates take months to settle. Years even. We refer to this as a probate gap. I can guarantee your patience is going to be tried as this thing moves forward. Just be prepared for that."

Jay let out an exhausted sigh then spent the next half hour filling Karl in on every detail. When and where the will was signed. Who witnessed it. Mildred's final instructions upon her deathbed. The location of the property. The appraised value. The full name of Mildred's son, along with contact information.

And the name of the Realtor who'd listed the property about a week ago.

It wasn't until Karl heard Katie Walken's name that he realized just what a pickle he'd gotten himself into.

Chapter 14

Katie decided to take a stiff upper lip approach to the Hamilton property. She removed the listing at once, fighting the sick feeling that washed over her at the loss of such a hefty commission. *It's just for a few weeks,* she reminded herself. Afterward, she telephoned the Morrisons, bringing them up to date on the issues surrounding the property. They opted to wait it out, even if it took weeks. They wanted the house. Period.

Though this whole ordeal would surely try Katie's patience, she made a decision to see it through to the end, no matter what. Surely the reward would be great as long as everyone's tenacity held firm. And she would eventually earn the commission. No two ways about that.

Katie was thankful her evening meeting was canceled, giving her a few hours to spend as she pleased. On a whim, she decided to stop off at an appliance supercenter on her way home from work. She didn't believe in counting her chickens before they'd hatched, but she did believe in being prepared. If God saw fit to bless her financially, whether it was next week or next year, what would it hurt to go ahead and start putting a plan in motion for her kitchen? She wanted to be a good steward of her income and would take the next few months to shop carefully, finding the best possible deals on every appliance. That way, when the time came, she would know just what to buy and from which store.

With excitement leading the way, Katie eased her way into the massive appliance center, unsure of where to begin. She'd shopped for a great many things over the years, but rarely refrigerators, stoves, and dishwashers. Thankfully, her condo had come equipped with those, but they were in serious need of updating. No problem—out with the old, in with the new. Right?

As she looked at the goodies in front of her, Katie couldn't help but think of her mother. What would it be like to go back to life without electricity? Life without a dishwasher? Of course, Mamm used bottled gas to operate her stove and refrigerator, but she still washed every dish by hand. Katie shuddered as she thought about that. There would be no going back to some things.

Pausing in front of a stainless steel refrigerator, Katie found herself captivated by its impressive size and appearance. She opened the door on the right and let out a whistle as she saw the space inside. "Man." She could put a lot of food in there.

On the other hand, living alone meant she rarely kept a lot of food in the house, didn't it? Why did she need so much space?

She opened the door on the left and gazed inside at the more-than-adequate freezer space. With such a spacious layout, she could almost envision it filled with all sorts of yummy things—ice cream, veggies, french fries, different kinds of meats, and so on.

And why not? The more Katie thought about it, the more she realized—*If I had this much space, I could buy in bulk and save even more money.*

Her thoughts began to shift, and she imagined herself married to Karl, raising a family. How could looking at a refrigerator stir up such imaginings? Still, she could almost picture herself reaching into this freezer to pull out food for her family.

My family.

Just as she'd done that day with the Morrisons, Katie thought about what it would be like to be married with a houseful of kids. All of the things she'd run away from years ago now held a delicious appeal.

And, ironically, so did this refrigerator.

Had the Lord really used a kitchen appliance to soften her heart? She had to laugh at the idea. Katie stepped back to give the side-by-side unit another once-over.

Just then her cell phone rang, startling her. Katie scrambled around in her purse, trying to locate it. When she saw Karl's number, her heart began to beat double time. How did he know she'd been thinking about him? Was he somewhere in the store, spying on her perhaps? Looking at appliances of his own—ones that put him in mind of a wife and family?

"Hey, you," she said, finally catching it on the fifth ring.

"Hi. Do. . .um. . .do you have a few minutes to talk?"

Something in his voice sounded. . .off. Wrong. "I'm in an appliance store. Are you okay?"

"No. I. . .um. . .I'm wondering if you could meet me someplace for a cup of coffee so we can talk."

"Sure. I can do that."

"Meet me at the coffee shop near the library."

She sensed something was wrong and didn't want to give up that easily. "Do you know something I don't? Has something happened back home?"

"No, it's nothing like that. Please just meet me and we can talk things through."

"I'll be there in ten minutes." Katie shoved the phone back in her purse and headed for the door, nerves leading the way. She couldn't begin to imagine what had Karl so upset. Something from work maybe? Regardless, he needed to talk to her, and she wanted to be there for him. Even if it meant interrupting her shopping spree.

Ten minutes later she arrived at P. A. Perk and noticed his car out front. She could see through the driver's side window that he sat in the front seat, cell phone in hand. The call must be serious from the look on his face and the tightness in his jaw. His wrinkled brow did little to alleviate her concern. If anything, it deepened, particularly when he looked her way and frowned.

"Lord, help me," Katie whispered. "I don't have a clue what I've done, but I have the strangest feeling I'm about to be taken to the principal's office."

With a heavy heart, she took a step in his direction. If she could've found an open window, she might very well have jumped through it.

❧

Karl led the way into the coffee shop and took a seat.

Katie gave him a curious glance. "You don't want to order anything?"

"Not really." The smell of coffee permeated the air, and he breathed it in, hoping for a few more seconds of peace before he split the room open with his news. "You go ahead and get whatever you like." He reached for his wallet, but she gestured for him to put it away.

She flashed a dazzling smile, one that nearly caused him to lose sight of why he'd brought her here in the first place. "I'm a twenty-first-century girl. I don't mind paying for my own coffee."

After a playful wink, Katie made her way through the crowd up to the counter, where she ordered something with foam on top. Afterward, she joined him at the table, taking the seat across from him. "Now, tell me what's happened."

He drew in a deep breath and tried to decide how to begin. "Remember I told you about that situation at my church?"

"The legal problem?" She took a sip of her coffee then made a face. "Ooo. Hot."

"Yes." He paused, unsure of how to continue.

"Is there something I can help you with?" She put the cup down on the table and leaned forward to face him eye to eye. "Need some sort of help on my end? From a Realtor, I mean."

"That would be putting it mildly."

"Karl, what's happening?"

He started with great care, guarding every word. "A few months ago one of the older ladies in my church—a Mildred Hamilton—passed away. She was a spitfire in every sense of the word. We're talking about a really generous woman here, one who stayed involved in a variety of ministries till the very end."

"Right." Katie gave him a curious look.

"Several months before she died, she drew up a will, leaving her property to the church. It was a godsend, because the congregation had almost outgrown the current facility."

"That was very generous." Katie shrugged. "She sounds like a great lady."

"Mildred was the best, in every sense of the word." Karl tried to swallow the growing lump in his throat. Clearly Katie didn't see where he was headed with all of this. "But the church has run into a problem."

"What kind of a problem?" She took another sip of her coffee.

"Turns out her son, Brian, has a different copy of her will in his possession."

The color drained from Katie's face at once. She put the cup down on the table, nearly toppling it over. "Brian Hamilton?"

Karl nodded.

"*My* Brian Hamilton?"

Again he nodded. "I just found out today. The will we have is recent, very recent, in fact. But this Hamilton fellow says she wasn't in her right mind when she signed it. If you knew Mildred, you'd know he's grasping at straws. I've never known a woman of her age to be so levelheaded. She knew exactly what she was doing and involved a great many people to make sure she did it right."

"Oh, Karl." Katie leaned her forehead down into her hands and groaned. "This is awful. I pulled the listing immediately when I learned the property was still tied up in probate."

"You did?" Relief washed over Karl. Maybe this wouldn't turn out to be as complicated as he thought.

"Yes. I would never have listed it in the first place if Hamilton had been straight with me. And I can assure you, I had no idea this was, in any way, connected to a disputed will. Or a church, for that matter. Especially your church."

"It's connected, all right."

Katie shook her head, and he could see the anger in her eyes. "The worst part is Hamilton led me to believe this would all be settled quickly, that the house could be relisted soon. I have clients waiting to purchase that house the moment it becomes available."

"If I do my job, it won't ever become available."

"This is awful," Katie said with a groan. "Seventy-two thousand dollars' worth of awful. My commission just shot straight out of the window." She looked up with a stunned expression on her face. "I can't believe I just said that."

It took him a minute for her comment about the window to register. He responded with a simple, "Ah."

"What am I supposed to do? Lose the sale permanently?" She raked her fingers through her hair. "Brian made it sound like it would just be a matter of time before this situation would be squared away. He told me a good attorney could poke holes in—" Here she put her hand over her mouth, her eyes growing wide. "Oh my goodness."

"What?"

"When he told me that he needed an attorney, I gave him your contact information."

Karl let out an exasperated groan. "Tell me you didn't."

"I did. But, again, we don't really know. . ."

"I know one thing." Karl exhaled loudly. "I know that someone is trying to take advantage of my church, someone who only made an appearance after his mother died, not before. And someone who didn't think enough of his Realtor to tell her straight up she was listing a property that wasn't yet available. That's what I know."

"Oh, Karl."

"And I know that I've committed to help my pastor see this thing through to the end, which means I'm most assuredly going to end up in court."

"Facing Brian Hamilton."

Karl shifted his gaze. "And any Realtor who might try to move forward with a sale before this issue is settled. You can't sell a house from an unsettled estate."

Katie's eyes filled with tears right away, and he wished he could take back his insinuation that she might do the wrong thing. Still, it was better that she understood the worst-case scenario. If she or anyone else from Bucks County Realty tried to force a sale, they could all very well end up in court—on opposite sides of the bench. Better to duke it out here, in a coffee shop, than in front of a county judge.

Hmm. From the look of pain in her eyes, he might stand a better chance in front of the judge.

Chapter 15

The following afternoon, Katie sat alone in her office with the door closed, trying to collect her thoughts. She'd spent the better part of the morning on the phone with Brian Hamilton in confrontational mode. He admitted flat-out that he'd deliberately avoided telling her about the disputed will in their prior conversation. He also admitted his version of the will was the older one, written nearly ten years before his mother's death.

Still, he planned to file a motion with the court to stop the church from acquiring the land, claiming they'd coerced his mother into signing the more recent will. He insisted it would just be a matter of time before the true ownership was established, but Katie knew better, based on her earlier conversation with Karl, who had committed to see this thing through to the end. The two opposing sides would be hung up in litigation for months, if not years.

Katie grieved not only the loss of income from the potential sale of the property but the damage this had done to both her reputation and her relationship with Karl.

She thought back to his words about fighting things out in the courtroom. Did he really think it would come to that? Surely he didn't believe she would try to move forward with the sale of the property now, did he? He could accuse her of a great many things—breaking his heart, for instance—but she would never deliberately do something as unethical as that.

A wave of nausea swept over her as she thought about Brian Hamilton. Now that she knew the truth, his whole story smelled contrived. Their most recent conversation had made things abundantly clear: he hardly knew his own mother. In fact, he could barely remember the name of her church or her pastor when pressed. He couldn't remember the date of her death, or even her birthday, for that matter.

Katie contemplated this dilemma from every angle, drawing only one logical conclusion. She had to talk to Hannah, and quickly. Preferably before Madison's birthday party, which was scheduled to begin in two hours. Picking up the phone, she punched in her cousin's extension. Hannah agreed to meet with her in half an hour, after taking care of some important paperwork.

During that time, Katie rested her forehead in her hands and prayed. She wasn't sure which hurt more—the loss of income from the sale or the look in

Karl's eyes last night. Surely he didn't think the worst of her, not after the day they'd just spent together in Paradise. Still, the pain in his eyes surely reflected some degree of distrust.

And why not? Hadn't she hurt him before? Maybe he had a right to think the worst of her now.

With a heavy heart, Katie prayed. As the words poured forth, she did her best to release both the anger and the betrayal she felt. She also asked the Lord to guide her future dealings with Karl and to open his eyes to the truth—that she had meant him no harm. After a bit more wrestling on the matter, Katie also released her hold on any monies related to the Hamilton property. Clearly the Lord never intended that commission to come her way in the first place. Letting go of it, at least from a psychological standpoint, was the only answer.

As she wrapped up her prayer time, a knock sounded at the door. "Katie? You in there?"

She recognized her cousin's voice at once. "I'm here, Hannah. Come on in."

Her cousin entered with a concerned look on her face. "You wanted to talk to me?"

"Yes." Katie released a sigh, wishing the burden would ease. "It's about the Hamilton property."

"Yes!" Hannah's face lit up. "I heard you've got a potential buyer. Congratulations. A family from California, right?"

Katie shook her head. "It's not that simple, at least not anymore. I had a potential buyer. Now I've got a nightmare."

"What do you mean?" Hannah dropped into a chair and gave her an inquisitive look.

Katie dove in headfirst.

After hearing the opening lines of the story, her cousin's smile quickly faded. "Oh, Katie. This is awful."

After hearing the rest, Hannah added, "There's nothing you can do. You certainly can't move forward. He can't sell a property that doesn't rightfully belong to him."

"I've already removed the listing." Katie shook her head, defeated. "And who knows? Maybe it really will belong to him in a few months, after he pays some savvy probate attorney a hefty fee to tear apart the church's case. But even then I wouldn't relist his house. I just couldn't do that."

"Because of Karl?"

"No." Katie shook her head. "I mean, that's part of it, of course. And I'm heartbroken over what Hamilton is trying to do to the people at this poor church. But primarily, I could never represent someone who didn't fully disclose something of this magnitude, even if the judge happens to move in his favor."

"Good for you." Hannah gave her a concerned look. "But I know this has to hurt, Katie. I can see it in your eyes."

"I can't tell you what it's doing to my confidence to lose a deal this big. I guess I really had my heart set on this one." Such an admission was tough but true.

" 'The Lord giveth and the Lord taketh away.' " Hannah quoted the familiar scripture, and Katie's heart jolted. Hadn't she said the same thing the day Sara's baby was born? Hadn't God reminded her that He alone would fill the empty spaces? No commission in the world could fill that spot.

"I think I had all my eggs in one basket," Katie said with a sigh. "I really can't do that again. I counted on that money too much. Maybe God is trying to teach me something here."

Hannah shrugged. "One of life's tougher lessons, to be sure. But you're a smart girl, Katie, and a savvy Realtor. This isn't the end of the world. It's a disappointment, sure, but at least you caught this before Hamilton accepted the Morrisons' offer."

"That's another thing." Katie let out a groan. "The Morrisons. They're such a great family, and they *love* that house. They were willing to wait as long as it took. But when I heard what Hamilton had done to the people at Karl's church, I called them back. Told them I wouldn't be relisting at all. They were devastated." She shook her head, remembering the disappointment in Debbie Morrison's voice.

"So, you'll sell them another house." Hannah smiled, as if it were just that simple.

"On the lake?" Properties there were limited, to say the least.

"The Chandler place is still available."

Katie frowned, thinking she'd misunderstood. "I thought Karl made an offer on the Chandler place."

"He withdrew it today, as well as his offer on the Wilcox property."

"Oh no. Poor Aimee."

Hannah shrugged. "It didn't make sense to me at the time, but I guess I understand it all now. Likely he considered working with anyone in our office a conflict of interest." A hint of a smile graced her lips. "But hey. . .don't give up the ship, and never underestimate the power of a mighty God. He can take what the enemy meant for evil and turn it to good. And you never know, the Morrisons might just fall in love with the Chandler farm. It's near the lake, too, and on some of the prettiest acreage in Bucks County."

"And much less expensive than the Hamilton property," Katie agreed. She was reminded at once of Karl's reason for wanting to buy that property in the first place. He wanted to see the land preserved. If the California transplants considered the idea, then Mrs. Morrison could have her garden and Karl would get the one thing he wanted most—someone who cared about the land and the home.

"If they go for it, I'll let Aimee keep the whole commission."

Hannah laughed. "That's a generous offer, and one I'm sure she'll debate, but the purity of your heart is evident, Katie." She paused and offered a pensive look. "And that's another thing. . .your motives have always been crystal clear. Anyone who might think less of you because of this situation doesn't know you like I do."

Katie shrugged. She wondered if Karl would ever see her as anything other than a money-hungry Realtor, willing to break the rules to get what she wanted.

Hannah gave her a wink. "Stiff upper lip, girl." She glanced at the clock. "Yikes. I've got to get out of here. I have to wrap Madison's present and then get myself psychologically prepared for twelve screaming nine-year-olds at the pizzeria. Are you still coming?"

After a quick nod, Katie said, "Of course. I wouldn't miss it for the world." An e-mail from Karl had alerted her to the fact that he wouldn't be there, but perhaps that was for the best. At least Hannah knew the whole story now and had handled the news with grace and style.

With relief flooding over her, Katie gathered up her belongings and headed for the door.

ð.

The following morning Katie climbed into her car and pointed it in the direction of Paradise. She had to get out of town, to clear her head. Sara's words still echoed loudly: "Still running, Katie?"

I'm not too proud to admit I'm running, Lord, but this time I want to run straight into Your arms. I want Your will in this situation. Save me from myself.

As Katie made her way out of Doylestown, she thought about the issues she now faced at work. Perhaps Hannah's response had been right: *"The Lord giveth and the Lord taketh away."* God had given her so many amazing opportunities over the years. She'd been blessed time and time again, not just with the sale of homes, but in so many other ways. And yet she'd faced several losses, as well.

As she contemplated her losses of late, Katie's thoughts went to Brian Hamilton. She began to pray for him. That he would come to his senses and do the right thing. That the Lord would intervene and soften his heart toward the church. That Karl wouldn't have to face him in court.

And as she drove, Katie prayed for something else, too. For the first time ever, she prayed that Karl would figure out she had left town. . .and this time, come running after her.

ð.

After an extensive night of wrestling with the sheets, Karl awoke to a slit of sunlight peeking through his bedroom curtains. He squinted and closed his eyes. As he filtered through the dozens of thoughts in his head, only one rose to the surface. He had to call Katie, and he had to call her now. Somehow he must undo any damage he'd done with his earlier insinuations.

He tried her home phone, but she didn't answer. Afterward, he signed online to see if he could locate her there. Nothing. Finally, he punched in her cell number.

She answered on the third ring with a tentative, "Hello?"

"Katie?"

"Yes?"

He paused as he heard the strain of a familiar worship song playing in the background. "I'm glad I got you. I really want to talk to you." The sound of a horn honking in the background threw him for a second. "Are you in the car?"

"Yeah. I'm headed home."

"Home?" His heart began to work overtime. "Spending the weekend with your family?"

"I thought that would be a good idea."

Except that it foils my plan. "I'm sure your mamm will enjoy having you."

"She doesn't know I'm coming. I might make a couple of stops first, do a little shopping. And, to be honest, I'm not sure if I'm going to stay at her house. I'm just feeling a little. . .unsettled. I had to get away from Doylestown for a while."

"Because of me?"

"No. Just everything."

"Katie, I really need to talk to you. I feel awful about something I said. I made it sound as if I thought you might deliberately do the wrong thing, and I'm sorry about that. I know you better than that."

He heard the break in her voice as she responded. "You. . .you don't know me at all, Karl. I've never let you know me."

I want to. The words got stuck in his throat. Perhaps they couldn't find their way across the huge lump that suddenly rose up at the idea of not having a chance to win her heart. Just the thought of it broke his. He'd already lost her once.

He wasn't going to lose her again.

Chapter 16

As Katie neared the Amish country, she opted for a slight detour before heading to the farm. For whatever reason, she felt drawn to a group of shops several miles away from Paradise. A tourist trap, that's what Mamm had always called it. A place for the Englishers to stop and gawk. To take photographs and ponder the oddities of the Amish lifestyle.

Today, however, the whole thing just seemed quaint. The growth of the community astounded her. Shops presenting everything from fudge to dresses, candles to quilts had sprung up. Parking lots, filled with cars and tourist buses, stood next to acres and acres of beautiful green countryside. Ironic, the two coexisting alongside each other. Was such a thing really possible?

And how interesting, to suddenly see things from the opposite point of view. As a child, she'd been the object of stares and whispers from tourists. Today she found herself gazing with curiosity at the workers in the shops. Had it really been twelve long years since she'd been in their spot? Did they feel as awkward as she did now? If so, they certainly didn't let it show.

Katie shook off these questions and made her way through several of the stores, taking her time to really breathe in the ambiance. On and on she walked, taking her time, drinking it in. Her past. Their present. Merging the two felt more comfortable with each passing minute. And the minutes passed with ease here, unlike in the city. Here people strolled about, laughing, talking, and shopping.

She made it a point to do the same. Today was all about rest and reflection. And good food.

After stopping off for an apple fritter, which she quickly consumed, Katie entered the candy store, ready to do some serious shopping. This had always been one of her favorite places, though the fudge in this shop could hardly compare with Aunt Emma's.

At once, Katie thought of Hannah and the unmended fences between the two women. Mother and daughter had hardly spoken in years, and all because of rules and regulations. Katie prayed for a miracle in that situation and also prayed that her recent run-in with Karl wouldn't cause a rift of such immense proportions. It would take a great deal of time and prayer to heal something of that magnitude.

She redirected her focus to the candy. "I'll take a half pound of maple." She

ointed through the glass case at a luscious brick of tan-colored fudge. "And a
ull pound of chocolate with pecans."

As she waited for the candy, her mouth watered. She would only pinch off a
ibble from the maple fudge; the rest she would take home to her family. Emily
vould be thrilled, as would Mamm. The boys would probably consume most of
t, though. As always.

After finishing up in the candy store, Katie moved out to the hub of the shops,
he area where an older fellow charged tourists for buggy rides. Datt would've
rowned on such a venture, no doubt, but this fellow looked to be having a grand
ime. So did his guests.

As Katie walked, she noticed a clothing store, one she'd somehow overlooked
arlier on. She found herself staring through the window at the most beautiful
vlue dress she'd ever seen.

Wow. The soft chiffon overlay took her breath away, and the trim at the neck-
ine only served to further draw her in.

For the first time in twelve years, she contemplated the unthinkable. *Blue?*
Where she would wear it, she had no idea. Certainly it wouldn't do for work. But
:omething about it called out to her.

I've got to have that dress.

To wear blue again would signify the end of an era. Was she ready to let go of
the past and face a more colorful future? With a smile on her face, she pondered
the idea.

Yes. Relief flooded over her as she realized the truth of it. *I'm ready.*

A familiar voice rang out from behind her, sending a shock wave through her.
"I think that color would look amazing on you, Katie Walken. I always thought
you looked especially pretty in blue."

With her heart now pounding in her ears, she turned to face Karl, who stood
behind her with an impish grin on his face.

"W–what? What are you doing here? How did you know I would be—"

"I know you better than you think, despite what you said earlier. I know that
you love maple fudge, for instance." He pointed to the bag in her hand, which
she quickly tucked behind her back. "And I know that you could never resist an
apple fritter."

"How did you know I ate an apple fritter?"

He reached to wipe a bit of powdered sugar from the edge of her mouth, and
she sighed, feeling like a kid caught with her hand in the cookie jar. Only, in this
case, it felt good to be caught, even with sugar on her lips.

"I also know that whenever you got stressed as a teen, you always wanted to
go to town, to the shops. Remember that time you snuck off and bought a pair
of high-heeled shoes when your parents were at your aunt Emma's? You actually

thought you could get away with wearing them."

Katie groaned. "I can't believe you remember that. I buried the box behind the barn with the shoes still in it. Wrapped the box in plastic, in case it rained. Those silly shoes are probably still there to this day." She paused and gazed at him in wonder. "But you haven't answered my question. What are you doing here?"

"You didn't think I'd let you get away twice, did you?"

The bag of fudge began to tremble in her hand, and she did her best to stay calm. Had he really just said that? Karl had come looking for her, just as she'd prayed.

"But how in the world did you find me in this crowd?" She gazed into his twinkling eyes.

"I move fast. Nearly as fast as you *used* to. Looks like I'm catching up with you." He gave her a wink, and Katie's heart flip-flopped.

"I'm glad you did." She offered up a shy smile.

"Me, too." Karl drew close, and for a moment she thought he would wrap her in his arms. Instead, a shopper brushed past them, forcing them apart. Karl shifted his gaze to the dress in the window. "So, are you going to try on that dress or not?"

She shook her head, suddenly reduced to a stammering child. "I—I don't need it."

"You might. Someday." He took her by the arm and ushered her into the store. When they approached the clerk, an elderly woman with silver hair, she happily pointed Katie in the direction of the changing room.

With nerves leading the way, she slipped the beautifully designed dress over her head. Staring at herself in the mirror, Katie had to admit, she felt pretty. The color was just right, but something more jumped out at her. It had more to do with how she felt, not how she looked.

As the "I'm happy in blue" truth registered, something amazing happened in her heart. Joy took over, and before long, giggling followed.

"Everything okay in there?" She heard Karl's voice ring out.

"Mmm. . .yeah." She twirled around to see the dress from the back. Another giggle erupted. "I like it."

"Come on out and let me have a look."

She felt her cheeks warm. "Oh no, I'd feel silly." *Happy, but silly.*

"Katie. I'm not moving until you come out."

She laughed. Some things hadn't changed. He still had the patience of Job, with or without a fishing pole in his hands. Katie gave herself another quick glance, then pulled back the curtain and stepped out into the store, curious as to what he would say when he saw her.

Karl took one look at her and let out a whistle. "Katie." He shook his head and stared. "You look. . ."

"Ridiculous?"

"Um. . .no."

"Amish?"

He laughed. "Hardly. But I've got to say, you look like something straight out of paradise." He drew near, and Katie felt his breath warm on her cheek. "Katie Walken. . ."

"Yes?"

He gently traced the freckles on the end of her nose with his fingertip. "I can't tell you how long I've waited to do this."

Her heart fluttered, and she looked around the shop to make sure no one else was watching. "D–do what?"

He slipped an arm around her waist and drew her to himself, planting a row of kisses along her hairline. She felt her legs turn to mush and thought for a moment she must be dreaming this. Only a dream could feel this wonderful. She closed her eyes to ponder that possibility then opened them to double-check the reality.

Nope. Not a dream. Karl gazed at her with the most hypnotic look, one that left her speechless, a rarity.

"I like you in blue," he whispered in her ear.

"O–oh?"

He lifted her chin with his fingertips and forced her to stare into his eyes. Beautiful blue twinkling eyes. Eyes she'd avoided for twelve years. As he leaned in to kiss her—right there in front of anyone who might be looking—she gave herself over to the sheer joy of the moment. Their lips met for the sweetest kiss she ever could have imagined, one most assuredly worth waiting for.

After just a few seconds, she felt the presence of someone nearby and took a step back, her cheeks growing warm. The clerk flashed a wide smile and spoke with a sigh in her voice. "Ah, to be young again."

The words made Katie want to laugh. Being with Karl *did* make her feel young again. And wrapped up in his arms, his soft lips brushing against hers, she finally felt whole. Complete.

Karl gave her a wink then glanced down at the dress once more. "So, what have we decided about the dress?"

The clerk joined him, adding her two cents' worth, and before long, they'd both convinced Katie she must purchase it.

"But I really don't have anyplace to wear it," she argued. "My church is really casual, and we rarely wear things like this to the office. If I had a party coming up, maybe, but. . ."

"Regardless, that dress was made for you." Karl whipped out his wallet. "And it's my treat."

"What?" She couldn't possibly let him make a purchase like this.

"I'm buying the dress, and you're not going to argue. Remember, I just saved a fortune by not buying the Chandler place."

Katie let out a groan.

"And you just *lost* a fortune *not* selling the house on the lake. So, I think you'd better let me take care of this one."

She offered up a salute and a playful, "Yes, sir!" Then, standing back, she took a moment to collect her thoughts and her emotions. With her heart in such a state, she could barely process what had just happened, let alone where she might end up wearing that beautiful blue dress.

On the other hand, what did it matter really? As long as Karl liked her in blue ...she might very well wear it every day from now on.

ชื่ะ

Karl couldn't seem to stop smiling. Not that he tried. But, as he paid for the dress, only the crowd of people kept him from screaming out, "She's mine!" He wanted to whoop and holler, to jump up and down, and to shout to the masses that the woman he loved clearly loved him back. That the Lord had truly redeemed the time they'd lost. And Karl wouldn't waste another minute lingering over anything in the past, including real estate disputes. God would take care of all of that anyway.

Karl simply paid for the dress and turned to Katie with a smile. "What else would you like to do today? You choose."

She grinned. "I've already done most everything. Eaten too many sweets, decided to give up on my moratorium against blue. Kissed you. I'd say it's been a pretty full day."

He drew near and pulled her into his arms once more. "Say that last part again."

"It's been a pretty full day?"

"No, the part before that."

"Ah." She smiled. "Kissed you."

He leaned down and pressed his lips against hers once more, this time not releasing his hold for some time. Karl found himself forgetting where he was. Not caring one bit who might be looking. He could go on holding the woman he loved forever, as far as he was concerned.

When he finally let go, he tipped his head back and gave her a playful wink.

"Whoa." She looked up into his eyes with a grin. "That's one for the record books."

"I just didn't want you to forget." He gave her a wink. "And now you can say I've kissed you twice."

"You've kissed me twice," she echoed, reaching for his hand.

And I'd like it to be a thousand times more, he wanted to shout. But didn't. There would be plenty of time for shouting later. Right now he wanted to relish every moment with their hands firmly locked together. He wanted to forget the outside world existed at all, that problems and real estate woes would ever again rear their ugly heads.

They browsed a few more shops then wove their way through the throng of tourists toward the parking lot. Karl nibbled on a piece of fudge, enjoying its flavor, then glanced up into Katie's eyes—eyes filled with love.

He found himself captivated. Hypnotized. And for a moment he wasn't sure which was sweeter, the maple-flavored candy. . .or the feel of Katie Walken's hand in his.

Chapter 17

Katie smiled all the way from the shopping center to her mother's hous Every now and again she glanced in the rearview mirror to make su Karl still followed along behind her in his car. Just the tiniest glimpse his face sent her heart soaring.

She thought back to the moment he'd taken her in his arms. The feelings th had washed over her far surpassed anything she'd ever experienced. Her hea once hardened to the idea of love, had obviously softened. And oh, how wonde ful that softness felt! How blissful! From the moment he touched the tip of h nose with his finger, she had melted like a scoop of ice cream left sitting in th sun. And that kiss—she'd wondered if such a thing were even possible. Now sh knew it to be true.

As she drove, Katie prayed. She called out to God for His perfect will to k done in their relationship—to smooth over any troubled places, take care of ar unsettled work-related issues. If the Lord could bring Karl after her, surely H could handle those pesky little issues. Never again would she allow her love fc things to come before her love for people. Never. She would toss every commis sion right out the window before she would sacrifice her relationship with Kar Or anyone else in her family, for that matter.

As she pondered work-related things, Katie happened to pass the same farr she'd noticed a week before, the one with the FOR SALE sign out front. Funny n one had purchased it, the land being so pretty and all. She thought of the Mor risons at once, of their desire to plant their family in a big house with sprawlin acres. She could almost see herself in a similar frame of mind, running hand ir hand with her children across the backyard of such a house. Someday.

Winding down the curvy road, she drank in the beauty of the land. How muc prettier it looked now that Karl had kissed her. How much taller the trees hac grown, and how much bluer the skies overhead appeared.

Bluer.

Katie giggled like a schoolgirl as she glanced in the rear-view mirror, this tim looking at something other than the car behind her. The blue dress hung from hook in the back seat, causing her heart to sing. Oh, the joy of it!

I own a blue dress. She could hardly believe it. And it had only taken twelv years to work up the courage.

She would wear blue every day if Karl would look at her with love pouring from his eyes. Blue shirts. Blue slacks. Blue dresses. Blue everything. If he would only kiss her every morning, noon, and evening as he had kissed her today.

Yes, she would surely wear blue.

She pulled her car into the driveway at the farm just as the late afternoon sun lit the fields with an amber light. At once Buddy rushed the car, his tail wagging. Funny to see the Amish dog so excited about a car in his driveway. He jumped up and down, offering his usual greeting. Just the sight of him made Katie want to visit the puppies once more, to see if Miracle had found a home.

As she parked, Katie glanced back to catch a glimpse of Karl pulling in behind her. She couldn't help but wonder what Mamm would think if she saw them together. Would she put two and two together and come up with four?

Karl met Katie at the door of her car, opening it for her.

She offered up a "Thank you" with warmed cheeks. How long had it been since a gentleman opened her car door for her? She couldn't remember the last time. In truth, the few men she'd dated over the years had been far more into themselves than she would've preferred, spending little time on time-honored traditions such as opening a woman's door.

Now, as she gazed into Karl's eyes, Katie thanked God that none of her prior relationships had worked out. She also thanked Him that somehow, in the grand scheme of things, Karl had managed to stay unattached.

Till now.

Together they made their way to the front door of the house, where Mamm greeted them with a smile and a hug. "You're right on time. Emily is in the kitchen fixing supper, and the men are due in from the fields anytime now. Come in, come in!" She ushered them into the house, where they were greeted with great joy.

"Where is the baby?" Katie asked, anxious to see the little darling.

"Sara's in the bedroom with her," Mamm explained. She lowered her voice to whisper, "Nursing her."

"Do you think she would mind if I snuck in for a peek at Rachel?"

"Surely not," Mamm said. "You go on in there, and I'll put Karl to work peeling potatoes."

Katie turned back to look at Karl, to get his take on the matter. He followed along on her mother's heels, a contented look on his face—as if peeling potatoes was something akin to slaying dragons. She knocked on the bedroom door, not wanting to disturb her sister, but hoping for a moment with the family's new addition.

"Come in," Sara's voice rang out.

As Katie entered the room, her sister's face lit in a smile. "I thought I heard your voice out there."

"You did." Katie drew near and reached out to touch the wisps of Rachel's hair. "I had to sneak in here to see my baby girl."

After a few more seconds of oohing and aahing over the baby, Sara looked up at Katie with a suspicious gleam in her eye. "Was that Karl Borg's voice I hear out there?"

"It was." Katie tried to hide the smile but couldn't.

"Tell me everything." Sara gestured for her to sit on the bed.

They spent the next several minutes giggling like schoolgirls with childhood crushes. Katie told her sister everything that had happened at the store then confessed her feelings for Karl. All the while, Sara's face remained aglow with excitement.

"I knew it when you were here a few days ago," she said.

"You did? How? I didn't even know."

"Oh, Katie." Sara laughed. "You can't keep love hidden. You're like an open book, every time you look at him. And when he looks at you, well. . ."

"What?"

"Let's just say he has trouble finishing his sentences. Or walking straight. All he can see is you."

Katie contemplated her sister's words as she made her way back into the kitchen to join the others. She kept a watchful eye on Karl all through supper, noting the many times he glanced her way with a glimmer in his eye. She longed for a few moments of privacy with him but knew better. They would have plenty of time for that tomorrow if he stayed in Paradise through the night.

After the meal, Mamm shooed them off to the living room. A summer storm lit the skies, and Katie looked out the front window, a bit anxious. "Mamm, is there anything I can help you with?" she called out.

"I'm nearly done in here. You just make yourselves at home."

Minutes later, her mother joined them in the living room. As she settled into the rocker, she looked at Katie with tears in her eyes. "I'm so glad you're here, Katydid. I do hope you can stay awhile."

"I'd planned to stay at a bed and breakfast in town," Katie explained, giving the sky another glance, "but it looks as if I'll have to stay here instead."

"Well, of course you'll stay here," her mother admonished. "Why, I would never have you waste your money on a room in town when there's a perfectly good one here." She dove into a lengthy discourse about finances and one's ability to be thrifty, and Katie smiled. Some things never changed.

"Your datt would never let me hear the end of it if I let you spend money on a bed in town. Can you imagine the look on his face at such a suggestion?"

Everyone in the room broke into a lovely discussion about Datt, one that

334

nded with tears in every eye. Katie tried to picture the look on her father's face
t the news she'd finally kissed Karl Borg after all these years. Surely he would
e grinning ear to ear.

After a few minutes of chatter about the new baby, Katie glanced across the
oom at Karl, who observed them both with a crooked smile. Oh, how she wished
he could read his thoughts right now. After their kiss earlier this afternoon, he'd
ever left her side. With hands tightly clasped, they'd made their way through
everal more stores, finally landing in the baby store, where she'd oohed and
ahed over a precious little pink dress, one she wanted to buy for Rachel.

Common sense had won out, of course. Katie knew that some things would
ever change—like her family's desire for the plain life. However, she also knew
hat several things had changed already. Her heart, for instance.

Yes, her heart had surely undergone a transformation over the past couple of
weeks. In spite of her childish struggles, she'd finally come to grips with the fact:
I love Karl Borg. And I'm going to make up the lost time.

And now, as she stared at the man she loved from across the room, her heart
elt as if it could burst into song. She wanted to run through the field behind the
house, this time with his hand in hers—not in mourning, but to celebrate the
wonder of what she now knew to be true. *God has given us a second chance. And
I'm not going to blow it.*

Her mother drew near and looked out of the window into the darkened skies
above. Turning to Karl, Mamm said, "Looks like you're not going anywhere tonight either, Karl. We'll find a room for you, as well."

"Oh, no," he argued. "I couldn't put you out like that. Besides. . ."

Katie knew his thoughts before he spoke them. It would be inappropriate for
him to stay in the house now that they'd expressed their feelings for one another.
Not that anyone knew, but still. . .

"I can stay in the barn," Karl said. "If that would be okay."

Katie looked at him, stunned. "The barn?"

"Sure, why not?" He laughed. "Do you know how many times my older brothers and I slept in our barn as children? We never minded. In fact, the hay was
softer than our mattresses. It won't be a problem, I promise."

Katie had to wonder at his willingness to do such a thing but didn't argue. If
he wanted to sleep in the barn, so be it.

In the meantime, she would enjoy their last few minutes together before everyone turned in for the night.

With a happy heart, she glanced across the room at the people she loved. *I
could be very happy right here. Forever.* She looked over at Karl and added one final
thought on the matter. *Right here. . .with him.*

❧

Karl sprinted across the yard with an umbrella in one hand and a lantern in the other. Under his arm he'd managed to hang on to a folded blanket. Avoiding the pouring rain proved to be a problem, but not nearly as tricky as guessing the location of each mud puddle.

Had he really offered to sleep in the barn? Karl chuckled as he thought about it. After years of city life, curling up on a bed of hay would be interesting, to say the least.

As he opened the door to the barn, he heard a low growl in the distance. He'd already been warned that a particular mama dog and her pups would likely welcome him in their own special way. "Be a good girl, Honey," he said in his most soothing voice. "I'm not here to hurt you. I'm just here to. . ." He glanced around, looking for a place to sleep. Finally his gaze shifted upward, to the loft. With a groan he approached the ladder and added, "I'm just here to catch a few winks."

With the blanket still tucked under his arm, he began the climb. Thankfully, up this high the dogs wouldn't be a problem. He prayed nothing else would either. Like bats, for instance. They had a tendency to make an appearance at this altitude, especially in the summertime.

Locating a spot off in the corner that looked doable, Karl eased his way over on his knees. No point in trying to stand; the loft area didn't appear to be more than four or five feet high, at best.

After a bit of wrestling with the blanket and the straw, he finally settled in. From down below he could hear the sound of the pups nursing, and from up above, the patter of raindrops on the roof. He closed his eyes and leaned back, taking it all in. Something about being here, so close to the land he'd always loved, did something to him. Instead of resenting the fact that he had to sleep away from the house, he celebrated it. Surely God had ordained this.

And, as he lay there, cozy in the softly piled straw, a plan began to take shape in Karl's imagination, one that surely had to have come from above. He glanced up at the ceiling and allowed his thoughts to wander back to what had happened in the dress shop. Had he really kissed Katie—right there in front of an audience even? And had she lingered in his arms, looking up at him with love?

Certainly he had not imagined it. No imagination could produce such wonderful memories. She had really been his—if only for a few minutes. If only he could turn those few minutes into a lifetime, then everything would be perfect.

Karl closed his eyes and offered up a prayer of thanks to God for orchestrating the events of the day, right down to his night in the barn. Surely it was meant to be a sanctuary, of sorts.

Unfortunately, as his eyelids grew heavy, other, more troubling, thoughts surfaced. He reflected on the church's situation and the role Katie had played. Her sacrifice had been huge.

Of course, the sacrifice on his end might turn out to be huge, as well. After all, the church could hardly afford to pay him for his representation. Working gratis didn't bother him; Karl knew the Lord would provide for his needs. But making sure he gave this case his all did. With such a heavy caseload already, he would have to keep everything in balance.

Which brought him once again to the question of why he happened to be sleeping in a barn in Paradise when an ordinary night like this would find him propped up in his own bed, plugging away on his laptop.

From outside, the sound of the rain against the rooftop lulled, wooing him to sleep. Turning over on his side, Karl decided to concern himself with work matters another day. Right now, he simply needed to sleep.

❧

Katie crawled into her bed—the same bed she'd slept in as a child—and gazed out of the window into the dark, troublesome sky. A flash of lightning streaked across the darkness, and she shivered, thinking of Karl in the barn. Of course, his willingness to sleep there had certainly shown his kindness and concern toward her family.

Funny. It seemed she'd learned a lot about Karl today. She rolled over and shaped the pillow to her liking, smiling as she thought back to the moment when he'd kissed her. Oh how perfect, how truly wonderful she'd felt in his arms. How right.

Katie looked again at the window, giggling. Had she really slipped through that same narrow corridor twelve years ago to escape Karl? No, she had to admit. She'd been running from far more than that. And how ironic that the Lord had led her back to the very spot where everything started.

Or maybe it wasn't so ironic after all.

Chapter 18

Karl awoke even before the sun rose. His back ached from the position he'd kept through the night, but that's not what prompted him to rise extra early. No, he had something else on his mind, something altogether different.

He rose from the bed of hay and made his way across the barn, bumping into all sorts of things along the way. If he could just make it to the door, perhaps there would be enough early morning sun to give him a clear shot of the car.

At some point in the night he'd come up with a plan that just might work, one that would set the wheels in motion for an exciting future. Oh, it involved a compromise, of sorts. And there were a few details to iron out, to be sure. Hopefully it wouldn't take long to get things squared away.

He reached the door and eased it open, then took a peek outside. As he'd hoped, no one had yet risen. Unfortunately, that also included the sun. With the skies above lingering between black and blue, he tiptoed his way across the yard, aiming for what he prayed was the driveway.

As he made his way along, the fresh scent of the dew on the grass threw him back in time to the many mornings he'd risen at this hour to tend to the animals with his datt at his side. How he missed those days, and how he ached for his father, especially now.

This morning, a variety of early morning sounds greeted him. Off in the distance a rooster crowed, and Karl instinctively whispered, "Not now!" He didn't want anything to wake the others. If they rose too soon, he'd be caught in the act.

He squinted, and his car came into view. Thankfully, he'd parked behind Katie. That made his getaway a bit easier. Still, he would have to pray for God's favor once he turned the key in the ignition. Likely the sound of the car starting would awaken everyone in the house, including her.

Without thinking about the noise it would make, Karl pressed the door unlock button on his remote. The beeping nearly sent him out of his skin. He looked around to see if the sound had caused anyone in the house to stir. No, thankfully everything remained peaceful and still.

He slowly opened the car door and slipped inside. So far, so good. He turned the key in the ignition, thankful the engine didn't roar to a loud start. Instead, it eemed to purr. Another God-thing.

Just as he began the process of backing out of the long driveway, however, something unexpected happened. Buddy, the golden retriever, appeared, barking like a maniac. Karl tried to calm him down, but from inside the car there was really little he could do. Instead, he kept easing his way backward, down the driveway.

As he neared the road, Karl noticed a light come on in one of the downstairs bedroom windows. Then another upstairs. By the time he shifted into drive and hightailed it down the road, nearly every light in the house had popped on.

So much for making a clean getaway.

❧

Katie watched through the downstairs window with a heavy heart. Karl must have wanted to slip away unannounced; otherwise, why would he have gone to so much trouble to leave before dawn?

The heaviness in her heart matched the weight of her eyelids. She'd hardly slept a wink, thinking of the possibilities, of the life she and Karl could one day share together. The children they would have. The merging of their two businesses.

And now this.

I had it coming. I did this to him—got his hopes up then dashed them. Maybe it's payback time.

She thought back to their kiss in the dress shop. Was it all just an act, part of his plan to crush her hopes as she'd done to his all those years ago? How convincing it had been. The twinkle in his eye had drawn her in, like a spider spinning a web. And she'd apparently stepped right into it.

A rap on the bedroom door caught her attention. She quickly dabbed away tears and called out, "Come in."

"Katydid?"

"Yes, Mamm?"

Her mother drew near and lit the lantern on the bedside table. Katie could read the concern in her eyes. Mamm wrapped her in her arms and whispered, "I'm sure it's not what you're thinking."

After a reflective sigh, Katie asked, "How do you know what I'm thinking?"

"Oh, honey." Her mother laughed. "I know you so well. We're more alike than you know."

"We are?"

"Oh yes." A hint of a smile graced her mother's lips. "We're from the same stock, after all. We are both hard workers."

"True."

"Both extremely passionate and driven."

Katie gave Mamm an inquisitive look. She'd never really thought of her mother as being passionate before. However, as the thought took root, she couldn't deny it. Her mother's passions were for family, faith, and community.

"I guess we are alike," Katie said after a moment. Not that she minded. There were few people she'd rather be more like than her mother.

Mamm smiled. "There are so many things I could tell you. A few might even stun you."

Katie turned to her mother, more curious than ever. "What do you mean?"

Mamm took Katie's hands in her own. "Did you know that I left the Amish country when I was seventeen?"

"W–what?"

"Yes." Mamm sighed. "I was in love. At least I thought I was."

"With Datt?"

A moment of silence was long enough to convince her otherwise.

"With an English boy I'd met in school," her mother admitted with flushed cheeks. "Back then, the Amish children were integrated into the public schools and learned alongside the English children. At some point in my midteens, I met this boy, Chuck, and fell head over heels."

Katie could scarcely believe this story. Her mother. . .in love with a boy named Chuck? Why had she never heard this story before? "He wanted to take you away from the Amish lifestyle?"

"That's just it." Her mother sighed. "He didn't want to take me away at all, but I was too naive to see it. I went to the trouble to run away from home, thinking he was interested in marrying me, and he didn't even want me at all. Turns out the other boys in the school had put him up to it—making me think he liked me when he really didn't."

"Oh, Mamm, that's awful."

"It was humiliating. But here's the funny part"—her mother's eyes took on a faraway look—"I left late at night, planning to meet him in town. When I got there, he didn't show up, so I located a public phone and called him."

"What happened?"

"Nothing. He told me the whole thing was a joke. Apparently the boys had placed their bait, and I took it. Anyway, I walked back home again, crying all the way." Mamm sighed. "My parents never even knew I left, and I never told them."

"You're kidding."

"No, but the Lord knew, and He certainly had a lot to deal with in my heart. The pain and rejection, of course. And then there was the issue of my leaving to marry an English boy. I carried quite a bit of guilt over that."

"Ah." Katie understood such guilt.

"The next morning I woke up with huge bags under my eyes and I was congested from all the crying. My mamm took one look at me and assumed I had the flu, so she started doctoring me right away."

Katie hung on her mother's every word, mesmerized.

"My heart mended, and the funniest thing happened—your datt's family moved to Paradise that same fall from Indiana. When I met that man. . ." Her eyes filled with tears. She took Katie by the hand. "I knew from the moment I met your father that he was the man for me. And I have thanked God every day since that Chuck Brower broke my heart."

"Like I broke Karl's heart," Katie acknowledged.

"Oh no." Her mother shook her head. "Karl was hurt when you left, of course. Like a wounded puppy for the first few months. But his wounds healed over nicely. Until his parents passed away. I think that was the thing that damaged him most."

Katie looked out of the window with longing. "I was so foolish back then, Mamm. A silly young girl who didn't know what she wanted." Her eyes filled with tears. "But I know now." She turned to face her mother. "And I think it's too late."

Mamm grinned. "Oh, sweet girl, it's never too late when the Lord's in charge." She gave Katie's hand a squeeze. "You just commit this to prayer and see what the Almighty does. He has a way of turning pain into something quite beautiful." Her eyes filled with tears as she gave Katie a kiss on the cheek. "If I hadn't met your father, I wouldn't have you. Don't you see? You have Chuck Brower to thank for that."

Katie giggled. "I guess." Her eyes now filled with tears. "But I'm most grateful to you and Datt." After a lingering sigh, she added, "I miss him so much, Mamm. And I regret not coming home more."

"You're here now." Mamm stood and gave her a knowing look. "And that's all that matters."

As her mother made her way out of the room, Katie pondered her words. *You're here now. And that's all that matters.*

With a sigh, Katie realized the truth of it. She *did* feel at home in Paradise. But what in the world could she do about it now?

Chapter 19

Karl drove all the way to Lancaster, the nearest big town, stopping off at a local diner for breakfast. As he ate, he put together a to-do list. A lengthy one. He scribbled through a couple of things on the list, but the others could not be overlooked.

Buying a ring, for instance.

He would have to do that, and quickly.

Leaning forward, he looked at the paper, deep in thought. The Amish didn't exchange weddings rings, so offering one to Katie in the Walken house was out of the question. He'd have to find a spot. . .just the right spot. And then he'd have to think of something brilliant to say, something that would seal the deal.

At once, the plan came to him. He'd take care of it, and in the most remarkable of ways. Surely she would accept the ring and agree to be his wife.

Now for the second part of the plan—the compromise. The part where his world would merge with hers. The part where they would both learn to lean a bit, meeting in the middle. Surely he knew just how this would work.

After leaving the restaurant, Karl drove up and down the streets in search of a real estate office. Thankfully, he located one within minutes. He entered with a particular plan in mind and exited nearly an hour later, joy flooding his heart. At this point, motivation growing, Karl stopped in at a pricey jewelry store, locating the most exquisite ring he'd ever seen, one sure to make Katie's eyes pop.

Now to perform the deed.

Karl drove to the Walken farm, praying most of the way. Afterward, he thought about the love he now felt for Katie. Surely it was a love born of waiting, but time had only served to strengthen it, not the other way around. And besides, he could hardly compare today's feelings to how he'd felt about Katie all those years ago. Maybe it'd been puppy love back then, the kind that would have blossomed into something more real in time. With the right circumstances. Maybe they both needed to see where life would take them as individuals before they could come together as husband and wife.

Was that the real message here? Had God used their time apart to grow them as individuals so that they would make a stronger couple? Karl chewed on that awhile. He'd grown so much since his parents' deaths. Might not make much sense to those still living in the Amish community, but his faith had grown in leaps and bounds over the past few years away. And Katie had clearly blossomed into a mighty woman of God, too. One who was finally ready to be swept off her feet.

He hoped.

His heart soared as he thought about the ring burning a hole in his pocket. He could hardly wait to present it to his bride-to-be.

His heart swelled at the idea. She'd almost been his once before, but clearly God had a different plan. They were both just children back then, not ready for the changes ahead. Now, older and wiser, they could face the future together. Like-minded. In one accord.

He reached the farm and pulled his car into the driveway. Buddy greeted him, of course, but so did a host of Walken family members, appearing on the porch the moment his car pulled in.

"Uh-oh." None of them looked terribly happy. Maybe he shouldn't have left without telling anyone. Did they think. . . ?

He drew in a sharp breath as reality hit. *They thought I was running away—like Katie did.* A delicious chuckle slipped out as he made his way from the car to the driveway. *Oh, if they only knew!*

As he meandered up the porch, Karl did his best to play it cool. "Hey, everyone."

"Karl." Katie's older brother, Amos, gave him a stern look. "Urgent business in town?"

"I couldn't have put it better myself." Karl looked through the crowd to find Katie, but she was noticeably absent. "Where. . .um. . .is—"

"You looking for Katie?" Mrs. Walken appeared in the doorway. "She's in the field out behind the house. Want me to go fetch her for you?"

"No." He did his best to hide the playful smile that attempted to rise up. "I think I'd like to fetch her myself."

The twinkle in Amos's eye let Karl know he understood. With a wink to all family members, Karl trudged around the side of the house, through the mud left from last night's rainstorm, until he finally arrived in the backyard. He looked out across the field, finally able to catch a glimpse of Katie as she ran.

"Man, she's fast." He started to take off after her but decided to give it a moment. If she went out, she surely had to come back in, right?

A couple of moments proved the point. Katie turned and began to walk toward the house. When she saw Karl, however, her walk turned into a sprint. The sprint turned into a full-fledged run. And before he knew it, she stood directly in front of him, her breaths coming hard and fast.

He hardly knew what to make of the expression in her eyes. Pain? Betrayal? Hope? Excitement? Funny how a woman could say so much without uttering a word.

"Nice morning?" he asked.

The smirk spoke volumes.

"Feel like going for a walk?"

"I just went for one." She turned back toward the house, and he reached to take her by the arm.

"Oh no, you don't," he said with a laugh. "I'm not going to let you get away that easily. You're coming with me, Katie Walken."

Her eyes grew large as she responded. "Oh, I am, am I?"

"You are." He took deliberate steps away from the house, and toward the creek. Once they arrived, he would set his plan in motion. Until then, he just had to figure out a way to keep her feet moving in unison with his.

≥▲

Katie's heart thumped a hundred miles an hour as Karl led her beyond the field and into the clearing. Mud covered her sneakers. Nothing she could do about that. But after the prayer time she'd just had, her heart was as clean.

The first several paces were filled with questions. Why had he picked today, of all days, to run away and then come back? And what in the world was he doing, walking her through mud puddles? "Do you mind if I ask where we're going?" she asked finally.

Karl simply shook his head.

"Won't you even give me a hint?" she tried.

He responded by shaking his head. Then, as Karl's hand reached down to grab hers, as he turned to give her a wink, all prior fears melted into one blissful thought. *This is the hint. He's not here to break my heart. He's got something up his sleeve.*

As they approached the creek, Katie held her breath. Fishing? Today? Surely they couldn't fish, what with everything along the edge of the creek being so muddy. And besides, they had no poles. No bait. Nothing. Yes, something was surely up.

"Follow me, Katydid," he whispered as he led her toward the bridge.

Hand in hand, they approached the center, the same spot they'd stood at hundreds of times as children. This time, however, one of them did not appear to be standing. Katie looked down in surprise as Karl dropped to one knee.

"W–what are you. . ."

He reached to take her hand. "Katie, a man doesn't often get the chance to propose to the same woman twice."

She groaned. "I didn't exactly let you propose the first time, remember?"

He cleared his throat. "Um. . .no, you didn't. And thanks for the reminder. But you're going to let me finish what I've started this time, right?"

Katie felt her cheeks turn warm, and her hands began to shake in anticipation.

Unable to say anything above the lump in her throat, she stared down into Karl's love-filled blue eyes and simply nodded. As if she would stop him!

She watched in awe as he reached into his pocket, coming out with the prettiest diamond ring she'd ever seen. Her breath caught in her throat as she took it in. He'd chosen white gold, her favorite. And the marquis diamond was flawless, perfect.

But not nearly as perfect as the image of the godly man kneeling before her now. And certainly not as perfect as the grace of an almighty, all-loving God who had brought them back together in such a miraculous way. She blinked away the tears so as not to miss a thing.

"Katie, I love you even more now than I did twelve years ago, if that's possible," Karl said. "I know we have a lot of time to make up for, but I want to enjoy every minute with you. I'm asking you. . ." Here he lifted the ring, nearly letting it slip out of his hand into the creek below. He caught it before it hit the slatted bridge, but not before Katie let out a squeal.

"Whew! That was close." Her heart began to beat faster than ever, knowing he would soon slip the beautiful ring on her finger.

Karl started laughing. "I can't even propose without fouling it up." He looked up at her with pleading eyes. "I'm trying to ask you to be my wife, but I'm not doing a very good job of it."

"Oh, you're doing a great job," she said with an encouraging nod. "Don't let me stop you." *Please don't let me stop you.*

"Katie"—he reached for her hand, slipping the ring into place—"will you do me the very great honor of marrying me?"

"Will I!" Katie let out a whoop, startling a flock of birds in a nearby tree. They soared away with their wings flapping in unison. "Karl, nothing would make me happier."

He rose to his feet and swept her into his arms. As their lips met for a magical kiss to seal the deal, Katie felt as if her heart would not be able to contain the joy. What she had ever done to deserve this she had no idea.

Chapter 19

S o here's what I'm thinking." Karl took hold of his fiancée's hand as they walked back toward her mother's house. "I'm thinking we're both a little homesick for Paradise."

"Are you suggesting we come back here to live?" Katie asked. "Surely you don't mean—"

"I'm suggesting we move to the area," he said. "I wasn't suggesting anything more than that. Returning to the lifestyle would be—"

"Tough?"

"If not impossible." He sighed as he thought it through. "There are so many things I want to do for people, and I know God can use my skills as an attorney." Here he paused, trying to work up the courage to broach the subject near to his heart. "But I've decided it doesn't really matter where I practice. And for that matter, unless your heart is set on Doylestown, you could sell real estate here in Lancaster County."

Katie's eyes lit up as she gazed at him. "You're really talking about moving back."

"I am, but only if you're in total agreement." He reached into his back pocket and pulled out a piece of paper, unfolding it. "I stopped and picked this up at a real estate office in Lancaster. It's a piece of property for sale not too far from here."

"You've got to be kidding me." She gave him an incredulous look. "I've been by this farmhouse twice. Both times it caught my eye."

"Mine, too, but I didn't want to admit it, at least not to anyone but myself." He paused for a moment then added, "You know how I feel about the land." Karl tried not to let his emotion take over as he spoke. "I'm always telling people I'm not a farmer, but in my heart I am. I'd like to try something on a small scale, something that would allow me to get my hands in the dirt and still run my own practice."

"So you're saying you want to be a dirty-handed lawyer?" The corners of Katie's mouth tipped up in a playful smile. "You think that will go over well in this neck of the woods?"

After they both stopped laughing, Karl shrugged. "Why not? Maybe we'll start a new trend. And you. . ." He took her by the hand. "You will thrive here in Lancaster County. There's land in abundance here. Plenty to sell."

Katie shrugged. "Maybe."

"Maybe?"

"Well, I don't know. Maybe I'll turn out to be one of those women who prefers to have a houseful of babies. A stay-at-home mom." She looked up at him with fascinating look in her eye, one he'd never seen before.

"You?" He couldn't believe it. "The girl who jumped out of a window in search of a bigger life? You'd be willing to stay home and change diapers?"

"Well"—she shrugged—"I'm not sure at the moment, of course, but maybe someday. And besides, raising children *is* a bigger life."

"True."

She leaned against him and kissed him on the cheek. "If our kids are half as troublesome as I was, they're going to need a parent to stay with them full-time, don't you think?"

"No doubt about that. But we'll find a good church to raise them in, one we can both agree on."

"Of course."

"And speaking of parents being close to their children"—he paused before unveiling the rest of the story—"the primary reason I'm suggesting all of this is because your family is here." A lump grew up in his throat and he did his best to quelch it. "My parents are gone, and now your datt has gone on, too. But your mamm is still here, and she needs you right now."

Katie's eyes filled with tears, and she gazed up at him with joy. "Yes, she does."

"And with all of your brothers and sisters nearby, I just think we'll be more at home in this area."

"You don't think it will be strange, since they now consider us Englishers?"

Karl shrugged and gave the matter some thought. "There will be hurdles to jump, no doubt, but they will be easier to jump from Paradise than Doylestown, wouldn't you imagine?"

"Yes." She gave him another kiss on the cheek. "I think you're brilliant, Karl Borg."

"Far from it." He shook his head, recognizing his own weaknesses far more than his strengths. "I'm on a learning curve in so many areas. But I think I'll be a better student with you at my side." He looked down into Katie's eyes and realized. . .he'd be a better *everything* with her at his side.

❧

The joy in Katie's heart consumed her all the way back to the house. She could hardly wait to tell the others. How would they respond? Emily would surely jump for joy. And Sara would be thrilled. Mamm. . .

Katie drew in a breath as she thought about her mother. What would Mamm think, after all these years? Would she expect her daughter to ease back into the

Amish lifestyle then have a traditional Amish wedding ceremony? Katie ha‹ something a little different in mind, but surely Karl was right. Perhaps they coul‹ merge the two worlds, come to some sort of comfortable arrangement.

As she thought back over Karl's plan—to move back to Lancaster County— a thousand thoughts went through her mind. She'd have to call Hannah, o‹ course. Would her cousin be disappointed to lose her at Bucks County Realty‹ Likely, but she'd be just as thrilled to attend her wedding with the children i‹ tow.

Katie smiled as she thought about that. If Hannah really came to the wedding‹ she would finally get to see her own mother again. Katie whispered up a praye‹ that God would eventually allow them to reconcile, for Aunt Emma to see th‹ beautiful woman Hannah had become. And to meet her grandchildren. What ‹ joyous day that would be—for everyone involved.

"A penny for your thoughts."

Katie looked over at Karl as he spoke the words. "Oh, I'm thinking abou‹ how good God is. He's already mended my relationship with my family, and I'‹ hoping He'll do the same for Hannah and her mother."

"Time is a great healer." Karl gave her hand a squeeze.

"Yes, it surely is." She pondered his words. Time had healed more than he‹ relationship with her parents and with God. It had mended her once-shattere‹ relationship with the man she would now spend the rest of her life with. "The‹ problem with time is. . .there's so little of it."

"When you live in the city," he offered.

She laughed. "I suppose you're right about that. It does feel like the cloc‹ speeds up when we're away from Paradise. But I have a feeling. . ." A smile crep‹ across her lips.

"What?"

"Well, I have a feeling the clock's going to move at warp speed during ou‹ engagement. We have so much planning to do. We'll have to settle on a dat‹ and figure out where the ceremony will take place. And, of course, I'll have t‹ find the perfect dress. We'll have to decide how many guests to invite then selec‹ invitations. And we'll have to talk about who will perform the ceremony. Oh‹ and then we'll have to see about bridal showers. Surely Hannah and Aimee wil‹ want to host one for me, maybe a lingerie shower at that." She dove off into ‹ lengthy list of things they would have to do together over the next few months‹ totally lost in the joy of it all.

"Whoa." He interrupted her with a laugh. "I can't believe you're already think-ing about these things."

Katie stopped dead in her tracks and stared him down. "Are you kidding? A girl has to think about these things. Why, I've been thinking about my wedding ever since. . ." She paused and put a hand to her mouth.

"What?"

"Since I almost married you the first time." She giggled.

"Oh, really." He pulled her close. "So you actually gave thought to marrying me back then?"

"I always loved you, Karl," Katie confessed with a sigh. "And what I said that night at the restaurant still holds true. It wasn't *you* I was running from. It was the lifestyle. Maybe I wasn't ready for marriage yet, but I am now. And I'm the happiest girl on planet Earth. I don't know if I've mentioned that or not, but I am."

He leaned in to kiss her then ran his fingers along the tip of her nose. "Well, if planning our wedding makes you this happy, then let's go for it." He chuckled. "Now, give me details. Are you thinking about a big fancy church in town? And if so, which town? Doylestown or one of the local villages near Paradise?"

"That's the funny part. When I was younger, I thought I wanted a ceremony with all the trappings, something a young Amish woman would never get to have. Fancy dresses, lots of bridesmaids, beautiful decorations for the reception hall, caterers, a huge cake. . ."

"And now?"

"Now. . .?" She allowed herself to dream a bit. "Now I think simple and sweet would be nice."

"Simple and sweet." He gave her a wink. "Kind of like the groom."

She reached over and gave him a peck on the cheek. "You are sweet, Karl Borg. You're the sweetest man I've ever known." Thinking she would catch him while the catching was good, Katie asked one final question. "Um, Karl?"

"Yes?"

Katie dared to brave the question on her heart, one she could simply not avoid. "How do you feel about golden retrievers?"

"Golden retrievers?" He gave her an inquisitive look. "To be honest, I think the breed is highly overrated."

"Oh."

After a wink, he added, "Unless you happen to live on a farm."

Katie reached up for one more kiss and whispered, "Thank you."

As he took her hand in his own and they began to walk together across the field, she was reminded of that little hummingbird she'd seen on her mother's porch less than a week ago. Katie now envisioned it returning to its feeder, its iridescent wings holding it slightly aloft as the slender beak dipped down into the water below.

This time, instead of taking to flight, he settled in, taking advantage of the sweetness. A feeling of peace settled into Katie's heart as she realized she'd finally stopped running. Finally stopped flying away.

Soon. . .she would be Mrs. Karl Borg. She would live in a house on several acres in Paradise. And she would do it all, after having tasted of the things of the world. . .and leaving them far behind.

Epilogue

The following spring, on a particularly breathtaking Saturday, Karl Borg approached the center of the bridge at Pequea Creek. This time there were no fishing poles involved. Thankfully, he'd already made the right catch, snagged the one elusive fish who'd slipped away thirteen years prior. This time she promised to stay put. Forever. Today Katie Walken would join him at the center of the bridge and link hands—and hearts—with him forever.

With joy flooding his heart, he took his place at the center of the bridge next to Jay Ludlow, who looked at him with a warm and inviting smile. Of course, Jay had a lot to smile about these days, what with Brian Hamilton finally relinquishing his hold on the church's property. Still, Karl had a feeling Jeff's current smile had more to do with the fact that he was about to perform a special wedding ceremony, one they had planned for months.

As Karl looked out over the small crowd of friends and family members stationed on the side of the creek, excitement took hold. Somewhere, hiding behind a tree perhaps, his bride-to-be awaited. From what he'd been told, she looked like a million bucks. He could hardly wait to see the dress she'd selected, one—he'd been told—that rivaled any in a fashion magazine.

Suddenly, off in the distance, he saw a shimmer of blue. His beautiful bride came into focus, and he almost laughed at the sight of her. Instead of a traditional wedding dress, she wore the beautiful blue dress he'd purchased for her last summer. *Oh, Katie. You've done it. You've made your statement loud and clear, for all to see. You're wearing blue.* She drew near, making her way beyond the throng of family and friends.

Off in the distance, he saw Hannah and her children standing next to Emma. The tear-filled eyes spoke what a thousand words could not. He would have allowed his gaze to linger on them awhile longer, but his beautiful bride required his attention right now.

As Katie made her way to the center of the bridge, he couldn't take his eyes off of her. How many years had he been in love with her? Fifteen? Twenty? And how long had he trusted God for this moment?

Suddenly, the years melted, dissolving into a blurry haze. As he gazed into her twinkling eyes, Karl realized that time meant nothing. The wait meant nothing. The pain of losing her the first time around was gone forever.

Another thought surfaced. Surely the Lord had wanted—even needed—to let the two of them go through the necessary changes before they were ready for one another, ready to face life together.

Oh, but as he gazed into that beautiful face, he was reminded of little Katie Walken, the girl he'd waited for at the creek all those years ago. Her impish grin. The freckles on her nose. The sight of her sprinting across the backyard.

As he looked at her now, took in her beauty in that amazing blue dress, drank from the love in her eyes, he had to admit—no matter how long it had taken, she'd certainly been worth the wait.

❧

Katie clutched a fistful of wildflowers in her hands, willing them to stop trembling. Oh, how she wished Datt could be here, to walk with her, arm in arm. She brushed away a tear and made her way through the crowd of people—beyond her many family members. Past Hannah and Aunt Emma. Past Aimee Riley. Beyond the Morrisons, now faithful friends. Straight into the arms of her husband-to-be, who waited with Jay Ludlow at the center of the bridge over Pequea Creek.

If only she could get her feet to cooperate, everything would be just fine. Katie seemed to trip with every other step as she made her way toward the bridge. The shoes presented a bit of a problem, no doubt. Wearing heels to a creek-side wedding might not have been the best choice. Still, she had her reasons.

On the other hand, her clumsiness might have something to do with the fact that her focus remained fixed on the handsome man in the center of the bridge, the one in the stunning black tuxedo. Or maybe it had even more to do with the fact that he'd waited on her. For thirteen years he'd waited.

She would keep him waiting no longer. Hence, the clumsiness.

Katie stifled a giggle as she looked into his eyes. He'd clearly figured out the logic behind the dress, and the joy registered in his expression. *I'm done with running*, her heart cried out with every step.

She met Karl at the middle of the bridge, noticing at once that his gaze shifted to her feet. Yep. The same high-heeled shoes she'd buried behind the barn, thirteen years prior. Thanks to the plastic wrap and a sturdy box, they'd held up through the many storms.

Just like her relationship with Karl.

She flashed another impish smile in his direction, one that spoke a hundred I love yous without saying a word.

Then, just as the pastor began to lead them in their vows, Katie's thoughts shifted to that little hummingbird, swooping down upon its feeder, drinking in the sweetness of the sugary water below.

This time the elusive creature had come home. . .to stay.

A Letter to Our Readers

Dear Readers:

In order that we might better contribute to your reading enjoyment, we would appreciate your taking a few minutes to respond to the following questions. When completed, please return to the following: Fiction Editor, Barbour Publishing, Inc., P.O. Box 719, Uhrichsville, OH 44683.

1. Did you enjoy reading *Allegheny Hopes* by Janice A. Thompson?
   ❏ Very much—I would like to see more books like this.
   ❏ Moderately—I would have enjoyed it more if _____

   _____

   _____

2. What influenced your decision to purchase this book?
   (Check those that apply.)
   ❏ Cover   ❏ Back cover copy   ❏ Title   ❏ Price
   ❏ Friends   ❏ Publicity   ❏ Other

3. Which story was your favorite?
   ❏ *Red Like Crimson*   ❏ *Out of the Blue*
   ❏ *White as Snow*

4. Please check your age range:
   ❏ Under 18   ❏ 18–24   ❏ 25–34
   ❏ 35–45   ❏ 46–55   ❏ Over 55

5. How many hours per week do you read? _____

Name _____

Occupation _____

Address _____

City _____ State _____ Zip _____

E-mail _____